Critical Praise for

Hideaway

"Genuine humor and an interesting cast of characters
keep the story perking along...and there are
a few surprises.... An enjoyable read."
—*Publishers Weekly*

"...*Hideaway* is gripping and romantic.
It may also have crossover appeal to fans of
medical suspense and of such authors as Tess Gerritsen."
—*Library Journal*

"...special care is taken to be accurate with medical
terminology. The author also writes beautifully about
those who struggle with the apparent hypocrisy of
Christians... Outstanding real-life dialogue...
is naturally sprinkled throughout the book."
—Laurie Copeland, *Christian Retailing*

"High-stakes medical issues, compelling story lines,
spiritual depth and characters so authentic you'd know
them if you met on the street, Hannah Alexander
knows how to weave stories that hang on to your heart
long after you finish the books. Bravo!"
—Susan May Warren, bestselling author
of The Deep Haven Series

"*Hideaway* is absolutely the best book I have read this
year.... The strength of emotion packs a powerful
punch, and the suspense sits on the edge of a
knifepoint.... Each and every secondary character is
captivating, and the events are traumatic as the story
moves quickly through the pages.... The inspirational
qualities are by far the most superior I have read....
Hideaway is an absolute must read for everyone....
I am pleased to award this novel *RRT*'s Perfect 10."
—*Romantic Reviews Today*

HANNAH ALEXANDER

Safe Haven

Steeple
Hill®

Published by Steeple Hill Books™

STEEPLE HILL BOOKS

Steeple
Hill®

ISBN 0-373-78517-8

SAFE HAVEN

Copyright © 2004 by Hannah Alexander

www.SteepleHill.com

Printed in U.S.A.

ACKNOWLEDGMENTS

For many years, Lorene Cook (Cheryl's mom) has been an active participant with us as we work on our books, and we wish to thank her for all the hours of reading, computer work, addressing, printing, filing, encouraging, errand running, cooking and, most important, praying for us. Mom, you've been a lifesaver.

We also wish to thank Mel's parents, Ray and Vera Overall, for your constant support and love.

Many thanks to Linda Sartin, our claustrophobic cave guide, who taught us everything we wanted to know about caves—and a few things we'd rather not know, but hey, it's too late now.

Jack and Marty Frost are good friends who have always encouraged us, and who always see to it that our books are available locally in their own print shop, where they frighten away countless customers with our picture prominently displayed in the front of the store. Yikes!

Barbara Warren, of the Blue Mountain Editorial Service, has been privately editing our work for many years. Thank you for your diligence in slicing and dicing until everything works.

Jackie Bolton, brave teacher of high school students, often lends us her insight into the teenage psyche. Fascinating.

Thanks to Ron and Janet Benrey, partners in some of our favorite crimes (on the page). Also thanks to our friend Lori Copeland, a dynamite writer who never fails to encourage.

Many thanks to our editor, Joan Marlow Golan, and the staff at Steeple Hill. You have a special insight we very much appreciate.

We thank Ellie Schroder, our friend far "down under" in New Zealand, who has been a firm supporter and encourager since our first meeting online. Also thanks to our friends on WritingChambers, who are always willing to pray and encourage.

Our friends "in the business," Nancy Moser, Annie Jones, Deborah Raney, Stephanie Whitson Higgins and Colleen and Dave Coble, helped brainstorm this book, and we are forever in their debt.

Mark and Janelle Schnieder and Athol Dickson gave us vital information on how we would build a foundation for a condominium on the lake—not that we would ever try to build one ourselves. That would be a horror story.

Many thanks to Stacy and April Frerking, our talented and beautiful Branson celebrities, who allowed us some insight into the setup backstage. Thanks, also, to Dennis Frerking for your healing touch, and to Dennis and Bonnie for your friendship.

Many thanks to our Webmaster and beloved cousin, Eugene Patterson, who definitely knows his way around a computer, and constantly keeps us out of trouble. We love you, Eugene!

If God did not bless us with our many friends, we would never be able to write another word.

"For I know the plans I have for you," declares the Lord, "plans to prosper you and not to harm you, plans to give you hope and a future. Then you will call upon Me and come and pray to Me, and I will listen to you. You will seek Me and find Me when you seek Me with all your heart. I will be found by you," declares the Lord, "and will bring you back from captivity."

—*Jeremiah* 29:11-14

❧ Chapter One ❧

Fawn Morrison glided across the atrium of the crowded country-music theater, enjoying the glances aimed in her direction. So what if the stares weren't all filled with admiration? Those jealous women could learn to apply makeup the right way and emphasize their few positive qualities. Everybody had at least one or two. Almost everybody.

With a grin and a wink at the old geezer who stood behind the ticket counter, Fawn eased herself past a group of chattering people and strolled toward the ATM machine in the corner.

Some of these people probably thought she was one of the entertainers in the production—she'd never looked better in her life. She wore a calf-length gown of blue silk that Bruce had selected, telling her it matched the color of her eyes. The plunging neckline raised a few eyebrows, and the thigh-high slit had almost caused an accident out in the parking lot. She sure wasn't in Las Vegas anymore. Branson, Missouri, seemed like a different planet. Hokey, maybe, but she kind of liked this place.

As she waited for the cash to click out of the machine, Fawn enjoyed the sight of her reflection in the mirrored wall. She looked hot. Sophisticated and grown-up. She'd come a long way in eight months—from earning money the hardest way, to flouncing through the casino in her cutesy little monkey outfit, smiling and calling "Keno, Keno, Keno" like a brain-injured parrot, to riding in limousines and living in luxury, eating lobster and drinking champagne.

All because she didn't mind a balding man with a paunch, and pockmarks on his face.

Okay, sure he'd been acting a little wacky the past couple of days, but what did that matter? He could afford to act wacky. Besides, he knew how to treat a lady—if the lady didn't expect him to open doors for her and if she didn't mind a burp or two during the dinner conversation.

She used the entry card and stepped into the elevator reserved for special guests, then rode up to the seventh-floor penthouse suite—Branson didn't have skyscrapers like Vegas. It didn't have casinos, either, and smoke didn't hang in the air like a cloud of poison.

Bruce was talking on his cell phone when she glided through the door. She allowed it to close with a muted clunk, and he glanced around at her. She smiled as she slid the thin spaghetti strap of her blue beaded purse from her shoulder and placed it on the counter by the minibar.

His gaze darted away and his fingers whitened on the tiny phone. "No, Vin, I told you what I'd do if you didn't stop the purchase."

Fawn sighed as Bruce paced to the other end of the carpeted great room. Okay, so he didn't seem as distracted by her hot looks as the old geezer at the counter downstairs.

He lowered his already deep, gravelly voice. "I've got everything I need to...no, you listen. I don't need the cash from this deal, I was just doing you a favor, but I'm not risking no lives for this." He grunted and held the phone out from his ear.

Fawn heard the angry rant all the way across the room, and she winced at the threat in that voice. Bruce frowned at her, then put the phone back to his ear. The lamplight made his face look as white as mashed potatoes. "No? Well, you didn't tell me about their new little discovery, did you? How many other investors know your dirty little secret? I'm not taking the heat for—"

He sighed and glanced over his shoulder toward Fawn, then disconnected with a push of a button. "Stupid jerk can have his little temper tantrum on his own time. Sorry you had to hear that, Princess. You got back fast." The edges of his voice softened as his gaze caressed her.

"What am I, your errand girl now?" she teased in the husky, seductive voice she'd practiced for months before she ever went to Las Vegas. She crossed the room in slow, easy strides and reached up to trail a fingertip along his shoulder, then rubbed at the bristles on his chin.

He jerked away as if she'd zapped him with electricity.

She pouted at him.

"Did you get the show tickets?"

"They're in my purse."

"And the cash?"

"That, too."

Bruce nodded, though she couldn't be sure he'd even heard her words. He reached into the front pocket of his slacks and pulled out a beautiful steel cigarette lighter, strolling slowly, thoughtfully, over to her purse on the counter. He opened the purse and slid the lighter into the tiny zippered pocket inside, then zipped it shut.

"I don't smoke," she said.

He sighed, the plump lines of his face drawing down with concern. "Whatever you do, don't lose the purse."

"You know I won't." Two weeks ago, some loser had tried to lift it from her shoulder, and he'd nearly lost his future children. He'd limped away, hopefully wiser.

"Are you done being serious?" Fawn asked. "Can we go play now?"

The question brought another frown. Bruce chewed on his lower lip for a moment, then pointed toward the satiny cushions of a Victorian love seat beside the wall of windows that overlooked Branson. "We've got to talk."

She blinked up at him. This was a new thing with Bruce since they'd flown here from Vegas two days ago. He seemed to want to talk a lot more, and he'd barely touched her since they arrived. Although in one way that was a big relief, in another way...

"Have a seat, Princess," he rumbled.

She smoothed the silk dress beneath her and sat, making sure the slit fell away and revealed her leg. She patted the cushion beside her. He ignored her gesture, pulled a chair from the dining set and sank down across from her, hands on his knees as he leaned forward and narrowed his heavy-lidded eyes.

She quietly sucked in her breath. Was she getting dumped?

"First of all, that isn't a lighter, it's a computer data storage device. It's called a flash drive, and that's all you need to know for now. Hopefully, you'll *never* need to know."

"But what if I do?"

"Just remember that it has important information in it—information that lives could depend on. If anything happens—"

"Anything like what?"

He closed his eyes. "Don't ask me that. Please. You're smart, and you'll know. If anything happens, find someone you know you can trust and give them the flash drive."

"You're not making sense."

"Just remember what I said. I'm asking you to do the right thing." He gave her a firm look, and she forced herself to behave like a lady and shrug, as if that would be no problem. "Second of all," he said, "I've got to tell you something, Princess, and this won't be easy." He straightened and shoved his right hand into the pocket of his gray slacks. "But first, I got a little present for you." He pulled out a small jewel case.

"Is that another storage device?" she asked.

He smiled gently—sadly. "It's a ring."

The air escaped her lungs in a loud whoosh, but before she could react, he lifted the lid.

Quietly and slowly, Fawn started breathing again. Okay, no huge solitaire diamond, nothing like that. What he pulled from the case was a beautiful gold ring encrusted completely by heart-shaped pink-red stones. He raised her right hand and slid the ring onto the little finger. It fit perfectly.

"Rubies?" she whispered.

"Vietnamese." He cupped both his hands around hers for a short second, then hesitated, watching her. He chewed on his lower lip again, then scooted his chair back and stood to pace across the floor. "How old are you, Princess?" He swiped at beads of sweat on his shiny scalp, watching her the way a horse would watch a strange object in the road.

Her stomach suddenly felt icky. "You know I'm twenty-three. I told you I didn't care much about—"

"Know what I think? I think I'm old enough to be your dad."

She tried hard not to react. *Don't let on. Don't stutter. You're past that now.* "I thought you said you were thirty-five." Her voice sounded smooth even to her own ears. In control. "That would mean you were...what...twelve when I was born?" She forced the corners of her lips upward.

He stalked across the room and back, once again rubbing his scalp. "You know what? I've got a daughter who's fifteen." He stopped and looked at her. "Haven't seen her in five years, but every time I see a kid around her age, I think about her." He gestured toward Fawn's hand. "I got my girl a ring just like that."

Fawn watched him without moving, barely daring to blink.

"Why is it I think more and more about my daughter when I look at you lately?"

She leaned back in the sofa and crossed her legs, keeping her spine perfectly straight. "You saw my driver's license."

"I've seen enough fake ID cards in my lifetime to fill the public library in Las Vegas. You know what, Fawn? Even though I don't see my kid, if I knew a big fat guy my age was shacking up with her, I'd shoot the loser right in the face. Why isn't your dad chasing me down?"

She couldn't prevent the scowl, or the gut response. "What dad?" The words bit into the air, making Bruce blink.

He wiped at the sweat again. "Are you even legal?"

"Of course I'm legal." She was old enough to drive. That was legal.

He reached down and fingered several strands of the blond hair that curved past her shoulders. "What year did you say you were born?" His voice strained tightly in his throat.

Get back in the act. Quick! She forced a husky laugh. "Bruce, don't be silly. Of course I'm flattered...I think. But I can't help it if I remind you of your daughter. Do I act like some little sixteen-year-old?" *Please believe me, Bruce. I can't go back to the Keno job. And I sure can't go back to the street.*

"Not when you're awake, except when you bite your nails."

She held up her perfectly groomed hands. She'd had a manicure just yesterday. "A woman needs her little vices. You should be glad mine are so innocuous." That was the right word, wasn't it? Bruce wasn't exactly an English professor, and tossing in an intelligent-sounding word now and then helped keep him guessing.

He continued to stare at her, as if he couldn't quite remember the true color of her eyes behind the brown contact lenses—lenses that, according to the advertisement, made her look friendlier and more approachable. More exotic as well.

Or maybe he was trying to make a decision about something. Fawn held her breath for a long moment, until the sound of a horn blast reached through the sliding glass door that opened onto the lanai.

Bruce glanced toward the door, then at his watch. "I want you to run another errand for me, Princess."

She pouted again. "So I really am your errand girl?"

"Let's just pretend that you are for now, okay?" He reached down and patted her cheek. "I think you can handle playing a role."

She watched him for a moment, fighting back a horrible fear that skittered through her stomach like a line of swarming termites. With as much cool as she could project, she reached for her purse on the counter. "Tell me what you need, oh master."

She endured his gaze. She would not beg.

"Did you withdraw the cash limit?" he asked.

"Only from one card. I don't know why you suddenly want all this—"

"Use the other card and withdraw that limit, too, but don't do it downstairs. I want you to take a taxi to an address I'm going to write down for you."

She didn't argue. How could she? He was trying to get rid of her. "You'll be here when I get back?" she asked, voice soft, conciliatory.

"I'm not leaving you, Princess, but I have some work to do, and I've got to be alone to do it."

Karah Lee Fletcher yawned for the third time in less than five minutes as her eyes glazed and she struggled to maintain her attention on the highway ahead of her. She was too close to her destination to give in to sleep now, or to the slight nausea she'd battled ever since eating that greasy hamburger in Springfield.

She was going to have to start eating healthier. And she needed to get more sleep. Working with sick people all the time left her open to just about every virus in Missouri, and when she didn't take care of herself, her immune system let her know about it.

The center line of the road blurred, and Karah Lee jerked the steering wheel to the right. "Come on, focus," she muttered to her ten-year-old Ford Taurus sedan, as if the car were the culprit weaving back and forth inside the boundary of her lane. "It isn't that late, and we're almost there. Only a few more miles."

Actually, it would be closer to ten miles before she reached Hideaway, and darkness had descended over Missouri some time ago. She glanced at the glowing numbers on the dash. Nine-thirty. Okay, not that long ago, but she'd worked last night. Big difference.

She felt another yawn coming on, and reluctantly closed the vents that allowed the sweet Ozark air to drift through the car. Time for the big guns.

She switched on the air conditioner full force and took a few deep breaths, aiming all four vents toward her. Ah, yes, that chased away most of the nausea and blew off some of the fog that hovered in her brain. The improvement wouldn't last long, judging by her experience of the past hour. Highway 76 west of Branson had very little traffic to keep her occupied, and it made her wonder: Did someone know something she didn't? Or could she be lost?

She pulled over to the side of the road and checked the directions Ardis Dunaway had given her. Follow the Highway 76 signs and ignore the strangeness of the new roads that had been added in the past few months. This place had changed a lot, but she still knew how to follow directions.

The stars congregated in the darkness of the country sky, but the moon was nowhere in evidence. The trees on either side of her seemed to swallow any excess light. Another attack of the yawns beset Karah Lee as the night invaded the car with increasing heaviness...and her eyelids drooped ever closer to catastrophe....

She jerked upright. "Time to get serious." Karah Lee hated talking to herself. To her, it meant that, after thirty-four years, the loneliness of single life had finally affected her mind. People who talked to themselves became so addicted to it that they did so in public. Death knell for a social life. So she wouldn't get into the habit of it, but if she fell asleep now and ran off the road and killed herself, that, too, would end future prospects.

She reached for the radio knob, then thought better of it. The blare of noise would only cheapen the experience of driving into this magical land that had made such an impact on her when she was a teenager—when the roads had been so much narrower than they were now.

Finally, she cast a quick glance into the back seat, where her huge black cat, Monster, lay snoozing in his pet taxi, strapped safely in place with the seat belt. "You know, you could learn to carry your weight in this family, and at least rattle your cage a little, give me one of those good deep snarls when I start to nod off. Your life is dependent for the next few moments on my ability to keep my wits, and they're threatening to scatter out across the Ozarks like leaves in a tornado."

She heard a grumpy cat-mutter and nodded. "That's better. I probably should have put you up here in the front with me, but I thought I'd be nice and let you sleep through this trip. It's stupid to drive when I've barely had eight full hours of sleep in the past three days."

The husky-hoarse sound of her own voice in the confined space of the car would probably keep her awake for a few moments. "How many patients have I seen in the past three years who'd fallen asleep at the wheel? I don't feel like becoming another statistic."

Just last week a father of three was fatally injured on I-70 during rush hour when he veered over onto the shoulder, then apparently overcorrected and slammed into a car in the next lane. His friends said later he'd gone thirty-six hours without sleep. Countless accidents were caused by irresponsible drivers who...

Her head nodded forward. She took a deep breath, slowed her speed, flexed her hands. She should have given herself more time, should've asked for an extra day to get here, but no, good ol' tough Karah Lee could do anything. She'd been accused by co-workers of having the stamina, pain tolerance and size of a redwood tree. At times, she was proud of the comparison. Other times, it made her feel lonelier. Few people took the time to venture past the facade of indomitable redhead and get to know the real Karah Lee Fletcher.

Monster, given to Karah Lee by a colleague recently engaged to a cat hater, wasn't exactly what she had in mind as a lifelong companion. In fact, they barely knew each other, and the relationship wasn't improving with time. When she complained about him at work, however, the staff teased that Monster sounded a lot like his new owner.

She was not amused.

The road blurred. She could *not* keep her eyes open. She desperately needed sleep.

Maybe if she just pulled over to the side of the road for a short nap...but experience had taught her that if she allowed herself to close her eyes for a few moments, it would take a loud beeper in her ear to bring her out of it before morning. Just a few more miles, and—

A shadow separated itself from the darkness of the trees, followed by another shadow and another, into the glow of her headlights, barely twenty feet from her front bumper. She slammed on the brakes and swerved as three deer darted back and forth over the road in confusion. The tires of Karah Lee's car skidded into the brush at the edge of the shoulder, and she couldn't prevent the slide, couldn't veer from the tree that came at her with sickening swiftness.

The impact thrust her forward, but her seat belt grabbed and held. The crash stunned her. She sat in horrified aftershock.

Monster yowled and scratched at the pet taxi with frantic cries, but Karah Lee sat frozen. Suddenly, she realized that she did not have the stamina, or the pain tolerance, of a redwood.

She fainted.

∽ *Chapter Two* ∽

Fawn stepped from the elevator on the seventh floor, heart still pounding, hands shaking harder than they had been when she left. She reached into her money-stuffed purse for the key card. Would he be here?

It wasn't as if she'd never been dumped before. It had happened twice in the past few months, but each time it had been harder to return to other kinds of work. And here she was in Branson, Missouri. She didn't even *know* these streets, and she had a strange feeling she wouldn't be able to do as much business here, even if she could force herself to do that business again.

But what else could she do?

The card slid into the silent-lock mechanism, and to her relief the door opened at the slightest pressure of her hand. Hearing Bruce's voice, she broke out with a sweat of relief. He was still here.

"Vincent didn't have the guts to come and talk to me himself," she heard him say from the other room, "so he sent you."

She stopped in the doorway and frowned as she caught sight of a tall, dark-haired man in an expensive-looking dark gray suit. His back was to her, and Bruce stood facing her, the shadow of his big body outlined in the neon lights that flashed into the room through the lanai windows. He didn't even glance toward her when she entered.

"He doesn't like associating with traitors" came the visitor's voice, which was rougher than Bruce's deep bass.

Fawn grabbed the door to keep it from shutting and disturbing the men. Bruce wasn't finished with his business. She'd come back too soon. She was about to turn around and leave without saying anything, when Bruce spoke again.

"I'd only be a traitor if I allowed my clients to pour their money down the drain with bad deals."

"It doesn't have to be a bad deal," Gray Suit grumbled. "You tell your clients to leave their money where it is for six more months, and you can guarantee seventy percent return on their investment. They won't want to pass that up."

"Vincent can't guarantee that, Harv, and you know it. How many dupes are you going to find to buy a worthless space of air over Hideaway? The condominium isn't even built yet."

"Construction's already begun."

Fawn saw the anger spill over Bruce's face. "How can that be?"

Harv gave a low grunt of laughter. "You're not the only man who can be bought. I've got good information that says you're carrying a vital report around in your pocket. You don't have any business with that inspection report, and Vincent wants it back."

"It's not on me," Bruce said.

Out in the hallway behind Fawn came the sound of the penthouse elevator doors opening and dishes rattling, probably a meal on a room-service cart. Harv half turned at the sound, until Fawn could see the outline of his long, heavy-boned face, with thick jawline and overgrown, black eyebrows. He looked really edgy, and the fingers of his right hand tensed, muscles flexing beneath his suit.

Bruce caught Fawn's gaze, frowning hard at her and jerking his head toward the door in an unmistakable command for her to leave. "Harv, this whole mess is going to come down on Vincent's head, and I don't want to be here when it happens. I'm not getting blamed for his stupid decision."

Harv returned his attention to Bruce. "Then what are you doing here? You didn't fly all the way here just to give Vincent the brush-off. You could've done that on the phone."

"I didn't—"

"You've got contacts here." Suspicion laced the man's voice.

"I wanted to see some of the shows, check out the—"

"I know what kinds of shows you like, and they aren't these country-music comedy shows."

"Vincent sent you here to do his dirty work, didn't he?" Bruce asked. "He doesn't care about a bunch of strangers in Hideaway as long as he can make his money and get out before tragedy strikes. Don't you care that lives could be at stake?"

"Since when did you care about other people?"

As if against his will, Bruce's gaze gave an imperceptible flick toward Fawn, then he looked back at Harv.

Harv's shoulders stiffened. He started to turn, reaching beneath his suit jacket.

"No!" Bruce shouted. "Princess!"

A deadly-looking pistol with silencer seemed embedded in Harv's hand as he drew it from his pocket. He aimed at Fawn and squeezed the trigger as she ducked at Bruce's command.

The doorpost beside her splintered. "Bruce!"

"Run, Princess!" Bruce shouted, charging the man. "Get out now! Hurry!" He was still six feet from his target when the man swung back, aimed, squeezed the trigger.

Fawn shoved the door wide behind her, barreling past a bellman with a room-service cart. The cart and dishes went flying with a clatter across the hallway.

"Get out of the way!" she screamed. "He's a killer! Run!" She raced to the elevator, jabbed the button, then realized she could be trapped. She ran to the stairwell and plunged downward, expecting to feel a bullet in her back any second. She heard another clatter of dishes, heard a man cry out above her just as the stairwell door closed— the bellman?

Her feet barely touched the steps as she raced down them. When she reached the third-floor landing, she stumbled and twisted her ankle. Gasping with pain, she didn't slow her stride. At the second-floor landing, she paused long enough to look up and listen.

She didn't hear the sound of pursuit. She kicked off the strappy, high-heeled sandals and looped them over her purse. Where was he? What was happening up there? *Bruce! What happened to you?*

She wanted to turn and race back up those stairs. She needed to get help, fast. Bruce could be up there bleeding to death.

Did Harv shoot the bellman, too? *Where was the man?* Harv could have taken the elevator down—he could be waiting for her when she stepped through the door on the ground floor.

But that would be crazy. Too many witnesses.

Instead of continuing down the stairs to the first floor, she rushed to the second-floor entrance. But as soon as she placed her hand on the knob to open the door, she let it go and drew back. What if Harv was on the other side of that door?

"Stop it!" she whispered to herself. She had to get to safety—reach the lobby and cry out for help, find the security guards and have them call for an ambulance. She cracked the door open and peered into the hallway. All she saw was a serving tray of empty dishes on the floor at the far end of the hallway. She glanced back over her shoulder toward the stairwell, then stepped into the hallway. She took the main elevator to the lobby. No way Harv could get her there.

The moment her bare feet sank into the plush wine-and-gold carpet of the lobby, she saw him. The man named Harv in the expensive-looking gray suit stood talking with two uniformed guards. He gestured toward the stairwell door, looking the part of a frightened man. One of the security guards drew his gun.

Fawn gasped.

Harv glanced her way and sighted her. "There!" he shouted. "That's the killer. Don't let her get away!"

She plunged into the midst of a group of elderly ladies.

"Stop that woman! She's a killer!" someone called across the lobby.

A couple of women screamed as Fawn stumbled to the exit and shoved open the door.

She ducked past another crowd of oblivious people, keeping the colorfully dressed theatergoers between herself and the guards as she slipped into the shadows at the edge of the property. Wishing desperately for a pair of sneakers, she slung the strap of her purse over her head and plunged into the darkness, barefoot and sure she would be shot in the back any second.

Taylor Jackson sped along the tree-shrouded road as fast as he dared, and watched for moving shapes in the beams of his headlights. He dreaded what he might find, and he hoped backup was on its way.

How many times had he warned tourists to avoid driving this stretch of road at night? And how many runs like this had he made in the year he'd been working this area? The local communities needed to buy space on radios and hometown papers daily, alerting the world that humans did not own the roads in the

Ozarks, especially at night. The deer, opossums, raccoons and coyotes did.

Sometimes he thought the four-footed variety of animals obeyed the rules of the Mark Twain National Forest better than the two-footed ones.

The only times he ever prayed were on runs like this, when he didn't know what he would find, how many victims would be involved, how much damage there would be. He especially hated finding children hurt. Highway 76 twisted through the hills with such diabolical suddenness it caught travelers unaware, making them think it was veering right, then veering left instead, in hairpin curves that seemed to make no sense.

Meanwhile, oncoming cars accidentally bright-lighted one another with vicious intensity. On summer days, when traffic was heavy and they got a slow driver bottle-necking thirty sightseers in a hurry to see Hideaway in a couple of hours, people got injured, even killed. Hideaway Road had earned a bad reputation in the past few months, since tourists had discovered its beauty.

But on a weeknight he knew he could probably blame a deer.

The glow of two flashlights hovered ahead of him in the darkness, and he cut his speed. Sure enough, fresh deer scat on the road told the story. He was relieved to find no big hairy bodies lying beside the pavement. As far as he could tell, not even any blood. Now, if only the humans had been so lucky.

He saw the bright red Ford Taurus sedan kissing a maple tree in the darkness. As he maneuvered his vehicle across the road to illuminate the wreck site with his headlights, Taylor saw Mary and Jim, who lived down the road, leaning over someone in the driver's seat. The door was open. Good. The damage might not be as severe as he had first feared. Also, he saw no passengers other than the driver.

He pulled in behind the car, left his emergency lights flashing on the dash and got out. As he ran to the car, the guttural scream of a nightmare screeched through the air, and he caught his breath at the animal sound. He'd never heard a deer cry like that before...and then he realized it was coming from inside the car.

As he approached the others, Jim and Mary stepped back, and the sound accosted him more directly. For a brief moment he hesitated, unwillingly reminded of the horror movie he'd watched years ago about a human possessed by a demon.

But the woman in the front seat behind the steering wheel did not look grotesque in any way. She looked sane, though slightly dazed. She groaned, and Taylor realized the screech did not come from her but from the back seat. He rushed forward, peered past the driver's seat, and caught the double gleam of terrified eyes, two black paws stuck through the wire mesh of a pet taxi. It was the biggest black cat he had ever seen—and the loudest he had ever heard.

"Would you *shut up?*" The deep, irritable tone of the driver mingled with the cries of the cat.

Taylor stepped back slightly from the car and bent low enough to get a good look at the victim. She had wildly curly red hair and an unhappy expression in a very pale face. In the residual glow from his headlights he saw a streak of blood outlining the left side of her face.

"I didn't mean you," she said. "It's Monster." Her voice was husky and authoritative, though slightly hoarse.

"Ma'am, it's okay, we'll take care of you. Just remain still until I can ascertain the extent of the damage."

"No need. I'll be okay. I just need to get out and stretch my legs a little." She closed her eyes and groaned again, lifting a shaking hand to her forehead.

Taylor raised his voice to be heard over the screeches of the cat. "Ma'am, I'd like to check you over first." He turned to Jim. "Would you go get my medical case out of the truck? I want to get her vitals and—"

"My vitals are fine." The victim's voice deepened. "I just want some fresh air." She reached down to unfasten her seat belt and fumbled with the release.

"Here, let me help you with that." Taylor leaned forward, but before he could assist her, she made her escape from the belt and turned to look into the pet taxi.

He got a close-up view of a long, graceful neck above shoulders that were surprisingly broad and muscular for a woman. She wore cutoff jeans and a faded blue T-shirt, and her arms and legs were untanned, well-shaped.

"It's okay, Monster, you're safe." Her husky voice was suddenly melodious and soothing. "Cut the noise a minute, will you?"

To Taylor's amazement, the racket lowered to the growl of a stressed-out tiger.

The woman turned back and looked up at Taylor. "Sorry about that. Is there a vet around the village any-where? I'd like to get him looked at."

"Don't you think we should concentrate on you first?" Taylor asked as Jim approached with the kit of medical supplies.

"I told you, I'm fine." She reached up and grasped the side of the door frame, then swung her feet to the ground. Her face and lips were pale except for the streak of blood that matched the color of her car.

Taylor placed one hand gently on her shoulder as he reached for the bag Jim held out for him. "Ma'am, please humor me and remain seated for a moment. You don't *look* fine. I'm a paramedic, and I'd like to make sure about you first. I need to ask you a few questions."

She blinked up at him, then frowned and looked pointedly at the gun hanging at his hip. "Since when do paramedics have to carry guns and wear ranger uniforms?"

"When they're also law-enforcement rangers. We're short staffed."

She took a deep, audible breath and leaned against the steering wheel, meeting his gaze squarely. "My name is Karah Lee Fletcher, I'm on Hideaway Road in Missouri, and the date is Wednesday, June 11. Those were the questions you wanted to ask me, right?"

"Done this before, have you?"

"You might say that." A hint of humor flashed across her expression and disappeared almost before he caught it.

"I can see you've hit your head—did you experience any loss of consciousness?" Taylor continued to look into those eyes. They were more golden than amber brown. She had a high forehead and cheekbones, and a strong, firm chin line.

She glanced away briefly at his question, and he noticed her hesitation. "Ma'am?"

"Some." Her voice grew irritable again.

"Some? Any idea how long you were out?"

"Couldn't have been more than a few minutes. That racket in the back seat works better than a sternal rub." She held her arm out. "Go ahead, take my blood pressure. It stays about 125 over 75. I already took my heart rate. It's steady and normal. Respiration's normal."

He pulled the cuff out of the bag and did as he was told, curbing his curiosity about her apparent medical knowledge. The cuff made a firm fit around her arm. She had a large frame for a woman, but in spite of her muscular form she didn't look like a bodybuilder. He pumped the cuff and took the reading, nodded and released the pressure.

"Elevated?" she asked.

"It's 140 over 85."

"Not bad after all this excitement," she said. Her cheeks were gaining some color. "*Now* do you want to let me up?"

"If you'd give me a couple more minutes, Ms. Fletcher, I'd appreciate it." Why did he always have to get pushy patients in the middle of the night? "Have you had any alcoholic beverages this evening?"

Her expression revealed her irritation, and the color in her face deepened. "A herd of deer ran me off the road, okay? I'm not a drunk driver. Do you smell alcohol on my breath?" She blew a puff of air into his face. All he caught was a whiff of onions. A strong whiff. "Just let me out of the car and I'll walk a straight line for you." She reached for the door handle to steady herself and scooted forward.

"Not yet, please." He leaned over her and palpated the back of her neck. "Sometimes you can be hurt worse than you think at the time. It's always best not to take chances, Ms. Fletcher."

She gave a long-suffering groan. "It's Karah Lee."

He frowned. "Excuse me?"

"I go by Karah Lee, not Ms. Fletcher."

He pulled out his penlight and dropped to one knee in front of her so he could get a more level look. "I'm going to shine this light into your eyes briefly, Karah Lee."

She gave another sigh of impatience. "Go ahead, do your thing. I'm telling you, I'm fine. I'd like to see about my cat, though."

He checked her pupils, and they were equal and reactive. He looked at the wound on her temple, which could use some attention but was no longer actively bleeding. "You obviously haven't been out of the car yet, right?" To his discomfort, the cat's voice did seem to be reaching a higher decibel again.

"No, but if you'll give me a chance, I'll go for it."

"I'm sorry, I'd like you to remain in the vehicle until we can get an ambulance here to do a more thorough—"

"No." Her voice was firm. "I told you I'd be okay. I am willing to sign a PRC form so you can release me without getting into trouble."

Taylor bit back a sharp retort. A Patient Refusal of Care form would release him from any liability if she should develop complications later. She sounded as if she was accusing him of trying to cover his backside.

"Look, *Ms. Fletcher,* I'm not interested in covering for myself, I just want to make sure you don't have any—"

"It doesn't look like there's too much damage," she said, gesturing toward the front of her car. "And I wasn't speeding. I realize that the damage to the car isn't always the best indication of injury to the occupants, but you'll have to trust my judgment. I promise to check in with the local clinic first thing in the morning." There was a hint of sarcasm in her words and a touch of irony in her gaze, and he wondered what that was all about.

"By the way," she said, "I tried to start the engine and it refuses to budge. Know of anybody I might call for a tow in the morning?" Her voice mingled with the cat's in a grating duet.

Taylor didn't bother to curb his own sarcasm. "The engine won't start?" He raised his voice to be heard over the yowling in the back seat. "Doesn't that tell you something?"

She rolled her eyes and sighed, then reached out and took his left arm in a firm grip. With that grip she urged him backward. "You don't listen too well, do you?"

She released him and stood gingerly to her feet. She was tall. The top of her head came to his eyebrows, and he was six-three.

"I'm refusing care. End of...discuss—"

Her focus seemed to waver, and the color drained from her face once more. She grabbed her stomach and doubled forward. He reacted quickly to step out of the line of fire, but not quickly enough. His uniform pants would never be the same.

❧ Chapter Three ❧

Sirens blasted through the air and bounced from the side of the building where Fawn Morrison crouched, panting from the run, terrified. She was at least three city blocks from the hotel-theater complex she'd escaped, and panic continued to shake her body so hard she could barely get enough air into her lungs. Red-white-blue lights reflected across the parking lot. She could only gamble that no one driving into the lot would catch a glimpse of her dress from beyond the thick hedge that shielded her.

She knew that if she moved quickly, she had a better chance of escape, but still she squatted in the shadows. All she wanted to do was pull herself into a tight little ball and block everything out.

She reached into her purse for a hair clip, twisted her long blond hair into a knot at the back of her head and anchored it. She pulled her bangs out of the stiff helmet of dried hair gel she'd used to keep them off her forehead. They made her look younger. Too young for her taste—like about fourteen—but it might save her hide to look younger, just for tonight. Now if she could get out of this dress, and scrape off some of this makeup....

As the whine of the sirens died, she limped along the edge of the building to a tall privacy fence that she guessed shielded the cast entrance for this theater. A searchlight flickered across the treetops at the theater next door. In spite of her ankle, she ran to the fence, jumped up and grasped the top edge, pulling herself up, kicking hard to swing herself over. Splinters gouged her arms and legs, and she gasped with the pain as she dropped to the asphalt on the other side.

The shriek of sirens continued to split the air as Fawn limped to a concrete loading dock. She climbed the steps and tested the door. It slid open, and she slipped inside to be overwhelmed by the smell of roast beef and onions, and the clatter of cookware. A kitchen. As late as it was, they would be cleaning up after a banquet, maybe. Or this could be a dinner theater. Judging by the size of the five-story structure, this, too, was a hotel-theater complex, which was a good thing.

She passed by a broad doorway and crept as quietly as she could along the shadowy hall. If she could find her way to the connecting hotel—

"Hey, you!" came a sharp male voice from the bright kitchen.

Going cold all over, she turned to see a thin-haired man standing beside a stack of pots and pans at a huge sink. He wore a white shirt and slacks and an apron.

"You lost?" he asked.

"Uh, yeah. Where's the ladies' room?"

"Back out the Staff Only entrance and to your right," he said drily, tossing a towel over his shoulder as he gave her a once-over.

She nodded and continued along the service corridor until she knew she'd be out of sight of the kitchen, then she opened a door to her right. The lights were off, of course, but the hallway fluorescents revealed a small office. No good place to hide. She checked the next room down on her left, but it was locked. Several yards farther, the next door on her right, was a linen room, complete with huge stacks of towels, aprons and uniforms.

This could work! They did it in all the movies—people sneaking into the closet of a hospital and pulling on a doctor's lab coat so they could blend in with the hospital staff. She could blend in. She'd worked at a hotel for a couple of weeks.

After a hopeless search for a light switch in the room—this must be one of those places where a master switch was located elsewhere—she pulled a tiny key-chain flashlight from her purse, stepped into the room, closed the door behind her. The thin stream of light flickered, threatening to go out as she grabbed a set of whites from the top of a stack in front of her. The pants would've fit an elephant. The next set in the stack looked as if they might fit. She pulled a hairnet from a package on the shelf beside the clothes. Of course there were no shoes.

She stripped off her dress and shoved it deep behind a stack of tablecloths. The clothes fit—the bottoms were a little too snug around her hips, but she could still move without ripping them. She pulled the black hairnet over her head and tucked her bangs beneath it. With the clip holding her hair up off her shoulders, she might get away with this. Except for her shoes. Still, she couldn't go barefoot.

The tiny flashlight flickered out as she tugged on her shoes. She couldn't coax any more from it. Should've changed the battery last week.

She felt around in the darkness for her purse, and was slinging the strap over her head when she heard the sound of purposeful footsteps and a man's deep voice.

"...police department. I need to ask you some questions."

The footsteps stopped, and Fawn caught her breath.

"I don't think any crooks or bad guys came through here tonight, if that's what you mean," came the voice of the dishwasher who'd given her directions to the bathroom. "Just people from the dinner theater."

"Is the show over?"

"Should have been over about fifteen minutes or so ago."

"Did anyone come through this way recently? A woman in a blue dress, blond hair?"

Fawn bit the inside of her cheek. *No, please don't tell him.*

"Hey, you kidding? Sure did," came the reply. "Blue dress? Really pretty?"

"Sounds right."

"She was in here just a few minutes ago. Looked a little spooked, if you ask me. What happened, Officer?"

"We just need to question her." There was a sound of static, like one of those walkie-talkie things Fawn's Uncle Ralph used to have. "We need to have a look around."

"Okay by me, but I'm not the one you have to ask. My boss—"

"We'll take care of that. If you don't mind, you just ease out of the building for a few minutes. There's been a double murder, and we're investigating."

"Murder! You're not kidding me? Right here in Branson?"

Fawn froze. *Oh, Bruce, no.* She squeezed her eyes shut and moaned softly.

There was a thunk on the linen-room door, and then the knob turned slightly. "What's in here?"

Fawn braced herself to make a dive for the floor.

"Towels and stuff."

"Okay, we'll want to check it, too. Why don't you go ahead and get hold of your boss, and I'll have a talk with him, get the master switch turned on down here. But meanwhile we need to get some backup in here." The voices became somewhat fainter, but they didn't go away completely. Fawn slid down beside a rack of towels and buried her face in her hands. She was trapped.

Oh, Bruce...he was really dead. Harv had killed him. And who else had he killed? The bellman?

And what was she going to do?

* * *

Karah Lee huddled against the passenger door of the ranger's SUV, doing her best to control Monster's movements within the circle of her arms as the ranger took the sharp curves at a sedate speed. "It wasn't the bump on the head that made me sick. Really. Ouch!" She eased Monster's front paws up and away from her shoulder, wincing as the sharp claws dug into her flesh in an effort to remain attached. "I was sick long before I saw those deer in the road."

"Look, it's never convenient to have to seek medical care in the middle of the night, but there are times—"

"I heard you, okay?" she snapped, then bit her lower lip. She knew the speech. She'd given it enough times, herself. And here she was behaving like one of her most obnoxious patients. Next time she would remember how irritable pain could make a person. "Trust me," she said more gently. "I'll be fine."

"Oh, really?" His sarcasm was still in evidence. "You have a sixth sense about these things, do you?"

She frowned at him. What was his problem? So she was refusing care—it shouldn't be a big deal to him. "I'm not trying to be a jerk," she said, then grimaced when her loving pet attempted to tenderize her right leg. "You know what, Monster? Some people think cat tastes just as good as chicken. I'm tempted to see if they're right."

Ranger Taylor Jackson skidded a glance her way.

"Joke," she said. "It's a joke. See? I'm making jokes, I'm thinking clearly, I'm—"

Monster yowled, and the impact of the sound reverberated through the interior of the SUV. Karah Lee covered the cat's face with her left hand. He nipped at her thumb, and she jerked away.

"Do you think he's hurt?" Taylor asked.

"If you're asking if he's behaving abnormally, no." She'd checked him over, as much as he would allow, and had found no damage. "I'd still like to find a veterinarian. You say there's none in Hideaway?"

"There's a kid at a boys' ranch across the lake who could probably look at him. Everybody around here takes their pets to him. Besides him, the closest vet is Kimberling City."

"A kid?"

"About seventeen, good kid."

Monster yowled again, and again Karah Lee attempted to comfort him.

"You say he's always like that?"

She nodded, then realized he probably couldn't see the gesture in the dim glow from the console. "He misses his previous owner. We aren't exactly soul mates."

There was a soft snort of laughter, and Karah Lee glared at the ranger's silhouette.

The amusement left his expression. "Sorry. You're staying at the Lakeside?"

"That's right. I'm renting a house in town, and it won't be ready for a week and a half."

"You're staying alone?"

She gave him a sharp glance. "Except for Monster. Why?"

"I simply wondered if you'd be alone tonight, without anyone to check on you."

"You offering?" The words slipped out before she could stop them, and she wished she could tie a knot in her tongue. She hadn't meant that the way it sounded. Not at all.

Even in the faint light from the dash she thought she could see him blush. He had the coloring for it, with faint freckling across the bridge of his nose, and hair the color of aged bronze. He had straight, fierce eyebrows—no, not exactly fierce, they just made him look earnest, like a younger version of Billy Graham.

She sighed. She had spent too much time in the company of a sarcastic hospital staff, and she'd grown accustomed to the cynical, occasionally coarse joking. "Look, I appreciate your concern, but I'll be fine, and if anything happens, I promise not to hold you personally responsible, okay?"

"That *isn't* what I—"

"I know about head-sheet protocol, I know what to look for and I know what to do in case of emergency."

There was a short silence. "That's fine." The reply was tight and clipped, and she realized she'd probably offended him. In fact, thinking about it, what she'd said had sounded offensive. Again. Disgusted with herself, she sighed and leaned back.

They rounded a curve, and there was a break in the heavy overgrowth of trees. Moonlight reflected from the glassy surface of a lovely lake below, and Karah Lee caught her breath. "I'd forgotten how beautiful it is down here."

From the corner of her vision, she saw him glance at her. "You've been here before?"

"My family came here a lot when I was growing up. It was one of my favorite places in the world."

There was a brief silence. Even the cat had settled into Karah Lee's lap without destroying any more flesh or further taxing her eardrums.

"I think you're going to find a few changes," he said softly.

"The roads have changed, for sure. When I was a kid, this was a gravel road. I like the improvement."

"It might have backfired on us."

"What do you mean?"

He steered the vehicle along the downhill curve of the road toward town. "We've been overrun by tourists this year. Some company came in last fall and bought several of the houses along the shore of the lake, then opened a shop on the square this spring that rents out mountain bikes, canoes and kayaks. They take excursion trips into Branson for evening shows, by boat. They've been advertising big-time online, and all over Branson. The crowds are swarming here. I can't believe you even found a place to stay."

"I made reservations early."

"You're lucky."

"No, I'm smart enough to think ahead."

"These people have also purchased some prime property at the eastern end of town, and they're building a ten-story condominium. Can you believe that? Right here in Hideaway."

She glanced at him as he pulled into the circle drive in front of the bed-and-breakfast. "You sound like you think that's a crime."

"I transferred here from the Grand Canyon. I've seen the kind of damage overcrowding can cause. It could devastate the whole area. Our mayor called a council together to try to enact some zoning laws, but by then it was too late."

"I'm sorry." But was she? After all, she owed her new job to the sudden increase in tourism. "Maybe it won't be such a bad thing, though."

Taylor parked and got out of the Jeep, then walked around the front to open her door. "The crime rate has already begun to rise," he told her. "I think it could be a disaster. I'll help you with your things."

She shoved Monster back into his pet taxi and braced herself. The yowling commenced. She noticed the ranger grimace. "I'll be fine," she said, raising her voice to be heard over the sudden din. "I can take care of my own luggage." The sooner she could haul this animal to her own private cottage and block out the sound, the happier everyone would be.

"I'll make sure you're settled," he said as he carried both her heavy suitcases along a lighted footpath to a broad front porch. Someone had left the porch light on, and he set the cases down and reached for the screen door.

She grabbed the handle before he could. "Look, I'm serious, I'll be fine." She regretted the rough tone in her voice, but the guy was a ranger, not a bellman, and he'd already gone out of his way to help her. She refused to take advantage of him. She didn't need a chaperon to see her inside. She knew small towns—had grown up in one, herself—and word could get out in a hurry that she'd had to be escorted to her room by a law officer.

"Really," she said more gently. "I'll be fine, and you probably have work to do. I'm a big girl, I can take care of myself. Thank you for the ride, and I'm sorry about the...the mess I made."

Without waiting for a reply, she shouldered past him and pushed open the door, carrying her angry cat with her. She'd suffered all the humiliation she planned to endure tonight.

Darkness and silence settled into the linen room like one of the thick quilts Fawn's great-grandma used to tuck around her when she spent the night. The sounds outside had faded just a few seconds ago—but not before Fawn heard the crackly voice of the policeman's radio informing him they were surrounding the place.

She pulled off her shoes once again. She couldn't run well in them, especially with the twisted ankle. She crept through the darkness, feeling her way along the edge of the shelves until she reached the doorway with the narrow line of light edging the bottom. No sound came from beneath that door.

Holding her breath, she reached for the doorknob and started to turn it. The hard metal felt cold in her hand. There was a soft click, and she froze again.

"Check all these rooms," came a man's voice, echoed by the sound of brisk footsteps. "Don't take any chances, she could be armed."

There came the sound of a latch turning, and Fawn caught her breath. It wasn't this door. They must be searching the room across the hall. They would come here next.

She plunged her hand into her purse and felt for the book of matches she'd taken from an ashtray in the suite. As the sound of new footsteps reached her, she ripped a match out and struck it hard against the base. It flared, and she held it high to search for any vents or removable grates along the wall or ceiling—she'd seen people escape that way a lot in movies.

The footsteps drew closer. The flame burned her fingers and she dropped the match, stifling a cry of pain. Tucking her purse beneath her arm, she struck another match, then braced herself and touched the flame to the entire book of matches, holding the tip of the cardboard cover.

It flared brightly, startling her. She gasped, bit her tongue.

There was no grate, no vent she could squeeze into. But she *might* be able to scoot beneath two stacks of towels in the corner, if she curled herself into a tight ball. She shook the flaming matchbook before it could burn her fingers again, just as a door closed across the hall.

"Not in here. Block this—"

The scream of an alarm shot across the room, smacking Fawn with an almost physical force. The ceiling started to rain.

Instinctively, she scuttled toward the stacks of towels where she'd intended to hide, and plunged through a tumble of terry cloth. She heard muffled shouts from the hallway and more footsteps, but the door remained closed.

Her teeth had begun to chatter before she realized *she* must have been the one to set off the alarm with her matchbook flare. If she hadn't already been in big trouble, she would be now, for sure. What happened to a sixteen-year-old convicted of murder and attempted arson?

She had to get out of here!

The shriek of the alarm continued to blast her as she worked up the guts to climb from her hiding place and creep back across the room. She opened the door, bracing for a gang of uniformed men to surround her and shove her to the ground.

No one stood outside the door. She peered out, both directions. Nobody. That wouldn't last long. Tucking her purse under her arm, she turned right and plunged along the brightly lit hallway, hopefully in the direction of the hotel section of the building—and an exit door.

The alarm paused, and a tinny voice came from a speaker overhead. "Attention. Attention. The automatic fire alarm has been activated. Please proceed to the nearest staircase to exit the building. Do not use the elevators."

If she could find a service elevator, maybe she could get upstairs. That way she could blend in with the crowd of hotel guests who would be making their way to the stairwells.

"Guard those doors!" came a voice from up ahead, just past a corner in the hallway.

Another alarm blast nearly deafened her from a speaker just overhead, followed by the same announcement.

"...can't block the people from getting out of the building," came the reply, and the echo of footsteps, and the sound of excited breathing...coming closer...

"Of course we can't stop them," came the sharp retort. "Just look for the woman!"

She came to a door and shoved it open, stumbled inside just as the sound of footsteps echoed through the hallway. She hovered in the darkness, afraid to breathe for several seconds, until the men continued along the hallway in the direction she had been going. She waited until the sound dwindled, then scuttled back into the shadows. In the dim light that came through the open door, Fawn could tell this was a prop room, with a black cape and top hat on a table in the front right corner. She saw a chest—or a cart—beside the table. A magician's cape? A magic show of some kind?

"Did you check that room?" came another man's voice as footsteps once again echoed in the hallway. "Hurry. Search where you can."

"But the alarm—"

"Just check the room!"

Fawn skittered toward the cart and dived behind it. She had worked backstage at a theater with a magic act in Las Vegas. These carts were big enough for someone to hide inside...if she could just remember how to unlatch—

"Can't find the light switch."

She found the latch and slid the panel sideways, scrambled inside just as the overhead light came on. Under cover of the echo of footsteps, she slid the panel shut behind her, plunging herself into the protective blackness, afraid to breathe.

"Anything?"

"Of course not. I told you she wouldn't still be here, even if she was here in the first place, which I don't think—"

"Just cover the exits and make sure she doesn't slip through." The voices faded.

Fawn crouched in the dark for a few more seconds, then slowly, with the alarms still sounding all along the hallway, she slipped out of the magician's cart and skittered to the open door. The corridor was empty. She caught sight of an elevator door a few yards down and sighed with relief. After another quick glance along the hall in both directions, she ran to the elevator doors and pressed the button, hoping this wasn't one of those places that disabled their elevators during a fire alarm.

Once again came the sound of footsteps. She tensed, ready to run, but the door slid open. She plunged inside as the footsteps grew louder, and tapped the third-floor button desperately. The doors took their time, then slowly closed as the footsteps quickened.

Fawn closed her eyes and slunk into the corner, sure the searchers would catch sight of her before she could escape. They didn't. The doors clanked shut, and she finally allowed herself to breathe again.

When the elevator deposited her at the third floor, she rushed into the hallway and joined a small crowd of sleepy-eyed, confused-looking people. She limped along beside a man dressed only in a pair of boxer shorts and a hotel terry robe. The woman with him wore a night-gown. As Fawn joined the others on the guest stairwell, she glanced down at her clothes, then reached up to feel her head. The net was still there, and her hair was wet, which would darken its blond color. They would think she was an employee, or someone in her pajamas.

More people came up behind her as she limped down-stairs. They reached the ground floor and stepped through the emergency exit out into the night, where three men in uniform stood watching them closely.

She yawned and rubbed her eyes.

They didn't stop her. Nobody called out as she joined the rest of the growing crowd in the glow of the outside lights.

As the first fire engine raced into the parking lot behind the building, Fawn crept closer to the edge of the crowd, then slipped out into the night. She hadn't needed her shoes, after all.

❧ Chapter Four ❧

The telephone beside Karah Lee's bed rang long before the alarm clock did on Thursday morning. Without opening her eyes, she reached for the receiver. Her left hand knocked it from the cradle and she barely caught it before it could hit the hardwood floor. This wasn't going to be a good day.

"Hello." She sounded like a frog.

"Hi, this is Taylor Jackson doing damage control," came the baritone-gilded voice.

She cleared her throat and pried her eyes open. Good grief, it was practically still dark outside. "Damage control?"

"You had a wreck last night, remember? At least you're awake and talking."

She tried to sit up in bed, but the movement made her head pound, and she lay back against the lilac-scented pillow. "Don't you ever have downtime?"

"Not lately. I've seen some bad reactions after an impact like last night's. I didn't want to take any chances."

Her nausea was almost gone, but her head hurt where she'd bumped it, and her shoulder ached where the seat belt had grabbed her. Even worse, she cringed with humiliation every time she thought about her nauseating display in front of—and on—the poor guy.

"Well. Okay." She glanced toward Monster through the semidarkness, and saw his huge outline, belly up, legs in the air, paws clinging through the holes in the top of the pet taxi. It was the way he usually slept—except he usually avoided the pet taxi.

"How are you feeling this morning?" Taylor prompted.

"I'm doing fine, no blurred vision, and I feel a lot better."

"Usually after an impact like the one you sustained, the victim feels worse the next day."

She gave a quiet sigh. Nothing better than a skeptic paramedic—unless it was a cat that snored. "Okay, but when you factor in the bulldozer running me over, I'm doing pretty good."

No reply.

"You know, considering." He obviously had been born without a sense of humor, or the gift of gab. "Look, Taylor, I'll be fine."

"The tow truck picked up your car." He had a very attractive voice. "The mechanics will be checking it out today. I gave them the number of the Lakeside in case they need to get in touch with you."

"You're kidding. You did all that?"

"The guy's shop is just three blocks from the square." Yes, that was definitely a nice voice, maybe a little impatient because she wasn't admitting to her misery. Maybe he was wondering why he'd even gone to the trouble to help her in the first place.

She was touched in spite of his curtness. After all, she was definitely a noncompliant patient. She wouldn't have been nearly so forbearing in his place.

"Well. Thanks again, Taylor. And really, don't worry about me. I'll be checking in at the clinic about eight-thirty this morning."

"Oh." He sounded surprised. "You will?"

"Of course." To work. She had specifically not mentioned that fact to him last night, because she knew how quickly word traveled in the medical community, in spite of the new Federal regulations about patient confidentiality. She did not want her stupid behavior last night to precede her. "Thanks a lot for calling, Taylor." Her head continued to throb. She needed aspirin, and fast. "Goodbye."

There was a pause, and then, "Goodbye." It almost sounded like a question, as if he still wasn't convinced she was okay.

She moaned and allowed the receiver to fall back into its cradle, hoping she wouldn't have to face him again until the stain faded from his uniform. Unfortunately, one did not easily forget a six-foot-tall woman with red hair.

Her stomach rumbled, harmonizing with Monster's early-morning growl of welcome, and she dragged herself from the comfortable bed to open the pet-taxi door. She had assured the elderly proprietress of the Lakeside

Bed-and-Breakfast that her furry ball-and-chain had the intelligence to use the ever-present litter box, and that he didn't scratch furniture because he'd been neutered in a former cat-life.

Monster rushed to the kitty-litter box in the bathroom while Karah Lee followed him and dug aspirin from her overnight case. Checking her appearance in the mirror, she groaned aloud. Her forehead was mottled red and blue and the skin was broken. She might possibly pull enough bangs down over it to conceal the bruise from the clinic staff, but it would take a better actress than she was to conceal the fact that her head was throbbing so hard it nearly crossed her eyes.

But she would be there, no matter what.

Fawn Morrison opened her eyes to dim, green-shaded light and the sound of tires on blacktop only a few yards from where she lay. She unwound herself from the tight-little-ball position in which she always slept, and brushed aside a pine branch that scratched at her cheek with the puff of every breeze. Her stomach cramped. Her feet hurt from the cuts and bruises she'd gotten from her barefoot run through the hazard-pocked darkness last night. Her ankle ached.

From the jumbled-together restaurants up the hill on Highway 76, she caught a whiff of frying bacon, and it reminded her how hungry she was in spite of her stomachache. It also reminded her where she was, and why.

Last night, she'd raced away from the crowd as fast as she could run, tripping over curbs in the dark, stumbling into bushes she couldn't see and, finally, scrambling down a steep, muddy embankment to this place. Unable to go farther, and hurting too much to care if she got caught, she'd curled up and cried.

Again this morning, the tears blurred her vision. *Bruce was murdered!* The police thought she was the murderer, and Harv knew what she looked like. He couldn't afford to let a murder witness live. And if she was right about that flash drive storage device in her purse, Harv would be after it. *She* couldn't afford to let him—or the police—get to her.

She couldn't let anybody find her—which meant she couldn't let anyone recognize her.

Another car swept past, and Fawn eased herself farther down the muddy, tree-lined bank to a tiny creek that trickled over some rocks in the shadows. It didn't smell like a sewer, so she stooped down and splashed some of the chilly water on her face. She couldn't believe this hidden place was so close to congested Highway 76.

Her head ached, and her eyes felt swollen from crying. For the past couple of years she'd been sure she'd never cry again. She thought she'd seen everything—and done everything. But just as Great-Grandma used to say, life had a way of changing. Why couldn't things just settle for once? Why couldn't people learn to be nice?

Fawn missed Bruce. He'd been good to her—as good as he'd known how to be. He wasn't one of those fine, law-abiding citizens or anything. He had a business, and it wasn't banking. But she'd also seen him give money to the soup kitchen down the street from the mall in Las Vegas, and he was a big tipper. He was good to a lot of people. So much better than her stepfather had ever been to her...considering Bruce didn't know how old she really was...considering he'd never forced her to do anything she didn't pretend to want to do.

Teardrops joined the creek water on her face, and again she let herself cry. "Oh, Bruce," she whispered. "Why'd you have to blow the whistle on those people? Why'd you have to make it such a big deal?" People broke the rules every day. *He* broke the rules every day. Why'd he have to pick yesterday to change his ways?

And then she couldn't help wondering about the big, ugly crime he said they were committing in Hideaway. What kind of danger were those people in? And what would happen to them now that Bruce wasn't there to stop whatever was happening?

Now she knew why he'd planned to take her there this weekend. He'd told her they could play—riding jet bikes and floating down a local river and hiking on some fancy new trail—but she'd known from the beginning he'd had something else on his mind.

A loud truck muffler startled her with its racket on the road. She sniffed and wiped her face, then slumped back against the bank of the creek. "What am I going to do now?"

She picked up the purse she'd used as a pillow last night, and pulled out the tiny lipstick with mirror Bruce had given her last week. From what she could see in the reflection, she had mud all over her face, and her hair was one big mat of tangles and dirt and leaves. One of her contact lenses had come out, and now she had one blue eye and one brown.

She'd have to clean up before anybody saw her.

She sniffed and blinked away the tears, then dropped to her knees and rinsed her hair and clothes as well as she could in the cold creek water to get some of the mud out. The gravel dug into her knees, adding to the pain of her cut and bruised feet.

Last night, she'd scrambled through the deserted parking lot of a mall about a half mile or so up the hill from here. Maybe she could go back there and get some clothes before it got busy this morning. And maybe she could get some other supplies, as well.

She pulled the cash from her purse and stuffed it into the pocket of her pants. She transferred the rest into her shirt pocket—including the teensy computer data storage device Bruce had told her to keep—and buried her pretty, blue-beaded purse that matched the dress she'd looked so good in. And so grown-up.

Now it was time to be a kid again. Maybe she could get away with that here in Branson, at least for a little while. Branson was nothing like Las Vegas.

Except there were murderers here, too.

The rumble of Monster's outraged cries still echoed in Karah Lee's ears as she stepped through the entrance of the two-story Victorian lodge that held the main office where she had checked in last night. The cat did okay alone most of the time, but he hated new places, and he let everybody know about it. Karah Lee only hoped he didn't blast the windows out with his caterwauling today.

Maybe someone at the clinic could tell her how to contact that kid who treated animals. Monster didn't appear to be injured, but she didn't want to take any chances with the life of her grumpy roomie.

Drawn by the irresistible aroma of a country breakfast, Karah Lee strolled through the comfortable-looking lobby, with its Victorian sofa and chairs and fireplace, to a wide hallway that led to a large dining area with fifteen tables decorated with cut-glass vases holding fresh carnations.

This morning, the only diners in evidence sat outside on a deck overlooking the lake. Karah Lee glanced toward a steam table near the wall to her right. A white-haired octogenarian stooped over the table, stirring a pot of gravy. There were steel trays containing sausage patties, omelettes, waffles and all kinds of toppings, fresh fruit, biscuits, hash browns with onions...the aromas made Karah Lee dizzy with hunger.

"There you are." The lady set down her platter of biscuits and gestured toward a table beside a window that overlooked the deck—and the sparkling blue lake just a few yards away. "You're Dr. Fletcher, ain't you?" she called across the room.

"That's me."

She studied Karah Lee's scrubs and lab coat. "Cheyenne sure is looking forward to seeing you."

"Good. I'll walk over there as soon as I finish my breakfast."

"She'll be glad of that." The woman dusted her floury hands on her apron as she crossed to Karah Lee's table. "Nobody can believe how fast her business grew this year, and what with her signed on to work down at Dog-wood Springs for the rest of the summer, to boot, she's been working night and day sometimes, it seems like to me." She held her hand out.

Karah Lee took it in a gentle grip, looking for a name badge that wasn't anywhere in evidence. "You must be Edith Potts's business partner."

The lady's dark eyes lit with a gleam of amusement. "Called me that, did she? 'Idiot partner' is more like it. I'm the one whŏ talked her into this fool idea last fall when the former owner retired."

"You mean this bed-and-breakfast?"

"That's right. Can you believe it?" She gestured around the room, then plopped a biscuit in a plate, split it in half, and stepped to the warming table to spoon some gravy over the top of it. "Two old women, each with a foot in the grave, and we're buying this place from somebody younger than we are by ten years." She shook her head as she set the plate in front of Karah Lee. "You look like a gal who likes rib-sticking food. Oh, where're my manners? My name's Bertie Meyer. I'll get you some coffee and freshly squeezed juice. You can have anything here you want to eat, you don't have to eat what I stick under your nose."

"I love biscuits and gravy."

"You sure? Red always griped at me for being too pushy."

"Biscuits and gravy are my favorites for breakfast except for waffles and strawberries and cream. Who's Red?" Karah Lee took a bite of tender biscuit and perfectly seasoned gravy.

"That was my husband," Bertie said. "He died last year. He was eighty-five or eighty-seven years old, we're not sure which."

"How could he not know how old he was?"

"When he applied for social security he thought he was seventy, and those people told him he was two years older than he thought. We knew better than to argue with the government, so we just let 'em think what they wanted."

"Why do you think buying this bed-and-breakfast was a bad idea?"

Bertie snorted. "You kidding? I must've lost my senses when I talked Edith into buying this place."

"Obviously Edith didn't think it was a bad idea."

"Most folks didn't at the time, but that was before a bunch of greasy-handed scoundrels called the Beaufont Corporation bought up most of the town." She glanced toward the steam table, then leaned toward Karah Lee. "You like black walnuts?"

"Love 'em."

Bertie's face crinkled in a pleased smile. Nearly a foot shorter than Karah Lee, she moved with a quickness that contradicted her professed elderliness as she poured coffee and juice and decorated a plate with a thick Belgian waffle, strawberries, whipped cream. White running shoes peeped out from beneath crisp green slacks as she quick-stepped back to the table.

"This here's my specialty." She set the platter in front of Karah Lee with a flourish. "Black walnut waffles made with milk and eggs from our own private supplies. My pet goat, Mildred, donated the milk."

Karah Lee held her breath for a moment, then sniffed, closed her eyes, exhaled slowly. "Black walnut waffles," she whispered. "I haven't had one of these in years."

"Aha! So you do appreciate fine dining." Bertie glanced over her shoulder, then leaned forward, lowering her voice. "Don't tell Cheyenne I said so, but she could use a little culture. Poor gal can't tolerate black walnuts." She pulled a chair out and seated herself across from Karah Lee. "You go ahead and eat, and I'll fill you in on some of the stuff that's been going on around here lately."

"You mean like the greasy scoundrels who bought up the town?"

"Two men in nice coveralls and bill caps, posing as farmers, came along with a deal I couldn't pass up. I should've known they was fakes when their hats didn't have a single sweat mark on 'em, and the overalls were brand-new. Red and I worked hard on that farm all our married life, and you know what? Those frauds couldn't farm a two-bit garden. I should've seen it, but I was so crazy with loneliness after Red died, I couldn't think straight."

"They offered you a lot of money?" Karah Lee asked between bites of a delicacy so scrumptious it was making her high.

"The money wasn't bad, nosiree. To boot, I told myself they was real farmers, and the land needed to be farmed. Now those so-called farmers are subdividing my home, and I can't hardly stand it. I'm just glad I sold our milk goats to the boys' ranch across the lake. No telling what those idiots would've done to my babies."

"Someone mentioned there was a local boys' ranch."

Bertie nodded. "Dane Gideon—he's our mayor?—he runs it. Wouldn't be surprised if your boss ended up over there at that ranch with him. Wouldn't be surprised at all."

"Dr. Allison?"

"Cheyenne. She and Dane've been sweet on each other since before Red died—that's how I count time now—Before Red, and After Red."

The food was so distractingly delicious, Karah Lee couldn't keep up. She blinked in confusion.

Bertie gave an inspection of Karah Lee's empty coffee cup, then carried it over to the pot for a refill. "Dane Gideon also owns the general store down the street from the clinic. I should've listened to him. He warned me to check out that offer a little closer, but did I listen? Oh, no, not me. In a few months, when they change the whole look of our town and get that monster condominium built and sold to the poor saps who've been flocking in here, Edith and I'll be out of a job, sure enough."

"Why do you say that?"

Bertie shook her head. "Honey, I've seen the tourists pour in here like this before. It was a regular holiday boomtown back when Branson got put on the maps with all those singing stars. Half those famous people came right here to this little place to stay when they wasn't performing. Then the developers built more of them fancy hotels closer to Branson, and we lost a lot of business. Mark my words, when that condo building's finished, it'll suck all the attention away from our little bed-and-breakfast. Tourists are fickle folk."

"I bet you're wrong." Karah Lee savored the final mouthful of strawberries and whipped cream, then wiped her mouth and pushed away from the table. "You've got what, ten cottages along the shore?"

"That's right, and three more rooms upstairs in this building, though the top floor ain't finished yet. Too quaint for the crowd the big boys are trying to reel in. Why, they're building them an honest-to-goodness hiking trail, and renting out kayaks and bicycles, and running one of them starlight-dinner boat rides into Branson. Ain't any way Edith and I can compete with that. And jet bikes! I never heard of such a thing around here. It'll scare all our fishermen away. They'll hate it."

"Seems to me you'll get a good clientele from those who just want peace and quiet, not all that crazy activity," Karah Lee commented.

Bertie leaned forward, the skin around her eyes crinkling with worry. "But I know our customers, and they ain't going to stay around here with all that activity. That company is set to take over this whole town. We won't be the same."

Karah Lee remembered what Taylor had said on that subject last night. Was his forecast of a disaster accurate after all? Bertie seemed to think so.

Dressed in new jeans, a pink T-shirt with LOVE BRANSON in big blue letters across the front and white canvas tennis shoes, Fawn carried the rest of her purchases across the parking lot of the outlet mall with the bright blue roof. Her ankle still felt stiff, but she tried really hard not to limp. She wanted to continue blending into the crowd—until she could escape it.

As soon as she reached the quiet backside of the mall, she cut behind the strip of buildings where no one could see her, then pulled out a compass and a map of Branson and studied the map for a minute to get her bearings.

She'd gone on a wilderness trek with a church youth group a couple of years ago—some friends of hers had tried for a few months to "save" her soul. All that Jesus and God talk didn't make much sense to her. Why would she want another father? They weren't good for anything but leaving. Or worse.

Anyway, the trek had been fun, and she'd learned some great stuff, like how to use a compass and how to wrap a sprained ankle. Judging by the map, she needed to cross Highway 76 and find a nightly condo-rental place down by Lake Taneycomo. If she pulled her con right, without getting caught, she might be able to find a place to hide out for a few days, until the police decided she'd left town.

But first, she needed to make a few changes. Still trying not to limp, Fawn scrambled back down to the bank where she'd slept the night before and opened her bags of purchases. She pulled out the denim backpack she'd gotten for half price at the wilderness outfitter store, tore off the tags and opened the zipped pockets so she could stuff it full. She stuck toiletries into the pockets, along with food, extra underwear and some shorts. By the time she filled the compartments, they would hardly zip shut.

She shoved the pack to the side and pulled out a food-coloring kit she'd purchased at the kitchen-supply outlet. In that whole mall, she hadn't found a single hair-color kit, so she'd have to make do. She was allergic to the hair-color developer, anyway.

Beside the little plastic bottles she set a tiny bottle of shampoo, a pair of rubber gloves, a mirror, comb, scissors. When she got finished with this rig, nobody'd recognize her from last night.

Before Fawn went to Las Vegas, she'd been an emancipated minor living with two older girls. One of her roommates had been a beautician and had taught her some of the basics, but there wasn't time for anything fancy right now. She whacked her hair off in long chunks, then buried the telltale blond strands beneath the mud along the bank, just in case someone came looking for her here. She couldn't afford to let them know what she might look like after she finished this.

She washed her hair, combed it out, trimmed it again. Using the rubber gloves, she mixed the food coloring until it was the same sort of burgundy brown a lot of kids sported, and spread it onto her hair, adding water from the creek to get it soaked through. The food coloring stained her cheeks—she had to scrub hard and even then didn't get it all off. Still, it looked like a big birthmark, so maybe she'd get by with it.

By the time she finished her makeover, Fawn didn't even recognize her*self*. She was a new person. Again. She'd done that a lot lately.

Sometimes it seemed as if she might go through the rest of her life becoming a new person every few weeks—as if the old person wasn't good enough.

When would the real Fawn Morrison ever be accepted as she was?

❧ *Chapter Five* ❧

Taylor Jackson inhaled the sweet scent of honeysuckle through the open window of his truck as he pulled into the scenic overlook above Hideaway. The Beaufont Corporation had just completed their new hiking trail along this ridge, and even though he wasn't crazy about all the disimprovements those people were making, he liked this trail. It was the only smart move they'd made, in spite of the difficulties with zoning laws and purchase of the land. Their efforts would help draw the business they would need to fill that ten-story condominium eyesore under construction at the east edge of town.

He might even use that trail himself, from time to time. One thing he missed about his job at the Grand Canyon— one of the only things—was the hiking.

As the echo of hammers, saws and the rumble of the crane drifted up to the cliffs from the construction site,

Taylor climbed out of the truck, taking his coffee with him. He glanced at the ashtray and considered, for just a moment, pulling a cigarette from the pack he kept stashed there. But he was trying hard to quit. He'd managed to do it three times already in the past year. Amazing how hard it was for a guy to live healthy when there were times that he saw the futility of living at all.

Gravel crunched beneath the soles of his boots as he strolled to the edge of the pavement to gaze down on the village of Hideaway. Settled comfortably on a small peninsula along the shore of the Table Rock Lake, the tiny town with a population of barely over a thousand always held him spellbound. He came to this spot often to remind himself why he'd requested the transfer to the Ozarks. The contrast between this view and the view from the South Rim of the Grand Canyon often made him feel as if he had traveled to a different planet.

Of course, he loved the starkly angled vistas of one of the greatest natural wonders of the world. He couldn't imagine anyone who wouldn't gaze in awe across the shadowed gorges from the South Rim to the North Rim and marvel at God's artwork. Part of his heart would always belong to the Canyon. But he no longer wanted to live with the memories the place continued to evoke.

Here in Missouri, he'd made no memories except those from childhood, when he had traveled historic Route 66 with his parents on vacation, and they'd made a detour south to this place.

The beauty of this area began with the lush June green of an abundant Ozark Garden of Eden, brilliant with flowers that dotted the grass and trees like enormous jewels. Generously proportioned gazebos dotted the broad lawn that reached into the lake on a peninsula down below. The Victorian angles and gingerbread trim of those gazebos blended with the bright yellow, green, blue and pink cottages of the Lakeside along the shore at the west edge of town.

Okay, so a guy could live without the pink, but the overall effect wasn't bad.

A large new dock, crowded with boats, extended from the shore, and it appeared as if construction had begun on still another dock to the east—another project of Beaufont. Across the lake, a tree-topped cliff—twin to the one on which Taylor stood—embraced the water and held captive vines of honeysuckle and wild roses.

The village municipal district was a square of connected brick-front buildings facing outward to the street that surrounded it on four sides. Each doorway had a flower box, and each box held red, blue, yellow or purple blooms. From Taylor's position, he could see nearly everything that went on below, from the dock all the way back to the ancient, abandoned barn directly below him in the shadow of the cliff. The barn was old, constructed of weathered gray board, old corrugated aluminum roof, loft door broken, barely hanging, old hay spilling out. A dilapidated wood fence caged nothing more than a herd of wildly tangled weeds in the corral.

A movement redirected Taylor's attention as the front door to the lodge at the Lakeside opened and a woman with curly red hair stepped onto the quaint, wooden front porch. She wore a long white jacket and a pink jumpsuit of some kind, though he couldn't tell the design from here. He was pretty sure, however, that the woman was Karah Lee Fletcher. She ducked beneath a low-hanging potted plant and descended the steps to the walkway. When she reached the street, she strolled toward town. Except for the new sidewalk that encircled the town square, Hideaway had no paved public walkways.

Taylor thought about his telephone call to her this morning. He'd obviously awakened Karah Lee, and he felt badly about that. He ordinarily had a little more finesse than to call someone barely past sunrise. After last night's conversation and this morning's—during which she'd made clear her eagerness to cut the talk short—he'd decided not to bother her again.

She frustrated him. Last night she'd shown obvious signs of injury, and yet she'd refused any kind of treatment. Her hostile response to his concern still rankled. His main concern had been her physical safety, and even though she looked perfectly healthy to him now as she walked along the road, last night she had not seemed well.

Too many people delayed medical care after an accident, and they paid the price for it later. Was he wrong to show a little human compassion this morning, knowing she was alone, with possible brain injury?

He just needed to keep reminding himself this wasn't the Grand Canyon, where the hot, dry climate had added a dash of danger to every situation during his shifts. The climate in the rolling hills of these Missouri Ozarks was more forgiving. But this was about an accident, not heatstroke, and on his watch, nobody was going to die from neglect.

The figure below crossed the street as she reached the square, and Taylor nodded with satisfaction. She was going to the clinic, just as she'd promised.

Static from the radio on his belt interrupted the rumble of the crane below, and Taylor returned to the truck as he listened to a message about the manhunt—which was actually a woman hunt. The murderer who had killed the Las Vegas businessman and the hotel employee last night in Branson had not yet been apprehended. No surprise there.

He glanced at the faxed report he'd received this morning and studied the unfocused picture of a sexy blonde in a blue dress. The image had been caught on a security camera as she ran from the scene of the crime last night. The police had lost her trail in a theater-hotel complex a few blocks away when a fire alarm went off. They'd been forced to evacuate the building. Details—and a better picture of the woman—were to follow sometime today.

Since murders were not a common thing in this area of the country, the press would be all over this. It wouldn't surprise Taylor if the picture of this woman made the front page of the local and regional papers.

He took a sip of his coffee and automatically reached for a cigarette. He had it out of the pack and halfway to his mouth before he caught himself and returned it. He hated these things.

On impulse, he carried the pack to the trash can alongside the trail, squashed the cigarettes as if they were a hand-exercise ball and tossed them in the can. People were murdering each other in Branson, Missouri, the heart of the Bible Belt. He didn't need any help to put himself in the grave.

Of course, he knew he'd probably break down and buy another pack tomorrow, but it felt good to make this gesture, expensive as that gesture had become lately.

He was just about to drive away, when he received another call, this one more typical for Hideaway. A child had bumped his head this morning, and the parents were concerned about a concussion. Taylor answered the call. He could get to their location in five minutes. Seemed as if he was on a roll with the concussion patients lately.

Karah Lee raised her face to the morning light—the sun had not yet appeared over the tall pine trees that stood sentinel over an outward-facing, redbrick town square. The majority of commerce in this thriving little town concentrated itself on a peninsula of land surrounded by the diamond-blue glitter of Table Rock Lake.

As she stepped across the street from the broad lawn to the sidewalk that encircled the square, she caught sight of the reflection of herself in the front window of the general store next to the brick-front clinic. She grimaced at the same tall woman with flyaway curls of red hair who watched her from the mirror every morning—and whose image she tried to avoid every chance she got.

She had never taken any delight in her appearance. She not only towered over other women, she was also taller than most men, and many of her male colleagues seemed intimidated by her.

This was her first job outside the supervision of the hospital or her trainer, and Karah Lee felt awkward. It wasn't that she doubted her skills—her grades had always been good, her supervisors and trainers had always given her excellent reviews, and she'd breezed through med school and residency with surprising ease. If only social situations had been so easy.

When she was growing up—and up, and up—Mom had always encouraged her to hold her head high and be proud of her height. Even Dad had told her to "suck it up," because someday she was going to be a beautiful woman.

So when did "someday" come? At thirty-four, Karah Lee did not feel attractive.

She knew what she looked like. One elderly patient a couple of months ago had called her "handsome," whatever that meant. At least her facial features were even, and her waist was still slightly narrower than her hips. Slightly.

This morning she wanted to make a good first impression, instead of blurting out the first thing that entered her brain—which was a habit she hadn't been able to break. People who knew her became accustomed to this tendency, but strangers didn't always know what to think about her—last night with poor Ranger Jackson being a prime example.

She took a final breath of the sweet, cedar-scented air and pulled open the glass door on the right. The sign on the window beside it stated Hideaway Walk-in Clinic. For Emergencies, call 911.

She walked quietly across the tile floor as the door whisked shut behind her. The clinic brooded in dim silence, not quite open for business this morning. To the immediate right were two vending machines, one with candy and chips and one with drinks; they combined with the row of windows behind her to provide the sole source of illumination at the moment. Another set of doors stood open to an empty, seemingly deserted hallway that held the smell of an old building, scrubbed to a shine with a lemon cleanser.

Voices and laughter reached her from the left, and she turned and glanced through another open door to find a waiting room and reception window. Lights blinked on in the office behind the window as she watched. Good, she wasn't late.

She took a step in that direction, but then she saw a movement in the shadows at the far side of the vending machines. There was a thump, and a grunt, and she recognized with amusement the posterior section of someone bent forward from the waist, squeezed between the machine and the wall.

She cleared her throat. There was another thump, and a low mutter of words she couldn't decipher. Definitely male.

"Hello," she called out to him.

"'Morning," he said without straightening. Though muffled, his voice sounded deep and youthful.

"We need to call an electrician to get this outlet fixed," he said. "Dane'd kill me if I tried to do it. The light was blinking when I came in. Is it okay now?"

Karah Lee turned her attention to the steady glow against the potato-chip wrappers. "Looks fine to me."

"Great, maybe that'll hold it until they can get over here. I'm glad the pop machine didn't kick off in the night." There was a shuffle of feet as he backed out toward her, then straightened to turn. "I'd hate to have to replace all those cans of—" He saw her, and his thick, black eyebrows raised in surprise.

The young guy was obviously in his teens. He had broad, muscular shoulders, ebony skin, and very short, kinky dark hair. He wore green scrubs that matched the color of the cedars outside. As all this registered with her, Karah Lee saw the realization dawn in his expressive brown eyes that he hadn't exactly greeted her—a stranger—with dignity. He grimaced with dismay.

He recovered quickly and gave her a broad display of straight, even teeth. "Hi, you must be our new doctor."

Karah Lee nodded and held out her hand. He took it, and she was pleased by the confident grip. "Karah Lee Fletcher."

"Gavin Farmer, but nobody calls me by my real name. You can call me Blaze."

She gestured to his clothing. "Are you a nurse or a tech?"

"Tech and chief flunky. I help out here when I'm not in school." He gestured toward the machines. "I've just been placed in charge of potato chips and soda, and I've already failed." He didn't sound upset about it. In fact, he struck Karah Lee as one of those terminally cheerful morning people who tended to get on her nerves.

"College?" she asked.

His grin broadened with pleasure. "Really? I look like a college kid?"

She nodded.

"Not for another year. Come on, I'll introduce you to the rest of the staff and show you around the place, if they'll let me." He led the way across the cozy waiting room toward the reception window where a woman sat with her back to the room, listening to an ambulance radio at the far side of the oblong office space.

"Hey, Jill, look who I found," Blaze announced as he stepped up to the window. "Our newest staff victim, Dr. Karah Lee Fletcher."

Without turning around, the woman held her hand up to silence him. She had short hair that resembled a brown football helmet. Karah Lee thought that style had gone out of fashion in the last millennium, but she'd never been one to keep up with fads.

Blaze gave Karah Lee an apologetic glance. "Believe it or not, she's usually friendly," he muttered.

"Hush a minute, Blaze," Jill said, her voice deep and raspy. "I'm waiting for some news."

He shrugged and leaned toward Karah Lee. "Jill's our nurse and general troublemaker. And she's doing secretary-receptionist duties since we don't have one right now."

A voice shot over the radio. "Nothing here, Jill. Over."

She pressed the talk button. "You're sure about that?" She released the button and glanced over her shoulder at Blaze and Karah Lee. "A friend of mine got a call this morning from Mary Coley, who lives out by the road a few miles from here. Said somebody swerved to miss a deer and ran into a tree last night. That shy ranger, Taylor What's-his-name, took the call, but he's tight as a clam and never shares details. You hear anything about a wreck?"

Karah Lee felt a sudden buzz of discomfort.

"Not a peep," Blaze said. "I want to introduce Cheyenne to Dr. Fletcher before we get too busy to—"

The radio chugged its static over the line again. "...the crew didn't make any runs to Springfield last night...either dead or alive. Over."

Blaze gave a long-suffering sigh and stepped forward. "Jill, would you quit playing?" There was a cajoling edge to his voice now. "This is our new doctor. At least say good morning."

Jill turned from the radio and straightened, grimacing ruefully. "Sorry. Hi, Dr. Fletcher. Nice to meet you. We've got a bet going on how many car-versus-animal accident patients we'll have for the month of June." She raised her voice, as if speaking to someone in another room. "So far it's three and I'm winning."

"Last night doesn't count until it's confirmed," came a slightly familiar voice from down the hallway. "And besides, our bet was on how many patients we _received_." The sound of the voice drew closer. "I haven't seen any patients yet this morning, have you?" The speaker stepped into view, and Karah Lee recognized her new employer, Dr. Cheyenne Allison.

Dr. Allison had hair the color of midnight, cut in a wash-and-wear shag that barely reached her shoulders. She had dark brown eyes and an olive complexion that suggested a Native American heritage. At about five feet seven inches, she had to tilt her head to look up at Karah Lee.

"Oops, you caught us being unprofessional." Dr. Allison opened the door between the waiting room and the treatment area and stepped out to shake Karah Lee's hand with the same firm grip Karah Lee remembered from their interview in Branson earlier in the spring.

"Hi, Dr. Allison."

"Shy."

Karah Lee frowned.

"Call me Shy. Short for Cheyenne."

Ah. Chey.

"First order of business," Cheyenne said, "we're all on a first-name basis around here, patients, doctors, staff. Some of the older patients like to be called Mr. or Mrs. and they insist on calling me Dr., it makes them feel more secure, but other than that we have a more relaxed office. Call me Chey or Cheyenne."

"Chey. Fine." Karah Lee pulled up an office chair and sat down. "I go by Karah Lee. So this is what you do for entertainment around here? Keep tabs on car wrecks?"

Jill and Cheyenne glanced at each other sheepishly.

Blaze chuckled. "Serves you right for betting."

Jill shrugged. "We're not betting for money, we're just competing for one of Bertie's black walnut pies."

"Oh, no, you don't. I've got dibs on a goat cheese," Cheyenne said. "*Not* black walnut."

"Ah, that's right," Karah Lee said. "I heard you didn't exactly have a sophisticated palate."

The gently angular lines of Chey's face filled with amusement. "Who told you that?"

Jill laughed. "Anybody in town could've told her that. Hey, I heard the dummy who caused the accident last night had a cat in the car. Does that count as a patient?"

"No way!" Cheyenne protested. "That's cheating."

Karah Lee forced a smile. Time to get this over with. "Since the dummy's cat suffered fewer injuries than even the dummy herself, I don't think you can count him as a patient. We might be checking out the dummy later. Depends on how the day goes."

If she hadn't been the victim of this unintentional joke, she would have laughed at the expressions of surprise on their faces. Blaze did laugh. Loudly.

She reached up and pushed back her bangs to expose the injury. "Deer ran out in front of me and I swerved and hit a tree. Actually, it was my car that hit the tree. I had sunglasses clipped to the visor, and my head made contact during impact. End of story. My cat's okay and everything is fine. You got any coffee? I could use another dose of caffeine."

Static jerked through the ambulance radio and drowned out Jill's abject apology. A disembodied voice announced the pending arrival of a small child who had slipped and smacked his head against the rocks while chasing a squirrel.

As the radio voice gave specifics, Karah Lee turned to Blaze. "You'd better give me that tour while we've still got time."

Chapter Six

Taylor led the way to the clinic in his truck, checking the rearview mirror to make sure the parents of the injured child were keeping up in their own car. The damage wasn't bad, but Dr. Allison—who preferred to be called by her first name instead of her title—would probably want to do a suture or two.

The radio buzzed at him again, and he received an updated report about the woman hunt in Branson. For some reason, authorities believed the suspect was still in town. To Taylor, that was stupid. With all the roads that led out of Branson, no murderer was going to hang around to get nabbed by the police.

Taylor switched off the radio as he parked in front of the clinic. He had more important things to take care of right now. Branson could keep its murderers.

* * *

Blaze opened the door to the fourth and last exam room. "I'll never make fun of my patients. If I ever have any."

Karah Lee glanced at him curiously as she stepped into the room and inhaled the familiar scent of iodine and alcohol. "You're going to be a doctor?"

"A vet. If I can make the grades. What were you saying about your cat?" Blaze followed her inside. "Did he get hurt in the wreck?"

"He seems fine this morning, but I'd like to have a vet take a look at him."

"You staying over at Bert's place?"

"Bert?"

"You know, Bertie Meyer. She and Edith run the Lakeside."

"Oh, that's right." A small town, where everyone knew everyone, just like Karah Lee's hometown. "Yes, that's where I'm staying."

"I can run over there this morning when I get a chance and take a look at him for you. What's his name?"

"Monster. You already take patients?" She remembered Ranger Jackson telling her about him.

"Right now I'm all Hideaway's got. My dad was a vet, and I worked with him."

"So where's he?"

There was a slight hesitation, then, "He died. My mom and I don't get along. They were divorced. That's why I live at the boys' ranch now."

"Oh." *There you go, Fletcher, putting your foot in it again.* "When did he die?"

"Last year."

"Oh, man. Sorry. I lost my dad when I was just a little older than you."

"How'd he die?" Blaze asked.

"He didn't die. He left."

It was Blaze's turned to grimace, and he did it with his whole face, his thick, dark eyebrows drawing close above beautifully expressive eyes. "I think that'd be worse than having him die."

Karah Lee nodded. "But I don't think he'd agree."

Blaze's grimace lifted.

"So when can you see my cat?"

"Lunch break."

"Karah Lee?" came her new boss's voice. "You want to come in here a minute? I need a big, strong, brave patient."

Karah Lee frowned at Blaze. "Patient?"

He shrugged at her. "Better do what she says. She's a dead-on shot with pepper spray."

"I heard that!" Cheyenne called from the other room.

Blaze grinned and rolled his eyes. "I'll explain later," he whispered.

After giving a report at the clinic, Taylor left the little boy and his parents in Dr. Allison's capable care and strolled back toward his truck, glancing along the sidewalk in both directions as he stepped from the curb. He'd seen no tall woman with red hair in the waiting room, and she was nowhere on the street. No way would he ask about her at the clinic. It was no longer his business.

It wasn't as if he wanted to run into Karah Lee—she might suspect him of stalking her.

He climbed into the Jeep and glanced toward the front doors of the general store next to the clinic. No, he would *not* buy another pack of cigarettes.

He was driving west on Hideaway Road, when he saw a late-model white Toyota Camry sedan parked alongside the road beneath a heavy overhang of trees. One man crouched beside the right front tire while another man was bent over, apparently searching through the trunk for something that didn't seem to be there.

Taylor parked and got out of the truck. "Lose your jack?"

Both men looked up at him. He noticed the motor was still running. "Engine problems?"

The man stooping at the right front tire straightened and hurried around the car toward him. He wore a sleeveless white T-shirt, which revealed a tattoo of an eye on his left shoulder. "I'll say. Thing's been dying on us all morning, and then this." He gestured with disgust toward the front, just as a car came speeding around the curve.

Tires squealed on blacktop as the driver caught sight of them and swerved to avoid a collision.

"You say you've got a jack?" Tattoo asked. "The one in the trunk's busted, and it's a little dangerous here on the road. Trouble is, there's no shoulder."

Taylor could only pray a car with a less cautious driver didn't come barreling around the curve before they could get out of the way. "I'll get my tools."

Working as quickly as possible, Taylor helped the guys with their tire and had them on their way within ten minutes.

The last thing he did as the car disappeared from sight around the bend was write down their license number. It was a habit he'd picked up years ago, working the Canyon. Ordinarily, he'd have done a more thorough check immediately, but not with cars screeching around the hairpin curve at double the speed limit.

Thirty minutes later, he received a call about a stolen vehicle.

Karah Lee had her first taste of Cheyenne Allison's bedside manner in exam room three in the presence of a frightened, screaming five-year-old boy named Jonah.

"There, now, it'll be okay, sweetheart." Chey's voice settled into the room like a soothing blanket. "Let me tell you what I'm going to do. You see this big strong doctor?" She placed a hand on Karah Lee's shoulder. "She has a bump on her head, too."

The child and his parents turned their attention to Karah Lee, and she suppressed a groan. So much for confidentiality in this office. Hadn't these people ever heard of government regulations?

Chey's hand tightened on Karah Lee's shoulder, urging her to lean forward; then, with her other hand she brushed Karah Lee's bangs aside. The child's eyes widened at the sight of the uncovered wound.

"Why don't you watch how we fix her head," Chey suggested. "Then, if she doesn't cry, you won't mind letting us do the same thing to you, will you?"

Like magic, Jonah's tear faucet stopped. He studied Karah Lee with serious intensity, hiccuped, then sighed. "Does it hurt bad?"

"It did when I hit it." Karah Lee leaned closer to him. "Want to compare? Hey, I think mine's bigger than yours." Truly, his injury didn't look too deep.

From the periphery of her vision she caught sight of Cheyenne winking at the parents. Okay, this could work. Karah Lee had been mothered by manipulative medical personnel before. In fact, she tended to be that way, herself.

With the observant child watching, Cheyenne sat Karah Lee on a stool and cleaned her wound with gentle pressure. She dabbed away the excess moisture and applied a dermatological adhesive instead of sutures or bandages. Her style was a little unorthodox, but Karah Lee approved.

Ordinarily, a wound could be sutured without question up to six hours after the injury. Between six and twelve hours, closure of the wound could be questionable, and after twelve hours Karah Lee never attempted it. No one did. Even though it had been more than six hours after Karah Lee's injury, the facial skin had a good blood supply, and this should heal quickly in spite of the delay of closure.

"All done," Cheyenne said a moment after applying the adhesive.

Jonah's eyes widened. He studied the repair job a moment. "Did it hurt?" he asked Karah Lee.

"I didn't cry, did I?"

"Grown-ups never cry."

"Well, it wasn't as much fun as eating chocolate chip cookies, but it feels better than being socked in the nose by my sister when I was five. Can I fix your forehead now?"

"Will you stick me with a needle?"

Karah Lee glanced at the mother. "Has he ever had a tetanus shot?"

"Last year when he stepped on a piece of tin and cut his foot," she said.

"Then I don't think we'll need to use a needle." There would be no need for sutures on this one. Kids healed quickly, and Karah Lee held a minimalist approach when it came to risk of traumatization.

As she cleaned Jonah's wound and soothed him and chatted with him about her big cat named Monster, and his dog named Bo, and her sister who was a bully, and his little brother who still wet his pants, she began to enjoy herself. Kids were so much easier to talk to than adults.

A couple of years ago, when Karah Lee was nearing the end of her first year in residency, one of the third year residents casually remarked that she shouldn't go into pediatric medicine because her size might scare the kids. Instead of giving in to her knee-jerk desire to punch the dolt in the stomach, she'd challenged him to a duel to see who could finish up the year with the fewest crying kids. According to the nurses, Karah Lee had won by a huge margin.

"Are you done yet?" Jonah asked as Karah Lee held the skin together for the bonding agent to set.

"Can you count to a hundred?"

"Yes," he said, as if the question were an insult.

"Let's hear it."

Though aware Cheyenne was watching her, Karah Lee didn't feel uncomfortable about being observed. She'd had plenty of that in the past few years.

The staff here seemed friendly, in spite of the disparaging remark Jill had made about reckless drivers. Karah Lee had made a few comments like that, herself, from time to time. Today she was learning a valuable lesson about pre-judging patients.

Cheyenne left to take a telephone call before Jonah finished counting, and the treatment ended without mishap, or more tears. As Karah Lee walked the relieved family to the waiting room, Blaze stepped to the reception window and handed Jonah a bright red balloon animal in the approximate shape of a poodle. Jonah laughed and played with the poodle while Jill talked to the uninsured parents about the fee for treatment.

Blaze tapped Karah Lee on the shoulder from behind. "Chey wants to see you in her office as soon as you're finished."

"I'm done."

"Okay, but tell her to make it quick. We've got incoming."

"Tell her yourself. This is my first day on the job, and I have to make a good impression on the boss."

She found Chey sitting in her office at the desk, reading a medical chart. "You wanted to see me?"

Setting the chart aside, Cheyenne glanced up at her thoughtfully. "Close the door and have a seat."

"I guess you have paperwork for me to fill out." The red tape could be daunting for doctors on a new job. Licenses, permits, clearing for insurance—both professional liability and various types of coverage for patients—took up a lot of a doc's time, and it never seemed to end.

For a moment, Cheyenne remained silent. She didn't smile as she glanced out the front window that overlooked the broad lawn and the lake.

The silence grew uncomfortable. "Did you have a problem with the treatment I gave Jonah?" Karah Lee asked.

Cheyenne shook her head, still frowning. "You're good with kids, obviously. If I'd had any doubts about your skills, I wouldn't have hired you." She folded her hands together and leaned forward. "But keep in mind that I'm the only one who makes decisions about personnel in this office."

Oh, great, Fletcher, what have you already done to tick off your boss? "Excuse me?"

"Do you know anyone named Kemper MacDonald?"

Karah Lee flinched. Ah. Ugly enlightenment. "He's a state senator."

"Any reason why his office would be calling to check on you?"

For the second time within twelve hours, Karah Lee felt the flame of humiliation heat her face. "He called here?" He had no *right*.

"His office called, whoever that was. Asked to talk to me."

"Did they say why?"

Cheyenne tapped the tip of an ink pen on the desktop for a moment, then looked back up at Karah Lee. "So you're not aware they've called here previously?"

Karah Lee's fingers gripped the arms of her chair as if by instinct. "When?"

"Three months ago, after I interviewed you for this job." Cheyenne held Karah Lee's gaze.

"And what did they say then?" She didn't really want to know, but forewarned was forearmed when it came to that overbearing, arrogant, self-serving—

"Only that you came highly recommended by his office," Cheyenne said. "And that you had received the governor's award for—"

"My *father* tried to pull strings to get me hired here?" Karah Lee's voice filled the room with a burst of unprofessional outrage, and she heard the chatter in the outer office grow quiet. She was going to strangle the man.

Cheyenne sat back, her dark brown eyes narrowing slightly. "Your father is Kemper MacDonald?"

"He wouldn't be my first choice," Karah Lee snapped. She was acting like a jerk in front of her boss. She needed to cool it. "I'm sorry, Chey. I didn't ask my father to help me get this job, if that's what you're getting at. I didn't even know he knew I was applying. It isn't as if I communicate with him on a daily basis." Or even a yearly basis when she could help it.

Cheyenne sighed, still tapping the ink pen on the desk. "You and your father are estranged?"

"You could put it that way." He'd done the estranging years ago, splitting their family right down the middle. It hadn't helped family dynamics when she'd changed her last name. "So, what did he want today?"

"He wanted to thank me for taking his advice."

Karah Lee groaned and slumped in her chair. "What did you tell him?"

For the first time since the beginning of their conversation, a trace of humor lifted the corners of Cheyenne's mouth. "Well, after insisting that his secretary put me through to him personally if he was so bent on contacting me, I asked him if he was getting his information from you."

"He wasn't."

"That's what he told me, but since he's a politician, and I'm not very good with some politicians, I chose not to rely on his word for it."

"You're even smarter than I thought. He fools most people."

"Not that it's any of my business, but your name is different from your father's."

"I changed my last name when my parents' divorce became final and my mother reverted to her maiden name. I was eighteen, so I could do it legally. I know it sounds like a spiteful thing to do, but I was feeling spiteful at the time. So what did you tell my father on the phone?"

"I told him that he had no right to interfere with the way I ran my practice, and if he wanted you to keep your job, he'd better not try it again—not that I'd planned on letting you go now that I've got you tied up with a contract for a year." Cheyenne winked and grinned. "Then I hung up on him."

Karah Lee relaxed completely. She was going to like this woman with the irreverent attitude. "I'll get a message to him that he needs to stop interfering, just in case he didn't hear you."

"Don't worry, I think he already got the message. If I've offended you by speaking to your father like that—"

"You haven't."

"Good. I'm glad you're here. We lost our nurse-practitioner a month ago, and then our secretary got married and moved out of state. I'm under contract until September to work part-time as an E.R. doc in the hospital at Dogwood Springs. That's about fifteen miles south of the lake."

"I heard business was picking up here at the clinic."

"Yes, and if I'd known that would happen, I wouldn't have been so quick to sign a contract somewhere else." Cheyenne yawned and stretched, settling back into her chair. "I try to be here in the clinic at least four days a week, plus work a couple of nights in the E.R. It's becoming too much. We're getting a lot more patients than I'd anticipated. I can't believe how it's picked up, especially since spring. How are you with emergencies?"

"I've done my share at the University Hospital, and I'm a paramedic."

Cheyenne nodded. "I read that on your curriculum vitae. With the number of traumas they get at University,

I'm sure you've had plenty of clinical experience. That means I can leave you on your own and you're not going to panic."

This time Karah Lee did hesitate. "I won't panic."

Cheyenne studied her expression and leaned forward. "Is there something I should know about?"

"Let's just say that the only person who's ever been able to undermine my confidence has been Kemper Mac-Donald. When he discovered I quit the university to stay home and care for my mother when she developed cancer, he tried to have me declared incompetent to care for her. My sister tried to convince me he was only doing it for my own good, so I would continue college, but his efforts came to light later when I tried to get into med school."

Cheyenne's eyes narrowed. "He sounds ruthless."

"So you can see why I want nothing to do with him."

"Yes, but—"

An intercom speaker crackled at the corner of the desk. "Chey, they're backing up out here in the waiting room. We've had some walk-ins. We need help out here."

Cheyenne pressed a button atop the speaker. "We're coming." She released the button and looked at Karah Lee. "Are you ready to hit it?"

"Let's get to work."

Chapter Seven

For the second time that day, Taylor pulled into his favorite parking area at the crest of the cliff overlooking Hideaway, and saw a slender, balding, middle-aged man in khakis and a burgundy pullover walking toward him. The victim of the crime.

The police were already on their way to intercept the thieves—one of whom had an eye tattooed on his shoulder—but for an experienced ranger to have actually stopped and *helped* the thieves escape? Unforgivable. Taylor smarted with the humiliation.

He parked and got out of the truck, then immediately reached back inside and pulled a bottle of water from his cooler. He handed it to the man. "Are you Mr. Freise?"

"That's me. Thanks." He took the water with one hand, while dabbing the sweat from his forehead with the other.

"I can't believe it. I was just away from the car for a few minutes, thought I'd check out the trail."

"Was there anyone else at the trailhead at the time?"

"Nobody. I didn't see anything suspicious." The man reached down and pulled a key ring with two keys from the right front pocket of his khakis. "I took these with me and everything. I couldn't have been gone more than ten minutes." He looked as if he'd been hiking much longer. His thin hair was matted with moisture, and his glasses looked as if they'd steamed over, and droplets had formed on them when he tried to wipe them clear.

Taylor had heard of a car-theft ring working the Branson area, but they'd never had trouble with it here. No one wanted to come this far out of their way to steal a car, and there was only one paved road out of Hideaway.

Mr. Freise took a long swallow of water, his Adam's apple working up and down his throat, then caught his breath and wiped at his mouth, raining more droplets of moisture over his sweat-dampened shirt. "I've already called the rental-car company in Springfield. Can you believe it? I'd have expected this in the city, but here?"

"It's unusual," Taylor agreed. "Unfortunately, we don't have electric fences to keep thieves out, Mr. Freise. There are a lot of places to hide on these back roads and in the overgrown brush. Did you lock the car when you left?"

The man frowned, then shook his head. "I thought I did. I always do, but that wouldn't matter, would it? A thief with one of those jimmies can open a car as fast as they could with a key."

"And hot-wire it just as easily." Which was probably why they hadn't turned off the engine all the time they were changing the tire. Taylor didn't have the guts to tell this poor man about his having helped the crooks get away.

"I don't suppose you could give me a lift down to the village, could you?" Mr. Freise mopped the moisture from his head again. "I need to find a place to stay until I can get a replacement car, or catch a ride down to Harrison. They got my luggage, my water bottle, everything."

"Hop into the truck and I'll give you a lift to the general store. They have travel supplies, and you can catch a shuttle from there."

Mr. Freise shook his head again as he climbed in and settled back in the passenger seat. "I just wanted to get a look at the trail. The wife and I thought we might buy one of those condos if the price was right. I've got a meeting in Harrison this afternoon, and I thought I'd check the place out, take a look at things while they were building. You know, make sure it would be a good deal."

"And was it?"

The man shrugged. "Hard to tell at this point. Getting my car stolen isn't a good sign."

"I've heard rumors about the big plans they've got to turn Hideaway into a resort area."

"You must've seen the brochures they're mailing out," Mr. Freise said.

"Brochures?"

The man unsnapped his seat belt, reached into his back pocket and pulled out a glossy advertisement folded into thirds. He tossed it onto the seat and resnapped his seat belt as Taylor cruised around a curve in the road, descending into town.

A quick glance at the brochure showed a beautifully landscaped village bright with flowers, picket fences, perfectly trimmed hedges, man-made waterfalls and pools.

"It looks like a theme park," Taylor said.

"That's right. The guy I talked to this morning told me they thought it would be more popular than Silver Dollar City, because tourists would get to stay in the town."

Taylor felt a renewed wave of discomfort. "But the Beaufont Corporation doesn't own the whole town. This place isn't a sideshow."

The man shrugged. "That's what I told the guy this morning. You know what he said?"

Taylor was silent.

"He said he knew a lot of folks were willing to sell at the right price. He thinks they'll own the town before the end of the year."

"What do you think?" Taylor asked.

"I'm not willing to buy into it just yet."

Taylor couldn't help wondering how many people already had.

They arrived at the general store, and Taylor let Mr. Freise out. He was about to go inside for a soda, when he received word that the thieves had been apprehended. Unfortunately, the car had to be impounded. Mr. Freise had to go to Branson to pick up another rental, and Taylor arranged for transportation via a tour bus that was going that way.

An hour later, after watching the bus leave, Taylor strolled along the shore toward the building project. He didn't like the new skyline, with a crane and steel girders jabbing into the bright blue canopy of this summer day, and the echo of hammers and drills and men shouting. The activity seemed like an intrusion.

Taylor wondered how much more intrusive it would have to get before the citizens of Hideaway decided to preserve their town.

By noon on Thursday, Karah Lee had a good feel for the routine of the office, and decided she was going to enjoy a more relaxed atmosphere among the staff—the very small staff. Cheyenne had been searching for someone to work the reception desk for two weeks.

All morning, however, one irritant had nagged at Karah Lee mercilessly, and she decided to stay and eat her lunch alone while the others went out. Blaze apparently knew the ladies at the bed-and-breakfast, and as he walked out the door he assured her that Bertie would let him into the cottage to check on Monster.

Karah Lee wasn't worried about Bertie, but she wished him lots of luck with the cat.

When the others were gone and the front door closed on the final patient of the morning, Karah Lee picked up the cordless phone and punched in her calling-card number, then a number she had unintentionally memorized many years ago. An unfamiliar voice answered.

"Kemper MacDonald, please," she said.

After several seconds of wrangling with the overprotective secretary, she was put on hold for several minutes. She was about to hang up, when her father came on the line.

"Karah Lee? Is this really you, or am I getting another crank call?" The voice, masculine and professionally smooth, with just the right emphasis on just the right syllables, immediately produced a visceral response in her. She stood up and leaned against the counter.

"It's me, Dad."

"Hmm. This sounds like my daughter's voice, but since it's been so long since I've had the pleasure of actually speaking with her—"

"Cut the sarcasm." She'd always hated his guilt trips, and he'd always been a master at them. She refused to squirm this time.

He paused long enough to give her a little more time to think about her many offenses. "So. What is my favorite doctor doing today? You aren't in Jefferson City, are you? We could have dinner tonight—oops, no, wait a minute, I have a dinner appointment, but—"

"You spoke with my boss this morning, so obviously you're aware I'm at work."

"Actually, your boss wasn't in the mood to discuss your whereabouts."

In spite of the tension, Karah Lee grinned as she thought about Cheyenne's reaction. "She isn't a team player." Or at least not the kind of player Dad liked.

"Then it sounds as if the job will be a good fit for you."

The grin died. Okay, so he did still have that special way of manipulating her feelings. "It'll be a good fit if you don't call and interfere again."

There was a pause, and then, "I just wanted to check in on you and see if your new job was working out well."

"It's fine."

"You like your new employer, then?"

"She's excellent."

"But she's giving you trouble about my phone call? That doesn't sound—"

"You mean because you tried to use your position to manipulate employment for me in the first place? As if I couldn't do it myself?"

"I knew you would never resort to such *underhanded* maneuvering."

"And so you decided to do it for me."

"You can't blame a father for trying to help his youngest—"

"Okay, hold it right there. I don't think *help* is the word for it. I think the word you're looking for is *control.*"

"All I wanted to do was give you a little boost," he snapped. "You didn't exactly get in on the ground floor. Some people will wonder why, at your age, you're just now completing residency."

That stung. Karah Lee bit the inside of her cheek to keep from snapping back. She sank onto the office chair as an ugly new idea occurred to her. How many times had he used the tactic to "help" her in the past?

"Hon?" His voice was soft again. Conciliatory. Quick tempers ran in the family. She'd long ago grown tired of his endless apologies.

"You know what, Dad? You need to leave me out of your attempts to overcompensate for ancient history. Believe it or not, I'm very happy where I am in my career right now, and if it embarrasses you, just keep in mind that no one has to know your youngest daughter is such a loser. We don't even share the same name."

"Thanks to your mother."

Thanks to you. "I need to ask you a question, and I want an honest answer." Yeah, like that was going to happen. This was a question she should have asked many years ago.

"Okay, what is it?" The words came out in a resigned sigh.

"How many times in the past have you made your 'influential' telephone calls on my behalf?"

For a moment, he didn't respond, and she almost wished she hadn't asked the question.

"The Sebring Scholarship?" she asked. "The chairman of the committee, Reverend Donaldson—wasn't he a good friend of yours?"

"Karah Lee, why are you doing this?"

"So you influenced him to award me that scholarship on what? Grade-point average? Sparkling personality? Pity for the orphan?"

"Stop it."

Of course, he could have denied it. Michael Donaldson had died six years ago. Karah Lee was shocked by the rush of disappointment when her father didn't even attempt denial. She hadn't earned that scholarship, after all.

"Okay, tell me what strings you pulled to get me into med school after they had already sent me the rejection letter."

More silence.

"Okay, I see."

He cleared his throat. "Doesn't it mean a thing to you that your father cared enough about you to help you in any way he could, in spite of your constant refusal to even accept my phone calls?"

"What it means to me is that my own father had so little faith in my abilities that he didn't think I could do it on my *own*." And apparently, she *hadn't* done it on her own. "Dare I even ask about my appointment to residency training?"

"I'm honored to know you think I have that much political clout."

"You're a senator." And he hadn't answered the question.

"And you are a senator's daughter. Why can't you enjoy some of the amenities the family ties afford you?"

"Because if I didn't really earn those steps in my education, then maybe that means I'm not really a doctor, and if that's the case, then I really feel sorry for my patients. Do me one big favor, okay? Don't do me any more favors."

She replaced the receiver and closed her eyes. Before she had time to absorb the conversation, she heard a bell outside signaling the arrival of a patient.

◦ *Chapter Eight* ◦

Fawn awakened Monday morning to the sound of a motorboat nearby on Lake Taneycomo, and the screams and laughter of what must've been a dozen kids out in the pool behind the complex where she had been hiding out since last Thursday. She'd love to go out there for a dip herself, but couldn't risk it. Besides, she didn't have a swimsuit. Somehow, that hadn't been important to her last week.

No longer limping, she stepped out the sliding glass doors of the two-bedroom apartment, which overlooked the narrow lake from the third-floor balcony. The bright sunshine soaked into her skin, and she wished she could lie outside and work on her tan. She would go nuts if she had to hibernate in this place another day, without television, radio, anything to keep her connected to the outside world except that stack of novels in the corner of the living room. She'd heard of "getting away from it all," but the owner of this place must've popped a cork.

Still, it was probably the lack of those things in this apartment that had allowed her to get away with the con for a whole, long weekend. Who could survive without television for even a *day?* Nobody was going to rent this place unless it was the last one left in Branson. And besides that, some of these condo-rental agencies must be hard up for good help.

All it had taken for Fawn to con her way into this place last week had been for her to get a key from the bubblehead at the rental office, who had been so busy talking to her boyfriend on the telephone that she'd barely looked up at Fawn, and hadn't even asked for ID or proof of age. Dumb!

If Fawn had a safe ID, she'd take that job away from Bubblehead in a neon minute. Even after Fawn had been gone long enough to copy the key and return the original to the rental desk, that dumb woman had still been talking on the telephone.

Of course, Fawn should probably thank the woman. Because of her, Fawn had been able to hide out in an air-conditioned place with a bathroom and a bed. It was more comfy than the average cave.

For the first three days after escaping the killer and the police, Fawn had nursed her injured feet and practiced disguises and makeup techniques in front of the bathroom mirror. She'd stayed inside, out of sight, and lived on the food she'd brought in her pack. Then yesterday, when she heard church bells echo across the lake, she'd worked up the nerve to step out onto the private balcony, and she'd discovered that the overhang of trees blocked the view of this place from most directions except for a small section of the lake.

Today she'd run out of food, and she couldn't hole up any longer. It would be okay. Nobody should be able to recognize her.

A car passed by on the street half a block away, and Fawn ducked back inside, even though she knew they couldn't see her. She hated having to hide out like this, always worrying that someone would come barging in when she wasn't alert, and shoot her or handcuff her before she could get away. She kept the dead bolt locked on the only access, but still...

She stepped into the bathroom and turned on the light, then stared at her reflection in the mirror. She'd gotten accustomed to the short, spiky haircut, the burgundy-brown hair from the food coloring. She'd practiced in front of this mirror for hours, experimenting with shades of face color, eye shadow and eyebrow pencil. She'd figured out how to line her face to look old, and she knew if she bought some hair color she could smear some on her face, neck and hands to irritate the skin just enough to make it look dry and patchy. She'd accidentally done that a few months ago.

But could she fool anyone by dressing up as a little old lady?

She picked up a light brown eyebrow pencil and smeared it onto her fingers, remembering what she'd learned from that makeup artist with the theater guild to shape her face with the color. She smudged it onto her eyebrows and drew it down the sides of her face and above her upper lip, like a guy trying to grow out his mustache.

Smudging complete, she frowned at her reflection in the mirror. Not quite right. She reached for the small pair of scissors beside the sink and snipped a few strands of hair. Ah. There. A little shorter around the ears, and she didn't look so girlish.

She looked like an underage kid who should be traveling with a parent.

She reached into the deep, right front pocket of her jeans. The money was still there. If she was careful, she could live on this for a while yet. Still, the fact that she even had the money to begin with made her wonder sometimes...why had Bruce sent her out to the ATM machines that night? What had he known?

When she did run out of money, what would she do?

If only she could get a new fake ID, but she didn't know anybody here, and couldn't risk trying to make contact with too many people, not with both sides of the law looking for her.

She tightened the strap of her backpack and stepped out onto the landing and down the two flights of steps. First thing she had to do was find food and a better disguise. Later, she could discover the best way out of town, if she decided to leave at all. If she could fool that ditzy woman at the condo-rental desk, she might be able to pull another con. With a little luck, she might even be able to pull this off for quite a while. Maybe the ID could wait.

* * *

Karah Lee washed her hands for at least the fifteenth time on Monday morning, scrambling to keep the patients straight in her mind in case she needed to add notes to their charts. She dried with paper towels, glanced through the reception window to make sure the waiting room was cleared out, and breathed a sigh of cautious relief.

Thank goodness Cheyenne had scheduled them to work together today. There had been three patients already waiting when Karah Lee arrived for work, and a steady stream came through the doors for two hours afterward. Along with the typical complaints of weekend sunburn, sprained ankles, minor injuries and tick bites, they dealt with more serious cases of asthma, chest pain and premature labor.

Neither Karah Lee nor Cheyenne had a chance to sit down until midmorning, because not only did they have an unusually heavy influx of patients, but they also had to help with office duties, since Jill was overwhelmed with nursing duties and they presently had no secretary-receptionist. Blaze was a great help, but his handwriting was atrocious, and he occasionally lost charts in the manual filing system.

Karah Lee took a cup of freshly brewed coffee and collapsed on the padded chair in Cheyenne's office. She selected a cream-filled doughnut from a small box that had been delivered from the neighboring bakery. She sank her teeth into the sweet, crisp parcel of temptation with a moan of pleasure. After oversleeping this morning, she'd missed her usual filling breakfast at the bed-and-breakfast.

Cheyenne slipped into the office a moment later, closed the door and sank into the chair behind her desk with a sigh of relief. "What a morning!"

"Is it always like this?" Karah Lee asked.

"Sometimes." Cheyenne selected a chocolate-iced doughnut from the box. "Especially Mondays, since the patients save up all their injuries and illnesses from the weekend, if they can. The closest urgent-care or emergency-care facility this side of the lake is at least a thirty-minute drive from here." She bit into the doughnut and leaned back. "How was your first weekend in Hideaway?"

"Quiet." And lonely, though Karah Lee wasn't going to admit that, especially since Cheyenne had invited her to church. "Jill told me I could go on a float trip with her and her family, and Blaze invited me to help him milk the cows and watch him train his pigs at the ranch. I opted to take a walking tour of Hideaway, instead. Why would a sane person try to train a pig to do anything?"

Cheyenne's dark eyes lit with affectionate amusement as she licked chocolate from her fingers. "You might be amazed at what Blaze can get those animals to do. Has he checked your cat yet?"

"Oh, yes, he and Monster became fast friends as soon as he walked in the door of the cottage last Thursday. My cat seems to love everybody but me."

"We should probably introduce Monster to Blue," Cheyenne said.

"Blue?"

"*My* cat. Bertie practically forced the kitten on me last year, and my life has never been the same since. I wouldn't want it to be. Those loving little animals can be such wonderful companions when we're feeling alone in the world."

Was Cheyenne Allison a mind reader? "Companionship, huh? I guess growling and snoring could be mistaken for companionship. Somehow, that isn't what I've always had in mind when I dreamed of connection to another living being. I get the impression my cat would prefer another companion, as well. He makes his feelings known with discouraging predictability."

"Don't take it too personally," Cheyenne said. "Maybe he's just got bad digestion."

"I'll give him an antacid next time he growls at me. So what's this deal about training pigs?" Karah Lee asked. "Doesn't Blaze have enough to do?"

"Yes, but the highlight of his year is the pig races at the community fair Hideaway has every September. He trains most of the racers, and I think it makes him feel a little more welcome in the community." Cheyenne wiped her mouth with a napkin. "Mind if I ask a personal question?"

"Ask all you want. I don't have to answer it, right?"

"That's right."

"Then shoot." Karah Lee took a sip of her coffee.

"Last week when we talked, you implied you and your father were estranged."

"That's right," Karah Lee said. "It's been that way for many years. If it's a part of my job description to make nice with a state senator, I'll—"

"It isn't."

"Good." She took another bite of heaven, surreptitiously studying the contents of the box for her next selection as her stomach reminded her how long it had been since she'd last eaten. The chocolate frosted cruller looked scrumptious.

"I won't interfere," Cheyenne said. "It's just that family has always been important to me. My own parents live down in Florida, and I miss them. I try to keep up with them by calling them every week or two, but I still miss them. Do you have any other family besides your father?"

"My grandmother died two years ago. I have an aunt and cousins in Oklahoma, and one aunt in California who keeps in touch as often as possible." Aunt Phyl, Mom's older sister, had been in a wheelchair for the past twenty years, but she didn't let that stop her from living her life.

"No brothers or sisters?" Chey asked.

Karah Lee grimaced. "A sister who works for my father."

"Sisters can make wonderful friends."

Karah Lee raised an eyebrow. "Shona is four years older than me, and she's a tad...I don't know...competitive." *Try hateful, overbearing, obnoxious at times.* It had been that way for years.

Cheyenne cupped her hands around her coffee mug, shoulders slumping. "That's a shame."

Karah Lee took a doughnut hole and dunked it into her coffee, then cautiously slipped it into her mouth.

"My sister was killed in an automobile accident a little over a year ago." Cheyenne's words came slowly, with obvious pain. "She was my...my best friend."

Karah Lee heard the catch in her boss's voice, and the appeal of doughnuts waned. "Oh, Chey. I'm sorry. That must have been horrible."

Cheyenne's eyebrows drew together as she continued to stare into her coffee, as if maybe she could see her sister's face there. "A living nightmare. They brought her to me in the E.R." She glanced up at Karah Lee. "I worked E.R. at Missouri Regional in Columbia at the time. I did everything to bring her back. Nothing worked. I was the one who pronounced her."

Karah Lee felt the shock of Chey's words all the way through her body. What did someone reply to a revelation like that? That truly would have been a living nightmare.

"A month later, I wasn't coping, and my director asked me to take medical leave." Cheyenne remained dry-eyed, but at an obvious cost. She swallowed hard, and her chin lifted a fraction of an inch. "That was when I came here to Hideaway for the first time. It didn't take me long to realize this was where I belonged."

"Your sister was your best friend? She must have been a wonderful person."

"My sister was the epitome of a Christian at a time when I resented the whole concept of Christianity. In the end, her example made a powerful impact on me, but not until after her death."

Karah Lee could identify with the resentment. Somehow, this didn't seem like the time for her to comment on it, however. "I know what it's like to lose someone," she said instead. "My mother was diagnosed with pancreatic cancer a couple of weeks after I completed my freshman year at the University of Columbia. She died two years later."

"Oh, Karah Lee, please tell me that wasn't when your father left her."

"He'd left her a year before the diagnosis. Mom refused to let me tell him about it. Since my sister, Shona, had gone to work for Dad's office as soon as she graduated from college, Mom didn't let me tell her, either. We just kind of fought it together, the two of us, for the next two years."

"And you never told the rest of your family?"

"Mom didn't want to. She was pretty independent."

"I wouldn't've guessed," Cheyenne said dryly.

"Anyway, even though my sister found every excuse she could think of not to visit much for the next year—Mom was never one to keep her opinions to herself about the divorce—Shona blamed me for keeping my mother's illness from her once the news was leaked to the rest of the family by my aunt."

Cheyenne studied Karah Lee silently for a moment over the rim of her coffee cup. "You carried an emotional load like that all by yourself and you were barely twenty? Did you have to quit school to take care of her?"

"She didn't want me to, but I had taken a paramedics course, so I was able to work with the ambulance service when Mom went into remission. When the cancer returned, I quit my job and stayed home to take care of her. Really, I couldn't have told Shona about it, anyway, because she'd have gone squealing to Dad, and he would have kicked up a fuss about my lost education. He did, anyway, when he found out."

Cheyenne leaned forward, elbows on the desk. "But then you finished school, and residency."

"I worked with the ambulance service during summer breaks and on weekends to support myself and pay for some of my education."

"And now you're here. Sounds to me as if things worked out in the end, because you took care of the most important things first."

Karah Lee felt uncomfortable about Chey's obvious admiration.

Cheyenne put her cup down. "Okay, I'll stop meddling. It would be nice to see you back in touch with your family, but I think you're the kind of person who can take care of that without my involvement."

"It isn't always death that takes people from you," Karah Lee said. "After all these years, I figure it'd be easier to just collect a good set of friends so my family and I won't have to intrude in one another's lives."

Cheyenne nodded, obviously still troubled but just as obviously unwilling to intrude further. "I just hope you make those friends right here in Hideaway. As you can see, we need you."

❧ *Chapter Nine* ❧

Karah Lee tidied up after her final patient of the morning and glanced at the clock in the hallway. Rats. It was already twelve forty-five. They'd had so many walk-ins this morning they'd had no hope of going out to grab a bite of lunch. The doughnuts had not lasted, and now they had fifteen minutes before their first afternoon patient was scheduled to arrive.

Once again, she slumped into her favorite chair in Cheyenne's office.

Cheyenne came in directly after her. "Lady, you'll be good for business if it doesn't kill us all." She sank into her own chair with a sigh.

"Knock-knock," Blaze said, stepping through the open doorway with a box that emitted the fragrant aroma of roast beef and vegetables.

"I thought you went to lunch an hour ago," Cheyenne told him.

"I did. This is for you, and Dane said to give you his love."

"Dane?" Karah Lee asked. Then she remembered. He was the town mayor, who was apparently seeing Cheyenne.

"The town mayor." Cheyenne straightened and reached for three bottles of water from the shelf behind her. "And Blaze's foster father."

"The love of Cheyenne's life." Blaze gave Chey an audacious grin and kissed the air as he opened the box, which held three white cardboard containers, complete with plastic forks and napkins. "He's late for another meeting. He said to say a prayer for him. We need another paramedic."

"I thought Taylor Jackson was a paramedic," Karah Lee said.

"The ranger?" Cheyenne reached for one of the containers and handed it to Karah Lee, then took one for herself. "Yes, but I think he's pulling double duty, and he can't be on call 24/7."

"Oh, right," Karah Lee said dryly. "Only doctors are expected to keep that kind of schedule. Where'd this food come from?"

"Our cook sent it from the ranch," Blaze said. "I took the boat across for lunch, and I told Cook the rest of you might starve, so he fixed you something. I'll take one of these to Jill." He picked up the remaining container and plasticware and left the room.

Karah Lee inhaled the intoxicating scent of the food and opened her container to find pot roast with gravy, salad and a square of corn bread. She picked up a fork and tucked into her food.

There was a short silence, and Karah Lee looked up to see Cheyenne with her head bowed, eyelids lowered.

Oh, yeah. Some people still asked a blessing on their food. Like Mom used to do. Like Karah Lee used to do, before she realized it was just a habit from childhood.

Cheyenne looked up and opened her container.

"*I'm* a paramedic, remember," Karah Lee said.

Cheyenne buttered her corn bread. "You mean you've kept up your certification all these years?"

"Like I said, I worked my way through school. And I tried not to take out too many student loans. I'm single, no family involvement. I could pick up a few shifts a month until they find someone permanently."

"But you'll be on call as a physician part of the time," Cheyenne warned. "That would keep you pretty busy."

"It isn't as if I'm looking for another job, but I wouldn't mind helping out."

Cheyenne smiled and took a bite of pot roast.

"Dane sounds like a good guy," Karah Lee said.

"He is. The boys at the ranch love him."

"You guys getting married?"

Cheyenne's smile brightened further. "How did you guess?"

"When's the wedding?"

"We're thinking about September, during the Hideaway Festival, but don't tell anyone. We don't have all the details figured out yet." She filled her fork with more tender beef.

"Okay, I'll keep my mouth shut."

"Are you sure you want to be on call, and lose some of your spare time?"

"As a paramedic? Sure."

"Then be my guest. Dane will be ecstatic if he can have coverage until they find someone permanent. You'll report to Ranger Jackson."

Karah Lee swallowed. "Taylor?"

"Yep. I'll call Dane on his cell phone and let him know."

Fawn stopped dead in her tracks at the western end of the Tanger Outlet Mall as she stared at her own image on an old *Springfield Daily* newspaper, dated last Thursday, taped in the lower left corner of storefront plate glass. Large letters asked Have You Seen This Woman?

She wanted to turn and run, but that would only draw attention. Instead, she read the description of herself— brown eyes, blond hair, about five feet seven inches, a hundred and twenty pounds. Last seen...

Okay, except for the shape of her face, she didn't look like the woman in the picture. Without the contacts, her eyes were blue, and of course the hair was different. Without the heels she was two and a half inches shorter—and happier about it.

With round, wire-framed glasses over her eyes and a ball cap securely pulled down over her short, dark hair, she glanced around the parking lot and studied the group of elderly folks who were just now being deposited onto the sidewalk from a charter bus.

If there was some way she could hop one of those buses as it left town...maybe that would be her best chance. Problem was, most of the people she'd seen coming out of those buses were at least fifty years older than her. It'd be hard to fake that for long.

She picked up a schedule someone had dropped when stepping off the bus. There were a lot of buses in and out of this place.

This might be just what she needed, but not yet. Obviously, no one recognized her—and most of the tourists who had been here last Thursday wouldn't still be here. She could do this. As long as she relaxed and didn't give herself away, or give anyone reason to be suspicious, no one would dream that she was this supposed "escaped killer."

She just couldn't call attention to herself.

An hour before official quitting time on Monday, Taylor was catching up on the ever-present paperwork at the ranger station, reading a memo he'd received this morning about clues the Branson police had found in their continued search for the killer, and drinking a second cup of strong black coffee to stay awake. He needed rest. He didn't get a lot of emergency calls for a first-responder paramedic here in Hideaway, but last night had been one of those rare times when he'd received two in succession. He had treated the patients until the county ambulance service could reach them.

Something had to give before he gave out.

He glanced again at the memo from Branson. It amused him. The morning after the murder, two people had reported seeing a woman who fit the description of the murder suspect. One salesclerk had claimed that the woman had entered a kitchen-supply store wearing a white uniform liberally smudged with mud. Her hair was wet, and she was barefoot. According to the clerk, the woman had purchased scissors and food coloring.

According to the police report, a blue dress matching the description of the woman's attire the night of the murders had been recovered from a local theater-hotel complex—in the linen room, where worker uniforms were stored. Those uniforms were white.

Follow-ups had so far led them to several different locations in town.

Taylor grinned to himself. That was shorthand for wild-goose chase. He had nearly finished his coffee and completed his paperwork, when the familiar sound of tires crunching gravel interrupted the peaceful birdsong through the front screen door. He glanced out to see two cars pulling into the graveled circle driveway in front of the station. Taylor recognized the county sheriff's big cowboy hat, and even bigger belly, as the sheriff and his long-legged, blond-haired deputy accompanied a man in plainclothes along the path from the driveway.

Taylor had the door open when they reached it. "Hi, Greg. Tom." He shook hands with the sheriff and deputy.

As always, Greg's beefy hand was as uncommonly gentle as Tom's was overfirm.

"Hey, Taylor." Greg nodded toward the stranger. "This here's our guy from the state, Lieutenant Doug Milfred, come to ask you a few questions about those car thieves and take some items for fingerprinting."

Taylor sized the guy up as he shook hands. He looked young, neat, compact, with wire-framed glasses. All business. Since Taylor's fingerprints were already on file, he didn't have to suffer that humiliation, but the whole situation was embarrassing enough, especially with that tiny, knowing smirk on Tom's face.

The lieutenant needed a description of the vehicle, of the driver and passenger, distinguishing characteristics, the license number of the car.

"I've got all that," Taylor said. He'd taken copious notes. "But I thought they already apprehended the guys and returned the car. I was prepared to be called as a witness in their trial."

The lieutenant shook his head, leaning forward. "The guys got out on bail, then disappeared."

"Okay, but—"

"The sheriff up at Jasper County called this morning," Greg said. "They had some heavy rains up that way this past weekend, and when the floodwaters went down this morning, they found two guys dead along a creek bank. They aren't sure yet, but they think these guys might match the descriptions of your thieves. One had a tattoo of an eye on his upper arm."

"Dead?"

"Shot. Execution style," Tom said.

"We don't know that for sure," the lieutenant warned.

"Not yet, but I bet it's the real thing." Tom's left foot tapped the floor with nervous energy—the guy never sat still. "You know what I think? I think they were errand boys for some organized-crime ring, and they had to be wasted or they'd talk."

Taylor bit his lower lip and turned back to Lieutenant Milfred. Tom watched far too much television, surfed the Web constantly and had too much time on his hands.

Milfred picked up the stack of notes Taylor had given him. "May I take these with me?"

"Of course, they're yours." Taylor gestured toward his Jeep. "I haven't touched the tools since I used them to help the men change their tire."

"I'll need those tools for fingerprints."

"Of course." Taylor led the way out to his Jeep and opened the back so Milfred could retrieve the tools, then answered a few more questions before the lieutenant left.

Greg and Tom were still in the station when Taylor returned. "You guys want some coffee?"

Tom looked at his watch. "None for me. I'm off duty in twenty minutes, and I've got a date tonight with a Web site. I still think there's an organized-crime ring in this area."

"I know somebody who needs to get a lid on his imagination," Greg muttered.

Tom's left foot once more tapped the floor. "If you ask me, Taylor needs to learn how to *use* his imagination a little. I mean, come on, Taylor—didn't you even think to call in about them before you fixed their flat for them and sent them on their way?"

"Lighten up," Greg said. "You saw where that car was stranded on the road. Either of us would've done the same thing. Taylor just wanted to get the guys off the side of the road before somebody rounded the curve and rammed them. Besides, they got the guys, and everybody's living happily ever after."

"Those car thieves aren't," Tom said. "Did you hear they were probably working as contract labor for the Beaufont Corporation?"

"Don't go spreading those rumors," Greg warned. "We don't know that for sure yet."

"Okay," Tom said. "But doesn't it strike you as a little weird that they never hired any locals for that project? Just guys from outside?"

Greg shook his head and stood. "You need to start writing fiction in your spare time, work off some of that imaginary genius."

"Don't you mean imagina*tive* genius?" Tom asked.

Greg winked at Taylor as he opened the door and stepped out onto the small concrete front porch. "Nope. See you, Taylor. Get some sleep tonight, why don't you. Dane says they've for sure got another paramedic in town to take call."

"You mean that isn't just a rumor?"

"Nope. You know that new doc they've got at the clinic?"

"I heard they had one, but I haven't met him."

Tom's crack of laughter reverberated through the small station. "Taylor Jackson, you're the biggest ostrich I ever met. The new doctor isn't even a man, she's a woman. You need to start getting out more. Talk to people." Tom pressed past Taylor and followed his boss out the door. "I tell you, if you'd met this new doc, you'd remember her. She's as tall as me, with red hair."

"She's prettier than you," Greg said.

Tom shrugged. "She's staying at the Lakeside. The woman weighs in at two-twenty. Talk about a Goliath."

"Oh, would you stop it?" Greg called over his shoulder. "Come on, let's get out of here. No way that woman weighs any two-twenty."

"Hey, I know what she weighs, I'm telling you," Tom insisted. "I studied one of those sites online that tell you how to guess a person's weight. You should try surfing the Internet sometime. You're missing out on a lot. Such as, did you know there's an earthquake predicted to hit the general vicinity of Blue Eye?"

"When?" Taylor asked.

"When the contestants sprout wings at the pig races in September!" Greg called, laughing as he climbed into the cruiser.

"You didn't say what the doctor's name was," Taylor called after them.

"Fletcher." Tom opened the passenger door. "Carrie, or Carla, or something like that."

"Karah Lee," Taylor said, suddenly wondering at his own obtuseness. "Her name is Karah Lee Fletcher." Of course! *Taylor, you really are an idiot. She practically told you that first night, with all her hints about knowing medicine, and then the next morning, telling you she was going to the clinic.*

Tom paused before getting into the car. He glanced over the roof at Greg, who had also paused. "Well, what do you know? He knows the lady's name. Maybe there's hope for the guy."

As the two men left, Taylor stared after them. Now he remembered Karah Lee telling him she'd been a paramedic. And she'd volunteered to take call? That would be a relief.

As he went about the office cleaning the coffeepot and shutting down the computer, he thought about Tom's comments. He glanced at his reflection in the bathroom mirror.

Never in his life, before coming here, had anyone ever called him an ostrich. He was not an introvert. He'd never exactly been a party animal, but he'd always had friends. Lots of friends. Once upon a time he'd even had a happy family.

So why did everybody here in Hideaway seem to think of him as some kind of hermit? True, he didn't get out much, didn't know a lot of people here yet, but really, he'd been busy. A guy couldn't have a social life when he found himself working sixteen hours a day.

Not that he always worked that many hours...

Okay, he seldom worked sixteen hours a day, but he had to admit that when he did get some time off, he either went hiking by himself, somewhere besides Hideaway, or he drove to Branson to eat or see a show. By himself. He did get lonely, but the ranger staff here was barely a skeleton crew, so he had few colleagues. The others had families.

Set within a patchwork section of the Mark Twain National Forest, Hideaway was an overlap of his jurisdiction. He always felt as if he was on duty when he was here; therefore, he spent his leisure hours outside his area of responsibility.

He thought about Karah Lee again. Okay, so he was probably the only person in Hideaway who hadn't known that the new doc in town was another woman. People around here sometimes got a little too interested in other people's business.

He stepped out of the office and locked it behind him.

No way could Karah Lee Fletcher weigh two hundred and twenty pounds...could she?

❧ Chapter Ten ❧

On Friday morning, a week and a half after Karah Lee's ignominious arrival in Hideaway, she relished the feel of the steering wheel in her hands once again as she drove her newly repaired automobile to the far eastern edge of town—a total of eight blocks from the Lakeside Bed-and-Breakfast, which was on the western edge of town. She already missed Bertie and Edith, but—as she had reminded herself at least three times in the past ten minutes—renting a small house on a monthly basis, until she could afford to buy something nearby, would be a good thing in several ways.

First of all, it would be good for Bertie and Edith, because Karah Lee had discovered two days after her arrival that, for the tourist crowd, those cottages cost twice as much as she was paying. When she'd attempted to pay more, Bertie had refused.

"Cheyenne needs you," Bertie had said as she stirred the gravy at the steam table. "She did so much for Red and me last year when he was sick, treating him for free, buying medicine for him, helping me with the goats when he turned up missing."

"She helped you milk goats?" Karah Lee asked.

"That's right. And Cheyenne was the one who found Red in the end." Bertie opened the window over the deck to allow the cool morning breeze into the stuffy dining area. "She's a good soul, and I aim to help her any way I can. I'd've let you have that cottage for free all year, just to help Cheyenne keep good help, if it weren't for that fancy accountant who keeps our books. He thought we was crazy in the first place for setting our rates so low."

A dog wandered out onto the street, and Karah Lee returned her attention to traffic as she pressed the brake. Not that there was much traffic on this residential street. The tourists tended to hang out at the lake and the town square and that sandy beach that stretched eastward along the shore for several hundred feet. Folks said the Beaufont Corporation was crazy for spending so much money on a free beach, but it sure was drawing the people.

Another good reason for Karah Lee to have a place where she had to cook breakfast for herself was to benefit her waistline. No way could she cook like Bertie Meyer. She could avoid temptation much more easily if she didn't smell the breakfast aromas drifting through the air every morning.

So if this was such a good idea, why did she feel so sad at the thought of leaving the Lakeside? She could stroll down the street from the clinic anytime to visit with the ladies. It wasn't as if this was such a big town. Like Branson, this little village burgeoned to probably ten times its actual population during the summer months. There was even talk of building a music theater.

Some people got carried away.

Hideaway's main residential street curved beneath a lush overhang of maples, oaks and cedars, with enough overgrown shrubbery in the yards to satisfy the most privacy-starved villager, and enough colorful flowers to please the most demanding artistic eye. Karah Lee had already fallen in love with her two-bedroom rental when she walked past it last Saturday afternoon. Of course, she hadn't been able to check out the interior because it had been occupied by another renter at the time, but she knew it was surrounded by cedars and maple trees, and wasn't visible from the street. The only drawback was the condominium project, barely a block and a half away from her rental. The noise of construction would be distracting on occasion, especially with that huge crane.

"Monster, you're going to love this place," she said to her back-seat nemesis.

She received a casual *mireer* in reply.

"You'll see. Just think, a bedroom of your own, and room to roam."

After years of sharing rooms and apartments with other students and medical residents, and spending half her nights at the hospital, she was going to love this. As long as the roof didn't leak and there was a bed to sleep in—it was a furnished house—she'd be satisfied. Rentals

here were hard to come by, and it was even more difficult to find one furnished. In spite of the condo project,
the location seemed ideal to her.

Karah Lee rounded a final curve, then stomped on the
brake, gasping with shock as all her nice little daydreams
shattered. Monster roared his outrage from the pet taxi
in the back.

A big yellow bulldozer backed out from between two
cedar trees onto the narrow lane in front of her, bucket
raised, scattering red clods of dirt.

Karah Lee threw the car into Reverse and backed half
a block to the nearest street sign. It was Maple Drive. She
parked on the side of the road and got out. This was the
place. This was the route she had walked Saturday, she
knew, because she recognized the flowers around
the street sign.

With Monster protesting loudly, she shut the door and
ran up the road to the place where the bulldozer continued to work. The building that had rested within the
shaded protection of those trees no longer existed. It had
been dozed flat.

Her rental house was gone.

Fawn awakened Friday morning with an upset stomach, cramps, and the sound of metal scraping metal
somewhere nearby. Her eyes flew open and she gasped.

Someone was trying to get inside.

She heard muffled voices outside the window, and sat
straight up in bed as her heart double-paced its rhythm
through her chest. Had to get out, quick!

She scrambled from the bed and grabbed up the baggy denims and wild, overlarge Hawaiian shirt she'd worn yesterday. She pulled them on, stepped into her new high-top men's tennis shoes—which were two sizes too big for her, and which she'd stuffed with socks to aid her attempts to look more like a male. She still wasn't sure it had the right effect, but now she had no time to change her mind.

She jerked open the dresser drawer and grabbed her other clothes, stuffed them into her backpack and raced with it to the bathroom, where she'd stored her cosmetics and toiletries in a drawer, including the scissors she'd used to cut her hair and the empty bottle of dark brown color she'd put on it and which was already itching her scalp, and the other bottle of "silver lining" color for old ladies she might use if she got desperate. Last night, thank goodness, she'd taken the rest of her trash out to the Dumpster.

The voice went away and the scraping stopped as she rushed through the kitchenette and pulled open the refrigerator. She tossed sausage sticks, a loaf of bread, lunch meat, cheese and apples into her pack, forced it shut and grabbed her final bottle of water from the counter.

She tiptoed to the entry door and cautiously peered out. A family of four was climbing into a green car down below in the parking place for this condo. They'd be on their way back to the main office, complaining because they'd been given the wrong key.

Fawn was just glad she'd bought herself more time by keeping the dead bolt locked.

Bubblehead at the rental desk would probably be talking on the telephone to her even stupider boyfriend—anybody who loved her had to be bonko. The poor vacationers would try to explain to her that they couldn't get inside, and she would probably give them a different key to try again, without ever pausing for breath.

By then, Fawn would be far away, and nobody would guess the truth. She hoped.

Halfway down the stairs to the second-floor landing, Fawn felt the beginning of another cramp. Her stomach rolled in protest. The backpack slid from her shoulder as she doubled over with a groan. She snorted in air through her nose, breathed out through her mouth, twice, three times, until the cramp eased. She'd have to get some aspirin or something. Soon.

But first, she had to find another place to stay, or find a bus out of Branson.

Taylor caught sight of a bright red Ford Taurus sedan parked alongside Maple Drive and a woman with red hair standing on the street corner, apparently shouting at a man sitting on a big yellow bulldozer. All other sound, however, was drowned out by the idling motor of the big machine. A small emblem on the side of the dozer identified it as the property of the Beaufont Corporation. Bad news.

Pulling up behind Karah Lee's car, Taylor felt his hands tighten on the steering wheel. He had received a call less than five minutes ago about an altercation between a tourist and a construction worker on the corner of Elm and Maple. Although this was not in his job description, he had come because Greg and Tom were on the other side of the lake and would take too long to come back around by the bridge.

He got out of the truck, locked it and pocketed his keys. After the incident last week, he couldn't take chances. He walked past Karah Lee's car and heard the familiar sound of an angry cat. Monster, no doubt, but he didn't pause to investigate. Why the woman would drive through town with her cat to have an argument with a dozer operator...it didn't bear consideration.

He heard Karah Lee's distinctive voice from across the street, raised to be heard over the irritating growl of the dozer.

"You mean to tell me you owned this house?" she demanded, her inflection strong enough to bend steel.

"Beaufont owns it, I'm telling you, lady," the guy called down to her from his perch. "I work for them, and I'm just following orders."

"Then someone made a big mistake! I paid rent and deposit money. Where am I supposed to stay now?"

The man caught sight of Taylor crossing the street and looked relieved. Karah Lee followed the direction of the man's gaze. Her face was flushed, her curly red hair flying in every direction. Her eyebrows were drawn together like storm clouds congregating, and it sounded as if she had every right to be upset.

"What's the problem?" Taylor asked.

"Finally!" the man said from the dozer. "You straighten this out, Ranger. I've got work to do." He reached down as if to put his machine back into gear.

"You stay right there until we get this settled." Taylor's voice boomed through the air, obviously surprising the dozer guy.

Karah Lee blinked.

Taylor pulled out his cell phone and dialed the number printed on the Beaufont Corporation logo on the dozer.

"I was moving today," Karah Lee said as the telephone rang at the other end. "I was supposed to move *here!*" Her voice wobbled as she gestured toward a rubble of wood and dirt in the midst of mature cedars and oaks. "Now I don't have anyplace to stay, and this man tells me I'm trespassing."

"What about your place at the Lakeside?" Taylor asked. "Can you go back there?"

"I moved out, and they're booked for practically the rest of the summer," Karah Lee said. "I took off work this morning so I could move, and now look at this!" She jerked her hand toward the destruction once more.

Someone answered at the other end of the line. Taylor spent the next ten minutes seeking someone who knew what was going on.

He never found a soul.

Fawn doubled over twice again with cramps as she walked the mile or so to the local mall, which was connected to a Wal-Mart. At Wal-Mart she bought a bottle of aspirin, swallowed three tablets, then found another bus schedule on the racks of brochures at the front of the mall.

The place was crowded with people rushing from shop to shop, and the highway out front was thick with cars going in both directions. This place bustled like the Vegas Strip.

She glanced down at the schedule, then frowned and glanced again at the brochure rack, at a very familiar picture.

She nearly forgot to breathe. It was her! At least, the old her.

Still, that wouldn't have been so bad, except now there was a small poster of a composite photo taped next to the old picture—and it was her... *Now!*

She gasped out loud. People glanced toward her. She took a quick step forward, acting as if she was reaching for a brochure near the top, and covered the picture with her body.

Don't panic. Don't let 'em see you react.

Some screaming, laughing little kids ran past her, and she looked around to see if anyone was watching her. They weren't. Some doofus in a jackrabbit suit was entertaining the little ones, and while they got all crazy about it, she reached in front of her and yanked the picture down.

Afraid to check to see if anyone had noticed, she folded it next to her body and casually strolled toward the back of the mall. With every step, she expected someone to stop her, to call for a guard, to scream and yell, "Murderer!"

But no one did. She glanced over her shoulder, and no one followed. Why hadn't she changed out of this stupid Hawaiian shirt? The colors would attract a lot more attention than the pea-green pullover in her pack. At least she'd taken the time to flatten her figure with the elastic bandage when she'd pulled her clothes on.

In a dimly lit corner near the back of the little mall, she found the bathroom door and pushed her way inside.

A woman at the sink looked at her in the mirror, and her eyes widened. "This is the ladies' room!" she snapped.

"Oh. Sorry," Fawn said gruffly as she turned and rushed back out. Just great. At least she was still being mistaken for a boy and not a killer, but where was she supposed to go to the bathroom?

She saw the door to the men's room, but couldn't bring herself to go inside. Instead, she found an unoccupied corner and, with her back to the crowd, unfolded the picture. It didn't have the glasses or the hat, and the composite made her look like a woman and not a boy, but the photo looked a whole lot like her reflection in the mirror this morning. She had to get out of Branson fast.

How had they known about her change in appearance? Had someone seen her and recognized her this week? They couldn't have, because she'd worn sunglasses or these dorky, round wire frames every time she went out, and she'd never taken her hat off.

Anyway, it didn't matter. They knew. Someone must've recognized her buying those things the day after her escape. She needed more disguise...more makeup, maybe?

She studied the bus schedule and realized there was a bus stop right here. She looked around, relieved. There was a ticket counter in the front corner of the mall hallway. She was going to escape Branson, and the next bus left in thirty minutes. One of the routes went to Springfield, the largest city in this part of the state. Another route would take her south, through Harrison and on to Little Rock, Arkansas. Another would take her through Hideaway and over to a place called Bella Vista.

Hideaway. Something dangerous was going on there, according to Bruce. From what she'd overheard of the conversation between him and the killer, that was the whole reason for flying back here from Vegas.

A small, soundless voice reminded Fawn that Bruce had known about the danger back here, and he had brought her into it, anyway. In the end, that meant he really hadn't cared any more for her than anyone else ever had. It hadn't mattered to him that she might be hurt or killed.

But then, he had tried to make sure she was gone during his meeting with Harv, and he'd made sure she had enough cash to cover her for a few days.

She knew he was one of those people who never thought bad things could happen to him. He'd probably figured he could talk his way out of trouble once he got here. Not that she knew for sure, because he hadn't ever let her in on what he was doing.

All that talk about going to Hideaway to go canoeing or biking, then back to Silver Dollar City before they flew back to Las Vegas... Had that all been a lie?

Sudden tears stung her eyes, and she closed them. *Oh, Bruce. What's happening?*

She sniffed and straightened. No time for this. She folded the schedule and stuck it into the right rear pocket of her baggy jeans. She glanced toward the crowded mall, and realized that quite a few other tourists wore wildly patterned shirts in lots of different colors. So maybe she wouldn't draw that much attention, after all.

❧ *Chapter Eleven* ❧

Taylor strolled beside Karah Lee as they crossed the street to her car. The cat's offended cries had grown silent, and all they could hear was the angry rumble of the backhoe as it tore up concrete, dirt and tree roots. Taylor felt as if he had just witnessed a mugging. He could tell, with a sideways glance at Karah Lee's profile, that she felt like the muggee.

"Now what am I going to do?" Karah Lee moaned. "I can't believe this. I have no place to go. All the cottages and rooms are rented at the Lakeside, and Bertie has a waiting list half a page long. I'll have to drive all the way back to Branson West or Kimberling City to find a motel room."

"That won't work." Taylor opened her car door for her.

She rolled her eyes at him. "Well, I don't like it, either, but what else am I supposed to do? It isn't like I can camp out in the park. It'll mean I'll have to drive a whole lot farther to work."

"You volunteered to be on-call paramedic, right?"

"Yes, but isn't there an office or someplace to hang out?"

"In this town? Hardly. There isn't even enough money to pay for an office yet, it's strictly volunteer call."

"You're telling me the revenue from tourism doesn't help Hideaway pay the bills?"

"The mayor's trying to get the city council to designate more of the tax dollars for things like that, but everything takes time. The only time you'd get paid is if you actually took a call, and you can't be out of the area when you're on call."

"Just great," she said. "So what am I supposed to do, stand on a street corner or stay at the clinic the nights I'm on call?"

"Nobody's going to expect you to do that. We just won't be able to bring you on until you can stay in the area."

"Well, you're sure a bringer of glad tidings," she muttered as she slid behind the steering wheel of her car and looked up at him.

"I'm sorry." He was the one who'd have to take up the slack, but even worse was the look of despair in her clear gaze. This time of year, not only was the deer population a factor on the road, but it could be difficult for Karah Lee to find a decent place to stay anywhere near Hideaway, especially a place that would allow pets. "From what I've seen, this town's pretty good about helping people out. I bet if you told the ladies at Lakeside about this, they might have a spare room."

She spread her hands and shrugged. "I heard Bertie tell someone just this morning that they were completely booked through the month of August."

Karah Lee Fletcher had very feminine features, a delicate, slightly upturned nose and striking, golden amber eyes. There was something so vulnerable about her—which probably had to do with the fact that both times Taylor met her, she was in some kind of trouble.

"What about your boss at the clinic?" he asked. "You might room with her for a while until something became available."

"That would be a thought if she hadn't just moved to a small apartment over the bakery. I know that because she's always bringing doughnuts to the clinic." Karah Lee gripped the steering wheel of her car as if she'd like to steer it toward the dozer operator across the street. "I want to know what happened *here.*"

Taylor glanced over his shoulder at the dozer, grimacing at the noise. He wanted to know, too, but first things first. "You've got your scrubs on. What time do you have to be at work?"

"One. I'm doing the afternoon shift. Cheyenne's working at Dogwood Springs E.R. this afternoon."

He checked his watch. "That means we have forty-five minutes to find a place for you to stay, because you can't leave your cat in the car, and I don't want to have to cat-sit all afternoon. Follow me to the Lakeside."

After an undetected trip into the women's bathroom, Fawn strolled to the bus ticket counter, where several people stood in line. Glancing nervously around her—while trying hard not to look nervous—she stepped into line behind a man who was humming under his breath. As the ticket clerk chattered with another customer about area shows, Fawn tried to play Name That Tune with the guy in front of her.

It took a whole minute, at least, to decipher a butchered version of the "Star-Spangled Banner." The patriot needed voice lessons real bad.

The line moved forward, and someone stepped up behind Fawn, so close she could smell perfume and men's cologne mingled. Flowers and spice, with a little sweat.

Glad she'd changed her appearance so drastically, she kept her head down as the guy in front of her moved to the counter and requested a bus ticket via Hideaway to Bella Vista. Her ears perked when she heard the name. *Hideaway. Danger there.* She sure didn't want *that* bus. It would cost less for a ticket to Springfield.

As the transaction took place in front of her between the smoky-voiced agent and the bad singer, the couple behind her argued quietly about which show they wanted to see.

"*Raising America,*" the woman insisted. "It's just across the street, and I heard some ladies talking about how good it was."

"*Yakov,*" the man said. "You knew I wanted to see *Yakov.* I told you before we even left for this trip—"

"We've got all weekend to see that, and this one starts in an hour."

As the man in front of Fawn collected his ticket and charge card and stuck them, along with receipt, in the back pocket of his slacks, Fawn stepped forward. Behind the counter, the clerk turned away and held up a very familiar picture, gesturing toward the clerk working at the other end of the counter. The picture was a duplicate of the one Fawn had jerked from the bulletin board a few moments ago.

"Hey, Pat, you see anybody who looks like this, you let me know," the clerk told her co-worker.

"Oh, yeah?" Pat said. "Who's that?"

"That woman who killed her lover and a hotel employee last week. Come on, you remember. It's all through the papers. Police seem to think they're closing in on her."

"Yeah, sure, whatever. Like anybody cares." Pat shrugged and turned away. "Honey, I'm from Los Angeles. If the papers in L.A. made as big a deal with their murders as you people here do, there wouldn't be enough paper to print it all."

Before the clerk could turn back, Fawn stepped from the counter and, heart hitting her ribs like popping corn, she strolled as casually as she could away from the counter and blended into the crowd.

Closing in? What did that mean?

What now? How was she going to get out of Branson? Maybe she should've tried the old-geezer getup, after all.

She could do it, of course. She could turn herself into a woman again with a little soap and water and some accessories, a lot of makeup, some different glasses. She could even buy a dress in Wal-Mart, stash the backpack someplace safe and march right back up to that same counter in twenty minutes.

But, what if the clerk recognized her anyway? Maybe she wasn't as good at this disguise thing as she thought she was. After all, if the police were closing in on her, as hard as she'd tried to cover her tracks lately...

Maybe she'd wait until another clerk took over, one who didn't seem so sharp-eyed. Still, how many other pictures of her were tacked up on the brochure racks around town?

The automatic door slid open at the side entrance to the store, and Fawn followed some other teenagers in. She could change her appearance in twenty minutes, easily. But did she want to chance it?

She strolled to the clothing section to check out the dresses. She'd have to go back to Vegas, because that was the only place where she knew her way around and could get another ID. Without an ID, she couldn't work, and without a job she'd be back on the street.

She couldn't go there again. And she didn't have a home to go to, not with a wicked stepfather infesting the place, and a mother who'd rather play stupid than risk losing another husband.

She pulled a dress from the rack and automatically held it up to her body and glanced at the mirror. Ick. Boy with dress.

Too late, she saw a woman watching her from the dressing-room desk with upraised eyebrows. The dress went back to the rack in a hurry, and as Fawn returned to the main aisle, she saw a familiar man two aisles away, with a bus ticket sticking out of his back pocket. He peered at the watches in the jewelry section, then glanced at his own watch.

She studied his movements, and glanced again at the ticket. If she could figure out a way…but that was crazy. He was going to Hideaway, and she didn't want to go there.

Still, if she couldn't get a ticket, herself, what else could she do? And besides, how was she going to feel if she didn't come clean with the police—or *somebody*—and then a bunch of people got hurt or even died?

But what could she tell the police that they would believe? They thought she was the killer. She didn't really have any information of value…did she?

What about the flash drive? Bruce had told her that if anything happened, she was supposed to give the device to someone she trusted. Only she didn't trust anybody.

He'd asked her to do the right thing, but what was that?

Maybe if she knew what was on the device, she would have a better idea about what to do…and maybe if she knew what was going on in Hideaway, she'd be able to figure out whom to tell.

But then, why couldn't she just hand the little silver case over to some policeman somewhere, then run? Or mail it to someone?

No. Stupid idea. She'd learned from life on the Vegas streets that some cops couldn't be trusted. Bruce wanted her to give the information to someone she could trust.

So, taking a deep breath and fixing her gaze on the lame singer with the ticket to Hideaway in his back pocket, she casually strolled toward him. Back in Vegas she'd run with some pickpockets for a couple of weeks. Not fun. She'd lost those losers as soon as she got her fake ID and landed a job, and when she saw them on the Strip after that she'd avoided them. But when she was with them she'd noticed some of the tricks of their trade, and even practiced it a couple of times. Problem was, she could never make a living at it because she'd felt so guilty, she'd actually tried to return a woman's hundred-dollar bill to her one night.

Today, though, she was desperate. If she could just get that guy's ticket—it wouldn't be hard at all, with it sticking out of his back pocket—then somehow delay him from getting to the bus on time, she might have a chance.

That was the big problem. How in the world was she going to stop him from going to the bus?

But maybe that wouldn't matter. If he didn't have his ticket, then he couldn't get on. Simple logic. Of course, he could raise a ruckus, but so what? It would be his word against hers...

Hmm...maybe she'd better prevent that situation. But first things first—get the ticket, then worry about how to waylay the ticket's rightful owner.

She slipped up behind him on the aisle, and as he passed a group of kids in the toy section, she bumped into him from behind to divert his attention, then easily slid the ticket up and out and stuffed it beneath her roomy shirt.

"Excuse me," she said in her gruffest voice when he started to turn, then before he could get a good look at her face, she pivoted and joined the group of kids going the other way.

He didn't call out to her, and when she risked a glance at him over her shoulder, she saw him continuing down the aisle, obviously not aware of his recent loss.

And then she noticed where he was headed, and she stopped and smiled. Perfect!

The men's room.

She fingered the ticket, and felt an extra thickness behind it. She pulled it out and her blood chilled. Not only had she lifted his ticket, but she had also lifted the credit card he'd used to pay for it. She examined the name. Casey Timble.

Okay, she was *not* a pickpocket. She wasn't. No way would she steal more than a bus ticket from the poor guy. But this credit card could serve as her identification card, at least for the next few hours.

Maybe she'd be able to pull this thing off, after all.

Karah Lee sat in the lobby of the Lakeside Bed-and-Breakfast, munching on a black walnut dumpling—one of Bertie Meyer's newest recipes. Dear old Bertie knew how to cook the comfort food, and Karah Lee desperately needed comfort right now.

"Dozed down your new house!" Bertie exclaimed. "I'm telling you, those people are weird out that side of town. If that don't beat all." She shook her head and clucked her tongue. "You call the police?"

"I'll be checking it out." Taylor looked tall and awkward sitting on the delicate Victorian chair in front of the lace-curtained window. "The problem is, the house belonged to Beaufont, so if they had a permit, they could do whatever they wanted with their own property."

"But it just don't make sense to me, a place all ready to rent like that getting dozed down," Bertie complained.

"They oughta at least have to find a place for Karah Lee to stay."

"Oh, I plan to get my deposit and rent money back," Karah Lee said. "And I'll send them a bill for additional expenses, but right now I don't want to argue with them."

"They're a little difficult to reach," Taylor explained. "Do you know of anyplace she might be able to stay, Bertie? From what I hear, rentals around here are grabbed up before they hit the classifieds."

"Wish I'd known earlier," Bertie said. "She could've stayed where she was."

Taylor looked more disappointed than Karah Lee felt, and she was touched. Even though this was only the second time she had met him, it was obvious the man had a tendency to go out of his way for people. Since she struggled with the same tendency—and with being exploited for that trait—she couldn't help finding it attractive.

"Do you have any friends in town with a spare room?" Taylor asked Bertie.

The elderly lady frowned as she thought. "Well, I guess I could get on the phone and make a few calls...or here's an idea. You knew the ranch boys were doing some construction work for us on the third floor? It's kind of a work-study program for them. It's too small up there for two separate suites, but it'd be a good-size single unit, lots of room for a big bedroom, plus a sitting room, desk, couch, eating area. Only problem is, the bathroom up there ain't done yet, and half the outside wall's knocked out."

"How long before that's done?" Taylor asked.

Bertie scrunched up her face. "Well, we could probably get the wall back into place by the end of the weekend if the boys work a little overtime tomorrow. Tuesday at the latest, if the boys hop to it, but that won't help Karah Lee in the meantime."

Karah Lee glanced at her watch, then out the window toward the clinic. She didn't have time for this. "I'm due at work in fifteen minutes."

"Why don't you call Cheyenne and explain?" Bertie said. "She'll understand."

"I can't call in," Karah Lee said. "Cheyenne's already gone, and there'll be patients waiting by the time I get there."

Bertie shook her head and patted Karah Lee on the knee. "Don't let this get your britches in a knot. Somebody in this town'll have a room to spare you for a few days, then you can move right into our third floor. Mind you, it won't be nothing fancy, as we won't have time to do any decorating, but I can sure cut you a good deal on it."

"I'll take it," Karah Lee said. "As long as you'll put up with Monster."

"Oh, sure. You can leave him here this afternoon if you want. He can spend time down with Mildred in the goat pen, or I can keep him in the lobby with me. Now, you get on to work. Taylor, you want to hang around for some coffee and cobbler whilst Karah Lee heads for the clinic?"

He glanced at Karah Lee, then shook his head. "I think I'll walk her to work."

Bertie paused and glanced at him, then at Karah Lee, and nodded, a slow grin spreading across her face.

After leaving the irritable black cat with the doting proprietress, Karah Lee walked beside Taylor toward the town square. "Thank you," she said quietly. "I know this wasn't your problem."

"Want to bet? You're scheduled to take call this weekend."

She chuckled as she easily matched her stride to his. "Okay, you're right. I should've just dumped the whole problem in your hands and left you to it."

"I'd have probably thought of something dumb, like letting you stay at my place while I camped out at the ranger station."

"How far is the station from here?" she asked.

He turned and pointed behind them along the road to the west. "A mile down Turtle Creek Access. You wouldn't want to stay there. It's a twenty-foot-by-twenty-foot cabin, with hardwood floors and a leaky roof."

"You obviously live somewhere around here," she said. Then she added, "Not that I'm suggesting I stay at your place."

"I live in a motor home."

"You're kidding."

"Nope."

"You mean, like a fifth wheel or something?"

"No, I mean a motor home, almost as big as one of the tour buses that pull into town every day. I bought it used at a good price when I left Arizona, and it works well. If I want to change jobs or move, I won't have to worry about selling my house. I'll just drive it wherever I want to go."

"Where are you parked? Or do you call it parked?"

"There's a private hookup down by the shore, not too far from the station. I've been there for a year."

She looked at him again as they crossed the street to the clinic. His ranger hat shaded his face. He had laugh lines around eyes that were now solemn.

He gave her a quick glance, then looked away, obviously uncomfortable about the scrutiny. She had drawn erroneous conclusions about people in the past, but judging by the scant amount of information she had about this guy, he didn't abuse his authority, he was willing to work long hours to make sure people in Hideaway had access to medical care—and sometimes those people weren't the most appreciative.

"You don't get out much, do you?" she asked.

"Why do you say that?"

"Not many people know you, and you've been here a year? In a town like this, that's phenomenal. You're a loner?"

"It's hard to be a loner in Hideaway, but I try to get out of town on my days off."

She nodded. "Being in town probably feels a lot like work. It's almost like you're on duty whenever you're walking down the street."

He glanced at her again as he opened the clinic door for her, and she felt, rather than saw, his surprise. "Exactly."

"Good way to avoid burnout." She stopped when she saw the number of patients already sitting in the waiting room.

Speaking of burnout...

* * *

Fawn felt sick again. And guilty. Because of her, an innocent guy had missed the bus, and would have to pay for another ticket, and even though he hadn't come charging onto the bus before it pulled out of the parking lot, she still wondered if he might say something to the ticket agent about his lost ticket—if he got out of the bathroom some time today.

When Casey Timble—her unwitting ticket donor— had entered the men's room, she'd found a disgustingly simple trick to delay him. Instead of following him inside and announcing that the bus schedule had changed, she'd noticed the layout of the door, with a molded metal handle on the outside, although the door pushed inward.

The setup had been impossible to ignore. Too simple, really. All she'd had to do was get a long mop handle in the hardware section nearby, and jam it through the door handle. When he tried to pull the door open from the other side, it would be snugged shut.

Not that she'd waited to see how it worked. She'd made a run for the bus, rushed inside, handed the driver her ticket and found a seat with a view to make sure she wasn't followed.

She'd barely breathed until the bus snaked its way past Celebration City theme park on the western end of town. She'd leaned back in her seat and taken a deep breath, and then panicked when they pulled off the road at the first overlook for a photo shoot. Several passengers had jumped from the bus, cameras ready, while the rest sat and waited in air-conditioned comfort.

And now she wasn't the only person on the bus who felt sick. A lady across the aisle from her, who looked at least eighty, rested with her head against a pillow, holding her hand to her forehead. She didn't look too great. A couple of seats behind her, someone had mentioned not feeling well, and a couple of minutes later, Fawn heard the awful sound of an airsick bag being used. She'd heard it before, on a bumpy flight with Bruce, but they weren't in the air now.

Fawn dug into her backpack and pulled out her bottle of aspirin and unopened bottle of water. She stepped across the aisle.

"Hey, lady, you okay? Can I get you something?" She might have stolen a ticket in desperation, but Fawn wasn't going to let a bunch of old geezers suffer if she could assist them. After all, she might be an old geezer herself someday—if her luck held out.

❧ *Chapter Twelve* ❧

Taylor returned to the intersection of Elm and Maple and parked across from the silent dozer. In the past hour the small rental had been decimated and stacked in sections, each section ready for the recycle bin. The guy had even taken out a couple of the smaller trees, their roots raised toward the sky in helpless defeat.

Beaufont Corporation. Everywhere Taylor looked, he saw the top-heavy triangle logo. Not to mention the damage they had done in the name of their beautification campaign. He knew many Hideaway natives were getting sick of it, too.

Beaufont for Beautiful. What a sick joke. The idiots were actually trying to make the lakeshore east of town look like a tropical beach by importing sand and tearing out trees and boulders, destroying the natural beauty of the wilderness area in order to bring in more tourists.

It was working. Crowds flocked to the sand volleyball courts and unnatural beaches, the jet-bike stand and the windsurfing boat. And now they were destroying perfectly good historical buildings. For what?

He got out of the truck and strolled across the street. Silence hovered over the lot, where the dozer had so recently ripped. The air was fragrant with freshly turned earth. Taylor stepped across the loose dirt toward the place where the foundation had been, but before he reached it, someone yelled at him from the road. He turned to see a man jogging toward him from the direction of the condo construction site.

The man wore a carpenter's coveralls and a bill cap with the same upturned triangular logo. "Don't you see the postings?" He slung his hand toward the No Trespassing signs planted in the four corners of the lot as sweat dripped from his red face. "What do we have to do, string razor wire around this place?"

Taylor hadn't seen the signs here an hour ago. "It's an empty lot."

"Private property," the man snapped. "The Beaufont Corporation doesn't want any lawsuits."

"What kind of lawsuit?" Talk about overreacting.

The man glared at him, and Taylor relented, still curious. As he drove away, he glanced into his rearview mirror and saw the man striding carefully across the lot, as if afraid he might stumble over something breakable. Or harmful.

Taylor seldom smoked on duty, and never in the truck, but this afternoon he made an exception as he drove along the curving, forested road toward his favorite overlook, with the windows wide open and a warm breeze blowing through. He inhaled deeply from the low-tar cigarette between his fingers.

He remembered in detail the incident he blamed for inciting his resumption of this old habit. He'd arrived home to find a note from Clarice attached to the refrigerator with a magnet. After years of placing notes in the same spot, he'd expected something like, Home late. Dinner in fridge.

Instead, she'd been so callous—after seventeen years of marriage, of raising Chip, of loving one another!—as to leave a refrigerator message for him to read, alone, when he got home. In the end, she'd been too much of a coward to tell him to his face that she couldn't stand to look at him anymore, that she blamed him for Chip's death.

His marriage and family had been relegated, in the end, to a refrigerator magnet.

A week afterward he had been served the divorce papers, and had been forced to endure the stares and sympathy of his co-workers. It was the final humiliation. That was when his partner, Carl, had offered him a smoke, and he'd taken it.

He knew now, as he hadn't realized then, that his acceptance of the cigarette was a silent admission that he had truly given up on his life. After all, what was left?

That same day, he'd stepped to the edge of the canyon rim and stared toward the north, realizing he would never share this experience with his wife again. The sense of loss, the loneliness and the anger had made him stumble backward for fear that he might intentionally pitch forward onto the rocks, a couple hundred feet below.

He knew this resurrection of a bad habit from his youth was an act of rebellion, although he wasn't sure who he was aiming it at. God, for taking Chip away? Clarice, for leaving him? She'd vowed to stand beside him until death parted them. At the time, he hadn't realized that the death wouldn't be his or hers, but the most precious life of his son.

Reaching the overlook, Taylor parked between a tour bus and a small red sports car. Obviously, he wasn't the only one who liked the view. He climbed from the truck and stepped to the edge of the paved pullout to stare across the sunlit edges of the forest, thick with undergrowth.

Chip would have enjoyed a float trip down the gentle Flat River. Clarice would have photographed a hundred sunrises and sunsets by now, rhapsodizing about the shades of pink and gold and orange and purple and blue. Missouri had a grandeur all its own.

By now, back on the South Rim at the Grand Canyon, smart hikers would be staying out of the heat on the trail, and rangers would be kept busy rescuing those who thought they were tough enough to make it to the river and back in the heat of summer.

He didn't miss it. Much.

Here around Hideaway, the only hiking trails besides this new one were logging roads in the Mark Twain National Forest, and the only hazards were copperheads, rattlesnakes and poison ivy—and the meth labs, but those were everywhere.

This place was a gentle, healing garden compared to the Canyon. So why did he still feel so lifeless sometimes?

"Hello?" came a timid, hoarse-sounding voice at his right elbow.

He turned and looked down to find a teenage boy standing beside him. The kid sported round, wire-framed glasses and a baseball cap pulled down low on his forehead. He had on baggy denim jeans, an equally baggy Hawaiian-print shirt with a Branson logo on the sleeve and running shoes that looked too big for his feet barely peeping out from beneath the hem of his jeans.

"Are you a ranger?" the kid asked.

"Yes." He felt immediate heat rush to his face. A ranger caught smoking by a teenage boy. *Great example you are, Jackson.*

"Well, I'm on this tour bus?" The teenager spoke in a rushed, breathless voice. "And there're these old geezers who are getting dizzy and sick and stuff. One old guy in the seat in front of me almost keeled over on top of me. Could you do something?"

Taylor glanced toward the bus the teenager indicated. "Where's the driver?"

"He's in one of those ugly plastic Porta Potties, I think. He's old, too, and he's kind of a porker. Do you think maybe they got food poisoning from their lunch?"

Taylor turned and walked beside the boy toward the bus. "Possibly. Where'd you come from?"

"Branson, but we've been out awhile, you know? It's like the bus can't even pass a curve in the road without somebody hollering for the driver to stop for pictures."

The kid's tone of voice effectively relayed his impatience with the trip so far.

"And you're not feeling sick?"

There was a long silence. The boy's face was pale, and moisture beaded his chin. "I'm fine."

"Are you traveling with your grandparents?" Taylor asked. The kid seemed young to be traveling alone, judging by the soft-husky sound of his voice.

"Grandparents?" He sounded offended.

"I'm sorry. Your parents? Friends?"

"I'm by myself."

"My mistake. What's your name?" Taylor asked as they drew near the tour bus parked in the first spot.

"Casey." The kid raised a hand to his stomach, and his eyes shuttered closed for a moment.

Taylor heard the sound of wheezing before he stepped onto the bus. The lady in the front seat sat with her head braced against an inflated pillow. Her eyes opened when Taylor entered, but she didn't move.

"Ma'am, are you feeling okay?" He leaned toward her.

"I'm fine. I just need to rest a few minutes." Her voice sounded weak. "I've got half a roll to take by the time we get to Bella Vista."

Taylor noticed the pallor of her skin, then glanced around at the others. Of the twenty-something people on the bus, he doubted if more than three or four of them, besides Casey, were under the age of sixty. He knew why, too. Bella Vista was a popular retirement community just over the state border in Arkansas. Why was a kid like Casey on a bus headed for Bella Vista?

An elderly man two seats back leaned out into the aisle. He didn't look much better than the woman did. "Are you a ranger?"

"Yes. Are you feeling ill?"

The man scooted forward, gripping the armrest on his padded seat. "They say Hideaway's got the most picturesque town square of any place in the Ozarks."

"It's true, and I think you're going to get some good shots."

There was a slight shifting of the floor and a heavy grunt behind him, and he turned to find an extremely heavy uniformed man struggling his way up the bus steps, his face drenched with perspiration.

The man sank into the driver's seat. "Is there a doctor's office around here anywhere?"

Karah Lee had just finished discharging a patient with an infected tick bite on his ear, when Blaze hung up the telephone at the front desk and turned around, eyes filled with the excitement of a child in a new playground.

"That was Taylor Jackson. You know, the ranger? There's a busload of elderly sightseers with flu symptoms on their way here. A couple were having breathing problems, one guy says he has chest pains."

"Breathing problems and chest pain?" Karah Lee asked. "That doesn't sound like flu symptoms." Besides, this was June, not flu season.

Blaze shrugged. "That's just what Taylor told me."

"How big a busload?" Karah Lee asked, fighting down

a rising concern. No way could the three of them handle a crowd like that.

"Twenty-some, Taylor said," Blaze told her. His voice quivered with sudden excitement. "What do you think's wrong with them? Should we—"

"Taylor's coming with them, I hope," Karah Lee said.

"He's leading them here."

"They're all sick?" Karah Lee asked.

"Yes, but Taylor didn't have time to give me every patient's symptoms."

Karah Lee took a deep breath. Oh, great. Terrific. Cheyenne was working in Dogwood Springs. She couldn't just drop everything and come charging back here for this. "Make sure a couple of the rooms are set up with nonrebreathers for the ones with breathing problems. You're sure Taylor said flu symptoms?"

Jill came rushing from the supply room with a look of panic. "Did I hear you say there's a bus coming *here?*"

"That's right. We're all they've got." Karah Lee reached for her stethoscope. "Set up exam room one for the chest-pain patient."

"Gotcha." Jill pivoted and returned down the hallway.

Karah Lee followed to make sure the equipment was in place. "I'll have the patient brought straight in. Put him on oxygen, start an IV, do an EKG. Follow our chest-pain protocol if you think his pain is cardiac."

"Okay, but where will you be?" Jill asked.

"On the bus, doing triage. Blaze will be with me."

"All *right!*" Blaze grabbed a spare stethoscope from the central supply counter along the east wall, looped it around his neck and turned back to Karah Lee with a grin, rubbing his hands together. "Finally I get to triage. Do you know how long I've waited for this day?"

"Don't get your hopes up, Blaze," Karah Lee said. "If it's too bad, we'll have to try to send them on to Branson in spite of what Taylor Jackson says."

"So really, Karah Lee, what do you think's wrong with them?" Blaze asked. "Some kind of epidemic? Smallpox maybe?"

"I'd say food poisoning," Jill called from the other room. "Although food poisoning doesn't cause breathing problems."

"SARS? Anthrax?" Blaze suggested. "Oh, I've got it, West Nile—"

"Blaze," Karah Lee said, "would you relax? We can't afford to have you freak on us now."

"I'm not freaking, honest, but I'd like to know what to look for."

"I'm telling you," Jill called from the other room, "on a busload like that, it's probably food poisoning. Maybe the breathing problems are unrelated, a reaction to the air-conditioning on the bus."

"That wouldn't cause chest pain, would it?" Blaze asked.

"Acid reflux, most likely," Karah Lee said. At least that was the case in the majority of patients she'd seen when she moonlighted in the E.R. in Columbia. She wasn't going to blow this situation off, but she wasn't going to panic. She *couldn't* panic. She was the only available physician.

As she issued further orders for preparation, she ignored the insidious voice inside her head that reminded her what a disaster this could become...and that she was freshly out of residency, with no one more experienced to call. No backup. She was in charge. Dad would be apoplectic by now.

What colleague would he call to get her out of this mess?

But it wasn't a mess. She could do this. They were well stocked for a small clinic. Because they were so far out in the middle of nowhere, they had to be prepared for anything.

Everything would be okay. It had to be.

The rumble of a diesel engine reached them from the street, and Karah Lee led the way to the front door to find Taylor parking his Jeep a few yards away, leaving plenty of space in front of the clinic entrance. A large red and black bus with the title Happy Trails blazoned across the side pulled onto the lawn across the street in a conflagration of heat and diesel fumes.

"Let's go," Karah Lee said, pushing out the front door. "Blaze, bring the wheelchair."

"Coming, boss."

Taylor jumped from his vehicle and reached into the back seat for his "tool kit," which looked like a tackle box and which Karah Lee knew would hold basic medical equipment and supplies.

"Sorry to do this to you, Karah Lee," he said, "but I didn't think they should try to make it to Branson or Dogwood Springs without triage and some stabilization. Some of them look pretty sick."

Karah Lee turned to walk with him across the street. "What's your best guess on this?"

"I'm not sure yet. It's confusing."

Karah Lee glanced up at his grim profile. *Get this. A man willing to admit he's confused by something?*

"Typically, with something like this, especially with more than half the group traveling together, I'd suspect food poisoning," he said as they reached the other side of the street. "But not all the symptoms fit."

"Beep. Coming through." Blaze rushed past them with the wheelchair, obviously eager to become part of the action.

"Where's the patient with the chest pain?" Karah Lee asked Taylor. "We've got a room set up for him."

"He's near the back," Taylor said. "I'll carry him out."

They stepped up into the air-conditioned bus, and a moment later Taylor was carrying an elderly, overweight man from the bus as easily as if he were carrying a small child. The elderly man clutched his chest and murmured something to Taylor.

"It'll be okay," Taylor said softly. "We're going to check you out and take care of you."

In triage mode, Karah Lee continued down the aisle as she saw motion-sick bags, pale, miserable faces, and people holding their heads in obvious discomfort.

Taylor was just stepping back onto the bus, when Karah Lee caught sight of an elderly couple, also near the back of the bus, who appeared to be asleep in spite of the activity going on around them. She made her way to them and knelt, touching the woman's arm gently.

"Hello? Are you all right?" she asked.

No response.

"The Whites were sick," said a lady from across the aisle. "They're trying to sleep it off. They're almost deaf, so you'll have to speak up."

"Taylor?" Karah Lee called over her shoulder as she reached down to check the lady's pulse. It felt slow, weak, irregular. She rubbed her knuckles against the patient's chest bone—the best way to waken someone in a hurry.

No response.

Taylor leaned over her. "Unconscious?"

"Unresponsive." Karah Lee repeated the sternal rub on the man's chest. Barely a flutter of eyelashes. She took her penlight out of her coat pocket and opened Mr. White's mouth.

"Oh, Taylor," she murmured.

"The mucus membranes are cherry red," he said. "We need to get everyone off this bus *now*. This looks like carbon monoxide poisoning."

Karah Lee reached down to pick up Mrs. White. "Get her husband, would you?" she asked Taylor. "They need a hyperbaric chamber."

"Cox South in Springfield?" he asked.

She nodded and led the way down the aisle. "Everybody off the bus immediately," she said, raising her voice to be heard above the chatter. "We'll treat you at the clinic across the street. Follow us, please, everyone."

Chapter Thirteen

Taylor listened to Jill's voice drift down the hallway as he settled Mr. White on the bed in exam room three, making sure his oxygen mask fit securely and the flow was at its highest setting. Jill was making arrangements for an airlift for the Whites to the nearest hyperbaric chamber, and Taylor only hoped they would hold out long enough for the chopper to arrive.

The treatment for most of the patients would be the same, though not as drastic as with the Whites. They all needed oxygen. Especially for the elderly, this kind of episode could prove disastrous because of their decreased ability to break down the components of carbon monoxide.

Blaze had rounded up all the oxygen in the clinic, and with Taylor's small canister they had eight. Not nearly enough to treat all twenty-three passengers, but the pharmacist, Nathan Trask, had been contacted via his cell phone, and was on his way back to the pharmacy from a supply run to Springfield. He would bring a couple of extra canisters as soon as possible.

Several of the passengers had shown marked improvement simply by escaping the tainted atmosphere of the bus, and so Taylor could only hope—and at this point, pray—that they had enough oxygen for those who truly needed it.

The prayer might work, but he wouldn't count on it. He seldom prayed lately. He doubted God would listen to him, much less answer. However, in a case like this, when Taylor wasn't praying for himself but for the lives of others, maybe those Great Ears would be open.

"Ouch!" came a guttural cry from exam room one.

"Sorry, Mr. Walker," came Karah Lee's voice. "Had to get the IV started. Your heart's showing some irritability, so we wanted to be prepared. Is the oxygen helping any?"

Taylor raised the bed rails around Mr. White, then rushed back into Mrs. White's room next door and rechecked the cardiac monitor he had placed on her—using his own from the truck. The improvement was negligible. They both needed to be on ventilators, but that would have to wait until the helicopters landed. In the meantime someone would have to ventilate them manually, which meant he needed to intubate them—place a tube down each windpipe to help them breathe. He wasn't familiar with the setup here. He needed help.

He went down the hallway to the first exam room, where Karah Lee stood checking the heart monitor connected to their patient with chest pain. She looked up when he entered, and he could see the concern in her expression. He glanced at the monitor and saw the reason for that concern. Heart irritability was an understatement.

"I need to intubate both Mr. and Mrs. White," he said.

She nodded. "Jill, where are you?" she called, her strong voice carrying well over the beeps of monitors and chatter of a packed waiting room.

"I'm on the phone," came the reply.

"Are we getting an airlift?"

"Hold on, will you?" There were quick instructions, then the sound of a telephone receiver being placed in its cradle. "Air Care will be here in fifteen minutes," Jill called.

Karah Lee frowned at Taylor. "Fifteen minutes?"

"Count your blessings," Taylor said. "That's good time for here. Don't worry, we can do this. I'm not very familiar with the setup since they changed things around a couple of months ago, but I won't have trouble intubating if I have some assistance. After that, we'll need a couple of people to squeeze the ambu bags until Air Care arrives."

Karah Lee's gaze caught on the monitor screen. "Get Blaze." She raised her voice again. "Jill! Call for another helicopter, and then call Dane Gideon. I think he's at the general store. Have him come over for a few minutes and help us. Blaze? We need you back here." She turned back to Taylor. "I'll do one of the intubations, you do the other."

Blaze came lunging into the room. "Got something for me? Casey's taking care of the patients in the waiting room. The ones on oxygen seem to be doing better. The driver's arranging for another bus."

"Who's Casey?" Karah Lee asked.

"You know, the kid."

Karah Lee glanced at Taylor and shrugged.

"Come with me," Taylor said, nudging Blaze by the arm. "I need help intubating Mrs. White. Have you ever done an intubation before?"

"Sure have."

"Good."

"Just never on humans."

Karah Lee was reassessing Mr. Walker's heart condition when she overheard snippets of conversation through the open door to the waiting room.

"...not sure you'd call it breathing problems, maybe just a little tired. Don't worry about me...Casey, you okay?"

"Where'd that Dr. Blaze go? He's awfully young to be a doctor..."

Karah Lee grinned. Blaze would love that.

"...those things are making my nose sore. Think it'll rub a blister?..."

"No, just leave it in there, Flo... A headache's worse than a blister."

"...Casey, you oughta be a doc, too, someday. You've got a nice bedside manner, for a young boy...."

"...calling another bus for us? Before we can take any pictures? But I bought this camera just for this trip."

Karah Lee glanced down at her patient again, then at the monitor. It didn't look much better. "Mr. Walker, are you still having chest pain?" she asked.

He nodded and grimaced, rubbing at the moisture on

his wrinkled forehead with his right hand. "Some. Not like my headache, though."

"What about your upset stomach?"

"Not as bad."

"And on a scale of one to ten, what would you rate your chest pain now?"

The man grimaced again, his pale lips pursing as he appeared to consider the question from all angles. "About a four."

"You're not allergic to anything? Morphine?"

"Morphine?" He frowned up at her. "Why?"

"I don't mean to alarm you, but your EKG shows your heart's acting up a little more."

"What does that mean?"

"You could be having a heart attack. We have a helicopter flying in for you, and they'll take you to Springfield."

"But I felt fine this morning. I thought this was all just carbon monoxide poisoning. Why do you have to fly me to Springfield?"

There was a collective gasp from the other room. "Casey! Quick, catch him!" somebody called out.

"I've got him," came Taylor's voice. "You just sit there and relax. It'll be okay."

Karah Lee hesitated, then returned her attention to her patient. "They have a hyperbaric oxygen chamber, which will do more than anything to get your carbon monoxide levels down and prevent further damage to your heart. Don't worry, the morphine will help—"

"Doctor." Taylor stepped into the doorway, carrying the one teenage passenger in his arms. The boy's hat was knocked sideways and his glasses were askew on his face. "We need to get this one into a bed. He was helping one of the ladies with her nasal cannula and just pitched forward. We barely caught him in time to keep his face from hitting the floor."

Karah Lee once more checked the monitor, then squeezed Mr. Walker's hand. "I'm sorry, but we're very short-handed. I'll let Jill start you on the medication, then I'll be back in to check on you." She joined Taylor and directed him to exam room four, then gave Jill instructions to start morphine on Mr. Walker.

"What dose?" Jill asked.

Karah Lee called the numbers over her shoulder as she followed Taylor down the hallway to the exam room at the end of the hallway. As Taylor settled the young man on the bed, Karah Lee studied her new, young patient more closely.

"Do you know if he's traveling with one of the other passengers?" she asked.

"He told me he's traveling alone."

"Okay, I'll take care of him. You go back out and triage. As soon as Nathan arrives with oxygen, bring a canister back here."

Taylor left, and the patient shifted on the bed. "No," he said softly.

Karah Lee leaned over him. "Is your name Casey?"

His eyes fluttered open and he stared at her a minute, as if trying to focus. He nodded almost imperceptibly.

"You're obviously having a bad reaction to the carbon monoxide," Karah Lee said. "Just like the other passengers. We're going to get you some treatment as soon as possible. You'll need oxygen."

"No." His voice trembled as he struggled to raise himself on his elbows.

Karah Lee gently eased him back. "Just relax for a few minutes, okay? Just because you're young and strong doesn't mean you're immune to the poison that got your fellow passengers on the bus."

Casey took a deep breath and shrugged Karah Lee's hand from his shoulder. "I don't need any oxygen." He had a surprisingly soft voice. His hat slid from his head to reveal short, deep brown hair and a red, irritated scalp. He reached up to straighten the glasses. "Don't take it away from anybody, okay?"

Karah Lee studied the lines of his face, the slender neck, the delicate, sharply pointed chin. "We won't be taking it from anyone else, we'll be bringing you a new canister as soon as it arrives."

"I don't need it." He closed his eyes again.

"Casey?" called an old man from the end of the hallway. "You okay back there, boy?"

Blaze stepped to the entrance and set a well-filled denim backpack inside the door. "They said this was yours, Casey. What happened to you?"

"He says he's fine," Karah Lee said dryly.

"Doesn't look fine."

"Get back in the other room, I'll take care of him. Oh, and don't let Nathan get away when he gets here. He's an EMT. He can help us keep an eye on the other patients."

Blaze saluted and rushed back down the hallway.

Casey moaned and pressed his hands against his lower abdomen.

Karah Lee leaned over him, watching his response carefully. This was an odd presentation of carbon monoxide poisoning. "You want to tell me what's going on with you?" she asked. "You're obviously having some belly pain. Do you have a headache? Trouble breathing?"

He shook his head, then seemed to reconsider and nodded. "Some trouble breathing." He hefted himself up onto his elbows again and dragged his gaze toward the door. "You want to shut that?"

Karah Lee closed the door and took her stethoscope from around her neck. "Okay, let's check you out. How bad is the pain on a scale—"

He raised his hand as he sat up. Without warning, he grabbed his shirt and pulled it over his head to reveal an elastic bandage wrapped several times around his chest. While Karah Lee watched, he unfastened the bandage and unwound it.

"With something like that impeding your movement, no wonder you're having trouble breathing," she said.

The bandage fell away, and Karah Lee stifled a gasp.

This was no boy.

She reached quickly for a gown and wrapped it around the young woman's very feminine, very bare upper body. "Lie back down, please, you're white as the bed linens. You want to tell me what's going on?"

"Cramps." As Casey dropped the pretense, her voice softened further, cracking with pain as her eyes squeezed shut.

"Okay, I'm going to listen to your chest," Karah Lee said as she pressed the bell of her stethoscope against the white skin of Casey's chest. Breathing was irregular, heart rate fast. A quick check revealed low blood pressure. When Karah Lee pressed Casey's finger, she noted a slow capillary refill. Then she noticed the very strong smell of blood. She glanced down, and saw a stain slowly spreading across the white sheet on the bed.

"Casey," she said softly. "There are obviously quite a few things going on here that I know nothing about. This is more than simple cramps, and you're losing too much blood for this to be just a period. Is it possible you're pregnant?"

The young woman opened her eyes again, and tears filmed them as she held Karah Lee's gaze. "I've been taking the Pill."

"Have you missed any doses?"

Casey glanced away. "Only a few days a couple of months ago."

"That's all it takes. How old are you?" Karah Lee asked.

Casey hesitated, swallowed. "Old enough, obviously." The casual sarcasm wasn't consistent with her expression.

"Obviously," Karah Lee said. "For some girls, eleven is old enough, but I would be forced to handle their medical care differently than I would that of a grown woman. How *old* are you?"

Casey glanced toward the door. "Eighteen. You can't write a medical chart on me or anything like that."

"So there's some reason you're masquerading as a—"

"Keep it down, will you?" The young woman's blue gaze was shot through with discernible fear. "Don't you doctors have some code or something that says you can't spill information about your patients?"

With a sigh of frustration, Karah Lee pulled the stirrups out at the end of the exam bed. "If you're talking about doctor-patient confidentiality, that's right. I won't go blabbing about what you tell me. Okay? Satisfied?"

"No matter what?"

"I'm required by law to report the case if you or someone else is in danger because of what you tell me. Now, we need to get those jeans off and check you out, and then I'll need to take a urine test and draw some blood for—"

"No." Casey pulled the gown around her shoulders and struggled to sit up. "I'm the one who'll be in danger if anybody finds out about me. You can't even tell..." Her voice faded, and she fell back onto the pillow.

"Convinced?" Karah Lee asked softly. "We need to get some fluid back into your system or you'll become even more dehydrated. I also need to examine you and see what's going on." It could be a ruptured ectopic pregnancy, which might be deadly if allowed to continue untreated.

Casey closed her eyes as Karah Lee pulled out equipment to establish a large bore IV. She needed to check on her other critical patients, but she didn't want to leave this young woman alone.

"I'm going to call my nurse back here to draw some blood, Casey."

The eyes flipped open. "Nobody else in this room, or I'll leave this clinic, if I have to crawl out of here."

"Okay, look, I'll draw the blood myself as I establish an IV site, but you'll feel a lot better with some fluid in you. I'll also need a urine sample."

"Just tell me where, and you'll have enough samples for the whole busload. Is that door locked?"

"No one's going to come in, but, Casey, I can't run the lab equipment *and* help those people out there. I'll at least need to have my nurse help."

Casey frowned, focusing closely on Karah Lee, as if trying to glean some hint of subterfuge. "Promise?"

"I promise."

"Don't tell that ranger."

"Only if your life is further threatened. I'm not going to hurt you, okay?"

Casey glanced around the room, then looked back up at Karah Lee, again with that careful scrutiny. "What will you have to do to me?"

"It depends on what I find wrong, but I'll need to give you a pelvic exam at any rate, to see for sure where the blood is coming from."

"You mean I'll have to do the stirrup thing?"

"Yes."

At last, Casey relented. "Okay, but no one else in the room, okay?"

"Okay."

"And can I do the urine test first? I really gotta pee."

⨎ Chapter Fourteen ⨎

Taylor removed a nasal cannula from eighty-year-old Mrs. Jessup's face. "You're doing better," he said. "I'm sorry we can't top off your supply right now, but all the other canisters are in use."

She smiled up at him flirtatiously. "I don't think I'm going to need it, Ranger. You've got my blood pumping just fine."

"Oh, cut it out, Flo," muttered the elderly man at the end of the room. "The poor guy's got his hands full already without your threats."

"That's okay, Fred, let her flirt." Taylor straightened, holding the used equipment, grinning at his recovered patient. "It isn't like I have women flocking around me all the time. I'm enjoying this." He knelt next to another lady and checked her pulse. She, too, was doing better.

With everyone else taking care of patients in the treatment rooms, Taylor had been on his own in the waiting room except for the few moments Nathan Trask had joined him. At the moment, the pharmacist was tracking down more oxygen at the fire station.

"Can't get over the delayed reaction with Casey," Fred said. "You should've seen him on that bus, what with the rest of us all whining because we felt so awful. He was passing out aspirin and sodas from the cooler in front just like he worked on that bus. Never heard a complaint from him."

"Well, he was none too happy when we stopped the third time to take those pictures at the overlook. Still, he's a nice young man," another lady agreed. "I wonder what's going on back there? He just fell over all of a sudden-like."

"I sure hope he's okay," Fred said.

Taylor glanced at his watch. The first Air Care flight was due to arrive at any time, and Bertie Meyer was manning the telephone at the reception desk. She'd already cut off about half a dozen calls, inexperienced as she was with the system. Problem was, Taylor couldn't do much better, so Jill was answering the phone from the exam room, where she continued to watch Mr. Walker.

Flo put a hand on Taylor's arm and grinned up at him with a look of obvious entreaty. "Couldn't you just step back there and ask how Casey's doing?"

He returned the grin. "Why don't I go see how Casey's doing." With a final glance around the room at the rest of his patients, he strolled to the back and placed his used canister on the floor, disconnected the tubing and mask and tossed them in the biohazard-waste container, then washed his hands.

He could barely hear Karah Lee's voice beyond the closed door of the exam room at the end of the hallway. He approached it and knocked. "Mind if I enter?"

He heard a gasp, and a quickly whispered, "No! Don't let anybody—"

"One moment, please," came Karah Lee's response.

He blinked and frowned at the door. What was going on in there? Thirty seconds later the door eased open and Karah Lee slid through, her height and the breadth of her shoulders effectively blocking his view of the interior of the room. He stepped back.

She closed the door behind her. "Sorry, Taylor." She touched his arm to draw him down the hallway with her. "We apparently have a shy patient. Casey's requesting total privacy, and I'm bound by the request."

"But what's wrong with him?"

She gave him a noncommittal shrug. "I'm still checking. How are the others doing?"

"Better. Things have improved in the waiting room, and Air Care is due to land soon." He glanced down and noticed the vials in her hand. "You drew blood?" He noticed that she had apparently spilled some of the blood on the hem of her lab coat.

"Yes, and I need to check the results as quickly as possible." She turned into the lab across the hallway from the first exam room. When Taylor started to follow her in, she turned. "I'm sorry, Taylor, but privacy—"

"I know," he said, frustrated. "Casey has a right to his privacy."

She shrugged. "Regulations."

He gestured to her coat. "You should change."

She looked down and nodded. "Thanks, I will." Then she closed the door behind her.

Taylor shook his head as he returned to the waiting room. "Sorry, folks, I don't have any news about Casey yet. Maybe you should ask the doctor about him when she comes out."

Karah Lee took off her soiled lab coat, double bagged it in the red biohazard bags and placed it in the corner to toss in the laundry hamper later. She listened at the door until she heard Taylor's voice back in the waiting room, then cracked the door open again and stuck her head out into the hallway. Jill was still in the room across the hall.

"Hey," Karah Lee called softly, waving for the nurse's attention.

Jill glanced over her shoulder, caught sight of Karah Lee and stepped to the doorway. "What's going on? You're doing lab *now?* Air Care should be here anytime."

"Good. Come here, I need you right now."

Jill frowned and glanced at her patient. "I'll be right back, Mr. Walker."

"You go on," the man said weakly. "I'm feeling better."

Jill didn't look convinced, but she shrugged and crossed the hallway. "What's wrong?"

"I need to check out our patients, but I have a problem with Casey." Karah Lee held the door open and motioned the nurse inside.

Jill joined her in the lab. "Is he okay?"

"I need you to run lab work on...on the blood and urine I took."

"What kind of lab work?"

Karah Lee closed the door and leaned against it. "Not a word to anyone about this, Jill. No one."

Jill shrugged. "Fine, but are you going to tell me what happened to our mystery boy, and why you're taking all your time with him when we have a lot of other patients—"

"Casey's a woman," Karah Lee murmured softly.

Jill hesitated, and her slender eyebrows drew together in disapproval. "This isn't a good time for jokes, Doc."

"I suspect a spontaneous abortion, but I need to make sure it isn't a ruptured ectopic. I've got her on IV fluids right now."

The eyebrows raised slightly, and the blue eyes widened. "You're not kidding."

"In case you hadn't noticed, I'm not exactly a practical joker," Karah Lee said. "I need to check the other patients and prepare them for transport, but then I need to get back in and give her an examination."

Jill's professional posture settled back into place, and she was once again as unshakable as her hard-sprayed hair. "Then get to it. I'll run the labs and get them to you ASAP."

"Thanks." Karah Lee stepped out into the hallway and heard the familiar sound of helicopter rotors beating the air.

Taylor poked his head around the corner from the waiting room. "You hear that? Choppers are on approach. Both of them. Blaze and Nathan are outside laying the markers for them."

Extreme relief. "How are the others?"

"All are showing signs of improvement, though some continue to need oxygen. Those who had mild symptoms are now asymptomatic, and those who were moderate are now mild. Another bus is on its way from Branson."

Karah Lee knew it was far too early to relax her guard, but it felt good to have such competent staff covering her backside. "Thanks, Taylor. I don't know what we'd have done without you."

She crossed the hallway to check on Mr. Walker and reassure him. The results of his bedside blood test, which Jill had run while Karah Lee was in with Casey, showed that he indeed had had a myocardial infarction. Though the results weren't specific, Karah Lee was able to interpret the seriousness of the situation by reading the monitor and EKG. She knew better than to try to interpret past that, however. She'd leave that for the cardiologists in Springfield.

The rhythmic *chop-chop* of helicopter blades beat the air in counterpoint as they landed, and Karah Lee was glad this town had reserved such a broad lawn between the main street and the lake.

As Taylor bent over Mrs. White and checked her vitals, Karah Lee allowed herself a fraction of a moment to watch him with the patient. He was a natural. Amazing how much a person could learn about another person in just a short afternoon of extreme tension. To watch him, she'd have thought this was his primary occupation.

Even better was that he'd come to her rescue again, and this time she hadn't disgraced herself in any way.

Taylor straightened from Mrs. White's bedside, and Karah Lee turned away. "I'll be in exam room four."

She could feel him watching her as she left the room, and wondered how much longer she'd be able to conceal Casey's real condition from the rest of the staff. Government regulations were the pits at a time like this, although Karah Lee would have kept Casey's secret, anyway.

Something was going on with that young woman, and Karah Lee wished she knew what it was.

Taylor focused on preparing his patients for the switchover and flight. The oxygen was working, thank God. The hyperbaric chamber would probably restore them completely.

Yes. Thank you, God. Answered prayer. He immediately turned his attention to other things, but the gentle thought remained. It was almost as if God had made physical contact with Taylor, as if they'd had a rare communication— almost like a reassurance of some kind, as if God were gently nudging Taylor to let him know his prayers weren't useless.

There had been no lives lost this time around, and for that, Taylor was profoundly grateful. Even Mr. Walker seemed to be doing better.

The atmosphere in the waiting room grew livelier as Taylor propped open the thick wooden door that separated the entry foyer from the waiting room proper.

He reassured the passengers about their buddies on the bus and explained where the helicopters were taking them, and why.

"What about Casey?" Fred asked. "What's up with him?"

"The doctor is with him now, but I really can't give you any news about him yet." Thanks to Karah Lee. "However, I'm encouraged by the fact that she hasn't called for another transport to take him to a larger hospital."

"That poor boy," Flo said. "We should've guessed he wasn't feeling too well, either."

"I'm curious about him," Taylor said.

"So are we," Flo said. "He got on the bus alone just before it pulled out in Branson, found a seat by himself and never said a word until Myrt got sick across the aisle from him. Then he started that little activity of passing out aspirin and carrying drinks and even handing out those motion-sick bags. Who'd've thought it?"

"Just goes to show you never can tell about people," Myrt said from the far corner.

"That's for sure," Fred replied. "D'you get a load of that ring he wore? Hot-pink hearts. I'm telling you, kids've got a different style these days, for sure."

"We'll need to know who to contact about him," Taylor said. "Guardian or parent or someone."

"The kid told me he was one of them emancipated minors," Fred said. "But he's with us now. We'll keep an eye on him, soon as the doctor lets him out of here."

"Don't count on that," Myrt said. "The driver says they've got another bus coming to pick us up, and we're going to have to be ready to roll if we want to get home tonight."

"You mean just take off and leave him here alone?" Fred exclaimed. "Just like that?"

"Don't worry, we'll take good care of him," Taylor said.

The flight crew from the first chopper came across the street pushing a stretcher, and Taylor braced open the glass foyer door to give them free access inside. He cautioned everyone not to block the walkway, then began giving reports on the patients as the flight crews transferred each one to Air Care's equipment.

Finally, just when Taylor thought he would be stuck giving reports on all three patients, Jill stepped out of the lab and closed the door behind her, then greeted the crews and helped with the transfers. Karah Lee, at last, emerged from her stronghold and rejoined the staff.

Taylor saw Jill rise up on tiptoe to whisper something in Karah Lee's ear. Karah Lee nodded, gave a reply that was too soft to be overheard, and nodded with apparent satisfaction.

And Taylor was left to battle his curiosity alone.

Chapter Fifteen

Fawn stared at the white ceiling of the exam room and imagined she could feel the fluid trickle into her arm and through her bloodstream.

Product of conceptus? Even if Dr. Karah Lee hadn't explained, Fawn knew she was having a miscarriage. Which meant she'd been pregnant with someone's baby. Had to have happened when she'd slipped up and forgotten to take her Pill for a couple of days.

Stupid!

The fluid from the bag continued to drip into her arm. The doctor had told her it was on the highest setting, and the bag was already almost empty. That stuff sure worked. She felt better now.

Except she was having a miscarriage. If she'd been carrying a little baby inside her, and now it was dead, shouldn't there be a funeral or something? Had she done something to cause the miscarriage? Or maybe God had decided that no baby of hers deserved to live.

A baby. A little baby she could have taken care of and protected. She might have been a mom in a few months.

The ceiling blurred as tears filled her eyes. An innocent little child surely didn't need to be stuck with a mom who turned tricks for a living. What a horrible way to grow up. But she'd been doing so much better with Bruce...and maybe she'd've given her baby up for adoption with a good family. And yet, for just a moment, she allowed herself to imagine...a tiny child nestling into her arms, trusting her to keep him safe...

How could she keep anybody safe while she ran from the police and the killer?

Her brothers and sister had snuggled into her arms, feeling warm and sweet and cuddly, and gazing up into her eyes almost as if she were their mom. They were so cute...until they overburped or dirtied their diapers or screamed and cried, and Mom hollered for Fawn to keep them quiet.

Is that the kind of mom I would be? Grumpy and crying all the time, and letting my husband do whatever he wanted to my kids?

Well, now she wouldn't have to think about all that. At least not for a while. Maybe never. Maybe she was one of those people who should never have kids.

Could be she even already had some disease, like an STD or even AIDS. Had the doctor checked her blood for that?

The chatter out in the main clinic reached her, and Fawn heard a couple of the old geezers asking about "Casey."

More tears trickled down the sides of her face and into her hair. What would those people think about her if they knew what she really was?

Maybe they'd still like her. Sometimes old people were more understanding about stuff like that. Great-Grandma had been.

But she didn't have time to think about Great-Grandma. She had to get out of this clinic and find some place around here to hide. She didn't know much about this town, or about what was going on here, but she did know she should never have talked to Ranger Taylor in the first place.

But what else could she have done? The driver wouldn't even listen to her when she told him how sick the Whites were, because he was sick, too. She wouldn't've done anything different. Still, Taylor had to have seen a picture of her, at least the one in the paper, and maybe she'd even been a TV star for about thirty seconds on the local news—not that she'd have seen it, hiding out in that cave of an apartment.

Anyway, this place might be a hideaway for some people, but they had newspapers and television, and Fawn knew better than to trust strangers. Would the doctor keep a secret from the ranger? What if he started asking more questions? And then there was the *real* Casey Timble, whose ticket had turned up missing after he got jammed into the men's room at the store. If he could use his brain better than he could sing, then he might have figured out he'd been duped, and if he called the right people...

...had to get out of here.

She watched the bag empty into the IV tube and into her arm, and with every drop she continued to feel better. Now she had to go.

She flexed her fist. Dr. Karah Lee had said she had nice big veins. Cool doctor, but could she be trusted?

Before she could chicken out, Fawn grabbed the needle, held her breath and tugged the tape from the top of the needle. The tip jabbed her and she winced, but she grasped the base of the needle and yanked it out, then pressed her fingers over the hole in her arm before much blood could drip out. She shoved the IV pole away from the bed with her foot and sat up.

Voices seemed to suddenly fill the hallway, which probably meant the helicopters were landing. With all the commotion, this was the perfect time to get out.

She got up, took a deep breath to steady herself, grabbed a handful of cotton balls from the second drawer down on the exam-room desk. She placed one cotton ball over the hole in her arm and put some tape over that, then bent her elbow double. That should stop the bleeding soon.

She reached down for her pack, which that hot guy, Blaze—oh, what a name—had brought back for her, and pulled out some fresh clothes. After dressing, she swung the pack over her shoulder, then tiptoed to the door and cracked it open. No one in the hallway.

With another deep breath, she stepped out into the hallway and turned left, toward the back of the clinic. There had to be some kind of emergency exit that way. She could do this. Everything would be okay.

* * *

Karah Lee checked on two of the three patients who hadn't gone outside to watch the helicopters take off with their charges. All were looking good, so she left them on oxygen and rushed down the hallway to the back exam room. Casey's drip bag should almost be empty, and she—

She opened the door and stumbled to a stop. The bed was empty.

"Casey?" She stepped back out into the hallway and checked the bathroom. No one.

Blaze was the first staff member to return to the clinic.

"Blaze, did Casey go outside to watch the liftoff?"

"I didn't see him. You going to tell me what's going on with him now? Why all the secrecy?"

"Sorry, you know the rules." She checked the other rooms.

He followed behind her. "Maybe he started feeling better."

"Obviously he did, or he wouldn't—" She looked in exam room four again and gasped. "The backpack. It's gone. Did you put it somewhere else?"

"Nope. I guess Casey must've taken it." Blaze frowned at her. "Come on, Karah Lee, it just means he's feeling better."

"It isn't that simple." She scanned the room. Casey had obviously pulled out her own IV needle. The discarded gown and top sheet covered the majority of bloodstains.

"What'd you have him on IV for?" Blaze asked.

"Dehydration."

"From what?"

"Blaze, I'm sorry, but the case is confidential from here on out."

"Okay, I know the rules. Fine. So what *can* you tell me?" He followed her as she rushed out of the room. "For instance, I've been wondering—Mr. and Mrs. White were sitting in the back of the bus, right?"

"Right." She glanced into the lab and the reception office, and finally led the way out to the waiting room, which was once more filling with people—not only patients from the bus, but an increasing number of her regularly scheduled afternoon patients, who looked confused by the hullabaloo.

"And the driver thinks the leak was closer to the middle of the bus," Blaze continued, still following her. "Why'd the Whites take the hit harder than the folks closest to the leak? And do you have to walk so fast?"

Yes, she did. Taylor was going to get his wish, and she needed to find him quickly. "Could be any number of reasons, Blaze," she said as she led the way out of the clinic. "If the Whites had other physical problems, like diabetes or heart problems or asthma, the carbon monoxide would most likely have affected them sooner, plus several of the other passengers kept getting out to take pictures. Those who stayed inside the bus to rest and stay cool would have been affected more severely." *That would include Casey.*

Karah Lee saw Taylor's tall frame and bronze hair as he walked with some of the more spry patients back across the street from the landing zone. She motioned to him. "Taylor, may I speak with you for a moment?"

He excused himself and joined her on the sidewalk as the others trooped back inside.

"You wanted to know about Casey?" Karah Lee asked softly, out of earshot of the others.

"What happened to patient confidentiality?" Taylor asked.

"Priorities. I think she could be in danger."

"*She?*"

"Definitely."

Taylor's expression didn't change, but the ensuing silence screamed his curiosity.

"Casey is a young woman who is possibly septic, or could become that way," Karah Lee said.

The control slipped a little as Taylor's gray-hazel eyes narrowed. "From what?"

"Spontaneous abortion."

He obviously struggled with this information for a few milliseconds. "Then we need to transport her to Springfield?"

Karah Lee leaned closer. "Taylor, I know this is highly unusual, but could you keep this to yourself? I couldn't drag the story out of her, but it seems she's masquerading as a boy to protect herself. She's terrified she'll be found out. Something's going on there, and I get the feeling she's in physical danger in more ways than one, or at least she feels that's the case."

"So you want me to take her myself?"

"I want you to find her and bring her back here to the clinic. I don't know if she'd be willing to go anywhere—"

"You *lost* her?" His shoulders slumped, and he brushed his hand through his hair.

"I didn't *lose* her." This man could be irritating. "She yanked the IV needle out of her arm and took off while we were with other patients. I told you, something's got her really spooked. Maybe she's running away from home, maybe she's afraid her parents will find out she's pregnant...or she was."

Taylor sighed and rubbed his head, then stepped off the curb and marched toward his truck. "Let me get my hat. Looks like this search will be on foot."

"Not necessarily, but you might want to check the buildings on the town square first."

"Any idea which way she went?"

"Probably out the back door, because if she'd gone out the front way, someone would have noticed."

He opened the door and reached inside, pulled out his hat and placed it on his head, and looked back at Karah Lee. "Can I at least call for help? Greg and Tom can cruise the perimeter of town while I search the buildings. That way—"

"I don't think anyone else should know about this, Taylor, really."

"Then I won't give them details, I'll just let them know the patient is unstable medically, and if someone finds her, they should bring her back here."

Karah Lee felt like a traitor. "Okay, just find her."

Dressed in fresh clothes and having to pee so badly she knew she would burst if she didn't find a spot soon, Fawn reached the edge of Hideaway, with shrubs that thickened into a forest on one side of the road and an overgrown field of weeds on the other.

This town had a lot of trees, which meant shaded alleys that almost looked like tunnels of green and that hid a girl well when she was trying to keep from being seen by the guys in the sheriff's cruiser.

But what now? She was feeling better, but not perfect. Her cramps were almost gone, and she didn't feel as sick to her stomach, but she'd sure like to lie down someplace safe.

Before going farther, she dropped her pack and relieved herself behind a couple of big trees. Dr. Karah Lee had told her that the need to urinate was a sign she was being well rehydrated by the IV fluid. That was a good thing, but it wasn't very comfortable without a bathroom nearby.

As Fawn hovered deep in the shadows, she heard the sheriff's car go past on the road again. She knew it was them because she could hear that little *ping-ping-ping* in the engine that sounded as if they'd gotten bad gasoline.

They were looking for her. She knew it.

Had Dr. Karah Lee broken her promise? She'd said she wouldn't tell anyone unless it was a matter of life and death.

But then, if the doctor thought Fawn was really sick now—which she wasn't, not really, not too bad now, anyway—then maybe she thought she was doing the right thing by turning Fawn in.

Should've told her about everything else, maybe. But what if she'd spilled her guts and the doctor had called the Branson police? You just never knew who to trust.

Instead of walking down the main road that led from town—with tar bubbling from the old surface in black, shiny streaks—Fawn climbed through a rusty barbed-wire fence and cut through the field toward a weathered gray barn that looked as if it had settled itself comfortably beneath the cliffs that oversaw the town. It looked abandoned. Kind of the way Fawn felt.

As sweat trickled down her face and back, she heard the sound of another approaching car and ducked into the branches of the one lone, stickery-needled cedar tree in the center of the field. She peered out from the secure hiding place in time to see the ranger's light green Jeep cruising slowly along the road, tar bubbles popping beneath the tires. Ranger Jackson gazed from beneath the brim of his hat across the field, then peered into the trees.

She waited as he drove slowly out of town, then turned around and drove past her again. When he finally disappeared from sight, she plowed through the overgrown field to the barn lot. She scrambled over the wooden fence and dropped into the corral, looking for the best way to get in. When she tested the huge double doors in the front, they opened with a squeal of hinges. The smell of molded hay seemed to greet her in a cloud.

The rough wood scratched her hands, and something rustled in the darkness. This place was spooky, but nothing could be spookier right now than the people cruising around searching for her.

Fawn pulled her new little flashlight from her pack and entered the barn, closing the doors behind her. Her pack was heavy, and she didn't feel the greatest. For now, she was going to have to make this barn in Hideaway her own hideaway.

With an earsplitting hiss and the chugging of a diesel engine, the new bus lumbered off with the remainder of the ill-fated passengers Karah Lee had treated and released. She stood on the sidewalk beside Blaze waving at the grateful crowd of mainly elderly tourists, most of whom seemed eager to continue their touring.

The bus cruised past the Lakeside Bed-and-Breakfast, past the old Methodist church and cemetery and up the hill on the road back to Highway 76. Karah Lee turned and went back inside to a waiting room remarkably empty of patients, thanks to Jill's rescheduling expertise.

Jill waved to get her attention through the reception window. "I hope you don't mind working until eight o'clock tonight," she said.

"Not if you don't."

"Good. You've got a caller on hold. You can take it in Chey's office. The woman says she's your sister."

"My *sister?* Shona?"

Jill pointed in the direction of the office and picked up a clipboard. "I've got Mrs. Carlson in three and Melody Thomas in one. I'll let you know when I need you."

Karah Lee picked up the cordless on Chey's desk, pushed the door shut behind her and plopped into the cushioned seat in front of the desk. She hesitated before answering. The last few conversations she'd had with her sister hadn't exactly ended well, but maybe this time would be an exception. One could always hope. Maybe Shona wanted to see how she was doing on her new job.

She pressed the "phone" button. "Shona? Hi. How's it going?"

"Not well."

Karah Lee suppressed a groan, her hope short-lived. "I'm sorry. Anything I can do?"

"Yes, you can tell me what you said to Dad the other day, because he's been a bear this week, and he just *happened* to mention he received a call from you last week. Big surprise." The sarcasm could cut through rock.

"He didn't tell you what we talked about?"

"Something about a scholarship you received years ago."

"The Sebring Scholarship. He was friends with the committee chairman."

"And that would be a problem because?..."

She obviously didn't get it.

"Shona, Dad influenced them. He also threw his weight around for my admission to med school, *and* my residency."

"Sure he did. I wrote those letters. Come on, Karah Lee, what is *bugging* you? And please don't tell me you expected some kind of la-la land where all the good little boys and girls study hard to make good grades and get into college."

"It happens on occasion."

"Not where I come from." Shona's voice had taken on a new edge since they'd last talked—and it had already been bad enough. "Oh, that's right, you used to beg Mom to read you those Pollyanna books."

No wonder Karah Lee always went into a depressive state after a conversation with her sister. Had it always been like this? Hadn't they been friends at one time—between the fights?

"Okay, look, Shona. Just don't do it anymore, okay? I told Dad not to do me any more favors, and now I'm telling you. No more letters, no more chummy phone calls. If I can't make it on my own, without influence from my father, then I deserve to starve."

An irritated sigh, then, "Karah Lee, you are such a jerk. Are you going to make Dad pay for his mistakes for the rest of his life?"

"I'm not trying to make him pay for anything, I just want him to stop interfering in my life."

"It's what parents do. They try to help their kids. Not that you'd know much about that, since all Mom ever did was sap your energy and complain about—"

"Mom might not have complained so much if she'd had a faithful husband who didn't start arguments and run out on her at the first sign of trouble."

"Mom never argued, Karah Lee, she just shut 'em down cold, like no one's opinion mattered but hers, and the 'Gospel According to the Great Katherine May Fletcher.'"

"Stop it."

"And believe me, if Dad had run out on her at the first sign of trouble, neither of us would ever have been born."

"How would you know that? Has he been telling you all about his problems with Mom?" What kind of father would do that?

"He wouldn't have had to tell me a thing. You could've seen it for yourself if you'd just gotten in touch with reality every once—"

Karah Lee pressed her thumb on the "phone" button and disconnected. Nothing ever changed, and she refused to sink to the level of sibling rivalry that had pocked her family history with ugly memories. She had work to do.

Of course, she knew what would happen. The phone rang again, seconds later, vibrating in her hand. She let it ring two times before she pressed the button to reconnect. No use making Blaze or Jill answer for her.

"One more word about Mom and I'm hanging up again," she said.

There was a long silence, and then an unfamiliar voice, "Excuse me?"

Karah Lee spent the next couple of minutes in mortification as she changed a patient's appointment time. She would deal with Shona later.

❧ Chapter Sixteen ❧

Something rustled in the hay nearby, startling Fawn awake on Sunday morning. She sat up in the stream of sunlight from the door of the loft and squinted at the glare, shielding her eyes. Her ears rang and her stomach rolled—she was going to heave any minute. Her head ached. Maybe it was just more side effects from the exhaust leak on the bus. She'd have to wait it out, at least for a couple more days, until the sheriff and the ranger gave up. Right now, she didn't want to risk trying to leave town.

Another rustle in the hay, and she turned and peered through the gloom of the barn, forgetting to breathe. A mouse or a rat?

As she watched, a smooth, black, reptilian head emerged from beneath her empty backpack, followed by a shiny black body, undulating around the left shoulder strap of the pack, over her empty water bottle, toward her small stack of clothing.

Fawn screamed and fell off the hay onto the hard wooden floor. "No! Get away!"

The snake froze in place, its tail hovering beside Fawn's high-tops across the clearing.

She covered her mouth to prevent another scream as she scrambled to her feet, doing the creeped-out dance. Had to get him out of here, had to get rid of him, couldn't scream again and shout to the world she was here.

She'd cleared enough hay away from the right front corner of the loft to have room to lie down, and to spread the stuff from her pack around her, as a kind of shield.

Some shield! Skin still crawling, Fawn crept through the dim light to the loft wall, where she'd found a broken pitchfork that now had only two prongs. She grabbed the fork, then went into gross-out mode again when spiderwebs touched her fingers. This was a horrible place to hide out!

She carried the pitchfork back to where the snake had stopped, but the reptile was gone.

She shuddered. She hated this horrible place! She had to get out of here!

But where was she going to go?

Using her weapon as a tool, she shoved the hay bales farther back from the middle of the wooden floor, sneezing at the moldy dust the movements stirred into the air. She didn't find the snake.

By the time Fawn finished clearing the filthy floor, the

heat in the loft overwhelmed her. She barely had the strength to stand, and so she sat, cross-legged, in the middle of the floor, a sitting guard against any more crawling, creepy Sunday visitors.

"It's okay," she whispered to herself, as if she were talking to her little sister. "It's only a black snake. They aren't poisonous." *Were they?*

A sudden loud gong echoed across the town, and Fawn cried out again, stumbling to her feet even as she realized it was the sound of church bells. She waited for her heart rate and breathing to settle once again, still glancing around the barn for the snake.

Church bells. She'd never heard them in Las Vegas, but years ago, when she'd spent the night with Great-Grandma and went to church on Sunday, she always heard them. The sound gave her a feeling of peace and protection, because at Great-Grandma's she was always safe. Always loved.

She stepped closer to the open loft door and sat down in the sunlight, skin still crawling as she thought about what might be watching her from the darkness behind her.

What was she going to do?

Karah Lee sat on the back deck of the Lakeside Bed-and-Breakfast on Sunday afternoon, watching the boats come and go from the dock a few hundred feet away. The slightly fishy-mossy smell of the lake mingled with honeysuckle and drifted on the breeze, and she grew drowsy in spite of the high whine of an electric saw and the echo of multiple hammers upstairs. The mechanical noises blended with the bleats of Bertie's pet goat, Mildred.

Amazingly, Monster had taken a liking to Mildred. It wasn't unusual to see him slinking around the little goat corral over by the abundant garden between the main lodge and the first cottage to the west. Spending time in a goat pen didn't seem like fresh air to Karah Lee, but she'd finally grown accustomed to the odd couple, and Bertie kept Mildred's place scrupulously clean.

Hammers commenced once more. Dane Gideon and his household of boys were working to complete the suite where Karah Lee hoped to sleep tonight. She'd spent the past two nights scrunched up on Cheyenne's comfortable-but-short sofa, waiting for first-responder calls that never came.

At first, when Dane and Blaze and the others arrived with their equipment today, she'd felt guilty for making it necessary for them to work on Sunday—Mom had never approved of it. Bertie had reassured Karah Lee, however, quoting some passage of scripture about how a man should get his ox out of the ditch even on the day of rest. Or something like that. Karah Lee wasn't sure how she felt about being called an ox, but Bertie meant well, and the guys sounded as if they were having fun upstairs, especially when their shouts and laughter drowned out the sounds of work.

Karah Lee had almost dozed off, when she heard a telephone ring inside. Her eyelids had just shut, when she heard footsteps on the veranda.

"Karah Lee, you've got a call from your sister."

That brought Karah Lee upright in her chair. She glanced at Bertie in confusion. "My sister?"

"You don't have a sister?"

"Well, yeah." But they'd had their annual sibling squabble Friday.

The veranda was deserted except for Karah Lee, so she took the cordless from Bertie and thanked her.

"Shona? What's wrong?"

There was an impatient sigh. "Does it always have to be an emergency for us to just talk?"

"No." *Yes.* "Sorry." In order to head off another argument, Karah Lee gave up and let Shona take the lead.

"You hung up on me Friday."

"I know. I'll try to refrain from doing it again, but it would help if you wouldn't get all crabby about Mom."

"Fine. I'm worried about Dad."

"In what way?"

"He's still all stirred up about this problem with you, and it hasn't exactly come at the best time for him."

Karah Lee scowled at the lake. "Sorry to be such a burden to him."

"Now, don't get all hot about it. This whole thing has hurt Dad for a long time." Shona's voice grew suddenly soft. "It's no fun having a daughter hate your guts."

Oh, great, here came the guilt trip. And they always said Mom was so good at it. "I don't hate his guts, I just—"

"And it hasn't always felt so great to me, either."

"Oh, come on, Shona, you've had Dad to yourself all these years. You should be ecstatic."

"Lucky me, I got to listen to him complain about his prison sentence with Mom, and then I got to watch his office romance with a woman barely six years older than me. Great fun."

Karah Lee sighed and slumped back down into her chair. Just the way she'd wanted to spend her Sunday afternoon, pulling out and analyzing ancient dirty laundry. "So how's our socialite stepmom doing these days?" Irene was another reason Karah Lee had as little as possible to do with her father, but right now she'd be a welcome change of subject.

"Oh, her? She's got a nice little apartment by the Missouri River at the edge of town. She doesn't come around much."

Karah Lee swallowed. "They're *separated?*"

"I'm just waiting to see who files first. Dad's showing his age these days, and that's another reason I'd like to see you two smooth out your differences."

Karah Lee rubbed the back of her neck. She was beginning to get a headache. Here in Hideaway, she'd begun to feel as if she were living on a planet removed from her old life in central Missouri. It didn't appear to be a permanent pleasure.

"Karah Lee?" Her sister's voice grew softer still.

"Yes, I'm here."

"Geoff and I are getting a divorce, too."

That news hit Karah Lee like a kick in the gut, and she caught her breath audibly. "Oh, no, Shona. I'm so sorry."

Shona and Geoff had been high-school sweethearts, but then had gone their separate ways for college. After four years they had reunited when they both went to work for Kemper MacDonald after graduation. All that time, Geoff had been the one strong connection between Karah Lee and her family. Though she avoided her dad, and she and Shona had found it difficult to hold a single pleasant conversation, Karah Lee had always gotten along with her brother-in-law.

"Are you going to be okay?"

There was a sniff on the other end of the line, and Karah Lee's vision blurred through sudden, unexpected tears. "Sure, I'll be okay. Why wouldn't I? Isn't that what we MacDonalds do best? Divorce and get on with life?" There was a new sound of unaccustomed vulnerability in Shona's voice.

"Why?" Karah Lee asked.

Another sniff on the line. "I don't know for sure. Maybe I've just got too much of my parents in me. Geoff and I can't seem to stand each other lately. We've fought so much this past year, he's started staying gone half the time. After all this time trying, I guess it's a good thing we never had kids."

The sudden flow of words startled Karah Lee. Why was Shona telling *her* all this? And why, considering their relationship, did Karah Lee feel the sense of loss so keenly?

But this was more than just a loss for her sister. It was like the loss of hope for Karah Lee. Her father couldn't seem to find a way to hold a marriage together—he'd failed twice. And now her sister... What hope was there for Karah Lee Fletcher to find a happily-ever-after relationship?

But she was being selfish. "I'm sorry." More tears fell. She sniffed and grabbed a tissue from her pocket. "I'm really sorry."

"Me too. And you know what? I could really use a sister right now."

More tears. More sniffing, more tissues. "I'm here. I'm not sure I know how to be much of a sister, since I've been out of the habit for so long." *And whose fault is that, Karah Lee? You've wrapped yourself in bitterness just as much as the rest of your family.* "I'm pretty rusty at it, and I'm not sure we know how to do anything besides fight."

"Do you think we could give it a try?" Shona asked. "It isn't as if I have a crowd of bosom buddies up here, you know. Trusted friends don't come into a political aide's territory too often."

Karah Lee nodded to herself. "Yeah. We could try."

More sniffing on the line. "Thanks. And if I promise not to let Dad use any more political influence, will you promise to think about giving him a nice casual call? You know, to let him know you don't really hate his guts?"

"How about if I just send flowers?"

"Words are so much more powerful than flowers, Karah Lee."

That sounded like a campaign slogan. Actions were more powerful than words, and time would tell if her family would be able to get their actions right after all this time.

A few moments after Karah Lee and Shona ended their call, Bertie came to the veranda door again. "Karah Lee, it's your young man."

"I don't have a young man."

"You know, it's Taylor."

Amused, Karah Lee picked up the cordless once again. "He isn't my young man, he's just orienting me for the paramedic stuff." She pressed the phone button. "Yeah, Taylor."

"I just received a distress call. Are you doing anything?"

"Nope. Can you pick me up?"

"I'll be there in a couple of minutes."

"Okay, give me time to put my shoes on."

"Make them hikers if you've got them."

Hikers? She'd have to dig them out of her suitcase. "Are we going to run a rescue operation?"

"Yep."

"I'll be ready." She hung up and turned to see Bertie standing in the doorway looking smug, with her arms folded over her chest.

"If that's not your young man, why're you grinning from ear to ear?" Bertie looked pretty today, with a touch of lipstick and powder on her face—her concession to dressing up for church. She wore navy slacks and a navy and red pullover that offset the silvery highlights of her white hair.

"I'm finally getting to go out on a run."

Bertie shook her head and strolled into the dining room, grabbing a bib apron from a nearby chair as she set to work clearing dishes from the tables. "Call it what you want to, Karah Lee. I never saw Cheyenne that happy about taking medical call."

Karah Lee made a face as she passed the older woman on the way to the storage room for her suitcase and medical pack. Come to think of it, *she'd* never felt this excited about an ambulance run. Could be she was bored. Or maybe there was just something about a lakeside resort that made everything more fun.

* * *

Taylor waited for Karah Lee to snap on her seat belt, then he put the truck in gear and sped onto the street. It felt good to have a partner after making these runs alone for so long. Of course, this wouldn't last. He was just orienting her.

"Want to tell me what's up today?" she asked.

"I got a call from someone on a cell phone in the northeast sector of the trail. A woman collapsed."

"Heat?"

"Probably."

"Any symptoms?"

"The usual. Confusion, leg cramps, nausea. Probably someone exercising too much without food. Where I come from, they call it the Canyon diet."

"Canyon?"

"At the Grand Canyon, people do it a lot. They hike the trails to lose weight. They drink plenty of water but don't eat, don't replace their electrolytes."

"You've got to be kidding. Hyponatremia? And they do it to themselves?" Karah Lee asked. "Sounds like they've already lost some weight—about two and a half pounds where their brains are supposed to be."

Taylor scowled at her. "Wow, Fletcher, you're all heart."

"Sorry."

She didn't sound sorry. "Not everyone has the privilege of your vast store of medical knowledge." He heard the sarcasm in his own voice and wondered if he was pushing it too far. Then, from the periphery of his vision, he saw her grin.

"That's right," she said. "But this victim will know better next time, if I have anything to say about it. I'll make sure she's medically stable before I start my free lecture. So you worked at the Grand Canyon before you came here? I hear ranger work is getting more and more dangerous."

It was, but that hadn't been the reason he left. "Any kind of law enforcement work is risky."

"Did you cycle out?"

He gave her a puzzled look.

"You know, stay there a certain number of years then get forced to transfer."

"No. Things have changed in the past few years. We have a promotion program now, and I wanted to stay at the Canyon with my family, so I chose not to ask for a promotion for several years. My wife did the same."

He sensed Karah Lee's interest level kick up a notch, but decided not to elaborate.

"How long did you work there?" she asked.

"Seven years."

"Your wife's a ranger, too?"

"She was an interpretive ranger."

"Interpretive? Somehow, I don't think that means she's multilingual."

"An interpretive ranger is someone who explains the natural world to visitors to the park. We used to call them naturalists."

"I heard the ranger program's tough on marriage. I'm glad you found a way to make it work for you."

He was sorry he'd even mentioned Clarice. "I didn't."

She picked up his binoculars from the console and raised them to her face to study something at the foot of the cliff as they drove up the side and around toward the top. "Divorced?"

"That's right." Not that it was any business of hers.

"Oh. Sorry. I was just wondering, because on Friday, when you suggested the possibility that I might stay at your place while you stayed at the ranger station, you never mentioned there might be someone else." She adjusted the binoculars. "Kids?"

"One."

She shook her head as she lowered the binoculars. "It's toughest on them."

"This kid was the reason for the divorce."

Another beat of silence. She replaced the binoculars and sat back. "You're blaming your kid." It was not a question, it was a castigation.

"I didn't say that."

"You sure did, you said—"

"I *said* my kid was the reason for the divorce, I didn't say I blamed him."

"I don't see the—"

"He's dead."

For the first time since he'd met her, she didn't have a quick reply. He kept his attention on the curving road, though he could feel her still watching him, could sense her shock followed quickly by sympathy, and he wondered, to his shame, if he'd subconsciously manipulated her for just such a response. He'd have to be a real jerk to use his son's death as a ploy for sympathy.

"How old would he be now?" she asked, her voice much gentler.

"Sixteen." And he didn't want to talk about it. Did he?

"Nearly Blaze's age, then," she said. "No wonder you get along so well with him. He seems to like you, too, amazingly."

Taylor glanced at her. Seeing the teasing glint in her eyes, he realized he hadn't manipulated her at all. And really, he wasn't trying to.

When he thought about it for a moment, he discovered his only intention had been to tell her the truth about himself, about where he was coming from. It had been such a long time since he'd been able to do that—since he'd allowed himself the luxury.

He also realized, to his amazement, that he was enjoying her company, though he didn't know how long that aberration would continue. When had he last enjoyed a woman's company, enjoyed the gentle teasing, the sharing...

He pulled into the parking area at the trailhead, turned off the engine and got out. "Let's go see if we can find our patient."

∞ *Chapter Seventeen* ∞

Another droplet of sweat broke loose from Fawn's forehead and tickled her in its race for freedom down her neck, and someone screamed with laughter far down on the beach. With the cliffs behind this barn reaching around to form a natural barrier behind Hideaway, noise seemed to funnel through the loft door and straight into her ears.

From what she could see from here, the shore was crowded with kids, teenagers, couples and gangs of girls in bikinis. Boats in all shapes and sizes kept the water in constant motion, flickering blue and green fire the color of the sky and the trees.

And Fawn sat in a rattly old prison with moldy hay and a snake to guard her.

Something moved in her line of vision at the construction site between the barn and the beach. A guy in jeans and a blue shirt stepped past a bulldozer that had been parked across an entrance to the site, obviously to keep people out. There were Keep Out signs everywhere, and usually there was a guard somewhere on the property, though Fawn didn't see him now.

So maybe this guy was a new guard coming on duty. He didn't act like it. In fact, he looked a lot like that guy who'd cruised around town with the sheriff yesterday. Maybe the deputy, out of uniform today.

He kept glancing over his shoulder toward the street as he stepped around cement mixers and stacks of lumber. He leaned over a hole in the ground and peered down into it, then reached out and thumped his hand against one of the supporting beams.

Curious. Maybe he'd decided to buy one of the units and wanted to check it out, make sure it was sturdy.

"Don't do it, mister," she muttered.

Yesterday, when she'd been too sick to do anything but watch out this window, a lot of things had started to make sense. That construction project was the only one in town, and it was obviously going to be a huge building—the condominium Bruce had been arguing about with his killer.

So something down there was dangerous. But what?

She wiped another stream of sweat from her face. And what could she do about it? Whom could she trust?

Again, she thought about Karah Lee. There was something about the doctor...something about her gaze that held steady when she was talking to you, as if she meant what she said. She never looked away or fidgeted with her hands or anything. Fawn had been lied to enough times, she could read it in a person's eyes. Dr. Karah Lee wasn't a liar. But she'd told on Fawn when she said she wouldn't. So that meant what? *Does she think I'm really sick?*

The man down below took out a cell phone, talked into it for a couple of minutes, then stuck it back into his pocket. He gave one last look around the concrete slab where he stood, then left the area to blend back into the crowd.

Before he disappeared, though, someone climbed out of the van parked nearby and watched him leave.

The sun glared down on Taylor as he stepped out. They'd been experiencing unseasonably warm weather this month, more like July or August than June. No wonder the heat-related illnesses were already striking.

As Karah Lee grabbed her pack and closed the door, Taylor reached into the rear seat for his own rescue backpack.

"My boy's name was Chip." He locked the door and turned toward the trail, leading the way past a truck and two cars and a motorcycle in the parking area.

"And was he?" She fell into step beside him, matching him stride for stride.

"Was he what?" he asked.

"You know, a chip off the old block. Was he more like you or your wife?"

"Ex-wife. She is no longer my wife, she's an ex."

"Gotcha, but it wouldn't hurt you to tone down the bitterness a notch."

"Just helping you get the facts straight, since you seemed so determined to know everything." He led the way along the broad trail, hoping this was the right direction. The dispatcher had told him the caller wasn't sure of her position.

"I'm just curious if your recent experiences might explain why you're such a hermit."

He winced. "I'm *not* a hermit." What had made him open up to this woman?

"Okay, so you're the life of every party." Her voice reflected the dryness of a desert. "What was Chip like?"

Taylor slowed his steps as they neared an overlook. He stared out over the surface of the lake, breathing the scent of the water that blended so effectively with the baked chlorophyl of the overgrown, lush jungle of the Ozark forest, so unlike the place where his son had grown up.

"People seemed to think he was a lot like me," he said at last.

"Serious, quiet, determined?"

Taylor blinked and looked at her. That was her impression of him? "No. Chip was never quiet. He talked a lot, laughed a lot. He had friends over to the house all the time. He made decent grades in school and he was active in church."

"He really does sound like Blaze, then." She looked up and caught his gaze, and she seemed stricken. "I'm sorry. I guess maybe I seem too nosy sometimes. I can't imagine what it must feel like to lose a son, and then a marriage. None of this is my business."

Taylor nodded. He had discovered, twenty-nine months ago, that he was truly unprepared for his situation. The emptiness was like hiking in the Canyon wilderness without water—forever.

Strangely, something about Karah Lee made him think of Clarice. Certainly, it wasn't her size. Clarice was a foot shorter than Taylor, part Navajo, with lots of long, straight dark hair and dark eyes. Before Chip's death she'd been one of those people who smiled and laughed a lot as well. After his death, it was as if her spirit had gone on vacation and forgotten to return.

Clarice didn't have Karah Lee's audacious, in-your-face attitude, and if she'd thrown up on someone's uniform, she would have died of embarrassment. Karah Lee had apologized profusely, but she'd seemed more worried about her cat.

So, really, Taylor couldn't put a finger on what it was about Karah Lee that seemed so familiar to him. In fact, there was a quality about her that he would've liked to have seen in Clarice, and it was that very same quality that also tended to irritate him if he allowed it to. Her forthrightness.

"So you left the Grand Canyon because of your divorce?" she asked.

He gave her an exasperated glance. "You don't exactly have a peaceful personality, do you?"

"Never claimed to. You don't have to tell me if you don't want to."

"My partner was killed in the line of duty. I decided then that it was time to leave."

Silence. He gave the lake a final glance as the trail took a turn into the woods. "A little over a year ago, my partner, Carl, answered a call late one night about a hiker who had fallen from the Grandview Trail."

"Grandview?"

"That's a nonmaintained trail that's steep and dangerous, and which most people shouldn't even hike in the daytime, much less at night."

She shuddered. "Now *that* scares me. I hate heights."

He glanced at her, surprised.

"Don't even say it," she said.

"What was I going to say?"

"You know, the typical snide remark about how tall I am, that I should be used to it by now."

"You get teased about that, too?"

"Too often. So what happened to your partner?"

"Carl wasn't supposed to be on duty, but he took the call anyway. He didn't call me. When he arrived to the rescue without the right gear, apparently the hiker panicked and grabbed him. He lost his balance and plunged a hundred feet to his death on the rocks below."

Taylor felt the graze of a spiderweb across his face. These brushy sections of trail were notorious for multiple spiderwebs from July through September, but June took a few hits as well, apparently.

"Wow," Karah Lee said.

Taylor knew what she meant, and again he felt ashamed of himself for spilling his guts like that. He didn't do it often. In fact, no one here in Hideaway knew as much as Karah Lee did now.

But why was he blabbing all this stuff to her, of all people? Maybe because she was the type of person to beat it out of him if he didn't tell her what she wanted to know.

Or maybe because, in spite of his macho self-sufficiency, which Clarice had resented so much, he had reached the point where he couldn't contain it all inside of himself much longer, and Karah Lee was the first person to supply a listening ear.

And maybe a listening heart, as well.

Or it could be his brain was addled by loneliness after he'd been living alone in the woods for a year.

Karah Lee drew up beside him at the same time that he stepped through another spiderweb. She spat and waved her arms in front of her. "Yuck! I forgot what a joy it was to hike out here in the summertime."

He chuckled. "You'll get used to it. At least the spiders out here are harmless."

She was flicking a final strand of web from her face when they rounded a small copse of trees and saw their patient seated on a log beside the trail, exhibiting typical signs of heat-related illness. The two women with her slumped on either side of their friend, looking none too great, themselves. They would feel even worse in a couple of days, once the chiggers began their meal.

Taylor held back and allowed Karah Lee to run the show. They had decided this would be an orientation run, and he was only supposed to observe. Karah Lee set to her treatment immediately, giving the woman an electrolyte-replacement drink and plying her with questions while wielding her stethoscope. Taylor pulled extra bottles of the beverage from his pack and handed one to each of the patient's companions.

They made their introductions, but Taylor only caught the name of Karah Lee's patient, Dorothy. The younger woman to his right accepted his offering, popped open the top and sucked down half the contents. "Thanks," she said breathlessly, seconds later. "We ran out of drinks about halfway around the loop, and it's hotter than we thought it would be."

He couldn't help glancing at her footwear. Sandals not hikers. Not even running shoes. "This is a twelve-mile loop," he said. None of the women even carried backpacks. "How much water did you pack with you?"

"We each had a bottle at the trailhead, and we thought it would be enough."

As Taylor listened to Karah Lee handle her patient with expertise and gentleness, he decided to forgo the usual lecture. After this, these three women would surely have learned their lesson.

"I told you we should have taken the skin-diving lessons instead of this hike," Sandals complained to her friends. "Then we wouldn't have run out of water."

"I didn't see any sign in town that advertised skin diving," the companion said. "Did you see a brochure or something?"

"No, but I saw that triangle logo on the boat with the divers. They're the same company that rents the jet bikes and kayaks and practically everything else in town."

"Where did you see the divers?" Taylor asked.

"You know where the trail cuts into those cliffs a couple miles down?" Sandals asked. "Some guys were diving out of a boat. Had that Beaufont thing right there on the side."

Taylor glanced at Karah Lee, who was focused on her patient. He hadn't heard anything about diving lessons, but he wouldn't be surprised. Beaufont was trying every other gimmick to make money, why *not* diving?

"Where's your vehicle?" he asked.

"Lookout trailhead," Sandals replied.

"That's only about a mile up from here. We can walk you out when you're ready."

Karah Lee helped her patient loosen her restrictive clothing, then pulled a nifty little battery-operated personal-size fan with a spritzer from her pack.

Taylor watched in admiration. "You come prepared."

She grinned and thanked him, then returned her attention to her patient. "Are you still feeling weak, Dorothy?" she asked gently. "There's no rush if you want to take a few more moments to regain your strength."

Taylor continued watching her. As he'd noticed on Friday, something about her seemed different when she worked with patients. She gave them all her attention, and although she was assertive, her voice held a tone of genuine affection. He realized she loved what she was doing.

How long had it been since he'd felt that way about his job?

He knew the answer to that immediately. It had been Friday. In the clinic. He, too, loved treating patients.

Taylor's cell phone chirped at him, and he stepped away from the women to answer. "Yes?"

"Taylor? This is Greg. Tom's all hot and ruffled about a call he took at the station a few minutes ago. You remember that busload of sick folks you helped take care of down at the clinic Friday?"

"Sure, what about them?"

"You remember treating a guy named Casey Timble?"

"Casey." Taylor said the word softly, but he saw Karah Lee glance up at him. "What about him?" Casey who wasn't a guy. Casey who'd been in the middle of treatment for a miscarriage when she skipped out, and no one had seen her since.

"He was by himself," Greg said. "Booked a trip to Bella Vista with a stop at Hideaway. Guy paid by credit card. Claims he never made it to the bus. He lost his ticket and credit card, then somebody barricaded him in the men's room. The bus company's trying to sort it out."

"Shouldn't they be asking the driver about all this?"

"They did, and the driver said Casey Timble got off the bus here at Hideaway with the rest of the passengers, but he wasn't accounted for when they loaded up and left on the replacement bus."

"I don't know what to tell you, Greg."

"You sure about that? Doesn't it seem a little strange, somebody like that just disappearing? And what about that woman you had us all looking for Friday? Said she needed medical care, but couldn't tell us any more than that. Too odd, if you ask me." Yep, that was definitely suspicion in Greg's voice...or maybe not suspicion as much as growing concern. The sheriff was astute.

Taylor risked a glance at Karah Lee, who was helping her patient to her feet but kept giving Taylor quick, intent looks. Obviously eavesdropping and not trying to hide it. When she caught his gaze, she narrowed her eyes and shook her head.

He gave her a helpless, open-handed shrug.

She shook her head more vehemently.

He sighed. "I'm sorry, Greg. I know it sounds coincidental, but due to rules about patient confidentiality, even I don't know what all that was about. Besides, whoever that patient was, she's obviously out of the area now." He just hoped the young woman was medically stable, because he knew how worried Karah Lee had been about her. She'd even called him a couple of times this weekend to find out if he'd heard anything.

There was a grunt at the other end of the line. Obviously, Greg was not mollified. "Well, could be this guy just didn't want to pay because of all that mess with the exhaust leak, but didn't want to wait around to get his money back, and all this other stuff really was a coincidence. You know what Tom thinks, don't you?"

"I'm dying to hear this," Taylor said. The deputy sheriff had a reputation to uphold as the man with the most active imagination in the Table Rock Lake area.

"He thinks it was the murderer passing through."

"He thinks this Casey guy is a—" He glanced toward the hikers, who were listening to a lecture from Karah Lee about dehydration. He lowered his voice. "He thinks the guy's a killer?"

"Not him. You know, that young woman, Fawn Morrison, who murdered her lover and that hotel employee, then attempted arson at another hotel-theater complex."

"I was under the impression she was only wanted for questioning."

"Try telling Tom that, especially after the media made such a big deal about it. He thinks he's got it all figured out. You know he's a bulldog once he gets his teeth into something, and he's decided there's a connection between the murdered lover and the Beaufont Corporation."

"What kind of connection?"

"Well, I'm not sure what he did, but you know what a computer geek he is. He practically lives on his PC at home, which is why he doesn't have any kind of social life." The sheriff paused, clearing his throat. "Not that there's anything wrong with not having a...well, anyway...sorry, Taylor."

"It's okay. What's the connection with Beaufont?"

"Well, like I said, I don't know how Tom gets all his information, but he says the victim was an investment manager for some high rollers out in Las Vegas, and some of his clients had invested in the Beaufont interests here in Hideaway."

Taylor allowed that to sink in. "And?"

"And the victim had just completed a transaction withdrawing the funds from Beaufont."

Taylor glanced at the others and strolled on down the trail a few yards, lowering his voice further. "So you're saying the killer worked for Beaufont?"

"I'm not saying it, and I'm not sure Tom's saying it yet, it's just something to keep in mind in case that patient happens to show up around here anywhere, if you understand what I mean."

"I understand."

"Right. Just be careful."

* * *

"He thinks Casey's a killer!" Karah Lee locked the clinic door behind her and turned to join Taylor on the sidewalk. She had just released her patient to the care of her friends with the promise that they'd keep an eye on her and call if she became ill again. The sun had settled behind the western hills, and the oppressive, unseasonable heat had diminished. It had been a good day, until now. She didn't like the idea that there might have been a killer in their clinic Friday. Didn't like it, and didn't believe it.

"I don't think Greg's convinced," Taylor said, "but Tom's all excited about this thing. They think our patient ran because she's trying to escape capture."

"Sure she did. But she wasn't a murderer. More like a kid."

"She didn't exactly seem dangerous to me, either, but now that I think about it, there are some close resemblances between our Casey from the bus and the composite picture I received on the fax machine last week."

"What picture?"

"Just a computer rendition of what Fawn Morrison would look like if she were attempting to drastically change her looks. The police questioned some Branson store clerks who claim to have seen a woman fitting the paper's description the day after the murders."

"Mind if I see the picture?"

They reached his vehicle, and he opened the right rear passenger door and pulled out a manila folder. He withdrew the black-and-white printout and handed it to her.

Karah Lee studied the short, dark hair, the high forehead with the widow's peak, the small, determined-looking chin. "The eyes are the wrong color, according to this description." She pointed at the list below the picture, but she could feel Taylor watching her.

"It's her, isn't it?" he asked.

"How am I supposed to know? It doesn't make sense that a killer would continue to hang out anywhere near the scene of the crime. A killer would be out of the state by now, establishing a brand-new identity, not catching a bus with a group of elderly tourists."

"You're right, it doesn't make sense."

"Especially when the supposed killer helps take care of those tourists when they get sick." She shoved the picture back at him and reached for her medical pack on the floorboard. "Look, I'm not the police, okay? There's no way I'll let myself get dragged into a witch hunt after a frightened teenager in trouble."

"That isn't what I'm trying to do."

"You're working with the police on this, of course it's what you're trying to do." She slung the pack over her back and marched across the street. She heard him shut the door, and heard the automatic lock batten down the doors as his footsteps quickened to catch up with her.

"Hey, I'm not the enemy, okay?" he said as he fell into step beside her. "All I'm doing is trying to figure out a few things of my own, such as how Tom thinks he has a connection between the Beaufont Corporation and the murders. If Casey *is* somehow involved in all this, then she might have some answers to a lot of questions."

"My only consideration was her physical well-being."

"Did you consider that if she *is* connected, then the exposure of her picture to the public in the paper and on television might attract the attention of someone besides the police?"

"Well, it doesn't matter much now anyway, does it? The girl has obviously found a way out of town. Case dismissed."

⚮ *Chapter Eighteen* ⚮

By late Monday afternoon Fawn decided she was feeling better. At least she wasn't cramping anymore. She'd felt thirsty all day, but at a thousand-degree temperature, anybody would be thirsty. Besides, she was tired of sitting around sick all the time, watching the world go by.

This morning she'd reached into the bottom of the middle pocket of her backpack and pulled out the flash drive. She'd stuck it into the pocket of her jeans—in spite of the heat, she wore jeans because the hay was too scratchy for her bare legs. She was going to try to find out what was on that device, and see if it had anything to do with the condominium.

Ever since Friday, when she wasn't watching the construction at the project or the constant beach party going on, she'd thought about that computer in the reception office at the clinic. She knew how to operate a computer, and even though she hadn't touched one since she'd left school—Bruce had never let her get near his desktop, laptop or pocket PC—she knew it wouldn't take her long to figure out how to download the stuff from the storage device. And then maybe she'd know what she was dealing with, and would be able to figure out whom to contact.

Now if she could just figure out how to get into that computer....

At four forty-five, Fawn placed sunglasses on her face, plopped an ugly gray fishing hat on her head—she'd found it floating in the lake the previous night when she went to the beach to refill her water bottles—and sneaked back into town toward the square under cover of the deeply shaded alleyways.

She kept a close watch on everything that moved around her. This latest disguise was probably her best yet, but why take chances when she didn't have to?

She'd used the hair-color kit last night down at the lake, and judging by her reflection in the tiny lipstick mirror today, she could tell it had worked. She had silver-gray hair. She wore an overlarge men's blue chambray shirt with sleeves rolled up to her elbows. She'd smeared the hair stuff on her face, neck, arms and chest and the backs of her hands.

Today her skin was red and irritated. In a couple of days, her face would look good and old, like any fisherwoman who spent a lot of time in the sun. Maybe the allergy burn would last long enough for her to do what she needed to get done and get out of town for good.

"You can do this," she whispered to herself. "Just act natural, like you're supposed to be here. Blend into Hideaway. You can—"

A thud to her right startled her, and she caught her breath, stumbling to a stop. She heard it again, and glanced through the thick, overgrown shrubbery to find an elderly man in faded overalls hoeing in a backyard garden.

She relaxed and breathed again. It was okay. He didn't look up. She wished she'd bought some overalls like that in Branson.

Rushing on, Fawn tried to recall exactly what route she'd used to escape town the other day without getting caught. This was the alley she'd taken, she remembered the honeysuckle in that sunny spot up ahead, only about a block from the square.

Now was when it got tricky. She skittered past the sunny spot, then ducked behind another shrub and studied the street. From here, she saw the entrance to the neat little courtyard in the center of the town square—actually all the buildings surrounded the courtyard, facing outward, but she remembered from her escape Friday that all those buildings also had doors and windows and balconies on the second and third floors that opened onto that courtyard. Anyone looking out one of those windows would see her sneaking in.

She stood staring at the square for several moments. Could she even do this? Was she crazy?

Fawn Morrison, P.I.

Stupid. She'd probably get caught crossing the street. But Bruce had said people were in danger. She had decided that she'd never turn out to be like her mother. She didn't want to be the kind of person who saw somebody in trouble and was afraid to do anything about it. She'd rather be dead. After this, she might *be* dead, but at least she'd die trying to help.

She thought about her brothers and her sister back home. Who was taking care of them now? Not Mom, for sure. And not their drunk dad.

But at least he was their father, not their stepfather. Maybe that meant he'd treat them better. After all, what kind of guy would rape his own flesh and blood?

Maybe the same kind of guy who would rape his stepdaughter?

For a moment, Fawn's nausea returned. But she couldn't do anything about her brothers and sister right now. She had to focus on what she *could* do.

Karah Lee was scrubbing at the sink in the minor-meds treatment room when Cheyenne knocked at the doorway and stepped inside.

"Done for the day?" Chey asked.

"Just finished with my last patient. Now I've got charts to complete." Karah Lee ripped off a couple of squares of paper towel and blotted her hands and arms.

Chey folded her arms over her chest and leaned against the counter. "I've noticed those stacking up today. Anything I can do to help?"

"Not that I can think of. I've just found myself getting a little overwhelmed."

"It was an overwhelming day. The workers' comp visits didn't help."

"I can't believe we got those four accident cases all at once," Karah Lee said. "I mean, what's going on out there?" These hadn't been the first cases they'd encountered. Today's injuries had been minor things—a sprained ankle, a bruised shoulder when a stack of two-by-four boards fell on one of the workers, a hammer misplaced onto a thumb. "I'm just surprised we're caught up." She was still trying to figure out how Cheyenne had handled the cases so quickly, with such confidence.

Confidence was one thing Karah Lee had lacked lately. She tried to blame it on the newness of the job, but she knew it was more than that. Several times today she'd sought Cheyenne's opinion on cases she would have breezed through a month ago. In spite of the praises Cheyenne had heaped on her for her performance last week, she continued to have doubts.

Yesterday she'd told Shona she would call Dad, but first she needed to think through a few key issues—such as how to forgive him for totally undermining her self-assurance.

"Karah Lee," Chey said, "is everything okay with you?"

Karah Lee looked down and discovered she'd been shredding the wet paper towels. And then she realized Chey was unusually quiet, almost apprehensive. "I'm fine, just trying to deal with the little matter of my interfering father. I haven't second-guessed myself so much in years."

Cheyenne nodded absently. "Looks like today is the day for family problems. Karah Lee, I need a favor. A big one, and I'm sorry to do this to you right now, when you're already struggling."

"Hey, don't worry about that, I'll work through it. What's going on?"

Chey closed her eyes and swallowed hard. "I just received a call from *my* father a few minutes ago. My mother had a heart attack this afternoon."

"Oh, Chey, no."

Cheyenne raised a trembling hand to her face and rubbed her temple. "I really need to fly to Florida and be with her. She's in emergency surgery now. I could be gone a few days, and that'll leave you to take care of things here by yourself, when we're already short on staff. I'm sorry about—"

"Make your flight arrangements and get to Florida. Your mother needs you. I'll put my personal problems on hold until you get back, okay? I'll be fine here."

Cheyenne pulled a tissue from the box on the counter and dabbed at her eyes. "Something you should keep in mind while I'm gone."

"Not to abuse the staff?"

"That, too," she said with a shaky smile. "But especially remember that even if your father pulled strings to get you into med school, his influence didn't earn your grades—*you* did."

Karah Lee wasn't so sure about that. She'd seen far too much political maneuvering in the medical field, but now wasn't the time to argue. "Thanks, Chey. Go to your parents, and don't worry about things here. We'll be fine."

* * *

Fawn studied the traffic circling the square and decided to wait a few minutes. Some blond-haired man eased a bale of hay and a bag of seed into the back of a pickup truck from a loading dock at the feed store, which was next door to the general store, which was next door to the clinic. If he'd just leave that loading dock open when he finished, she might get in that way, sneak out the back and slip through the back entrance to the clinic.

If only she could time this right.

All day, as she'd waited in the hot barn, she'd watched through the door of the loft as construction workers crawled all over the skeleton of that condominium down by the lake, dodging the crane as it carried building material through the air without knocking into anything, and without killing anybody.

Bruce had said people could die because of that building. But why?

Maybe someday she'd have her own condominium, and she'd have a couple of apartments where she'd let girls in trouble come if they needed help. Or maybe she'd have a whole building where kids like her could stay, so they wouldn't have to beg on the streets or steal from tourists or sell tricks to strangers.

Right now, though, she just needed to make sure she didn't get caught breaking into the back door of the clinic.

The truck at the loading dock drove off. The driver waved at the blond man, and the blond man waved back, then glanced up and down the street, dusted off his hands, disappeared through a side door.

Fawn braced herself and checked the street, then stepped from the alley and walked casually toward the square, trying to think like a gray-haired fisherwoman.

When she reached the loading dock, she casually looked around, peered through the plate-glass window of the general store, then climbed the steel-bar ladder to the dock. She entered the shadowed, hay-scented feed-storage area, rushed to the back door and found it unlocked. She hurried through the door to the back, ran two doors down and tested this door. It, too, was unlocked, but here she paused.

This door opened directly into the central hallway of the clinic. If she stepped inside, there could be someone in the hall.

But if she stayed out here, someone could come out any minute and catch her lurking, or they could lock up on her, and she knew it was a dead bolt. She couldn't break in.

She pressed her ear to the door and listened. All she could hear was her own nervous breathing. She placed her hand around the knob and turned slowly, then pulled the door open in time to hear someone from the front of the clinic call good-night to someone else.

Good. It was quitting time. The hallway was empty, and Fawn slipped in, ducked into the bathroom on her left and opened the cabinet door below the sink. No way she could fit in there.

Next she opened the door to the hot-water heater. There might be enough room to squeeze against the tank and hide there if she didn't have to wait too long for the others to leave.

Please, please, please don't come back here, anybody!

If she didn't get caught, she was going to sleep here tonight, in the treatment room where she'd gotten the IV Friday. That bed was a lot more comfortable than the bales of hay in the barn, and there weren't any snakes in the clinic.

As soon as the stranger stepped up to the clinic reception window, Karah Lee knew he wasn't a patient. He didn't look sick. He wasn't limping. There wasn't a speck of dust on his suit, and something about his expression gave him an aura of authority. Maybe it was the hard set of his long jaw, or the lack of humor in his hooded eyes.

Karah Lee was sitting at the other end of the desk, drinking a soda, while Jill manned the phones.

The man reached into his back pocket and pulled out a thin billfold. He flipped it open and shut in a quick second. "Hello, ma'am, I'm Detective Withnell with the Federal Bureau of Independent Investigators out of Springfield assigned to a missing persons lead in an ongoing investigation. We have reason to believe a suspect for a federal case has been seen in this area, and I need to ask you some questions."

Jill didn't hesitate or break a smile. "I'm sorry, Detective, but according to federal regulations, we aren't allowed to share information about our patients."

"I understand that," he said smoothly. "But I'm not asking for patient information, I'm simply eliminating possibilities. I'm sure you can understand the difference."

Jill's chin jutted out a little farther than usual. She slid a glance at Karah Lee, then looked back at the man.

"Sure. Shoot me your possibilities, and I'll eliminate them for you."

He opened a folder with several eight-by-ten color photographs of an attractive young woman with blond hair and a formfitting blue dress. At first, Karah Lee didn't recognize her.

"Sorry, but nobody looking like that has been in here when I was on duty," Jill said.

"Okay, how about this one?" He flipped to the next sheet, which appeared to be a computer-composite head shot of the same woman, with short hair. "Our sources tell us she might have been posing as a young male on a busload of elderly tourists. The bus developed a leak in its exhaust system. Several passengers became ill. Some of them remember a young male, dressed in typical teenager garb, with a cap and glasses."

Jill continued to shake her head. Her expression didn't change. Karah Lee saw her hand tighten around the ink pen she held, and hoped the visitor didn't notice.

The man glanced at Karah Lee's name badge. "Are you the doctor in charge?"

"I was on duty the day that bus came in," Karah Lee said. "I saw that picture in the paper last week. You sure those two pictures are of the same person?"

"We're just following up some leads. Are there any other staff—"

"What was it you say this woman did?" Jill interrupted. "You say you're a federal investigator? That'd mean murder or drug trafficking, wouldn't it?"

"Say! That's right," Karah Lee said. "This woman supposedly killed her boyfriend and another man at their hotel up in Branson, didn't she?"

The man's eyes narrowed. His gaze made her uncomfortable. "Someone said the kid called himself Casey. They said he collapsed and had to be taken to an exam room in the clinic." He studied her for another uncomfortable fraction of a second. "You say you can't remember a patient like that?"

"Oh, I remember those patients, all right. Sure I remember Casey." She scrunched up her face in an expression of disbelief as she stood and stepped to the reception window. "You're telling me they thought that pimple-faced, scrawny, smart-mouthed punk was a *woman?*" She hoped she'd placed enough outraged emphasis on the word. "Come on, Detective, I know some of those folks were mighty sick, but they'd have had to be falling down blind to imagine anything feminine about that boy."

"So can you tell me what condition he was in when he arrived?"

"Nope."

No change in expression. "I can get a subpoena."

She spread her hands. "Sorry, but you're wasting your time, Detective...what did you say your name was again?"

"Withnell."

"Sorry, Detective Withnell, but you aren't going to get any information about that kid even if you do subpoena us. You can't expect us to make a complete set of medical records on every patient we treated with oxygen that day. There's no information to be had. We didn't have the manpower to get it done. It was an emergency situation, and we were overwhelmed."

His eyes narrowed further. He leaned forward, as if intimidation might refresh her memory. It only served to refresh her suspicion. This man was not from the federal bureau, the state bureau, or any bureau she'd ever had any dealings with. Not that she'd had that many.

Karah Lee stood beside Jill as the "detective" replaced his photographs in his folder, promised to be in touch, and left the office.

"Karah Lee Fletcher, you should be an actress," Jill murmured when the door shut.

"Want to be my costar?"

"He'll probably be back, or send someone else."

"I don't have anything else to say."

"Neither do I, and for tonight, you're on your own." Jill closed her appointment book and placed it in the desk, picked up her purse, stood up and waved good-night.

Karah Lee watched the nurse leave, grateful to be working with someone who took patient confidentiality as seriously as it should be taken—not that she'd get any gold stars from the investigators on that murder case.

Still, it didn't matter. Casey was obviously long gone.

Karah Lee sipped her soda and studied the stack of files she had yet to complete. Someday she would learn to keep up with her charting as she saw patients, but since today had been another busy one, she'd fallen behind halfway through the afternoon. Cheyenne had left thirty minutes ago. That woman was disgustingly organized.

Karah Lee planned to emulate her someday. When she had time.

As she worked, deciphering her own scribbled shorthand to type into the computer, she couldn't help wondering, once again, about the young, frightened woman who had collapsed here last Friday. Was she okay? Had she found shelter far from here?

Blaze finished cleaning an exam room, ran the vacuum and straightened magazines and books in the waiting room, all the while humming a tune under his breath that was just enough off-key, and familiar, to distract Karah Lee.

After trying and failing for the third time to pull up a patient file, she swiveled in her chair and glared at him through the reception window. "What happened to our canned music?"

"I turned it off."

"Well, either turn it back on or hold off on the church music until I can get this stuff entered and get out of here."

"Having trouble with the program again?"

"What do you mean, *again?*"

He leaned through the window and peered at the computer screen. "Whose file you looking for?"

"I can't find the Wyzenstein file, and I know she's an established patient."

"Her maiden name's Corona, and it hasn't been changed yet."

"Why not?"

"Because we still don't have a secretary, and Jill won't let me near the files or stay overtime herself to catch up."

"Fine, if you'll show me how to do it, I'll stay and—"

"Aren't you on call tonight?"

"That's right. And the next few nights, until Cheyenne comes back."

"Then shouldn't you get some rest while you have a chance?"

"I'm not going to go home and sleep right now, Blaze." She might not sleep at all tonight, as keyed up as she felt at the moment.

"Okay, fine, then let me help you with it."

"I thought you couldn't file."

"No, but I can sure type."

Karah Lee scooted over and pulled up another chair. "I've got all evening."

Fawn stood squeezed next to the noisy hot-water heater with sweat streaming from every pore. She felt really sick again, almost ready to pass out, but she couldn't move because she still heard voices in the front of the clinic.

How much longer would they be here? She didn't know if she could take much more of this. It was way past quitting time, wasn't it?

She needed a drink, bad. If she could just sneak over to the sink and take a few swigs—but if they heard her, it would be all over.

It was okay. She could take it a little longer. Maybe.

Chapter Nineteen

Karah Lee squinted at the notes in front of her, trying to decipher her own writing as she transcribed it into the computer.

"I heard you had a date with Taylor yesterday," Blaze called to her from the far corner of the waiting room, where he was stacking magazines and books.

"That was no date, it was a rescue operation."

He snorted. "Like I said."

"Hey, watch it, pal. For your information, I clean up good for a date. I don't need rescuing." She glared through the reception window at him.

"How do you have time to date when you're in med school or working in a residency program?" he asked.

"I didn't say I'd been out *recently.*"

"That's the problem with a medical career," Blaze said. "Cheyenne worked for years in an E.R., had never been married. It wasn't until she met me that her love life started picking up."

Karah Lee completed the transcription of a page and flipped to the next. "What are you, a matchmaker or something?"

"Maybe something like that. I guess it just comes naturally."

"Right. I'm sure Cheyenne and Dane had nothing to do with it." She frowned at the monitor screen, still not understanding the program. "Did you write down what you did on this thing so I'll know how to do it next time?"

"It's already written somewhere. I'll dig it out for you in a minute."

"Do I need a password to log on in the morning?"

"Yes, and if you don't do it right the first time, you've got two more tries before it shuts down on you." He leaned against the reception counter. "When that happens, you practically need a computer programmer to set it up for you again, so don't even try unless you're sure you have it." He watched her enter more notes. "So, you want me to dust off my matchmaking skills and see what I can do for you?"

"I don't think I'm interested in a love life. Divorce seems to be a dominant gene in my family."

"That can change. My parents divorced, too, but someday I'm going to be married and have lots of kids. It all depends on a guy's priorities. Like Bertie says, a guy's got to put God first, his wife and family next, and not let anything get in the way of that."

"Oh, sure, like that's going to happen these days."

"It could, you know."

Karah Lee felt a change of subject coming on. "Okay, so you're telling me Cheyenne came here to start a clinic and fell in love."

Blaze shook his head. "Nope. She came here to heal after her sister died, then she met me, right off, in the middle of the night."

Karah Lee sighed softly. She wasn't going to get these files finished tonight if she didn't shut up and get to work. "Okay, I'll bite. How did she meet you in the middle of the night?"

"I was searching for some orphaned kittens in this vacant house across the lake from the ranch, and here comes Cheyenne marching in with a flashlight, like she owned the place. Like to've scared me to death, because I wasn't supposed to be there. I scared her, too. She pulled a gun on me."

"You're kidding." Cheyenne with a weapon?

"When Dane showed up a few minutes later, she shot him right in the face with pepper spray."

Karah Lee chuckled, then bit her lip. "So that's what you meant the other day when you mentioned her dead-on shot with pepper spray. That must have hurt."

"Yep. But she didn't know how to handle the stuff, and she caught herself with it, too. I ended up dunking them both in the lake until the burning stopped." He adjusted his position at the counter, grinning at the memory. "But you know what? I think Dane lost it right there, soon as he met her, pepper spray and all."

"Imagine that," Karah Lee said dryly. "My own personal technique is to throw up on them. That'll bring the guys running."

Blaze's laughter echoed through the empty clinic. "You threw up on Taylor?"

"Who said it was Taylor?"

"Something about the way you act with each other when he's around, and he's around a lot more since you came."

"I think you've got a good imagination. Now, you want to stop distracting me and let me get this work done?"

Fawn heard laughter, and glared through the darkness of the cramped closet. What were they doing out there, having a party while she was back here suffocating? Her hands were so slimy with sweat, they slid from the sides of the hot-water heater, and she was just glad the thing was one of those insulated models, so at least it hadn't fried her when she touched it.

Still, she was doing a slow roast, getting a whiff of natural gas every few seconds that made her gag. Not good on an upset stomach. This thing needed some routine maintenance about five years ago.

The flame on the unit kicked on while she huddled there, and she could feel the temperature slowly start to rise in the closet as she caught another whiff of gas.

She felt dizzy. She had to remind herself that she'd been through worse. A lot worse. *Just hang on a little longer. They can't stay out there all night.*

She closed her eyes and did what she always did during the worst times, when she couldn't face what was happening to her. In her mind she danced on the theater-guild stage back home, wearing a white satin dress, trimmed in lace and pearls and sequins, with a tiara on her head. The prince danced with her—he wore a white tuxedo instead of those stupid tights the prince wore in the musical they'd had two years ago at school.

This prince was strong, and kind, and he smiled at her as if he enjoyed dancing with her. He kept his hands where they should be, and she could tell by the way he looked at her that this was a prince who saw something more than just her eyes—he saw into her heart, and he liked what he saw.

Pure fairy tale. But it was hers, and this prince would never leave.

Now, if those overtimers out front would just leave...

"Do you believe in soul mates?" Blaze pulled out the other office chair and swept beneath it.

Karah Lee deleted a mistake on the screen and scowled at him. "You mean like love at first sight? Nope. What a load of—"

"I don't mean love at first sight, I mean like two people belonging together since before they ever meet."

Karah Lee sighed and sat back. Obviously, this kid was in a mood to talk. "Don't tell me you're in love."

"Me? No. I'm talking about Dane and Cheyenne."

"Ah. The couple of the century."

"I think they belong together. Dane was the one who talked her into opening the clinic, and she was the one who convinced him he'd make a good mayor."

"So Dane Gideon is new at mayoring?" Karah Lee asked.

"Yes, and he's great at it. I mean, the last one, Austin

Barlow, was a real jerk, always throwing his weight around, trying to hit on Cheyenne, trying to blame me for all kinds of stuff that happened last year."

"Stuff like what?"

"Fires. Sunk boats. Pets shot."

"Did they ever find out who did it?" Karah Lee asked. This place had an interesting recent history.

"Sure did. It was Austin Barlow's own son. He nearly killed Cheyenne before we caught him, too. Now the son's doing time in a juvenile detention center—he had some psychological problems, but they didn't meet the definition of criminal insanity—and I heard Austin's working real estate up in Springfield. I just hope he never comes back. Now, back to Dane and Chey. They're good together."

"I can tell you feel that way," Karah Lee said dryly. "So just because she's a good person, he decided to marry her?"

"Not that." Blaze stopped sweeping for a moment, as if deep in thought. "It's almost like they were meant to be together from the beginning. Both of them are the kind of people to help others, you know? It's like their hearts are in the right place, and that place is the same for both of them, and God meant for them to share the load. You know, to bless each other."

Karah Lee held her hands out in front of her face, as if to ward Blaze away. "Okay, sorry, but that's a little too much sweetness and sunshine for one day. Just call me a die-hard cynic, but if you think relationships are that simple, you'd better avoid marriage. It never works that way. Now, would you let me work? I'm just getting the hang of this program."

* * *

Trickles of sweat raced down Fawn's face. She was going to suffocate if she didn't get out of this closet. The voices stopped in the other room, and for a couple of minutes she thought maybe they had left and she hadn't heard them over the hiss of the gas flame at the bottom of this stupid hot-water heater.

Then the heater kicked off, and she heard the clatter of a computer keyboard.

Someone was still in there working.

Fawn wanted to scream! How much longer would they keep it up? If she had to stay in this stupid sauna much longer, they'd come in the morning and find her in a puddle, all sweated out on the floor.

This was a crazy idea, anyway. Coming to Hideaway was crazy. What made her think she was smart enough to figure out what was going on at that construction site when nobody else knew? And what made her think anybody'd listen to her even if she did figure it out?

She was a loser. Total loser. She deserved to sweat to death on the bathroom floor.

But she didn't want to die. She needed a drink. Now. If she kept it quiet, she could probably creep to the sink and stick her mouth under the faucet.

She'd never been so thirsty in her life.

She reached through the darkness until her fingers touched the wooden door. It wasn't latched, since she hadn't been able to squeeze completely inside the closet. Slowly and carefully, she eased the door open until she could see the gray outline of the toilet and the sink.

She started to step from the closet and tripped over the raised threshold, bumping against the closet door. It swung back and thudded against the wall.

She held her breath, eyes wide. She was caught!

"What was that?" Karah Lee asked, suddenly aware that they'd been working for nearly an hour—or rather, talking. Blaze was working while he talked, but Karah Lee couldn't do patient charts and hold a conversation.

"Probably the old water softener kicking into its cycle," Blaze said. "That thing needs to be replaced. Rinsing with the water here is like trying to rinse with pond scum. Cheyenne says it's the next thing on her list of items for replacement. I'll put it in as soon as she buys one."

"You install water softeners, too?" Karah Lee exclaimed. "Is there anything you don't do?"

He grinned. "Admit it, I'm quite a guy."

"Well, maybe you're not too bad for a—" She broke off. She did have a bad habit of blurting out exactly what was on her mind at any given time, and it was something she needed to learn to control better, especially when it might embarrass someone...or give him an ego trip.

He was silent for about ten seconds. The teasing light in his eyes grew less vivid. "Not too bad for a what?" he asked softly.

She hesitated.

"You meant to say I'm not bad for a black kid?" It was nearly a whisper, and it suddenly held a depth of hurt.

She glared at him. "I was going to say for a good-looking teenager who's too big for his britches, but you can forget the good-looking part. I don't like it when people are ashamed of their heritage."

He blinked at her, and the edges of hurt smoothed from his expression. Some of the light returned to his eyes. "You think I'm good-looking?"

"Oh, right, like you don't have any mirrors over at that ranch."

The grin broadened.

"Don't forget the part about being too big for your britches."

"I'm not even sure what that means." He looked down at his baggy scrubs.

"It's an expression my mother used when my sister and I got too cocky when we got good grades in school, or won an award." She heard another thump. "There's the noise again. Are you sure it's the water softener?"

Blaze glanced at the clock over the computer. "I think so. That thing's loud, and it's timed to start its cycle at six. I'll go check."

Fawn didn't have time to crawl back into the closet with the heater, so she stood in the bathroom shadows and listened to the footsteps grow louder. She was almost miserable enough to step out into the hallway with her hands up and beg for mercy. Maybe Blaze wouldn't turn her in, and maybe Dr. Karah Lee would help her.

But then again, what if the doc called the ranger and the sheriff?

"Like I thought, it's the water softener," came Blaze's voice less than a foot from where Fawn stood.

She kept her eyes closed and didn't breathe, tried not to even think as she waited for him to move away. She heard him humming under his breath as he moved toward the exam room across the hall from where she hid.

"Well, I've got my cleaning done," he called as he returned to the front of the clinic. "Got anything else for me?"

"Not tonight."

"You want me to leave you the keys and let you lock up?"

"Nope, I'll finish this tomorrow. Bertie and Edith are doing a new grand opening of their dining room tonight, opening it to the public. I want to get there ahead of the crowd. Let's go."

Fawn slumped against the wall with relief as she listened to keys jingling out front, the voices diminishing to silence.

When she was sure she was alone, she rushed to the sink and turned on the cold water, cupped her hands below the stream and filled them, then drank, slurping noisily, splashing her hot face. It felt so good she did it again and again, until she couldn't swallow any more. She took paper towels and dried herself as well as she could, then tossed the towels and rushed to the front of the office.

She still felt hot and icky, but she wanted to try out the computer. She pulled the storage device from her pocket as she stepped into the reception area, glancing warily toward the entry door at the far left corner of the waiting room. Unfortunately, if someone opened that door, they would see her through the reception window.

She sank into the chair in front of the computer monitor. The seat was still warm from where the doctor had been sitting.

It took a minute for the machine to go through its chatter phase, and when the final screen came up, it asked for a password.

Fawn stared at the screen and groaned. She pressed the exit button, but the screen wouldn't budge.

She bent down and studied the front of the computer itself, and found the USB port. She plugged the device into it, hoping it might jump-start some other program the way a CD would.

Nothing.

Okay. This could still work. She just needed to figure out the right password.

After a search around the desk for a cheat sheet—such as a slip of paper with some letters and numbers on it, she started pulling out drawers and rummaging through papers on the stackable files.

Nothing.

Okay, she could still do this. She started punching in likely words and numbers. HideawayClinic1...clinichideaway...doctorclinic.

After she hit enter the third time, the screen blinked off and the computer powered down with a mechanical whine.

She gasped. "No!" It wasn't supposed to be this way!

She tried to turn the computer back on, but nothing worked. She couldn't get the stupid thing to come back on!

She pulled the flash drive from the computer base and searched through the rest of the clinic for another computer, a laptop or something she might be able to use.

There was nothing. She stuck the device back into her pocket and slumped into a chair in the waiting room. What now?

She would have to find another computer, but how? She was sleeping in a barn! She wasn't crazy enough to walk up to some stranger on the street and ask if she could borrow a laptop for a few minutes. She had no one to trust.

People in danger...

But what was she supposed to do about it? "Bruce, why did you get me into this? How could you leave me like this?"

Her voice seemed to echo through the clinic, and then the telephone rang, startling her. She cried out, then sank into the shadows of the room beside the coffee table.

The answering machine went through its greeting, but no one left a message.

Silence filled the place except for the *thlick-thlick-thlick* of the clock on the wall, and the hum of the soda vending machine out in the foyer. The thought of soda made Fawn thirsty again. She reached into her pocket and pulled out her roll of bills, sorted through them and cursed aloud. No ones or fives. She didn't have change for a vending machine. She'd have to rob one.

That would have to wait, though, since the vending machines were out in the foyer, where anyone walking past the entrance could see in. Later, when the general store and gift shop, bakery and library closed, she would try to get some food from the machine. She might have to shake it, and the noise would attract attention if she wasn't careful.

For now, she would lie low, wait and rest. If only she felt better. She wished she had the guts to go up to Dr. Karah Lee and ask for help, but how much would it cost? Her life?

Fawn pulled out the tiny flashlight she'd brought with her, and after glancing toward the entry door again, she pressed the on button and shone the tiny beam over the coffee table stacked with magazines and books.

Last Friday, while she sat out here with Fred and Myrt and Flo and the other old geezers, she'd studied the titles of those books. Not the magazines or grown-up novels or self-help books, but the little hardbacks for children.

She'd wanted so badly to sprawl out on the floor and bury herself in those stories and forget about everything that was going on around her, forget the pain she was in...and the danger.

She placed the light between her teeth and picked up the first book. This was stupid, she knew. The book was written for eight-year-olds probably fifty years ago. *Lady and the Tramp.* The letters blurred as her eyes filled with hot tears that burned down her face.

She felt so feverish.

The next book was *101 Dalmatians.* She closed her eyes and could still see the black-and-white splotches behind her burning lids as more tears squeezed from between them.

She stuck the books under her arm and turned toward the hallway, feeling comfort in the very presence of the familiar books Great-Grandma used to read to her so many years ago. She'd loved those books. She could almost hear those puppies barking.

Now she could close her eyes and see Great-Grandma's face. As she crept into the back room and climbed onto the neatly made exam bed, Fawn pulled the books against her chest. She turned out the flashlight and closed her eyes and tried hard to think about puppies and sunshine and flowers and laughter.

Could life ever be like that again?

❧ Chapter Twenty ❧

Karah Lee's first solo distress call came at five-thirty Tuesday morning, thirty minutes before Taylor was scheduled to take over. She pulled on her old paramedic uniform, with the cargo shorts she'd worn Sunday, and checked her map to make sure of the location.

This one shouldn't be much trouble. It was two houses down from the rental that had been demolished last Friday. *Her* rental.

She was walking out the front door with her rescue backpack over her shoulder, when headlights slid through the early-morning grayness and pulled to a stop in front of her on the circle driveway. Taylor.

He reached across the seat and shoved the door open from inside. "Get in."

She didn't argue until she was buckled up. "I probably

shouldn't remind you that I took this job so you wouldn't have to be on call 24/7."

"You're off in twenty-five minutes, and I want to be ready to take over in case it's a long one."

"Right, and you probably overheard the address over the radio."

He gave her a quick grin. "That too."

Taylor Jackson had a devastating grin. Humor lit his eyes and caressed every part of his face, transforming him from the usually serious, intense ranger-on-the-job to someone who knew not to take life too seriously.

Karah Lee grinned back. "You plan to sneak over and do some snooping while I work?"

"Nope, I'm just going along for the ride."

"Good to have you." All they'd said was that a woman had fallen in her front yard. The neighbor was afraid to try to help her, in case she'd injured her back.

"Taylor, I thought about calling you last night, but you were off duty and I didn't want to disturb you."

"Call me about what?"

"You said Tom was suspicious about Casey."

"That's right."

"Do you think he might have called for federal assistance to search for her?"

"Not without going through Greg, and Greg didn't seem willing to do that when I talked to him on Sunday."

"Would he have told you if he had?"

"Yes. What are you getting at?"

"Some guy in a suit came to the clinic last night after Cheyenne left, showing us pictures of Casey and claiming to be a federal investigator."

Taylor's foot slid noisily from the accelerator and he gaped at her.

"Uh, you might want to watch for your turn," she said as a tree limb came at them from the darkness and brushed the left front fender of the vehicle.

He pressed the brake, belatedly signaled, turned, but didn't speed up after completing the turn. "No federal investigator's been in touch with us here."

"I didn't think so."

"Did he say he was FBI?"

"Federal Bureau of Independent Investigators."

"Never heard of them. Name?"

"Detective Withnell. Could we get a move on? There's a patient waiting for me."

Taylor replaced his foot on the accelerator, and the Jeep surged forward. "What did you tell him?"

By the time they reached their destination, Karah Lee had completed a replay of the conversation she and Jill had conducted with their visitor. "Jill thinks he'll be back."

"So someone thinks our runaway might still be in the area?" Taylor asked, releasing his seat belt and opening his door.

"Maybe so."

"Could be, but I haven't seen any signs of her since Friday, and I've been looking."

"Good. Will you please just keep your eyes open?"

"I'll do it."

They saw their patient sitting on the ground a few feet from her front porch, with a younger woman hovering beside her. In the glow from the porch light, the patient appeared to be about sixty years of age. The younger woman rushed across the grass to greet them as they climbed from the vehicle.

"Thank goodness you're here," she said, glancing over her shoulder toward the victim, then lowering her voice. "That old crank is driving me crazy. She's trying to bully me into taking her to the clinic myself."

"When did the accident take place?" Karah Lee asked.

"I heard her hollering about ten minutes ago through my bedroom window and realized it was a human and not a rooster crowing—though it's hard to tell the difference, if you ask me."

"I take it you two don't exactly get along," Karah Lee said.

"Like I said, Ethylene's a crank. She can't get along with any of her neighbors. I didn't want to move her, in case I did more damage."

"That was the right thing," Karah Lee said as she hurried to the patient's side.

"It's about time somebody showed up," the older woman muttered. "You know how long I've been sitting here?"

"I'm sorry, ma'am." Karah Lee knelt beside the woman. "We came as soon as we received the call."

"I know what's wrong with me, I broke my leg. Just like that." She snapped her fingers. "I stepped off the porch to get my paper, and somebody'd come up and dug a hole in my yard last night. I didn't even see it till I went down."

"Ma'am, I'm Dr. Karah Lee Fletcher. Are you Mrs. Hutchins?"

"I'm Ethylene Hutchins. You're the doctor? I thought you were the paramedic. Where's Cheyenne? *She's* my doctor."

"I'm the one on call this morning, Mrs. Hutchins. Your neighbor did the right—"

"I *said* my name's Ethylene."

"Thank you, Ethylene, you can call me Karah Lee."

"Some neighbors I've got," Ethylene grumbled, glancing at the retreating figure of the lady who had called for the ambulance. "Wouldn't even help me into the house, and sure wouldn't even think about loading me up and hauling me to the clinic just a few blocks away. How much trouble could that be?"

Karah Lee reached into her medical kit. "Are you in any pain right now, Ethylene?"

"No more'n anybody else would be with a broken leg."

"We'll see if we can help you with that pain, and I'd like to get you down to the clinic to check you out, but the ambulance is still a few minutes away."

"I told that blasted woman I don't need any ambulance. All I need's to have this leg set. Why can't you just haul me off the way you got here? In that gas eater over there." She pointed toward Taylor's Jeep.

Karah Lee suppressed a grin and looked at Taylor, expecting a protest—Taylor loved his SUV, and was always singing its praises. Apparently, he had other things on his mind at the moment, however.

"Ethylene, you say this hole wasn't here last night?" he called over his shoulder, inspecting the ground where she had fallen.

"That's exactly what I'm saying."

"It doesn't look as if anyone's been digging, it looks as if the earth caved in from below. The grass is still in place."

"Whatever caused it, I still fell, and I don't want to wait around on no ambulance when I can get a ride with you. Are we going or not?"

"We'll wait for the ambulance," Karah Lee said.

"You going to pay for it? Those ambulance trips cost money I don't have, and don't try telling me we can make arrangements for that later. Dr. Cheyenne can set my leg. She took care of my arm last fall."

"I'm sorry, Ethylene," Karah Lee said, "but Dr. Cheyenne is out of town."

"Fine, then you can set it."

"I'll take some X rays of your leg and check you out, but if you need an orthopedist to—"

"Oh, no you don't," Ethylene snapped. "You're not dumping me on some guy with a fancy title stuck to the end of his name, and you're not sending me out of Hideaway. I can't afford it. I'm a year away from Medicare, and I don't have insurance."

"Then it's important for us to get it right the first time, isn't it?" Karah Lee pulled her stethoscope from her medical kit.

"What kind of doctor are you?" Ethylene asked.

"Family practice."

"Haven't you ever fixed a broken bone?"

"Yes." Several of them, but in Columbia Ortho was always within shouting distance, and they always checked her handiwork.

"Good. Get me up from here and call your ambulance people off."

Again, the specter of doubt made Karah Lee hesitate. "Ethylene, please—"

"You can either call them off now, or I'll send them back home when they get here."

Karah Lee glanced helplessly at Taylor, then shrugged. "Okay, we'll immobilize your leg and take you to the clinic, but if the fracture is complicated—"

"We'll worry about that if it happens," Ethylene said. "Get me up from here."

Fawn woke up in hell. She felt the flames all through her body, and her skin felt like desert sand. Her eyes hurt too much to open them at first, but a quiet thump echoed through her mind, like a knife plunging, until she forced her lids apart.

The room where she lay was dark, but as she struggled to sit up, the light came on in the hallway.

She'd fallen asleep and now she was caught!

Quick, get off the bed. Get behind the door. Peek out into the hallway to see if anyone's out there.

But she couldn't move. She felt as if she'd been glued to the mattress, which suddenly felt hot and suffocating.

Voices reached her, then she heard footsteps down the hallway. Slowly, she sat up. Her body felt as if it had been poured full of wet cement. Hot cement.

They had her. They knew. This might even be the sheriff coming to handcuff her and take her out. Or maybe it was the ranger. Or what if it was Harv? The killer, himself? What if he'd discovered where she—

"In here, Taylor."

Fawn froze and waited for the end to come. And then she recognized the voice. It was Dr. Karah Lee, and she was talking to the ranger and somebody else... sounded like a grumpy woman. And they hadn't come in here.

Maybe there was time to get out.

Under cover of their voices, she climbed down from the bed, but when she straightened to rush across the room, the floor bucked with her, and she stumbled. The room spun around. She grabbed the end of the bed rail.

For a moment, she leaned against the bed and listened to the doctor's soothing voice in the other room. *What if I just stayed here?*

"...don't want to move unnecessarily and cause more damage, Ethylene. That's it, we'll be finished with this in just a moment, then I'll let you rest."

Fawn closed her eyes. The voice was so kind, so calm.

She was about to sit on the bed again, when she heard someone call out from the front of the clinic. "Okay, I'm here, but I have to leave again. Dane wants me to unlock the general store at seven. Karah Lee? Where are you?"

Fawn recognized that voice. Blaze.

"In X ray," Dr. Karah Lee called back. "I'll be out in a minute."

"Hey, who's been taking books from the stack this early in the morning?"

Fawn stiffened. She looked down at the children's books on the counter. He'd noticed as soon as he walked in. And there wouldn't be a chance to take them back to the waiting room. He was too sharp. What else would he notice?

"Keep it down, will you?" Karah Lee called. "We've got a patient."

"Sorry."

Fawn knew she couldn't stay. What had she been thinking? With Dr. Karah Lee, maybe it would've been okay, and maybe even with Blaze—he'd been so sweet to her Friday—but there were too many other people, and she wasn't supposed to be here. That meant Taylor would have to do something about it. She was a criminal, according to the police and the newspapers. Who was going to believe her?

She forced herself to stand up straight, then staggered to the door and listened. After making sure the hallway was empty, she slid out, holding on to the wall for support as she turned left toward the back exit. She fumbled with the dead bolt and pulled the door open, peered out, and tottered from the clinic like an old geezer, trying hard to be as quiet as possible.

She was never going to make it back to the barn.

Karah Lee sat down in Cheyenne's peaceful office while she waited for the X-ray films to develop on Ethylene Hutchins's leg. Taylor had stepped out for a few minutes, and Blaze was still wandering around the clinic somewhere, muttering about books missing from the stack on the table.

Except for that, the place was quiet. It felt strange, because usually by the time Karah Lee arrived for work in the morning there were patients already here, the telephone was ringing and Jill had everything under control—or at least as controlled as it could be.

This morning, for the first time, Karah Lee realized what Cheyenne had envisioned for this clinic. People like Ethylene depended on them for all her medical care, and she refused to consider other options. Sure, treatment of complicated medical problems here could be considered substandard care, compared to the treatment patients would have with a specialist in Branson or Springfield, but if they refused a specialist, what then? Dismiss them from the practice? Unthinkable.

And so Cheyenne Allison, knowing she could be sued, risked everything in order to treat everyone she could. Karah Lee felt overwhelmed. She had been taught from day one that those specialists were her safety net. She'd referred patients daily in Columbia, where the physicians, per capita, were much higher than elsewhere because of the focus on medicine in that city. There was almost always a doctor eager to take her referrals.

Her safety net had suddenly been removed, and now even Cheyenne was gone. Karah Lee was not an emergency physician, she was a new family practice doc.

She glanced around the sparsely furnished office. "What am I doing here?" she whispered.

Was she even really a good doctor? All this time she'd been so proud of her independence from her father's money, and now she was discovering how very dependent she actually had been.

"Karah Lee, something's going on." Blaze stalked into the office, holding two children's books up for her inspection. "You saw me stack everything just right on the table in the waiting room last night, didn't you?"

Karah Lee frowned at him for a moment, mentally switching gears. "Uh, yes, but I didn't—"

"I had these two right on top. Dog stories. Kids love the dog stories, and I knew we had some kids coming in this morning, so—"

"So what happened?"

"That's what I'd like to find out. You know where I found these? In exam room four. And you know what else? The bed was a mess. I cleaned that room before we left last night, remember? It's a good thing Jill didn't find it first, or she'd be nagging me about it all day."

"I don't suppose you found a book titled *Goldilocks* lying around anywhere," Karah Lee said dryly.

He gave her a blank look.

"You know, as in 'Who's been sleeping in my bed?'"

"I don't think we've got that one."

Don't kids even read the classics these days? "Never mind. What else alerted you?"

"There are potato chips and pretzels and a candy bar missing from the vending machine."

"How many?"

He held up three fingers. "One each. Somebody shook the machine to get them to fall. It's easy to tell, because they're missing from the front of each row."

"But we would have heard someone shaking it."

"Sure, if we'd been here when it happened." He spread his hands to his sides. "I'm telling you, something's going on here."

"Raccoons?"

He glared at her.

"Sorry. We locked up last night before we left, and I haven't been near the back door. Did you check it this morning?"

"Yes, but you know that dead bolt locks automatically. I've even locked myself out a couple of times. It's one of those old ones."

"Have you noticed anything else missing?"

"No, but give me time." He pivoted and left the room.

Now that she thought about it, she had heard a couple of noises last night. But Blaze had thought the sounds came from the water softener.

As Blaze powered up the computer in the other room, Karah Lee heard a strange series of beeps, and a moan.

She was pretty sure the moan came from Blaze.

"What is it?" she called.

He came walking slowly back into the office. "I think someone's been messing with the computer."

"Why do you think that?"

"Because it *told* me so. Remember I warned you last night that it'll shut down after three wrong password entries?"

Great, just what they needed. "Have you searched the rest of the clinic?"

"Yeah, but don't we have enough evidence? I think some little kid sneaked in here while we were still open and crawled into one of the cabinets or something until we locked up."

"A kid who knows how to power up a computer?"

"Why not? An eight-year-old can operate a computer these days."

"Taylor didn't say anything about a child missing from the neighborhood. Where'd he go, anyway?"

"I think he went outside for a smoke."

Karah Lee frowned. "For a *what?*"

Blaze winced. "Oops. Would you forget I said that? Taylor's bigger than me, and it's none of our business what he does on his own—"

"Fine, I'll talk to him later about any missing children. Right now we have a broken leg to set." She suddenly felt irritable "Where's Jill?"

"I'm here," came a voice from the other room, accompanied by the sweet aroma of fresh-baked cinnamon rolls and freshly brewed coffee.

Unfortunately, they would have to wait until later for breakfast.

Chapter Twenty-One

Taylor completed his report in the Jeep, then considered going back inside for one of the cinnamon rolls and a cup of the coffee he'd seen Jill carry over to the clinic from the bakery a few minutes ago. Blaze and Jill could both brew a decent cup of coffee, but the bakery used freshly ground beans first thing in the morning, and its brews were out of this world.

For now, however, they would all be busy with Ethylene and her harangues, and he wasn't in the mood to hang around and deal with those.

He opened the glove compartment for an extra ink pen, and his gaze flicked over the pack of cigarettes he'd stashed there yesterday. He didn't usually allow himself to smoke this early, but for some reason he'd awakened from a nightmare about Chip about four this morning. It had been the reason he'd switched on the ambulance radio and caught the message about Ethylene. In fact, he'd gone out on this call specifically to escape the memories crashing down on him with such alarming vividness—the aftereffects of his "sharing" time with Karah Lee.

He pulled out a cigarette and his disposable lighter and slid them into his shirt pocket, then closed the glove compartment and got out of the truck.

He was strolling across the broad, summer-green lawn by the dock when he saw a canoe gliding quietly toward him from across the lake. Dane Gideon waved from the boat. The man's white-blond hair and neatly trimmed beard and mustache—sprinkled more liberally with white than with blond—made him appear slightly older than his thirty-nine years.

"You're out a little early this morning, aren't you, Taylor?" Dane called out as he nosed the canoe into an empty slip and tossed a rope onto the wooden dock.

"We had an emergency call." Taylor moored the boat, then shook hands with Dane when he stepped out. "What are you doing with the canoe? Did Blaze steal your Mystique?" Everyone in town knew in what fond regard Dane Gideon held his motorboat.

"Karah Lee sounded like she needed help quickly when she called Blaze this morning, and I wanted the exercise, so I let Blaze take the boat, and told him I'd be in later for it." Dane patted his stomach. "Too many meetings lately, and everyone wants to conduct business over a heavy meal. I want Cheyenne to recognize me when she gets back from Florida."

"How's her mother?" Taylor asked.

"She's doing well, but I'm afraid Karah Lee's going to have the clinic to herself for a few days yet."

"She can handle it." Though she'd seemed a little hesitant with Ethylene this morning, Karah Lee had proven herself capable last Friday.

"That'll put the extra load on you again, since she can't take medical call and first-responder call at the same time." Dane turned and walked with Taylor, their footsteps echoing across the wooden dock and blending with the splash of water as a fish broke surface in a leap for breakfast. "Sorry to do that to you."

"I'll deal with it."

"We missed you at the town-hall meeting last night."

"I had to find some lost hikers and guide them out of the woods. How'd it go? Is everyone still up in arms about Beaufont's activities?"

Dane nodded, his craggy, farmer-tanned face growing serious as he stared across the imported sand and the lifeguard stand on the eastern edge of town. Even this early, they could hear construction under way. "Beaufont was well represented last night," he said. "That didn't improve the mood. Our deputy sheriff was pretty outspoken."

"Tom? I'm not surprised. He blames Beaufont for anything that goes wrong around here."

"Him and half the town. Last night he went so far as to warn about an earthquake that's being predicted down in Arkansas."

Taylor looked at Dane. "He mentioned something like that the other day. Him and his Web-surfing addiction."

"His concern is that any tremors that could reach this far up might endanger the town because of that 'monstrosity of steel and concrete,' as he calls it."

"What was Beaufont's response?" Taylor asked.

"They went into great detail to explain why something like that could never happen to their building. You know how deeply they blasted through the rock for a solid foundation. They also made light of Tom's concerns about a tremor. Said it would never happen here."

"They can't know that." Taylor had also disregarded Tom's prediction the other day. As had Greg. The Ozarks didn't have earthquakes. Sure, there were fault lines, but the last major earthquake to hit anywhere near here had been across the state near the Mississippi River. Tom would be the butt of jokes once again.

"I heard a rumor that you're planning to support our pharmacist for the next election for mayor," Taylor said.

"That's right," Dane said. "I never wanted the job in the first place, and Trask grew up here, he knows the town, and he'll do a good job, but that's not going to happen for a while, unfortunately."

"You're still taking heat from the locals?" Taylor asked.

Dane nodded, casting a glance toward the skeleton of the building. "I've always pushed for progress, but not their kind of progress." His steps slowed, and his voice lowered. "You know their party boat goes out twice a night now?"

Taylor nodded. Beaufont's paddleboat parties had become legendary in the past few weeks, with lots of on-board entertainment, lavish meals, free-flowing drinks and—it was rumored—other party "enhancers" that weren't legal. As a direct result, law enforcement was becoming more of a problem. The sheriff had been forced to request backup at least three times lately after one of the excursions.

"Marketing strategy," Dane said. "Their guests don't have to pay a dime for any of it."

All because Beaufont wanted to have all their condominium units sold before the project was complete. "I hope the investors will quadruple their investments, the parties will end, and all will be well," Taylor said.

"I'm praying that's what will happen," Dane said. "We did have one bit of good news last night. It looks as if we're getting closer to a vote to purchase an ambulance and hire a crew."

"For Hideaway?"

"That's right. Have you ever managed an ambulance service?"

"Me? No way. I've been a ranger for twelve years."

"Did you ever consider a career change?"

Taylor realized that Dane wasn't kidding. "They're getting that serious about an ambulance service? In a town barely over a thousand in population?"

"Branson was our size once."

"Yes, but—"

"Our revenue's based on tourism, just like Branson's, and we're already more than a sixth the size of Branson. We may be growing in ways we don't want to grow, but we still need good medical care, with good people running it." Dane grinned at Taylor. "I've seen you handle everything this town has thrown at you for a year, and you've earned all the locals' respect. Would you at least consider the possibility?"

"There hasn't even been a vote to do it yet."

"It'll happen soon, and I want to be ready when it does. Would you think about it?"

The offer was tempting. "I'll consider the possibility."

Dane's grin broadened. "Thanks. Now I'd better go open up the store before Bertie Meyer comes looking for me." He started across the street, then stopped and turned back, serious once more. "By the way, I don't suppose you've seen a stranger hanging around the square lately—female in denim with gray hair and a painful-looking sunburn?"

"You're kidding, right? This place is packed with sun-burned strangers lately."

"Junior Short told me he was driving past the feed store loading dock yesterday evening and saw some-one who fit that description climb up the steps and dis-appear inside. My customers always come next door and pay for their feed, then one of us goes over and loads them from the dock. I was just curious who it might be."

"Was anything missing?"

"I didn't notice anything last night when I went to close up."

"I know you've had some vandalism in the past."

"Not for nearly a year. Don't worry about it, Taylor, I'm sure it's nothing. You just keep thinking about that am-bulance service."

* * *

Fawn slumped against an old tombstone in a cemetery next to a little white church building down the road west of town. She couldn't take another step. In a minute, she'd try to crawl over to the lake and get a drink, but for now, she just wanted to sit here and rest.

Her ears had started ringing when she crossed the street to leave the town square, and for a few seconds she'd thought it was a police siren, that they'd finally spotted her. All she'd felt was relief. Nothing could be worse than the way she felt right now.

But as she looked around her at the headstones that filled this little cemetery, she knew she couldn't give up yet. *People could die.* Bruce and others already had. If a six-teen-year-old hooker named Fawn Morrison had to risk her own life to keep others safe, wouldn't it be worth it?

If she could just rest awhile, drink a lot of water, stay hidden, she'd get better. All she needed to do right now was break the fever.

Behind the church, the yard was shaded. There weren't any houses nearby except for the Lakeside Bed-and-Breakfast down the road a few hundred feet. She could stay in the shade of the hedge out of sight.

She just had to rest.

Taylor strolled toward a deserted section of the shore east of the boat dock, avoiding the imported sand on the beach. The fake-beach lovers would sleep until noon, and the only others he saw out on the lake this early in the morning were dedicated fishermen intent on their prey.

If he were still married to Clarice, he would never have started smoking again. If Chip were still alive, it would never have been a consideration.

But that was the whole point—Taylor had no one to answer to...except for Jesus, and that hadn't exactly been a steady relationship. Would the Lord even notice?

Taylor sank onto a concrete bench with a yawn, stretching his arms up and out as he gazed across the lake. The morning stillness of the water had enchanted him from his first day on duty here. There was a magical quality about the glow from a still-unseen sun outlining the hills and trees with ever-increasing detail. An Ozark sunrise could hold its own with anything the Grand Canyon offered.

So why had he never felt settled here?

True, he didn't like law enforcement. What he did like, more and more as time went on, was rescuing people. And now there might be a chance for him to do that full-time.

He lit up, took the first smoke-filled breath and imagined the calming drug entering his bloodstream. He exhaled, and with his second puff he felt a heaviness pass through him.

He relaxed a little and took another drag, watching an older gentleman across the lake help a sleepy-looking child cast his line. Two mallards swam toward the dock, where later in the day groups of tourists would lean over the wooden railing and toss bits of bread into the water to feed the fish. Taylor knew from experience they would be out of bread long before the ducks, or the fish, stopped coming.

Footsteps whispered in the grass behind him, and he stiffened a fraction of a second before Karah Lee's voice flicked over him.

"I *don't* believe it."

He didn't turn around. "What's that?" Stupid question.

"You smoke."

"I don't do it often, and when I do, I like it to be a peaceful process."

"Secondhand smoke is not peaceful." Though she didn't raise her voice, outrage curled around every word.

"There's no one else nearby, and I didn't expect you to come out gunning for me." *Cool it, Taylor. She's had a rough morning, with Ethylene's acerbic personality.*

"Cancer isn't peaceful."

"Neither are you, but I've never seen a warning label on you anywhere."

"I don't cause cancer. Why would a grown man experiment with the slowest suicide legally available today?"

"I've heard the sermon, so can the corn, Fletcher. I'm not giving any more excuses."

"There's no excuse—"

"Shut up, Fletcher. Okay?" Finally he turned enough to glare at her over his shoulder.

She didn't even wince. She looked wide-awake and fresh, without a trace of makeup.

"Has anyone ever told you how obnoxious you are when you're trying to be bossy?" He winced at his own words. Here she was, not only shouldering the responsibility for the whole clinic with Cheyenne gone, but also brave enough to show concern about his health, and risk getting her head bitten off. And he was doing the biting.

"The truth isn't always popular," she said quietly, "but sometimes it saves a life."

"Okay, never mind." Taylor got up from the bench, strolled casually over to the lake, and jabbed the smoldering end of his cigarette into the water. Without looking at Karah Lee, he took the soaked cigarette to the nearby trash can and flipped it in. He felt like a schoolboy caught by the teacher, and in spite of Karah Lee's obviously good intentions, he resented it. Because she was right, of course.

Dusting his hands together, he walked back to Karah Lee. His initial irritation disappeared with the last whiff of smoke when he saw the look of worried distraction in her eyes. "Happy?"

"For your information, I didn't come out here to sharpen my claws, I came out to ask if anyone called you about a child missing in the neighborhood last night."

"Why?"

"Someone's been sleeping in our beds, eating our food, playing on our compu—"

"Look, if you want to find Goldilocks, why don't you call Greg or Tom? I'm not even officially on duty yet this morning, and downtown Hideaway isn't my usual jurisdiction even when I am on duty." Okay, so he *was* still a little irritated with her.

He could tell by the brief flash of irritation in those golden-amber eyes that she'd taken the hit, and again he was sorry he'd been so sharp with her.

She slapped her forehead in an exaggerated gesture of dismay and pivoted back toward the clinic. "Of course. I'm such an idiot. What could I have been thinking, just taking for granted you might be concerned about some little lost child or his overwrought parents? I mean, you're not even on duty here, and just because you came rushing right up to my doorstep this morning when you also weren't on duty yet because you wanted to snoop around the property that also isn't your jurisdiction—"

"Okay, that's enough, I'm sorry, okay?" She didn't sound angry, she sounded as if she enjoyed goading him.

"No, I'm the one who should be sorry," she insisted. "I'll call—"

"Would you stop it?" He caught up with her and matched her long-legged stride. "Has anyone ever told you you're a bully?"

"Yes, actually, they have. It's a point of family pride. Bullying and manipulation are my most effective methods of coercion."

"And guilt trips," he said. "You're good at those."

"I learned it on my father's knee."

"You shouldn't be allowed to get away with it."

"Fine, I'll call Tom as soon as I get back to the clinic. I think he's on duty this morning."

"That wouldn't be my first choice. Tom's never been married, never had kids, and wouldn't make your problem a top priority like I will. He's more worried about some earthquake predictions in Arkansas."

She flicked him a gaze full of disdain.

"So tell me what's up," he said.

"Someone was apparently in the clinic last night after Blaze and I left a little after six. It looks like they slept in exam room four. Their choice of reading material was children's books. We thought maybe we had a young runaway on our hands. A neighborhood kid, perhaps."

"You're not joking?"

"Come and see. I'll let you check the place out while I find someone to drive Ethylene home."

"Doesn't she have friends or family?"

"If she does, she's not saying. How many cigarettes do you smoke a day?"

"A few."

"A few, as in three or four? Or a few, as in twenty or thirty?"

"What does it matter?"

"Well, even one is dangerous, but it'll probably kill you more slowly than, say, a carton a day. You know, like I'm sure you can tell I don't miss many meals, and that'll kill a person, too. So I don't want to sound like a hypocrite or anything."

"Why, Karah Lee Fletcher, I never thought I'd hear you backpedal."

"I'm not backpedaling, I'm just trying to come to terms with the disappointment of seeing you smoke."

She said it lightly, with just the right amount of teasing sarcasm, as if attempting to take the sting from her words this time. Still, they stung, because he realized he didn't want to disappoint her. And he didn't want to be so disappointed in himself. Clarice's father had died of lung cancer, and the doctors had made it abundantly clear that it had been a direct result of his two-pack-a-day habit.

"You know, I'm trying to be compassionate and identify with your pain," she said.

"Well, don't get stupid and start smoking to make the identification easier."

"Smoking isn't my weakness. Like I said, I go a little overboard in the eating department."

He glanced sideways in appraisal. She hadn't taken the time to change from her rescue clothes this morning, and she had the best legs he'd ever seen on a woman. They could be quite distracting at times. The rest of her could be, too. She didn't look overweight to him. *Full-bodied* might be the word he'd use, though not aloud. He knew she was muscular, because he'd seen her lift Mrs. White from her seat the other day as if the lady were a child. Muscle *did* weigh more than fat. And Tom was good at guessing age and weight. He had plenty of time to practice because he didn't have a life.

"It's not polite to stare," Karah Lee said.

"What are you, about two-twenty?"

She stopped at the side of the street, then blinked at him as if he'd slapped her. "What!"

Oh, no. *You idiot. Never listen to Tom.* The blood in Taylor's system chose this moment to rush to his face. "I'll kill him."

"Speaking of killing—"

"No, I'm sorry. I didn't mean—"

"Last physical I weighed one-eighty-three," she said. "And it's possible I've gained a pound or five since then, but—"

"Somebody played a practical joke on me." Face still burning, he glanced around, hoping no one had overheard him.

"Using my size as the butt of their jokes?"

He grinned at the pun, then glanced at her face and realized she wasn't smiling.

"You know, it's been a few months since someone made fun of my size."

"I honestly wasn't making fun, Karah Lee, believe me. I just don't judge weight very well, apparently, and—"

"It's not polite to try to guess a lady's weight."

"Really, I'm sorry." He touched her arm and stopped her before she could cross the street. "I wasn't using my brain."

She glanced at him. "One-eighty-three for a woman my height isn't bad."

"Obviously it isn't. Look, the guy who told me that isn't the kind of person who would think about your feelings."

"Sounds like Tom."

Taylor didn't respond. She was *good*.

"Maybe I'll make sure he has something to think about next time," she said.

"I'd better quit while I'm ahead. You're what…six feet?"

She glared. "Five-eleven and three-quarters. You fitting me for a body bag?"

"Okay, listen—let's call a truce? I promise not to try to guess your weight again if you'll promise not to mention my smoking."

Her gaze narrowed. "Forget it. Not a deal. What kind of a person would I be if I allowed you to use insults and subterfuge to keep me from telling you the truth about what you're doing to your health?" She stepped into the street.

He followed. "Oh, I don't know, the word *polite* comes to mind."

"Forget that. Women my size aren't expected to be polite. Why disappoint people?"

In spite of the situation, he smiled. To him, she was the perfect size. As long as he learned to keep his mouth shut about it.

Come to think of it, both of them could stand to learn that lesson.

❦ Chapter Twenty-Two ❧

Fawn opened her eyes, then squinched them shut against a blinding light and a world spinning out of control. Where was she?

Her clothes stuck to her skin and her head pounded. A bird chirped nearby and a breeze touched her face. The laughter and screams of children and the rumble of motorboats was closer than usual, and she could hardly hear the hammers and saws and the banging and clanging of heavy equipment at the construction site.

This wasn't the barn loft.

She shielded her eyes with her hand and eased her eyelids open once more. Lake water, a few feet down a rocky shelf of shoreline, reflected the sun back at her. She half turned and saw the church behind her through the trees. She had been in the shade when she collapsed here this morning.

"It's okay," she whispered to herself as she crawled slowly, painfully, back beneath the shade of the forest that edged the church. She was far enough from everything that probably nobody'd seen her. She felt so weak, it was hard to move. She needed water.

Right now, though, she just wanted to sleep.

The sun was nudging its way into the edge of trees in the west. Fawn slumped on the ledge of rock above the lake when a noisy paddleboat trudged by in front of her. Laughter and music echoed across the lake, and she caught a whiff of barbecue smoke.

Shading her eyes again, she watched the people on board—the women in their slinky-sexy swimsuits and the men baring their sunburned chests, already drunk and loud.

Only one man on board wore a suit, and Fawn leaned forward, squinting again to study him better.

She caught her breath when she realized she knew that face. The last time she'd seen it, he was shooting at her. Harv.

She wanted to jump up and run away, but she could barely drag herself to her feet and wobble across the uneven stone ledge.

Apparently, her movement caught the man's attention. He watched her for a few seconds as the boat paddled farther down the lake. He raised something to his face, but by now he was too far away for her to see what it was. She turned away, showing him her back. It could be a camera, or a pair of binoculars, but whatever it was, she'd bet he could see her better than she could see him. And *she'd* recognized *him*.

A rock tripped her. A tree caught her fall. She hugged the trunk and slid to the ground as everything went dark.

Karah Lee sat at a table overlooking the lake in a far corner of the Lakeside Bed-and-Breakfast dining area on Tuesday evening. This place rocked. Bertie's breakfast bar had become so popular that she and Edith had started opening it to the public in the evening, and now the place was packed with sunburned boaters and fishermen, water-skiers and hikers starved after a day of activity.

Karah Lee took a sip of her excellent coffee and settled back, watching the other diners as they carried their trays to tables near the windows overlooking Table Rock Lake. The mingled aromas of eggs, bacon, ham and onions— and Bertie's black walnut waffles—drifted from the food bar and filled Karah Lee's senses, helping her forget, for a few moments, that her own meager fare was dry toast and yogurt.

Ugh. Why couldn't Bertie and Edith do salads and soups for dinner? Why breakfast again? No one in their right mind did a breakfast buffet at night.

Although a lot of people seemed to be enjoying it.

Karah Lee loved breakfast, but even her comfy scrubs were showing a little too much affection for her growing curves. She didn't have time to drive into Branson and find an outlet mall, and she didn't want to shop for a larger size.

She bit off a corner of the toast and grimaced at the lack of taste compared to the aromas of sumptuous fare that filled her senses. Maybe if she smoothed just a little layer of cream gravy over this... It would be lower in calories than butter, wouldn't it? But as more people came through the entrance from the lobby, she decided not to take a chance on losing her seat to go back through the line.

A group of six young men and women, barely out of their teens, carried their trays to the long section of tables beside her and sat down with an echo of scraping chair legs on the wooden floor. Their talk and laughter mingled with details of the boat ride they'd taken the night before. They teased each other about hangovers and about the skiing they planned to do tomorrow, and discussed the possibility of pooling their money so they could make a down payment on a condo unit.

Taking another sip of coffee, Karah Lee tried to tune out the chatter as she gazed through the plate-glass window at the pink and gold sunset framed by a lacy etching of trees. The reflection of colors transformed the surface of the lake into a treasure chest of glowing coals.

She was so entranced by the sight that it took her a couple of seconds to notice that one tree trunk in the thicket of forest between the church and the lakeshore was shaped a little oddly—and it appeared blue.

As she continued to stare, the trunk seemed to take on the shape of a human.

This day had started weird, so why change now?

"Mind if I sit here?"

She looked up, startled, to see Taylor standing beside her table, tray in hand. "Where'd you come from?" She used her foot to shove a chair out for him. "Be my guest. I think this is the only place left in the dining room."

He sat down.

"I'm sorry about this morning." She glanced out the window again. Denim blue. A tree wearing blue jeans?

He poured maple syrup over his waffle. "What about this morning?"

She dragged her gaze from the tree. She was definitely losing it. "For nagging you like I was your mother or something. Unless you blow smoke in my face, I don't have any right to preach."

He didn't reply as he placed a napkin in his lap, then paused briefly, gaze lowered, before picking up his fork.

"It's a stupid, self-destructive habit," he said at last.

She watched as he cut a bite of the luscious, rich, fragrant black walnut waffle. "So you're trying to self-destruct?"

"I've never been a pack-a-day smoker. Maybe half a pack, at most. I guess since I don't have that many during a day, I'm trying to convince myself I haven't reached the danger point."

She bit down gently on her tongue and remained silent as he placed the delectable looking bite of waffle into his mouth. There were a lot of things she wanted to say, but she'd already harangued him too much.

"If I'd been through what you have in the past few years, maybe I'd be self-destructive, too," she said. "Besides, lots of people have self-destructive habits. Mine is eating, yours is smoking. But I'll tell you what—I'm on a diet. Maybe we could form our own chapter of Smokers and Overeaters Anonymous. I'll call you when I'm tempted to take a bite of Bertie's black walnut waffles, and you call me when you're tempted to take a smoke."

He grinned suddenly, and the expression transformed his face as he set his fork onto his plate. "You're kidding, right? You really think you need to lose weight?"

She waited for the punch line. He didn't say more. Okay, she really, really liked this guy.

"My son would have blasted me for smoking," he said. "I can almost hear him now, 'Dad, what kind of a Christian witness would you be if someone saw you doing that?'"

She set her coffee cup down. "Christian witness. I'd take a nickel for every time I heard those words."

"From whom?"

"My mother."

"You were raised in a Christian family?"

"Actually, you could say I'm the product of a mixed marriage. My mother was a believer, and my father attended church with the family when he thought it would serve a purpose."

"A purpose?"

"You know, earn him votes and improve his reputation. He's a politician." For some reason, instead of resentment, for the first time Karah Lee felt only sadness. Dad had failed in his relationships, and he was alone again, in spite of all his political success.

And Mom, in spite of her continued claims about her faith in God, had responded with such bitterness after the divorce and the discovery of her cancer that she'd alienated her oldest daughter. It wasn't until that final year of struggle that she'd come to terms with her situation and shown a more peaceful attitude.

"Earth to Karah Lee."

She blinked and refocused on Taylor.

"I asked if your mother's faith had an impact on you."

"You're asking if I did the whole 'walk the aisle' routine?"

"Did you?"

"Sure. I grew up Baptist. I said the sinner's prayer, I was baptized, the works."

"Okay, but I guess what I'm really asking is if you're truly a believer. In Christ."

She didn't hesitate. "Yes. I just avoid church, which I know is a contradiction in terms for some people. You?"

He nodded and looked away. "Hard to believe, huh?"

"Why?"

"Because someone whose Lord is Christ wouldn't pollute his body."

Karah Lee suppressed a snort. "Right. You tell me where you can find a church filled with slender, physically fit Christians. *Not* that I'm excusing you for smoking. I think it's a disgusting habit."

"You have such a forgiving spirit," he said dryly.

"So I've been told."

For a moment the noise of chatter in the dining room became too uncomfortable for them to hear each other talk, and Karah Lee contented herself by watching Taylor devour his waffle and bacon.

He didn't even offer her a bite.

The din grew louder as more diners entered. Two people grabbed the extra chairs from Karah Lee and Taylor's table, and Willy, from the boys' ranch, circled the room in his clean white apron, jeans and T-shirt, bussing tables for Bertie. This place would keep all the ranch boys busy if it continued, and it wasn't even a weekend.

When Willy pushed his cart through the swinging doors into the kitchen, Karah Lee caught sight of Blaze at the huge steel sink in back, and she shook her head. At this rate he was going to burn out before he graduated from high school.

Taylor polished off his melon, finished his milk and stacked his dishes back on the tray. His mouth moved, but Karah Lee couldn't hear him above the ruckus.

She leaned forward. "What?"

"I said let's get out of here!" he shouted.

She was glad to comply.

A splash of water reached Fawn through the darkness, and she tried to cry out, to move, to open her eyes so she could see to get a drink.

But her eyes wouldn't open. The refreshing sound faded away, until she was lost again in that nightmare place of heat and screams and frightening faces...until she found herself in a tacky bedroom with still another strange man she had to be nice to. Very nice.

Great-Grandma said nice girls never did things like this. What would she think if she knew?

Even in the darkness, Fawn tried to forget she was alive. Maybe she was going to die.

Then would everything be okay?

♣ *Chapter Twenty-Three* ♣

Taylor felt a surge of relief as he led the way onto the front porch, stepping from the racket of the crowded lobby and dining area into a symphony of peace.

"Ozark silence," he murmured, holding the old-fashioned screen door for Karah Lee.

"What's that?"

"It's a phrase I started using when I first moved here last year." He went down the wooden steps and inhaled the fragrance of sunbaked cedar and felt the touch of a fresh evening breeze. "It's never actually silent here in the Ozarks. There's always the sound of birdsong or wind in the trees or motorboats on the lake, but they're good sounds, filled with life." He ambled across the lawn to the street, and Karah Lee walked beside him.

"Motorboats are filled with life?" she said. "You're kidding."

"You obviously haven't spent much time in the desert."

"Nope, but I'd guess there must be something attractive about even the sound of a boat motor on the lake, if it's evidence of water."

"Exactly."

"That would work for a desert dweller, but I was raised next to the Missouri River, and the sound of a motor seemed like an intrusion to me."

They walked in the grass alongside the road for a few minutes. A whippoorwill shouted its echoing call from a treetop nearby, and a fox squirrel skittered across the road a few yards ahead of them. Taylor realized, suddenly, that he hadn't felt this content in a while.

They strolled past the ancient church building, with its private, fenced, fastidiously maintained cemetery that took up about an acre of ground west of the building. Weeping willows guarded the dead from six vantage points amongst the tombstones, but concrete benches welcomed visitors.

"I love this place," Taylor said.

Karah Lee gave him a strange look. "The cemetery? You come here often? I don't think it counts unless you attend the church next door."

Taylor smiled at the lame joke. "You said you avoid church?"

"That's right."

"Any reason?"

He didn't receive an immediate answer, and he glanced at Karah Lee to find her gazing thoughtfully back at the church building, with its Ozark stone exterior and freshly painted white trim.

"My parents got a divorce," she said. "It was so humiliating to have to face it, and to admit it again and again every time someone asked about Dad at church, that my mother and I both eventually quit going."

"I'd think your church community would have supported you through it."

Karah Lee gave a half shrug. "I think most of them would have, but at the time everyone was as shocked as Mom and I, and they asked a lot of uncomfortable questions. Some old jerk even had the gall to suggest that my mother must have been partly to blame."

"Was she?"

Karah Lee turned and focused her disapproving gaze on Taylor. "My father left my mother for another woman. Yes, my mother had her faults, but no jilted spouse wants to shoulder the blame for someone else's adultery."

"I'm sorry." *Stupid question, idiot!*

"Think nothing of it," she said dryly.

"So after that, you and your mother stopped associating with all those friends you'd made over the years, cutting off ties to your whole support structure."

"You could put it that way."

He watched her silhouette as she studied the tombstones in the cemetery. Her face might not be called classically pretty. She had a firmer than normal chin and a wider than normal mouth. Her eyes, though, struck him with their unusual beauty, the golden amber warming her face. It was said that eyes were the windows to the soul. With Karah Lee, that link seemed a little more firmly established. She was one of those people who didn't usually try to hide their thoughts.

A light breeze blew strands of red hair across her face, and he resisted the urge to smooth them away. She looked so vulnerable, and he felt a surge of sadness for the memories of a divorce that seemed to live with her still.

She turned back to him suddenly. "And you? Do you attend church?"

Uh-oh, back to him again. He shook his head. "To be honest, I guess you could say I quit for the same reason."

"Your divorce?"

He nodded, then strolled back toward the cemetery. "I drive past this place almost every day, and I've always felt drawn here, especially on Sundays, when the parking lot's filled with cars." He trailed his hand along the top of the white fence.

"So why don't you attend?"

He thought about that for a moment. "Maybe I don't feel as if I belong."

"Why not? Just because you're divorced?"

"Not just that. I guess the blow of losing Chip, then my wife, then my partner, all combined to make me wonder if God really was in control, after all, and if so, why was He allowing everything to hit me at once like that?" What was it about this woman that forced him to practice all this self-honesty? Maybe it was her own addiction to blurting out the truth.

"And is He?"

"In control?"

She nodded.

"Yeah, He just doesn't control things the way I want Him to."

"My sister stopped attending church long before our parents divorced," Karah Lee said. "She told me once that she could meet with God anywhere she wanted, and she didn't have to depend on church to communicate with Him."

"And does she communicate with Him?"

"I don't think so. She doesn't even communicate with *me*. At least, not until recently."

"What about you?" Taylor asked. "Do you pray?"

"Sometimes." She frowned, seemed to think about that for a moment, then grimaced. "I guess not very much, except out of desperation for a sick patient. You?"

"I'd like to get back in the habit." Once upon a time, he'd prayed every day, especially after Chip's death, clinging desperately to the knowledge that his son was truly with God. It wasn't until after Clarice left that he'd pushed God away.

She turned and strolled away from him a few feet, gazing up at the sky. "I guess it could be possible that I've tried to use my father as a scapegoat all these years to explain why I've been avoiding God." Her words sounded casual, as if she were repeating something she didn't necessarily believe—even as if someone had said those words to her sometime in the past, or that maybe she'd read them in a book.

"So why have you really been avoiding Him?" Taylor asked.

She tested the gate, then pushed it open and walked through. "I guess you would probably think it was because I've wanted to hold on to my bitterness all these years, and I know that in order to have a good relationship with God, I'd have to release that bitterness." Again the casualness, but this time he caught a thread of tension underlying the words, as if the casualness was feigned.

"Sounds like you've been doing a lot of thinking about it."

"I have an aunt who calls me every few weeks from California." She glanced over her shoulder at him. "She's my mother's older sister. She's quadriplegic, and she has a lot of time to interfere in family problems."

"It sounds as if she also has a lot of time to pray. And to think. Do you ever listen to her when she interferes?"

"Usually I can keep her off the subject, but lately she's been harping on me a lot."

"She sounds like a wise lady." Taylor followed her through the gate. *Oh, Lord, is that what I've been doing all this time? Hiding behind my bitterness? Blaming You for something someone else did? Please forgive me.* "You know, it's possible God's always been there, always waited patiently for us."

"Waited for what?" Karah Lee asked. "I'm a believer."

"You're estranged from God, you said so yourself. What kind of a relationship is that? Maybe He's just waiting for you to admit you want to restore the relationship. Maybe He's just giving us both a chance to get over ourselves and realize that what matters in life is really how we handle all the baggage."

She held his gaze for a moment, then nodded.

"Our churches could have helped us heal, but we rejected the help," he continued.

"What about the jerks who made us feel unwelcome?" she asked. "That *wasn't* a healing experience."

"Could be some are the tares among the wheat. People who weren't planted there by God, but are there to disrupt and destroy the true body of believers. But for the most part, the 'jerks' are just fallible believers like us, who make mistakes and misjudge."

A breeze blew those same strands of hair across her face again, and this time he did reach up and smooth them away. Her eyes widened, but she didn't withdraw.

"You never told me how your son died," she said.

He'd expected to feel pain at the question, but he didn't. It was perfectly natural concern, and it was a relief to share the facts about Chip's death. "He fell from a ladder when he was painting the eaves of our house."

"Did you have a tall house?"

"No, he just fell wrong and hit his head. He'd been doing a job I was supposed to have done months before, but I was too busy working overtime when we were short-staffed."

She stepped around a tombstone and paused at another one, reaching out to trace the dates on it. "This person died fifty years ago," she said softly. "He was eighteen. I wonder if his father took the blame for his death, as well."

Taylor caught the gentle inflection and nodded. "It's difficult not to. A father's supposed to nurture and protect his children." Here he was, spilling his guts to Karah Lee again. He wondered what nightmares would attack him this time. "Tell me about your father," he said, needing badly to change the subject.

"There isn't much to tell. It's the typical family divorce story. We lived in the tiny burg of Rockwell, on the shore of the Missouri River, just a few miles from Columbia, where everyone knows everyone else. It all fell apart when Dad filed for divorce the summer after I graduated from high school. He's tried to make up for it ever since, but he's gone about it totally wrong."

"How's that?"

"By using his influence to make sure I got into the right school, got good grades, got the residency I wanted."

"You didn't want him to do that?"

"I didn't even *know* he'd been doing it until my first day on the job here." She turned away from the tombstone and strolled across the grass toward the old church building. "I understand that he wanted to try to make up for the divorce, but now I've got all these...I don't know...all these doubts about myself. I mean, every time I get a challenging case, I agonize over whether or not I'll be able to handle it. If my *father* didn't think I was capable of earning my medical degree on my own—and he's in a position where he has to be able to judge people, judge abilities—then what if he's right about me?"

"Why don't you take your eyes off your earthly father for a while and turn your attention to Someone who knows a lot more about you?"

She turned and looked up at Taylor, and the play of emotions across her face went from confusion to gradual understanding to—

She glanced suddenly toward the road, and all expression froze. She grabbed Taylor's arm. "That's the man I told you about. That's 'Detective' Withnell."

He automatically scanned the late-model gold Buick sedan and studied the face of its occupant as he drove past. The man had a long, brooding face, dark features, and he wore a dark suit. "That's the guy who claimed to be a federal investigator?"

"It's him."

Taylor automatically read the license plate, repeated it in his mind, then repeated it again as the man drove away. "I'm pretty sure I've seen him a couple of times today." He pulled his cell phone from his belt, flipped it open and hit Greg's speed-dial number.

When the sheriff answered, Taylor explained the situation to him briefly, gave him the license number to check out, disconnected.

"What's up?" Karah Lee asked.

"He's going to check it out, see if he can come up with anything. Want to take a walk up to the square? Apparently, Tom's mingling somewhere with the party-boat crowd, and the first tour just returned a few minutes ago. I think we need to compare notes."

"I'll hang around here for a while."

Taylor glanced around them. "In a *cemetery?* It's getting dark."

"I'm a big girl."

Taylor glanced along the road where the car had disappeared. Could be the man was just headed out of the area for the evening. But what if he wasn't?

"I don't think so," Taylor said. "Why don't I walk you back to the house. That man may suddenly decide he wants to ask you a few more questions."

"I'll tell him the same thing I told him before. And I want to stay here for a while."

"Why?"

Her quick grin surprised him. "Would you relax and stop trying to take responsibility for the whole world? You're acting spooked."

"With good reason."

"Haven't you ever wanted to just relax in your peaceful Ozark silence and be alone?"

"Sure, but—"

"I'm not going to get that back at the lodge, even up in my room, with all the commotion downstairs. If you're so sure God is watching over us in spite of ourselves, then give Him a chance to work with me, okay? Now go. I've got some thinking to do."

He nodded and left her to her thoughts.

❧ *Chapter Twenty-Four* ❧

Karah Lee stood in the churchyard watching Taylor walk away, and it seemed to her as if the very air around her grew still. She couldn't believe she'd actually listened to a sermon for the first time in over a decade, and it had been preached right here in this cemetery by a man who, like her, also avoided church.

Talk about a miracle.

According to Taylor, God was waiting for her to speak. She could pour her heart out to Him right now, in this quiet place.

She'd known that since she was a little girl, but it had taken Taylor to remind her.

How did one make contact with God again after so many years of estrangement? All her upbringing reminded her she would have to apologize first, confess all her sins, and...and that could take all night. She wouldn't even get a chance to say hi.

She'd been raised to believe that she could pray anytime, anywhere, but the peacefulness of this place was especially conducive to prayer. In her suite at the house, she would have to keep her windows open and the fan going because the air-conditioning hadn't been installed yet, and the noise of the crowd could be distracting. So this was a better place for her to pray.

She just didn't know where to start.

She glanced toward Taylor's retreating figure. He had a long, powerful stride, wide, muscular shoulders and, even more important, he had a strong streak of honesty that was more attractive to her than all those physical attributes combined.

A car approached from behind Karah Lee on the road, and she turned to find that same gold Buick sedan cruising back toward town, coming a little too slowly past the cemetery again. Withnell's gaze skimmed over the tops of the tombstones toward the thicket of trees between the church grounds and the lake, then he looked at Karah Lee.

He was not smiling.

She didn't smile either.

His car slowed further, and he glanced toward the driveway, as if he might pull in. Taylor chose that moment to pause and turn, then casually take a couple of steps out into the road, hands on his hips, ranger hat pulled low over his face, though the sun had long ago settled past the tree-lined horizon.

The phony "investigator" cruised on past the church and continued his drive to town.

Karah Lee gave a relieved sigh and looked heavenward. "Thank you, Lord." She'd needed that gentle but powerful reminder that God was involved in every situation in her life. "I'm not feeling very talkative right now, and I don't even know where to start. I know you haven't left me the way Dad did, and yet it's been hard not to think that way." Taylor was right—*she* was the one who had left.

She thought about Taylor's grief over his son. Had God grieved that way when she withdrew from Him? "Oh, God, I'm sorry. I never wanted to cause you pain. I was only thinking of my own pain. When my own father rejected me, it seemed as if You rejected me then, too." But her human father wasn't God. Just because she'd felt she was unlovable by human standards, she wasn't unlovable by divine standards.

"Life's been confusing," she whispered to Him. "Especially where my faith in You is concerned." She closed her eyes and remembered a passage of scripture she and her sister had both been taught by a charismatic youth leader in their early teens. "For I am convinced that 'neither death nor life, neither angels nor demons'...nor something else I can't remember...'nor height nor depth'—which is a big deal because I'm scared of heights—'nor anything else will be able to separate us from the love of God that is in Christ Jesus our Lord.' That means Dad, too, doesn't it? He can't separate me?"

But she had allowed her dad's choices to impact her own in a destructive way, by convincing her that she had, indeed, lost God's love. And though nothing God created could separate her from His love, what if she just walked away from it? How long would He wait for her to return?

And what if she didn't return? Would she still be bound for heaven when she died, or had she walked away from that, too?

But none of that mattered for her any longer. "Lord," she whispered, feeling a long-lost sense of peace settle over her, "I'm back."

Taylor watched the Buick drive past, then called the sheriff again, still strolling with what he hoped was apparent casualness toward his Jeep, parked on the square.

"Yeah, Taylor," Greg said.

"Did you find any information on the plates?"

"Nothing outstanding, but that car isn't registered to any federal agency, or anyone named Withnell."

Taylor could have told him that. "I tried calling Tom and couldn't reach him. Do you know if he's still downtown?" He scanned the crowd of visitors who were presently boarding the paddleboat.

"He hasn't told me he was leaving, but he might have his phone turned off. You could probably find him at the construction site. Unofficially."

Taylor watched as the gold Buick rounded the curve at the far end of the square and then pulled onto the grass beneath a tree and parked. "I'll let him snoop for a while. I need to keep watch on this guy. He was showing a little too much interest in Dr. Fletcher a few minutes ago."

Greg chuckled. "Taylor, I've never seen you jealous before."

Taylor shook his head. The lack of professionalism around here was occasionally frustrating. "The man we're discussing entered the clinic claiming to be a federal agent seeking information about a patient who came in last Friday on that bus of sick folks. And now it appears he's lying about being a federal agent."

There was a thoughtful pause. "Well, that's a bad deal, I know, but why are you suddenly so hot about it?"

Taylor hesitated. "You know that young woman we were discussing Sunday?"

"The murder suspect?"

"Yes."

"What about her?"

"That's who he was looking for." As Taylor neared the square, the man got out of the car and closed the door, glanced around at the crowd, then immediately fell into step behind a group of tourists headed for the beach.

"You're talking about the woman Karah Lee had us searching for the other day?"

"That's the one," Taylor said, clamping the phone tightly to his ear as he hurried to catch up with the suit.

"What's your take on her?"

"I think that kid was no murderer."

"I'm not asking you to be judge or jury, I'm asking if you think that kid was actually the woman who's been accused of killing her boyfriend and the hotel employee. Fawn Morrison."

Taylor was not a liar. He said a silent apology to Karah

Lee. "I think it could be the same person whose picture's been circulated, but there's a lot more to this case than we've heard. A lot more. This investigator could be dangerous. Dr. Fletcher wouldn't have mentioned him if she hadn't felt it was significant."

"In other words, you think Fawn Morrison has been in Hideaway."

"Yes."

"But we never found that patient the other day, remember? If that woman ever was here, she's long gone now."

"Not necessarily," Taylor said. "She could be hiding, or in disguise again." He thought about the woman Junior Short had spotted entering Dane's feed store, and about the "child" who had apparently broken into the clinic. "In fact, Greg, I think it's likely she's still around somewhere."

"Obviously, so does the man with the gold Buick. Maybe you'd better tell Doc Fletcher to stay away from the guy."

The suit stopped at the dock, and for a moment Taylor was afraid he would get on board the paddleboat. But he didn't. A familiar-looking man stepped from the boat—the guard who had evicted Taylor from Karah Lee's destroyed rental last week.

"I think I'd better give Lieutenant Milfred a call," Greg said.

"Maybe you should." Taylor signed off and plunged through a crowd of laughing partyers who had apparently been on the previous boat cruise and had chosen to hang out on the shore and continue their party.

He brushed past a man wearing an indiscreet racing swimsuit that did nothing to hide his love handles or his paunch.

"People get weirded out on that boat, don't you watch them?" the man was saying to a woman in a one-piece. "I was standing right over there on the dock when somebody jumped overboard, and the boat went on without him, like nobody even noticed."

"What happened to the man overboard?" she asked.

"Swam ashore, shook off the extra water and walked away."

"You saw all that?"

"Sure. The party sounded like it was getting a little wild, if you know what I mean, but still, you'd think they'd keep a better watch on their guests."

Taylor heard no more as they walked away. Evening had deepened to the point that he couldn't see the cemetery in the gloom, and when a rowdy group of teenagers jostled past him, he lost his quarry. Withnell was gone.

Taylor rushed across the lawn toward the place he had last seen the man. Nothing. He had disappeared. Taylor's radio sounded the alert for a first-responder call. There'd been an accident at the construction site.

He had no choice. The ambulance was twenty minutes away. He had to answer the call.

As he ran back to his Jeep, he dialed the bed-and-breakfast and asked Edith to ring Karah Lee's room. Maybe she'd had the sense to return.

There was no answer.

By the time Edith came back on the line, Taylor was in the Jeep driving through town with his siren blaring and lights flashing.

"What on earth's that racket?" she asked.

"I've got a call. Edith, I need your help."

"Help me!"

Fawn awakened and realized she had cried out. Her throat felt as if that hot sand filled it. She tried to lick her lips. Her tongue felt crackly-dry.

She opened her eyes to see the treetops looming over her in the blackening sky, and for a few seconds she didn't know if it was really the sky or if she was delirious.

The sound of a motorboat reached her from the distance, and the familiar wash of water from the paddleboat she'd seen earlier. What she wouldn't give to be under that splash of water right now. She was so thirsty.

The lake was only a few feet away...if she could only crawl down there.

She struggled to get up, but she didn't have the strength. Rocks dug into her back as she collapsed again.

"Please," she whispered. "Help."

Karah Lee watched the sky deepen from dusty rose to dusky purple. The stars flickered, demanding attention. Whoever thought a cemetery was a spooky place at night? Out here, the crowd didn't chatter or clamor for attention, and she didn't have to worry if she was going to get a case she couldn't handle.

The cemetery also served to remind her that, no

matter what heroic steps she might take to save a life, eventually, and inevitably, she didn't have the final say. God did.

That was a strangely comforting thought.

Still, she didn't have a flashlight, and she didn't want to sprain an ankle on her way back to the bed-and-breakfast. She cast one last, lingering gaze at the night sky, and was turning to leave when she heard a rustle in the trees down by the water. She stopped to listen, and heard a faint cry.

It sounded like a wounded baby rabbit—they used to get those when she was growing up, when a cat would find the nest of babies. A couple of times, she and Shona had been able to rescue the babies and bring them into the house, but they never lived.

The cry came again from the woods. No, it wasn't a baby rabbit. It sounded more like a lost kitten this time.

Now she wished she'd thought to bring a flashlight. Perhaps it would be best to go back to her room and get one, then come back here and check out the problem. If Blaze was still working in the kitchen, he'd likely want to help.

She strolled across the church lawn, reading the little sign in front. It was Hideaway Methodist. She had cousins who were Methodists. She'd never understood the differences too much when she was growing up—

The cry came again.

Karah Lee stopped, frowning. This time it hadn't sounded like a kitten or a baby rabbit. It had almost sounded...

"...please...help..."

Human. Karah Lee retraced her steps to the cemetery fence, then turned and followed it around the back of the church. "Hello? Who's there?"

Again, the soft, unintelligible cry, like someone too hoarse to speak.

Karah Lee crept into the heavy night shadows of the woods, stepping cautiously toward the spot where she had last heard the cry. All she heard was the lap of lake water, driven against the shore by a fresh breeze.

"Who's there?" she called again.

A wisp of sound reached her from beneath a tree a few feet away. She took a step forward, recognizing this spot. The blue tree trunk. A woman with gray hair, dressed in denim.

She knelt beside the woman, and caught her breath. "Casey?"

Chapter Twenty-Five

Taylor stepped from the Jeep onto the rocky ground of the freshly dozed site and gazed up at the dark skeleton of the building. He caught the glow of a beam of focused light on the third floor.

"First responder," he called out. "Will I need climbing equipment?"

"No, but someone's fallen up here. Bring a backboard if you have one." The flashlight beam brightened as footsteps clumped along a wooden walkway. The beam angled downward on Taylor and flicked into his eyes. "Jackson, that you?" It was Tom.

Taylor winced and shaded his eyes. "Redirect that thing, will you?"

The beam withdrew. "Sorry. Watch your step," Tom called, his voice echoing against the cliffs to the north of them. "There's holes all over the ground down there, like some kid's been playing with the backhoe. There's rough wooden stairs to your left that the workers use."

Taylor pulled his emergency medical kit from the back seat and reached for his backboard fastened to the top of the Jeep. "Where's the patient?"

"Third floor."

Taylor entered the dark building and switched on his own flashlight. The stairs were obviously built for temporary use only. He found Tom at the top of the steps waiting for him. The lanky blond deputy was definitely out of uniform. *Shorts and a tank top?*

"Tom, what are you wearing?"

"The latest police fashion statement. Like it?"

"It looks wet."

"It is." Tom's voice dropped, and he gestured along the narrow, wood-planked walkway, which stretched the distance from the front of the building to the back. "Better get your board over there. I don't know how far he fell. I hate these tall buildings."

"You've made that clear to most of Hideaway."

A dark shadow of a man sprawled across the center of the walkway, and a ladder lay at an awkward angle beside him, upside down.

"I think he's one of the new guards they hired to watch this place." Tom led Taylor over to the victim—an extraordinarily muscular man with short, dark hair and a neatly trimmed beard and mustache.

"Could you tell if he was breathing?" Taylor asked, setting his backboard and medical case next to him.

"He was moaning when I found him, which is how I found him."

The victim lay on his back; he wore coaching shorts and a muscle shirt. His face matched the paleness of the wood on which he lay, and his eyes were closed.

Taylor inhaled the scent of freshly cut wood and recently poured concrete. And lake water. He sniffed, and as he knelt over his patient, he looked more closely at Tom. "You've been swimming?"

"I like to keep in shape. Be careful with this guy. He dropped his gun, but I think those arms are lethal weapons."

"Gun?"

Tom held up the weapon. "I've got it. Don't worry, I'll cover you."

Taylor crouched over the victim. "Hello? Can you hear me? Sir, I'm a first responder, Ranger Taylor Jackson."

Nothing.

Taylor did a sternal rub. It didn't rouse the man.

Tom hunkered down next to Taylor. "Is he still breathing?"

"Yes." Someday Taylor was going to teach Tom the bare basics of emergency medical techniques.

Taylor did a quick check of the patient's sugar level, blood pressure, heart rate and respirations. The man's breathing sounded as if it was becoming labored.

Taylor pulled an ambu bag from his supplies and was placing it over the victim's face when the man's eyes flew open and his arm swung up, knocking Taylor sideways without warning.

Taylor grabbed the arm and shoved it aside.

The man swung with his other arm, and Tom lunged for him, knocking the flashlight away in a rolling spin that cast strobing shadows around them. "Hold it, there, buddy, settle down."

The prone man's eyes flew open in the glow of the flashlight. One of his muscled arms escaped Tom's grip, and Taylor made a grab for it and held him down. The man moaned in delirium.

"We've got to get him restrained before he injures himself or us," Taylor said.

"Does it look like I've got handcuffs on me?" Tom complained. "Drug him. It's all you can do."

Taylor reluctantly agreed, and though chemical restraint could further depress the man's respirations, it would be preferable to risking further injury. He pulled a vial from his medical case, unpackaged a syringe and filled it, then plunged the needle. They held the patient down until the medication had time to work.

"Guess you know they've had their first tremors down in Arkansas," Tom said by way of conversation. "Earthquake's doing its thing."

"You've been online tonight?"

"I'm keeping my eye on it."

"Tom, we won't even feel it here."

"Want to bet? Down between Berryville and the state line? We're practically on the epicenter."

"What's the prediction on the Richter scale?"

"Good question."

"His muscles are relaxing," Taylor said. "Let's get him strapped to the backboard."

After the man was further restrained, Taylor took out his penlight and checked his eyes. "Looks like you've been on a bad trip, mister. Have you been taking some hard stuff?"

The man closed his eyes.

"Muscle builder?" Taylor continued.

"Maybe some GHB to keep the strength going?" Tom suggested. "That stuff's flowing hard and heavy on the boat parties."

"Oh, really?" Taylor asked. "You know that for a fact?"

"Just took a ride, myself."

"Don't tell me you were the one who fell off the boat," Taylor said.

"I didn't fall, I dived." Tom shook the patient's arms. "So what about it? GHB so you can work extra hours following people like me around town? Or maybe you just couldn't resist doing the stuff while you were on duty. Were you planning to jump me?" He cocked a bushy eyebrow at Taylor. "What do you bet he works for Beaufont? Maybe they pay part of their wages in drugs now, to stay ahead of taxes."

The guy slurred an obscenity under his breath.

"Want to tell me what happened here?" Taylor asked.

The man opened his eyes and glared. "The earth moved."

Tom nodded at Taylor. "See there? Told you we'd feel it this far up."

Fawn shrank against the trunk of the tree, mouth open in a silent cry for help. Her heartbeat seemed to pound through her head as the shadow knelt beside her, touched her chin, reassured her.

"I'm not going to hurt you, Casey."

In a wash of weakness, she thought she recognized that voice. "Who are you?" She could only mouth the words and hear the pitiful sound a little kitten made when it meowed.

"It's me," the woman said. "Karah Lee Fletcher. Don't you remember me? I was the doctor who treated you the other day."

Dr. Karah Lee. Fawn wanted to cry. She reached up and touched the doctor's arm, wrapped her fingers over it and squeezed. "I'm scared. Help me," she wheezed.

"I'm going to, but I need to check you for injury before I can move you," the doctor said.

Fawn shook her head. She wasn't hurt, she was sick.

Amazingly, the doctor seemed to understand. "Then I'm going to take you to the clinic." She reached down and placed her right arm beneath Fawn's shoulder blades, and her left arm beneath Fawn's knees and lifted her with a soft grunt. "Honey, can you put your arms around me?" The doctor's voice was firm and strong in Fawn's ear. "I don't want to have to carry you over my shoulder."

Fawn reached up and tried to grasp the doctor around the neck. She couldn't get a good grip. The strength had poured from her body with the sweat that had dripped from her all day long.

"Just hold on if you can," Karah Lee said.

Fawn pressed the side of her face against the doctor's collarbone and leaned into her, hearing the snap of twigs and the brush of branches against their clothing in the short trek through the forest. And she listened to the strong rhythm of the woman's heartbeat, and her own breathing.

Several times, Karah Lee turned and backed through the branches to keep them from striking Fawn.

As soon as they emerged from the woods, Karah Lee hefted Fawn up higher in her arms. Fawn reached around the doctor's neck and tried again to clasp her hands together, then turned her head to see where they were going.

Karah Lee stopped suddenly, catching her breath, her arms tightening around Fawn. A soft glow of light flickered around the side of the church building, highlighting the overhang of the eave and the outline of hedge.

Karah Lee stiffened, then took a step backward, then another step, and another until they were hidden once more in the deeper shadow of the trees.

The flashlight beam sliced through the darkness and skidded across the tops of tombstones in the cemetery, as if searching for something. Or someone.

Fawn's focus remained on that light until she heard the wailing cry of a siren slither over their heads from the hills.

She stiffened. No! The police were coming to get her! This wasn't a rescue, it was an arrest.

She struggled within her captor's tight grip.

"Shh. Casey, stop it!" It was just a breath of sound, and the arms tightened more firmly around her, then Karah Lee pressed her mouth next to Fawn's ear. "We could be in danger. Be still!"

I'm already in danger. Once again, she struggled in the woman's grasp. Like steel bars of a jail cell, the arms held her.

Taylor heard the echo of the siren against the cliffs. Thank God. The patient appeared to have a broken left ankle, and Taylor was glad he'd thought to strap the spine board to the Jeep last week. Now he only hoped he would get the board back sometime in the future. He'd learned long ago to keep a close eye on his equipment, or it could get "lost" in the shuffle of patients to other hospitals.

"You were really on that paddleboat?" he asked Tom.

"Sure was." Tom stepped over to the end of the building, flashlight in hand, to signal to the driver where they were.

Taylor joined him. "You're not exactly an undercover agent, Tom."

"Not trying to be."

"You don't have a gun or anything?"

"Sure, in my car."

"I don't see a bulletproof vest under that skimpy shirt."

"I took my chances," Tom said. "You'd be surprised what a guy can find out at one of those parties when at least half the passengers are either drunk or high on something."

"How did you happen to hear our friendly patient?" Taylor asked.

"Pure luck." Tom's sarcasm was palpable, his gaze fixed on the flashing lights as the ambulance came around the curve from the hillside into the western edge of Hideaway, past the church and the bed-and-breakfast.

Taylor shone his light on their patient to make sure he was still in place, even though the man was restrained and the monitor was beeping faithfully. "So you think he's with Beaufont? What happened on the boat?"

Tom leaned closer to Taylor and murmured, "I found out they're insured to the hilt."

"You heard that on the boat?"

"I found that out from some contacts in Springfield. An old college roommate of mine's been doing some research for me."

"So Beaufont shows some financial responsibility. I don't have a problem with that."

Tom gave him a disgruntled look. "Do you have a problem with this crazy guy packing heat? How serious does it have to get for you to realize these people mean business? I'm telling you, I had to hit the water and swim to shore, because they caught me in the cockpit and they were on me like mud in a pigpen." He raised his flashlight and motioned to the attendants with the doors opened on the ambulance. "We're up here, Joe."

"Karah Lee? That you?"

Karah Lee released a breath she didn't realize she'd been holding, and stepped from the shadows into the beam of Blaze's flashlight. "I'm going to tie a cowbell around your neck if you sneak up on me like that again." She felt Casey stiffen once more in her arms. "It's okay, honey. He's one of the good guys. You remember Blaze?"

The girl relaxed.

"What's going on down here?" Blaze hurried down the

gentle slope from the church. "Taylor called the Lakeside, all bent out of shape, wanting you to get indoors immediately, and he didn't say why, didn't have time to talk, but I think he meant what he said." He reached Karah Lee, keeping the beam of his light aimed at the ground, and not in her face or Casey's. Thoughtful kid.

"I'm glad you're here," Karah Lee said, repositioning her grip on her heavy burden.

"Casey!" Blaze exclaimed. "Where'd you come from? What happened?"

"She's sick," Karah Lee said.

Blaze's eyes bugged out. *"She?"*

"Do you have your keys to the clinic? She needs treatment now. She's dehydrated, barely functional, and we'll probably need another ambulance out here." She felt Casey stiffen in her arms once more.

"The keys are in my pocket." Blaze reached for Casey. "Give her to me. No offense, but you're about to drop her, and I've been carrying hay bales on weekends when I'm not working for Bertie. I don't guess your car's down here anywhere."

Karah Lee gratefully relinquished her load and took Blaze's flashlight. "Not when I can *walk* the two blocks. Let's get to the clinic."

Chapter Twenty-Six

The overhead lights in the clinic nearly blinded Fawn, but the pillowcase felt soft and cool against her neck and the right side of her face as Blaze gently lowered her onto the exam bed. It was the same bed where she'd slept last night. She automatically glanced toward the stainless-steel tray table she'd used as a nightstand, and where she'd left the books this morning in her rush to escape. They were gone, of course.

Had someone found the chip and candy-bar wrappers in the trash can yet?

It didn't matter. She was in such big trouble now, stealing some food wouldn't even count.

Water splashed somewhere behind her while Karah Lee quietly gave Blaze instructions that Fawn didn't completely understand—something about WD-50 or something, which sounded like motor oil to Fawn. Were they giving her a lube job?

The important thing was that they didn't make any telephone calls, and wherever that siren had come from earlier, it hadn't brought any policemen or ambulance people to this place.

And then Blaze left the room.

Fawn stiffened. "No," she squeaked.

"It's okay," Karah Lee said, leaning down beside her and holding her gaze with gentle concern. "He's just going to the supply room. If we were going to call anyone, we have a telephone right here, Casey. I'm not going to do anything behind your back."

Fawn studied the woman's face carefully. Some people could lie really well. She'd thought this doctor was different, but... "You called the police on me," she rasped, barely doing more than mouthing the words.

"You mean last Friday? I didn't have to call them, because Taylor was already here, remember? He called the sheriff for help, and I asked him not to give them any particulars about your case."

Fawn wasn't sure she believed that. She shook her head.

"Look," Karah Lee said. "I was concerned for your safety, and I'm legally bound to do anything necessary to protect my patient, even if that does mean calling the police."

"But you don't—"

Karah Lee placed a finger over Fawn's dry lips. "Don't try to talk right now. I know you're in some kind of trouble, and you need help. I'll do my best to treat you and protect you, and in order to do that I may still have to call for reinforcements, or send you to a larger, better-equipped facility."

Again, Fawn tried to speak, and again, Karah Lee stopped her with a quick shake of her head. "I need to ask you a question, and it'll help me a lot if you're honest with me."

Fawn wouldn't promise any answers.

"I know your real name isn't Casey," Karah Lee said. "Is it Fawn Morrison?" As she asked the question, Blaze came back into the room with a tray of supplies and didn't break stride. He didn't even seem surprised.

"Please," Fawn whispered. "Don't call."

Karah Lee closed her eyes and took a deep breath, then looked away as she exhaled and stood. "First we'll treat you. Then we'll talk—if we can manage to coax your voice back to life." She nodded to Blaze, then reached for the tray he'd carried into the room. "Get her vitals, then give her some water. I'll set up for the IV."

"Gotcha, boss." Blaze put a cuff around Fawn's left upper arm. "Fawn, huh?" he said in that actor-smooth voice. "Pretty name. You don't look much like the woman in the papers and on television. Was all that blond hair a wig?"

"Blaze, don't make her speak until we can soothe those vocal cords and plump up her cells a little," Karah Lee said.

Fawn shook her head.

"Did you cut it to disguise yourself last week?"

She nodded.

"Brave move. Good job, too. I think Karah Lee could use a good haircut."

"Hey!" Karah Lee complained as she worked across from him.

"Just a suggestion. Okay, Fawn, I'm taking your blood pressure and heart rate, then I'm going to get your temperature. After that, you can have some water, okay?"

She nodded, watching him work, and especially watching his face. He wasn't smiling, exactly, but he looked satisfied doing what he was doing, as if he thought it was the most fun job in the world. He was smart, too. She'd heard him coaching Karah Lee on the computer last night—though she hadn't heard much of what he'd told her because the stupid hot-water heater kept kicking on and drowning out the voices.

After jotting something on a clipboard sheet, Blaze glanced at Fawn and caught her watching him. He smiled, and those dark, dark eyes seemed to have lights in them. She tried to smile back and felt her lips crack painfully. She winced.

"I'll get some petroleum jelly for that," he said, his voice gentle.

She suddenly realized she stunk. Badly. He had to've noticed. How long since she'd had a bath? Yesterday? And she'd sweated like a horse all day today. She smelled like a street person—and since she'd *been* a street person a couple of times, she knew how that smelled.

Okay, so she didn't exactly smell like that yet.

Karah Lee pushed the IV pole to the side of the bed and hung a bag on the hook. "Honey, I'm going to get those fluids going on you now. You already know the routine, so just try to relax. I'll be as gentle as—"

"Wait," Fawn rasped. Before Karah Lee could take her arm prisoner, she reached into the right front pocket of her jeans and pulled out the flash drive. She held it up to Blaze.

He looked up from his clipboard and stared at it, then at her, then back at it. "I'm an idiot," he said softly, taking it from her. "Why didn't I realize it was you in here last night?"

"Okay," Karah Lee said. "Now that's established, can we get back to work here? Fawn, your arm, please."

"Take care of it," Fawn croaked to Blaze.

He held the device up to the light and studied it as Karah Lee opened a couple of small packets and rubbed alcohol on the inside of Fawn's right arm, near the place she'd inserted the IV needle last Friday.

"There must be something pretty important on here for you to break in and crash the computer last night," Blaze said.

Fawn nodded.

"Mind if I take a look at it?" he asked.

"I do," Karah Lee said. "This young lady's in deep trouble, wanted by the police and most likely someone on the other side of the law. You don't need to be messing with that stuff, you need to be helping me with Fawn."

"But this could be—"

"First, do no harm," Karah Lee said. "Which means keep an eye on her vitals, then do the labs on her blood for me when I get it."

"I'm not certified."

"You know your way around that lab better than I do, and right now we're breaking the law, anyway, because we haven't reported her immediately. All I want are some answers, fast."

Fawn shook her head. "But—"

"Hush," Karah Lee said. "Just close your eyes and relax. We'll worry about this other stuff later."

Fawn tried to do as she was told. She wished she could snuggle into the bed and cover up her face and sleep forever...after she had a drink of water and a bath.

"Blood pressure's eighty-eight over fifty-five," Blaze said. "Heart rate a hundred twenty. Temperature's a hundred two point two."

"We'll get that down quickly."

A needle pricked Fawn's arm and she jerked, startled. Her eyes flew open.

"So," Blaze said, leaning over her left side to place a straw in her mouth. "Thirsty?"

Her lips barely functioned, and for a couple of seconds she sucked air. He adjusted the straw, and she felt the first spurt of cool, sweet, filled-with-life water trickle over her tongue and down her throat. She closed her eyes and gave herself to the pleasure of four hard, fast gulps before the glass emptied. Small glass.

Blaze chuckled. "You're going to have to take it easy on the next drink. So, you like dogs, do you? Dalmatians and cocker spaniels, like in the books?"

She nodded, then looked at her arm in time to see her own blood flash up into a tube connected to the IV needle.

"I'm drawing some blood from the IV hub, Fawn," Karah Lee said. "Then I'm going to rehydrate you while we run analysis in the lab."

"You mean while I run the analysis," Blaze muttered, returning to Fawn's side with more water.

* * *

"I promise to get this board back to you," Joe the paramedic said as the four of them carried their patient down the wooden stairway.

"I'd appreciate it." Taylor followed them. He knew there was another backboard at the clinic he could borrow for runs, but he wanted this one back.

He gave his report to the ambulance team as he and Tom helped them place their patient on the stretcher, then watched with relief as the big red, white and orange van drove away.

Tom punched Taylor on the arm. "What do you want to bet Beaufont's going to have some wild tale to tell us about all this?"

"They can tell the feds."

"Not before I get a few questions answered."

"Then you'd better hurry, because Greg's already made a call."

"When?" Tom's voice picked up an edge. He hated it when anyone got the jump on him.

"A few minutes ago. Apparently, there's been someone hanging around town impersonating a federal agent."

Tom whistled. "Tell you what, Jackson, I think you're one of those guys who bring trouble with them. This place was never so exciting before you came to Missouri."

"Gee, thanks." Taylor aimed his flashlight across the pocked and rocky ground. "So when will you be back in uniform?"

"Soon as you stop trying to give me orders."

"Your wish is granted." Taylor glanced toward the Lakeside and reached for his cell phone. "I'll see you later."

He dialed the bed-and-breakfast as Tom sauntered away. Edith answered and relayed the unfortunate news that not only hadn't Karah Lee returned, but Blaze was gone now, too.

Taylor thanked her and hung up

Karah Lee placed a motherly hand across Fawn's forehead, checking her temperature the old-fashioned, though less reliable, way. The skin felt much cooler, though still not back to normal. Fawn's forehead was moist with slight perspiration—still not enough, but at least her body was functioning better. Blaze had given her two tablets of acetaminophen with her second glass of water about twenty minutes ago, and that, too, would have helped.

Karah Lee placed the tympanic thermometer in Fawn's ear and drew it back out. The girl's temperature was now under a hundred. "Your fever's broken, honey."

"I feel better." Fawn's voice was still soft, but it sounded stronger. "Are you going to call the police?"

"If I say yes, are you going to bolt again?"

Fawn blinked up at Karah Lee, and those clear blue eyes held hers. "Maybe. Can't you look at the flash drive first? Please."

"What's on it?"

"I don't know for sure, but Bruce gave it to me that...that night."

A frisson of horror trickled down Karah Lee's spine. "The night he was murdered?"

"Yes, and he said that there was important information in it that lives could depend on, and that if anything happened I should give it to someone I trusted to—"

"Okay, but I think we should just give it to the police and let them—"

"I don't *trust* the police, I trust *you.*"

"I couldn't do anything with any information I might find on there." *Lives could depend on it?* "Now just lie there and rest and let me do the worrying for a few minutes, okay?"

"But you're not worrying about the flash drive, you're just blowing me off," Fawn accused. "Let Blaze look at it if you don't want to."

"I'll talk to him about it." Karah Lee adjusted the tubing so that it lay more neatly across the side of the bed. "And let me warn you now, if you remove this IV catheter again, you won't be doing yourself any favors. The next needle will be bigger."

Fawn looked down at her arm, then narrowed her eyes at Karah Lee. "That's mean."

"No, it isn't. The only reason I didn't use a larger needle was because you were too dehydrated for me to get the stick." She gave Fawn a wicked grin. "Now you aren't." She went down the hall to the lab.

She didn't risk losing sight of the exam-room door, and was relieved to find Blaze just pulling a sheet from the lab's printer.

"You should get certified on that thing," she said.

"I will as soon as we hire someone else here, Bertie gets more help at the Lakeside, haying season is over, Dane sells some calves and the pig races are over." He handed her the sheet. "The CBC shows a high white count, and the automated differential shows that Fawn's body is losing the battle against infection. What else do you want me to do, fearless slave driver?"

She glanced down at the numbers and nodded. "She needed antibiotics last week."

"The sterile water is already on the supply-room counter, waiting to reconstitute whatever you want mixed with it."

"My hero."

"What do you want me to—"

"I'll mix the medicine, you check out that flash drive Fawn gave you. I want a better handle on whatever's going on with her, and she seems to think that drive will have some answers."

There was no mistaking the sudden light in Blaze's eyes. "I'll fire up the computer."

Chapter Twenty-Seven

Taylor sped from the construction site, watching the street for stray partyers on his way to the church. Why wasn't Karah Lee back at the bed-and-breakfast yet? Or maybe she was already in her room and Edith hadn't seen her.

Or maybe something else had happened....

In spite of the hour, several people still mingled in the park and on the sidewalk on the square. Taylor spotted a campfire down by the beach, and several people sitting on the edge of the dock. He was about to cruise on past the square, when he noticed light coming through the door at the clinic and screeched his tires as he pulled to the curb.

He jumped from the Jeep, pressed the automatic lock with his key chain and charged inside, through the foyer and into the waiting room—the entrance doors weren't locked, and the door to the clinic proper stood open.

Blaze sat at the computer in the reception office, and he turned around, looking frustrated, when Taylor arrived. "You know anything about computers?"

"Not much. Tom's the expert in that department, much as I hate to admit it. Where's Karah Lee? Have you seen her? Did she—"

"Sure, I saw her." Blaze picked up the phone. "I thought you were the one who wanted me to go find her at the church. She's back with a patient."

Taylor went weak with relief, then wondered why he'd suddenly started worrying so much about Karah Lee's well-being. Except for the fact that there were a lot of strange things happening in this town lately, and...

"What patient?" he asked.

Blaze looked up from the receiver in his hand. He hesitated. "Maybe you should talk to Karah Lee about that."

"Oh, great, now we're back to patient-confidentiality issues."

"Not exactly. Not this time." Blaze leaned to the left and called down the hallway, "Karah Lee? You might want to come out here."

While Blaze talked to Tom on the telephone, Karah Lee stepped from exam room four, looking incongruous in her khaki shorts and turquoise T-shirt in this setting. When she saw Taylor she closed her eyes and took a deep breath.

He watched her closely. *Something weird going on here...*

She glanced back into the exam room. "I didn't call the police, Fawn, but Taylor's here."

Taylor's mouth fell open. "Fawn?"

"No!" came a feminine, recognizable voice from the room.

"It's time," Karah Lee said. "You can trust him."

"She's *here?*" Taylor asked.

Karah Lee nodded and gestured for him to join her.

"As in Fawn Morrison?"

She rolled her eyes. "You know any other Fawns?"

He rushed down the hallway. Karah Lee gestured him into the room, and he saw a young woman lying on the exam bed.

Instead of the boyish disguise she'd worn last Friday, this time she had short, gray hair. Her frightened blue eyes contrasted vividly against the fiery red skin of her face. The glasses she'd been wearing Friday were nowhere in evidence. She wore denim. She was the mysterious woman in blue with the "bad sunburn" Junior Short had seen entering Dane's feed store yesterday evening.

Taylor caught a whiff of body odor as he stepped close to the bed. "Hi, Fawn." He kept his voice casual, gentle. She didn't look prepared to handle all the questions that desperately needed to be asked.

She waved at him with a trembling left hand. Her right arm was connected to an IV tube that looked as if it had some major stuff flowing through it.

"You must like this place." He reached for the molded-plastic chair against the wall. Then, instead of moving it closer to the bed, he left it where it was and sat down. Sometimes his size tended to intimidate people.

Karah Lee crossed to her patient's side. "You need to tell him what you've been telling me, honey."

"Which part? The part about how sorry I am I stole the food from the vending machine? I didn't have any change, or—"

"Tell me again about Bruce." Karah Lee reached for the backless exam stool and wheeled it to Fawn's bedside. She sat as close to the young woman as she could get, positioning herself between Taylor and Fawn.

Taylor stifled a smile. This young woman did seem incredibly young, vulnerable.

"I didn't do it." Fawn said the words quietly. She sounded as if she'd given up hope that anyone would believe her.

"Tell us what did happen," Taylor said.

"I was in Branson with my boyfriend."

"That would be Bruce Penske," Taylor said. The murder victim. According to the papers, the guy had been thirty-five years old. Taylor tried not to show his revulsion as he became fully aware of her youth.

Fawn nodded. "He sent me on this errand to get rid of me for a while so he could do business, and when I got back to our room at the hotel, he was arguing with some old guy in a suit named Harv, and I didn't realize I shouldn't be there until—"

"How old was Harv?" Taylor asked.

"Probably at least forty."

Yep, she was young. "So what happened?"

"They were arguing about that big building they're putting up a couple of blocks from here."

The Beaufont project? "You're sure that's what they were talking about?" Taylor asked. "The building here?"

She nodded. "Bruce was an investment manager, and he was withdrawing funds because the place didn't pass some kind of inspection, and—"

"Wait a minute, Fawn," Taylor said. *The earth moved!* "What kind of inspection? A safety inspection of the building? A survey?"

Fawn shrugged.

Taylor looked at Karah Lee. "I think I have a hunch about why the Beaufont Corporation's been so tight with security, and if we can find something to back up my hunch while the place is without a guard tonight—"

"Everybody's tight with security these days," Karah Lee said. "It's called legal protection."

"Hiring thugs with big guns to intimidate people? I think there's more to it than that."

"For instance?"

"Fawn said Bruce was murdered because he was blowing the whistle on problems with the property. Fawn, did he name any names? Give you any figures? Do you know—"

"He never talked to me about that stuff," she said, shaking her head. "The only names I know are nicknames like Vin and Harv, and then he gave me that flash drive Blaze is trying to pull up, but it doesn't sound like he's doing much better than I did."

"Okay," Karah Lee said. "What happened during the argument?"

"Well, the guy, Harv, got really hot, you know? And he pulled a gun out and shot at me, but Bruce told me to duck, and then the scum turned and shot Bruce while I was getting away." Her voice wavered, and she took a deep breath. "Bruce died saving my life." Tears spilled from her eyes.

Karah Lee pulled some facial tissues from a box on the counter and handed them to Fawn.

"Thanks." She dabbed at her face and wiped her nose with the tissues. "And Harv shot that poor bellman out in the hallway, who wasn't even involved in anything but pushing a cart with food on it. I mean, it's like the guy didn't even matter!"

"What happened after that?" Taylor asked.

Fawn wiped at more tears. "I ran down the stairs to the lobby, and I was going to tell the security guard, but Harv reached the guards before I could, and then the police came, and I didn't know what to do, so I ran. I mean, they were after *me*, with guns and everything."

Karah Lee handed Fawn more tissues and took the damp ones from her. "Where did you go?" she asked gently.

"I just ran through the dark until I reached another hotel, where I changed my clothes and hid. Then I accidentally set off a fire alarm when I was trying to see my way around with some matches because my flashlight went out on me and—"

"Fawn." Taylor leaned forward, elbows on knees. "Could you identify Harv if you saw him again?"

She nodded as she soaked yet another set of tissues. "I saw him today. I won't ever forget—"

"What do you *mean*, you saw him today?" Karah Lee asked.

"I don't remember a lot about it. I mean, I was so sick then, I even thought I might've been seeing things, you know? He was on the big paddleboat out in the lake."

"Did he see you?" Taylor asked.

"Yeah, but I don't really look like me right now, and when he tried to get a better look with his binoculars, I turned away so he wouldn't see my face."

"Describe him," Taylor said.

"Ugly."

Taylor exchanged glances with Karah Lee.

"Okay, okay, I know what you want," Fawn said. She closed her eyes as if to focus better on the memory. "He had a long, droopy-looking face with lines down the sides like a basset hound's. Black hair, and mean-looking lips— you know, thin, without any color. No beard or mustache, but with a shadow, like he hadn't shaved in a day or so."

"Withnell," Karah Lee said. She glanced at Taylor.

He nodded. "That's what he was after when he saw us at the cemetery. I'm calling for backup."

"No!" Fawn cried.

"We need to get you out of Hideaway."

"Why? If Harv really recognized me, I'd be dead now. He wouldn't've finished his little cruise."

"You're right," Karah Lee said. "But the fact is, he came to Hideaway to find you, and he's obviously still looking. He was curious enough after seeing you from the boat that he drove past us at the cemetery a couple of times, looking a little ticked."

"I'll get an ambulance," Taylor said.

"Oh, sure," Fawn said. "Call an ambulance to come shrieking into town and draw attention. That way, if he doesn't know where I am, he will soon."

"You watch too much television," Karah Lee said. "Ambulances don't use lights and sirens for a simple transfer. Go ahead and make the call, Taylor. I'll ride with her when they get here."

Taylor excused himself. After he called for the ambulance, he would phone Tom and Greg. The deputy was already itching for news about Beaufont. He could do some snooping.

Fawn watched Karah Lee adjust the bag and tubes. "You'll really go with me?"

Karah Lee sat back down in the chair next to the bed. "I don't think you want to be left alone with strangers right now, do you?"

Fawn shook her head.

"Why did you come to Hideaway?" Karah Lee asked.

"Because I thought I could find out what the problem was and warn somebody, and because they were looking for me in Branson." She looked down at her tissues. "And because the clerk working the counter was waving my picture around. I couldn't risk facing her, so I had to steal a ticket from poor Casey Timble."

"Fawn." Karah Lee touched Fawn's cheek, and her touch was so gentle. "Honey, how old are you, really?"

Fawn closed her eyes and shook her head.

"Okay," Karah Lee said. "Let's put it another way. Would Bruce have been in trouble with the law for statutory rape?"

"Nope."

"So you really are eighteen, like you told me the other day?" Karah Lee asked.

"He wouldn't have been accused of statutory rape if nobody testified, and no way would I have testified. I mean it, Bruce treated me right."

"Sixteen," Karah Lee guessed.

Fawn opened her eyes then, and stared up into that golden-brown gaze for a long moment. "I'll be seventeen in September. I'm an emancipated minor."

"But your family must be frantic—"

"My mother's husband raped me last year, okay?"

Karah Lee obviously tried hard to keep the startled expression from her face, but she wasn't the best actress in the world. She leaned back, as if struggling to recover from a blow. "Okay," she said at last. "Have you pressed charges?"

Fawn shook her head. "I just told my mother, and she wouldn't listen. The police wouldn't listen to me even if I did tell them."

"Yes, they would."

"I tried to tell my mother he was trying things even a couple of years before he did it, but she didn't want to hear. They've got a whole other family, and they don't need me, anyway." She felt the tears burn her eyes again, and closed them, turning away. Why had she suddenly become a whiny little dweeb?

Karah Lee squeezed her arm. "You've been through a lot lately."

Fawn nodded, still not opening her eyes.

"You want to tell me about it?"

What she wanted to do was forget this last year had ever happened. But she knew she was going to have to talk about it to a lot of people. They'd never leave her alone, even if they did find the real killer and let her off the hook.

She opened her eyes to find Karah Lee watching her, waiting. "Short version, and then I'm done, okay?"

Karah Lee nodded.

"And you don't tell anyone about it."

"Doctor-patient confidentiality."

"Yeah, but this is illegal stuff, and you'd have to report it."

"I'll see what I can do to get *you* to report it, instead."

"I told you, I already tried."

"I mean to the right people. When did your stepfather rape you?"

"It happened on my sixteenth birthday last September." What was it about this woman that made her want to spill her life story like this? "I tried telling my mother, like I said, and she freaked, got all in my face, calling me a liar, and so when I asked if I could move into an apartment with some older girls, so I could stay away from him, she was glad to shove me out the door."

"Where did you live?"

"Muskogee, Oklahoma."

"That isn't too far from here."

"Too close for me, okay? A couple of weeks after I moved out, my mother's husband caught me at the apartment alone and almost got me again, but I fought him off. One of my roommates loaned me some money to get out of town, and I took a bus to Vegas."

"What did you do there?"

"You don't want to know."

Karah Lee suddenly looked sick.

"I figured if I was going to be abused, I might as well be paid for it," Fawn said at last.

Karah Lee closed her eyes. "Oh, Fawn."

"I couldn't force myself to do it for long. I got a fake ID and did other stuff, and then I met Bruce this spring at a party." She looked at the ring he'd given her, with the hot-pink rubies, and forced herself not to cry again. "So," she said, swallowing and forcing a smile, "can we talk about something else? Like, do you and Taylor have a thing going on?"

Blaze whistled suddenly, startling Taylor as he hung up the phone. "You want to see what Fawn's been carrying around in her pocket?"

Taylor leaned over and looked at the screen, and for a moment he couldn't believe what he was seeing. It was a map. "Caves."

"Big ones."

"But that's here, below Hideaway." Taylor studied the screen more closely. There was a labyrinth of connected caves, and the only opening into the system was now far below the lake.

"Those things would be filled with water now," Blaze said, scrolling down the screen.

Another map came up.

"They're directly beneath the Beaufont property," Taylor said.

"Yeah, but those caves extend past that property. Look at this—it's the houses across the street, and City Hall."

"All the blasting they did into the rock for the foundation would have weakened the structure of the caves."

All the pieces fell into place, and the result frightened Taylor. First, they'd dozed down Karah Lee's rental, and then there had been several injuries at one time on the construction site. He also remembered what the sandaled hikers had said about divers Sunday afternoon—maybe checking out the cave to see if they could find a way to reinforce the foundation from below? Ethylene's accident this morning had also been caused by an unexpected depression in her front yard. And she lived near the site.

Taylor caught his breath and straightened. "The earthquake."

"What do you mean?"

That monstrosity of a building could be a danger to everyone around it, and Tom had just tonight mentioned the earthquake south of the state line.

He yanked up the phone again. They needed to evacuate some homes.

❧ *Chapter Twenty-Eight* ❧

Karah Lee checked Fawn's vitals one more time. Her temperature was back to normal and her color was better, her eyes clear and focused.

"So what do you think?" Fawn asked.

"You're looking stronger by the minute. How do you feel?"

"Like I don't need an ambulance. Can't I just stay here? I don't need to be in a hospital or anything." Fawn gave her a wide-eyed, pleading look that made Karah Lee wonder how anyone had ever mistaken this young lady for anything but a sixteen-year-old girl, in spite of the elastic bandage the other day, and in spite of the gray granny hair now.

"Thanks for that observation, Dr. Morrison," Karah Lee said, "but there's a room reserved for you at Cox South in Springfield. There'll be a guard at the door and everything."

"And handcuffs on my hands?"

"No."

"You'll be there?"

"That's right. So sit still for a few minutes. I've got to make a telephone call, and don't forget what I told you about the needle."

Fawn scowled, and Karah Lee winked and walked out the door to find Taylor coming at her.

"We've got trouble," he said. "Tom just called from the eastern end of the Beaufont property, and there's been a collapse around the foundation of the building. We've got to secure the perimeter. Greg's on his way in, and Blaze is going with me. We've tried to evacuate the affected homes, but not everyone is answering their phone. This needs follow-up right now."

"Do you want me to man the phones, make some calls?"

"No, we've got that covered. The ambulance won't be here for at least another fifteen minutes, so just sit tight."

"The town square isn't in danger?"

"According to the maps, the threat doesn't extend past City Hall, but when I came in here, people were still lingering out on the streets. We need to comb the area and clear them out before there's another accident. I've called out the volunteer fire department and there's backup coming from Kimberling City. Lock the door behind us when we leave."

She gave a brief thought to the man who'd called himself Detective Withnell. "I will. But Fawn's probably right. If Harv had recognized her, he would have—"

"Just lock the door."

* * *

Taylor stepped out the front door with Blaze and waited until Karah Lee slid the dead bolt home and waved at him through the window.

"Which way do we go?" Blaze asked, rushing eagerly toward the Jeep.

"First, I want to check on Ethylene." Stubbornly, she had refused to go home with her niece this morning, and so was alone in her house. Taylor wasn't sure her neighbors would think to check on her, particularly since she didn't have the most pleasant personality.

He glanced back toward the clinic as he pulled away. Maybe he was just being paranoid, but he felt uncomfortable about leaving Karah Lee and Fawn alone.

Blaze opened the glove compartment. "You got another flashlight in here?"

"I have three in the back. Let's do this as quickly as possible and get back to the clinic."

Karah Lee dialed Senator Kemper MacDonald's home number, using the cordless phone as she paced from Fawn's exam room to the reception office and back again, glad to be able to walk off some nervous energy.

He actually answered the telephone after the second ring, instead of letting the answering machine do it.

"Hi, Dad. It's Karah Lee."

"Okay, what have I done now?"

She winced at the tired tone in his voice. "Nothing, believe it or not." She closed and locked the door between the clinic proper and the waiting room, then turned to pace down the hallway again. "In the first place, I'm sorry I was so hard on you the other day." She thought about Fawn's experience with her stepfather, and realized she truly meant what she said. "I know you were doing what you felt you needed to do for me at the time, and I never thanked you for that."

Silence.

"Dad?"

There was a soft sound of a throat clearing. "Yes."

"I'm thanking you now."

More silence.

"And I need to ask you to help me again."

There was a heavy exhalation on the line, as if someone had just given him a playful punch in the stomach. "You're serious?"

"Very."

"Then this must be bad. What's going on? You didn't get fired because—"

"No, this is a special-interest case for a senator with some clout, and that would be you, Mr. Senator. We're having trouble here in Hideaway."

"What kind of trouble?"

"We have a corporation that needs to be investigated as soon as possible. Tonight, even, if it can be done, because there's a disaster happening as we speak." As briefly as possible, she explained about Beaufont, then added, "Also, there's a connection between this and the murders in Branson a couple of weeks ago, and we have a very ill sixteen-year-old who is innocent of the crimes and who needs protection, and she can't go back home."

There was a long pause, then a low whistle. "You can't be talking about Fawn Morrison."

"You know about that all the way up in Jefferson City?"

"You've got an alleged murderer there with you now? Karah Lee MacDonald, are you crazy?"

Karah Lee didn't correct the last name. Why pick at old wounds? "It's a long story, Dad. Would you please just help us with this? I promise to explain it all later."

"I'll call some friends of mine about the building problem. There had to be studies done on that land before construction began. Surveyors should have caught any problems. How they could even begin to get away with something like that—"

"Well, there's apparently been quite a cover-up by someone with a lot of clout. That's why I called."

"Why is that?"

"Because I figured if anyone had more clout than Beaufont, it was you."

There was another long silence. "I don't think I've heard you say anything like that about me since you were ten years old."

That stung. "I'm sorry." She swallowed hard and turned to pace back down the hallway. "And Fawn. She needs protection."

"That'll be a little trickier."

"The murderer still hasn't been apprehended, and she didn't do it."

"You have at least contacted the authorities about her, haven't you?"

"Yes."

"She's sixteen?" he asked. "What about her parents?"

"Family abuse situation. She's an emancipated minor. I'd like her to stay with me after everything's cleared up, if that's possible."

Several seconds of airtime passed. "You don't ask for much, do you?"

"Please. She needs shelter."

Another heavy sigh, then, "I'll do what I can."

"How much is that?"

"There are a lot of hoops to jump through, lots of legal ramifications, but at that age we can get Family Services involved—although I'll have to check my facts about the emancipated minor thing. I know some good people who can help."

"Thanks."

"One condition."

"What's that?"

"You meet Shona and me for dinner someday soon."

Karah Lee's hand tightened on the receiver, and for some reason her vision grew blurry. How long had it been since she and her dad had been on the same side of any problem? "Just the three of us?"

"We *are* a family, you know, as much as we've all tried to sweep that fact under the rug these past few years."

A dysfunctional family. But she didn't say it. "Sure, Dad. Soon. I'll be talking to you."

He cleared his throat. "We need to clear up an apparent misunderstanding about the Sebring Scholarship."

"You mean the one you obtained for me?"

"I think you jumped to the wrong conclusion about that. It's a natural tendency of yours, I suppose, to suspect me of the most corrupt behavior."

Karah Lee stepped into the reception office and glanced toward the front door through the window. She thought she saw a shadow of someone walk past on the sidewalk through the narrow section of the outer door she could see from this angle. "Now, Dad, I didn't—"

"Donaldson called me about you the year you were awarded that scholarship, but only because you were under consideration by the committee and they were reluctant to give the scholarship to the daughter of a congressman who could easily afford her tuition."

"But that wasn't—"

"Let me finish, please. I was forced to admit to Donaldson that my own daughter would rather struggle financially for the next twenty years paying back school loans than accept a penny from me."

Oh, man. "And you told him that?"

"Would you expect me to lie?" he asked quietly.

She continued to watch the sliver of sidewalk she could see from here, and once again she thought she saw someone out there, past the glow of lights from the outer foyer.

"Karah Lee, is everything okay there?"

She was being paranoid. "Sure. Let's just plan for that dinner soon, okay?"

"You got it. I'll be in touch as soon as I make a few calls."

"You'll be able to find me at Cox South a little later tonight. I'll be in Fawn Morrison's room."

* * *

Taylor scrambled through the darkness with Ethylene in his arms while Blaze held the flashlight beam to the ground. The tricky part was making sure the thick, unmowed grass in Ethylene's front yard didn't camouflage any new depressions.

"You could at least let me get my car out of the garage," she grumbled. "How come I never heard anything about any caves under my house? I think it's all stupid."

"We can't take any chances," Taylor said.

"Well, I don't—"

A loud crack like thunder shot through the air and echoed from the cliffs north of town.

"What was that?" Blaze cried.

Taylor turned in time to see part of the bare structure of the massive Beaufont building plunge downward, straight into the earth. A tremor shook the ground, and he braced himself to keep his footing. In the glow of streetlights, a supporting beam lurched sideways, crashing against other steel supports with a metallic explosion, like rapid cannon fire.

Then the lights went out. Their only source of illumination was the flashlight in Blaze's hand.

"Let's go," Taylor said. "Ethylene, I'm taking you to Junior Short's house. You can stay there until help comes."

"Okay, Ranger, your point's proved," Ethylene said. "Let's get out of here."

Karah Lee was hanging up the phone when she heard an explosion, then felt the jolt of movement beneath her feet. The lights went out, plunging the clinic into total darkness.

"Karah Lee!"

"It's okay, Fawn, I'm—"

Something slammed against the front of the clinic. Karah Lee turned to see a flicker of light, then the glass in the front door shattered. She hit the floor on her hands and knees and scrambled into the hallway. In the foyer, footsteps crunched through the broken glass into the clinic.

Karah Lee felt her way along the wall toward Fawn's room.

There was a *pop-thump* at the door between the waiting room and the clinic, which she'd locked when she was talking to her dad. Another *pop-thump,* and wood splintered.

Was he using a gun with a silencer?

The intruder kicked the door.

She lunged forward and into the fourth exam room, where she could hear Fawn's labored, frightened breathing.

"Who's there?" Fawn whispered into the blackness.

"Karah Lee." She closed the door and locked it as the waiting-room door crashed against a wall.

"It's him, isn't it?" Fawn whispered.

"Shh." Karah Lee felt along the bed until she reached the IV pole, silently removed the IV catheter from Fawn's arm and bandaged the puncture site.

A footfall landed outside their door.

Fawn grabbed Karah Lee's arm and squeezed, hands trembling.

Karah Lee eased her off the bed and against the wall, then felt her way over to the utility cabinet.

She was searching through a drawer for a wrapped scalpel, when the exam-room door handle jiggled, then came a loud *thunk-clack* of bullet hitting metal.

She found the scalpel. The door flew open, turning black to gray with the intruder's penlight. Fawn shoved the IV pole into the intruder's path. He yelled as the impact from a muffled shot hit the wall above Karah Lee's head.

Karah Lee leaped in front of Fawn, wielding the scalpel blindly as he shot again, this time hitting the sink. She stabbed at his gun hand, kicked up with her knee, then slammed him in the face with her elbow.

With an enraged scream, he lunged at her and shoved her to the floor, raising the gun.

Fawn rammed him from behind and his shot went wide. Karah Lee kicked upward. The gun flew across the room, bounced against the wall, spun crazily on the tile floor.

He grabbed Karah Lee by the throat and yanked her aside as she fought for breath. He snatched the gun and turned it on her as light suddenly blazed through the room.

Taylor rushed through the door, grabbed the bed and thrust it forward, catching the killer between the bed frame and the wall, forcing the gun from his bleeding hand. Taylor kicked the gun from the killer's reach.

"Karah Lee, get that!" he said as he jerked the man onto his stomach and secured his hands behind his back.

Karah Lee grabbed the heavy gun and backed away, looking for Fawn. The girl stood huddled in the darkened corner.

"You okay, honey?"

Fawn nodded, tears streaming down her face.

Blaze came rushing into the room, stopped, gaped at the destruction. He reached for Fawn, and she stumbled into his arms.

"You guys okay?" he asked.

"Blaze, get her out of here. Call some backup for Taylor."

As Blaze and Fawn left the room, Karah Lee gripped the gun in both hands and held her aim steadily at Harv's head.

"You need to get out of here, too, Karah Lee," Taylor said.

"I'm not leaving here until you do."

Five minutes later Greg and Tom came bursting into the room, guns drawn.

"We'll take it from here, Taylor," Greg said. "There's an ambulance pulling in outside, and the girl's asking for Karah Lee." He cuffed their prisoner and helped him from the floor, then frowned at Taylor and Karah Lee. "Either of you know the State Senator, MacDonald? He's calling out the FBI to come down here."

"We've met," Karah Lee said.

Taylor chuckled and threw his arm around her as they walked out.

∞ *Chapter Twenty-Nine* ∞

On Saturday morning, September 13, Fawn came banging through the back door of Karah Lee's two-bedroom cottage at the western edge of the Lakeside property. "Where were you?"

Karah Lee looked up from the medical supplies she had spread across the kitchen table. Fawn's super-short blond hair with the spiky gray tips stuck out all over her head. She had a fake tattoo of a pig on her face.

She pointed at the clock. "Hel*lo*. It's ten-thirty. You told me you'd try to get to the pig races."

"I'm sorry," Karah Lee said. " I did try, but my kit was low on supplies, I'm on call and I got to imagining what would happen and—"

"And you're hiding from Taylor."

"He's avoiding me, I just didn't feel like being avoided today." Not that she cared, really. He'd been acting like a jerk the past couple of weeks...since their last date.

"So how are you going to dodge him at Cheyenne and Dane's wedding?" Fawn asked.

Karah Lee sniffed and wrinkled her nose. "What is that smell?"

"You're changing the subject."

"Right now the subject stinks."

"I helped Blaze in the racing pen."

"The *pig* pen?"

"And I slipped a little."

Karah Lee recoiled and looked at Fawn's feet. They were bare.

"I fell in it, okay? I took my shoes off outside and I washed my legs off in the lake so I wouldn't track poop into the house."

"Turn around."

Fawn rolled her eyes, but she turned, flashing her shapely legs, wiggling her rear. Her dirty rear.

Karah Lee suppressed a smile. "Okay. How'd the race go?"

"Blaze won!" Fawn did a victory dance across the kitchen floor toward her bedroom, arms raised high, totally unselfconscious about the faded denim coverall cut-offs stained by pig manure.

"Change clothes before you sit down anywhere," Karah Lee called after her, chuckling at the seventeen-year-old's unfailing energy.

"You'd better believe it!" Fawn called back. "The wedding's in two and a half hours." She poked her head back out the door. "What dress are you wearing? Do you know it's already in the eighties out there? I can't believe they're going to have this thing in the *city park*. We'll sweat to death."

"It's shaded." And besides, the collapse in June had come a little too close to City Hall, undermining part of its foundation, and the church wasn't big enough to fit all the guests. Cheyenne and Dane had refused to be married anywhere but Hideaway, and most of the town was attending. That left the city park, directly east of town, far enough from the collapse that there would be no danger.

After changing into a long T-shirt, Fawn sauntered back into the kitchen, acting a little too casual for Karah Lee's comfort. She was up to something.

"So," she said, picking up a wrapped bag-valve mask, examining it, then setting it back on the table, "you think you might be interested in trying out some of that makeup we bought last week?"

"I thought that makeup was for you. It was *your* birthday."

"Sure, but it wouldn't hurt you to try some just this once."

"My face has worked for me for thirty-four years now, why change?"

"Because you could use some improvement."

Karah Lee glowered at her.

"I mean, you've got this great bone structure, but you never do anything with it. At least we've got you a decent wardrobe now, so you don't look like a hog anymore."

A hog! "You've got a real way with words, you know that?"

"Hey, all I'm saying is you've got a big chest, so you need to emphasize your waistline. I mean, at least show people you have one. I know girls who pay lots of money to get what you already have. I just think you need to learn to dress smarter."

"Right. When was I going to find time to do that during med school and residency training? I barely found time to eat."

"Looks to me like you ate okay."

Monster sauntered over to Fawn and rubbed against her legs. She picked the cat up and hugged him close, burying her face in his thick fur. And he took it like a gentleman. If Karah Lee had done that, he would have fought to escape her clutches.

"So, okay, you grew up geeky," Fawn said. "It doesn't mean you have to stay that way." She took a step closer, eyes narrowing as she made an obvious show of studying Karah Lee's facial features. "I could show you how to do it."

"Yes, I know, I've heard it all before." Fawn had told her weeks ago that she'd hung out with the theater guild since she was twelve to avoid being at home.

"I could remake you...if you're brave enough."

Karah Lee packed the last of her gauze into her kit and closed the top. "Bravery has nothing to do with it. Common sense has everything to do with it." She had been sharing this two-bedroom cottage with Fawn for two months, and these walls had heard some form of this argument at least once a week.

"Give me thirty minutes and I'll prove it to you," Fawn

said. "Give me your credit card and let me on your laptop, and I can change your world."

"I like my world the way it is."

"Okay, fine, just let me at your face and hair." Fawn put Monster down and headed for the bathroom. "Do you even *have* a curling iron and scissors? I've never seen them. No, never mind, I've got scissors and tweezers and all the rest."

"Tweezers?" Karah Lee followed her, still suspicious. "What do you want with tweezers? I'm not into torture. And I didn't say you could take scissors to my hair." A new wardrobe was one thing—actually two things, since during their shopping spree last week, Fawn had shown as much enthusiasm about selecting a new wardrobe for Karah Lee as she had over her own closetful of new clothes for school.

Karah Lee almost refused, but she loved the look of lively excitement in Fawn's blue eyes, loved the quick smile, the hint of mischief that often revealed her thoughts across those gamine features. The girl was now in danger of being spoiled rotten here in Hideaway, where she was a local celebrity.

After the media had gone wild about her story of escape from the murderer in Branson, she had reported her stepfather for rape. Her mother had disowned her, and she wasn't allowed to see her brothers and sister. As far as Karah Lee was concerned, this place would be Fawn's home as long as she needed it. Bertie and Edith adored her. Monster had obviously adopted her.

"Okay, get out your scissors and your tweezers and all

that goop for my face," Karah Lee said. "But if you disfigure me, I'll hold you personally responsible for making me miss the wedding."

Fawn walked proudly beside Karah Lee Fletcher from the car to the broad sweep of lawn that was the city park, and the festival grounds, and for the next hour, a wedding chapel. Thank goodness the place was shaded by a troupe of mature maples, oaks, hawthorns and cedars. A breeze blew in from the lake, making the temperature bearable.

Someone had cleared the grass of trash from the festival, and a band from Branson played in the bandstand. The rose trellis needed no additional decoration. It was where the ceremony would be held, and the crowd already filled the place. The ceremony wouldn't be formal—no hot, uncomfortable tuxedos for the men. No long dresses. Just lots of laughter and smiles, maybe a few practical jokes by the ranch boys, but it wouldn't be mean.

Unable to resist a glance at Karah Lee, Fawn once more admired her latest artistic miracle. Karah Lee wore a sleeveless dress of amber lace and silk that subtly hinted at the dynamite figure, emphasizing what needed to be emphasized. Her wild curls had been tamed to curve around her face in delicate tendrils. Her eyes—those golden-amber jewels—were luminescent. Karah Lee Fletcher was a babe.

Someday Fawn would be a makeup artist for the stars. Maybe royalty.

"You look great," she said. "Stop adjusting your dress."

"It's too low-cut."

"It doesn't even show your cleavage. Your pink scrubs

are more revealing than that dress. I mean, when you bend over just right, a person could see all the way to your belly button." Fawn caught sight of Blaze standing with the ranch boys. He wore white slacks with a blue dress shirt and a vest. He looked hot, even though he was standing in the shade.

Fawn excused herself and joined Blaze beneath a cedar tree while Karah Lee went to speak to the bride.

"Where is he?" she asked.

Blaze gestured toward the other side of the park.

"Did you ever find out what was going on with him?" she asked.

"Good question. Nobody knows. It isn't as if Taylor ever talks to anyone."

"Except Karah Lee."

He nodded.

"And you."

Blaze grimaced. "He's not going to go baring his soul to a seventeen-year-old kid."

She placed a hand on Blaze's arm and shoved him in Taylor's direction. "You can give it a try. Quick. Before Tom sets up camp beside Karah Lee for the wedding."

Taylor couldn't help staring. The tall, voluptuous woman with the red hair who arrived with Fawn really was Karah Lee Fletcher. Her hair was shorter, not quite as curly, and she was...hard to look away from.

"You know what?" someone said beside him.

He turned to see Blaze standing there, hands in pockets, gazing casually across the growing crowd.

"What?"

"For a hero, you don't have a lot of guts."

Taylor frowned at him, then followed his line of vision back to Karah Lee. "I have brains. Who needs guts when he has brains?"

"Your brain tells you to dump her without any explanation?"

As they watched, Karah Lee glanced toward Taylor, met his gaze, looked quickly away.

"I have the brains not to go rushing into something unprepared," Taylor said.

"Nobody'd ever accuse you of doing that."

Taylor gave Blaze a suspicious glance. Definitely sarcasm.

"Look, you don't have to go rushing into anything," Blaze said, "but how stupid is it to completely break off a relationship after two whole months of intense dating? No explanation, no fight, nothing. Just quit calling. How do you think that makes her feel?"

Taylor couldn't quite stifle his annoyance. "Since you seem to know so much about it, why don't you tell me?"

"Bad answer. You should know this one. Just put yourself in her place."

"I've done that, Blaze. Believe me."

Blaze nudged his arm and pointed toward Karah Lee. They watched a familiar, blond-haired deputy stroll casually to Karah Lee's side and gesture toward some chairs as the tone of the music segued into the Lord's Prayer.

"Yeah, sure, Taylor," Blaze said. "Take all the time you want."

* * *

Karah Lee had never seen Cheyenne look so happy, and she'd never seen a more beautiful wedding. The speaker system didn't reverberate and bust eardrums, and no one forgot their lines. Most important, Dane and Cheyenne sounded so sure of their vows, and of their love for each other.

Karah Lee sat between Fawn and Tom and tried really hard not to cry—first of all, because she didn't want to ruin Fawn's makeup job. Second of all, because she was afraid if she headed that direction, she'd be a weepy mess. It didn't look as if she'd ever have a ceremony like this of her own, so she didn't want to ruin this one with tears.

Dane looked so handsome, with silvery-blond hair that emphasized his craggy features. Cheyenne looked at peace with herself, and her dark brown eyes glowed with love as she gazed up into Dane's face. She wore a knee-length cream silk dress that enhanced the olive tone of her skin and shining black hair. She carried a single red rose, which she handed to Karah Lee at the end of the ceremony as she and her new husband walked down the aisle between the chairs.

The band kicked into high gear and the wedding party became a dance party. Tom asked her to dance, and she declined, and so he offered his arm to Bertie and led her to the aisle. Karah Lee was watching them leave when she felt a touch on her shoulder. She glanced around to find Taylor looming over her, his bronze-red hair glowing with highlights from the hot sun. His serious, gray-hazel eyes bored past the polite smile with which she greeted him.

"I forgot to ask," he said softly. "Do small-town church girls ever learn how to dance?"

"Sure they do, but they're more accustomed to long walks along the shore, where they can talk without being disturbed."

"To themselves?"

"Sometimes, if that's the only intelligent form of conversation they can find."

He held his hand out to her, and she looked at it.

"I don't promise to be intelligent, but you'll look silly out on the shore all alone talking to yourself while everyone else is dancing and having a good time."

"You're such a gentleman." She didn't take his hand, but she relented and strolled beside him across the lawn, sidestepping guests.

"What did you want to talk about?" Karah Lee asked.

"Well, let's see," Taylor said. "I have a good story. Hideaway City Council has decided to have an ambulance board, and they want me to be the director."

"You're kidding."

"You don't think I can do the job?" he asked.

"I know you can do that job, but I don't believe they're still going to try for an ambulance service now that Beaufont's pulled out."

"They may have pulled out, but they've sold out to the people who originally sold to them. Folks around here are tickled. They still want to be tourist oriented, but more laid-back. No condos, that's for sure, and if you'll notice, our tourist business hasn't dropped, it's just changed focus."

"Bertie and Edith got their loan approval for the purchase of the land between their property and the church. They've got plans to start building ten more units."

"Isn't Fawn already working for them part-time?" Taylor asked.

"Yes, but she's had to cut her hours back for the school year. I've made it a rule that homework comes first. So when are you going to clear up the big mystery?"

"What big mystery?"

"About why you've turned into a hermit the past two weeks."

He strolled beside her in silence for a moment. "Leave it to Karah Lee to cut to the chase."

"You have a problem with that?"

"No. In fact, it's something I've always liked about you."

"Oh, right. You were so complimentary the day we discussed your smoking."

"But you allowed me to verbally abuse you without getting hot about it."

"You didn't verbally abuse me. You're changing the subject."

"I know. It's because I'm a coward."

She slowed her steps. Here it came. He was going to explain why he didn't want to see her again.

"Three months of friendship is not enough time to tell if two people are right for one another."

"Right?" She glanced at his profile. "In what way? Can't a friendship just be a friendship without analyzing it to death?"

"Okay, look, I'm sorry. I'm saying this badly." He stopped and touched her shoulder. "What I meant to say was that three months isn't long enough to know for sure if you're falling in love, but that's exactly what I'm doing."

For a moment, the rhythmic thrum of the dance music and the shouts and laughter of the crowd on the lawn seemed to fade to silence as Karah Lee stared into Taylor's earnest eyes. "You are?"

"It's hit me like that proverbial ton of bricks," he said. "I'd almost forgotten what a brick looked like."

"They come in different shapes and sizes."

He grinned, shaking his head. "So you could recognize one if it hit you in the head?"

"I recognized the one that did."

His grin broadened.

"So if we both know what's happening, what's the problem?" she asked.

"I don't want to come into this relationship with a needy heart. You and I both have work to do in our relationships with others before we can build a solid foundation together."

"And that's what we're doing. I'm making amends with my father and sister, and with God. You've even stopped smoking—I mean, talk about your major steps toward rehabilitation, that's major."

He chuckled at her lame joke.

"Seriously," she said, "you told me yourself you've begun to come to terms with Clarice's defection, and you've made amends with God. So what's the problem?"

He turned once more and strolled toward the shimmering lake, and Karah Lee followed.

"You know what you told me the night we went walking in the cemetery?" she asked.

"That was June. This is September. You expect me to remember something like that?"

"You should," she said. "You said you realized God was in control, but He didn't control things the way you wanted Him to."

He sighed, and his shoulders slumped a little, and he nodded.

"And you also said that you thought He was always with us, but He was just giving us a chance to get over ourselves and realize that what matters in life is really how we handle all the baggage."

Taylor's eyebrows rose, and he glanced around to study her face closely. "Have you memorized all our conversations like that?"

"Just the important ones. Look, Taylor, we're always going to have baggage. Everybody gets hurt sometime by someone they love, and it colors the way they look at the world. I just don't want that to be a permanent thing, okay? I know you don't want to be hurt again. And I know you don't want to hurt me."

He touched her cheek, then cupped her chin in the palm of his hand. "I never want to hurt you."

"You will, you know. But you can't let that stop you from loving, because that would mean your fear is stopping you from living. Maybe we need to step back from the controls and allow God to handle things a little more often. If we do that, I think life will hurt a lot less."

"Karah Lee Fletcher, when did you become so wise?"

She smiled at him, then gently kissed him. "I have some very wise friends."

* * * * *

And now, turn the page for a sneak preview of

LAST RESORT

The third title in the exciting HIDEAWAY *series.*
On sale June 2005 from Steeple Hill Books.

❧ *Chapter One* ❧

Not again. I can't let it all start over again. I've got to stop this madness, even if it costs me everything. I can't bear to take another life…and now Carissa.

She's the light that fills this hollow. She brings sunshine from the gloom that seems to haunt this cursed place. I'll take my own life before I lay a hand on…

But she knows too much about me. She's been searching where she shouldn't be searching, telling everybody she's gathering information for that school report of hers. What if she's lying? Maybe the report is a cover-up.

Now that I think about it, she's been looking at me differently.

The kid is too smart for a twelve-year-old. Far too smart. She has other ways of knowing about me. I can't trust her. I trusted before, and look what happened. I can't ever let my guard down, or I'll lose everything.

I can't let Carissa tell what she knows.

* * *

Carissa Cooper stepped carefully along the muddy lane that led from the sawmill to the house, hugging the old business ledger Dad had sent her to fetch for him. Keeping her flashlight aimed at the track, she studied the darkness with fear that trickled up and down her spine like spiders on patrol.

She hated the dark. She knew she was too old for that kind of stuff, but she couldn't help imagining what might lurk there, evil that appeared as soon as the sun disappeared. If only Justin had come with her. If only he weren't still so mad at her for telling on him.

"Should've kept my mouth shut," she muttered under her breath, then stopped, startled by the sound of her own voice carrying along the lane through the darkness.

She thought she heard the sound of horse hooves, but as she froze and held her breath, all she heard was the puff of breeze through the trees as it brushed tips of leaves against each other in an eerie chuckle. The branches made shadows leap across the trunk of the old walnut tree in the glow of her flashlight...like bony arms reaching out for her.

The breeze died, and the movement stopped.

Carissa swallowed hard, aiming the light around her. No movement. She had less than an eighth of a mile to go. She could do this.

Returning the beam of light to the ground in front of her, she stepped forward.

What was all the fuss about with Justin, anyway? Why did he have those weird problems? Everybody talked about him now. It was embarrassing. His behavior drew more attention to the Cooper family, and the Coopers already had enough attention around Hideaway.

Something horrible had happened down here in Cedar Hollow when Carissa was only two years old. Grandpa and Grandma and Uncle Frank had died in an accident at the sawmill. The kids at school told her some of the stories their parents told them about what happened, but Melva, Carissa's stepmom, said not to listen to stupid stories told by silly busybodies.

Carissa repositioned the business ledger under her right arm. If she dropped it in the mud, Dad would kill her. He didn't like his stuff dirty. Why couldn't he have sent her down to the sawmill for the stupid ledger before it got dark? If Cousin Jill wanted to see the figures in the book, why couldn't she get the ledger herself?

But no, it always had to be Carissa. Who cared if she had homework to do? Who cared if she was afraid of the dark? Especially now that she was doing research on the Cooper sawmill, and the deaths nobody would tell her about. She could get a good grade on this report if she could dig up enough information, but did they care? No. What she wanted never mattered.

That sound again—that thump of hooves hitting wet earth. She stopped, shuffling the ledger beneath her arm to keep it from sliding from the grip of her sweaty hand. It continued to slide. She grabbed for it with her right hand, and dropped the flashlight straight down into a thick, gooey mud puddle with a splat. Darkness surrounded her.

She caught her breath and dived for the light, plunging her right hand into water all the way up to her wrist.

She came up with a handful of mud. Heart banging in her chest, she tried again, feeling through the slick mud for the hard plastic body of the flashlight. She searched with both hands, forgetting the book until it slipped from under her arm and fell into the water with a loud splash.

Oh no! Dad was going to go crazy! He'd warned her to be careful with it, not to—

A twig crackled somewhere close.

Still stooped to the ground, Carissa froze. Had she really heard that? Was her mind playing tricks on her? She waited, holding her breath, listening.

Nothing.

Her head came up. "Justin? That you? You'd better stop it or I'll tell Melva."

Still no answer.

"Justin, I mean it. Stop it right now." If anyone was out there, it had to be Justin. Didn't it?

Yeah, it was just Justin playing a trick on her. With a sigh of impatience, loud enough to show him she wasn't scared, Carissa searched again through the water for the ledger, found it, caught hold of its corner. Dad was going to kill her. Maybe she could convince him it was Justin's fault.

"Justin?"

She continued to glide her fingers through the muddy goo, feeling for the flashlight, but her movements grew slower and slower. She frowned.

Usually Justin would be making weird noises by now, just to scare her... Was that breathing she heard?

"Justin! Dad'll skin you alive when he finds out you made me drop the ledger."

Nobody answered. This wasn't like Justin.

Noelle Cooper's fingers stiffened in the process of making change for a customer. She caught her breath, biting down on a cry of unreasoning fear that gripped her.

"You okay?" the bearded man asked as he stared at the coins Noelle had poised over his outstretched hand.

His voice helped. She breathed again. Forcing a wobbly smile to her lips, she relinquished his change. "Sorry, Jack," she said, closing the cash drawer. "Guess it's past my bedtime. Hope you like that yogurt. If you want to cut your fat intake, you can skim it off the top, because that stuff isn't homogenized."

She waved him out the door, cast a glance around the natural-food store and reached for the keys to lock up.

It was eight o'clock, straight up. Everyone else had gone home. Mariah, Noelle's business partner, kept encouraging her to keep the doors open a few minutes past closing on Friday nights for last-minute shoppers, but there were hardly any cars in the parking lot of the shopping center.

Besides, Noelle felt strange...enervated...weak. No wonder, since she'd awakened the past three nights from old, familiar nightmares. They were probably brought on by her ex-husband's return to Springfield after three years of blessed peace while he was out of state. It had been too much to hope for that he'd disappear forever.

On top of everything else, Mariah was away on a buying trip to Kansas City, and Noelle had been here since seven this morning. Why was it every time her partner left town, all the grouches and complainers descended? For the past three hours Noelle's face had ached from forcing a smile, and if one more crank walked through that door...

She locked it. She dumped the keys back into the cash drawer, slammed it shut and slumped against the low shelf behind her.

What was happening to her? She felt awful, fearful, as she had several times these past few days. But why?

This time it felt worse, almost uncontrollable. She closed her eyes and breathed deeply, conjuring in her mind a picture of her favorite hiking trail. She would go hiking again soon. Very soon. The constant bustle of Springfield, Missouri, tended to get on her nerves if she couldn't escape town at least two or three times a month.

Stretching her arms over her head, she glanced around the store one more time. Everything looked in place. She straightened a package of pumpkin seeds on the sale rack, and returned to the counter to balance the cash register, unable to shake off the discomfort as she usually did.

There was something different about the way she felt this time. She knew it wasn't simply stress. The mingled emotions of fright, grief and confusion were too familiar, too painful.

The last time she'd felt this way, loved ones had died.

Carissa didn't move. Her heart pounded faster and faster, and her throat felt stiff when she swallowed. She prayed silently. That was what Noelle told her to do when the darkness loomed too heavy over her.

Something rustled the bushes to the side of the track. Carissa couldn't prevent the low whimper that slid up her throat.

Maybe it wasn't Justin. Maybe it really wasn't anybody she knew. But who else would be down here in Cedar Holler, a mile from the nearest blacktop?

More rustling...

Carissa forgot to breathe.

A footstep.

Abandoning the flashlight, Carissa swung around and ran into the darkness, back toward the sawmill. She held the muddy book to her chest like a shield as she stumbled over weeds down the center of the dirt track.

The footsteps came behind her, and she heard something else...a quiet whisper that almost sounded like the wind in the trees, except that the whisper kept time with the rhythm of footsteps.

Carissa tossed the ledger to the side of the road and ran through the darkness toward the sawmill, tripping over rocks and stumbling into branches that reached out from the black tree line on both sides of the lane. She stumbled from pitch black into the moonlit lumberyard and pivoted to her right, racing toward the door at the far side of the huge building that housed the sawmill.

The echo of footsteps behind her grew fainter, and when she reached the door she risked a glance over her shoulder. A shadow broke loose from the darkness, but she couldn't tell who it was.

She yanked open the unlocked door and ran inside, and immediately stumbled over something and fell hard on her face. The footsteps came closer. They slowed and stopped as her pursuer seemed to listen to her harsh, shallow breaths from the doorway.

She scrambled to her feet and turned to run into the darkness but stumbled over something else. She hated this sawmill! Too many things to trip a person up.

A hand touched her shoulder. She screamed and skittered backward, tripping again. The last thing she felt was her head smacking the concrete floor.

Tension surged through Noelle like an electric charge. She dropped the bills back into their slot and shoved the cash drawer shut. Time to go home and go to bed.

She looked up to find a customer reaching for the handle of the front door—the door she'd locked a few moments ago. Groaning inwardly, she motioned for the man to wait, then retrieved the keys from the cash drawer.

She could feel her neck muscles tightening even as she walked toward the front. She glanced at the dark sky outside, then at the white, impatient face of the waiting customer. She wasn't up to this, she really wasn't. She needed to get away sometime soon—away from the demanding customers, the complaints and traffic. She couldn't take—

Sudden weakness engulfed her. The floor seemed to rock beneath her, and she grabbed at a nearby shelf, knocking a bottle of oil to its side with a clatter. The lights dimmed and she stumbled. Her legs gave way and she fell to her knees. For countless seconds the lights disappeared completely and she held on to that shelf with all the strength she could summon.

A loud thud-thud-thud in her head kept time with the rhythm of her heartbeat, interspersed with the sound of muffled shouting...

The customer outside.

Gradually, the darkness receded and the floor returned to its stable foundation. Noelle shook her head and looked toward the door to find the panicked man frantically punching numbers on his cell phone.

Oh, great. All she needed was an ambulance arriving at the front door, drawing a crowd.

She waved toward him as she pulled herself to her feet. "I'm okay," she called. "I'll be okay."

From #1 CBA bestselling and
Christy Award-winning author

DEE HENDERSON

comes her first classic romance.

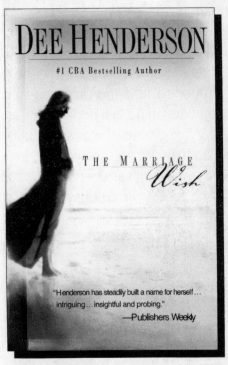

As Scott Williams's thirty-eighth birthday dawned, he was at the top of his game.
Or was he? Successful, blessed with friends and a rich faith, his life seemed perfect to others. But something was missing—a family of his own to love.

After making a birthday wish to meet the woman of his dreams, Scott encountered enchanting author Jennifer St. James strolling along the beach. But beneath her beauty lay a heart mourning her late husband and a faith once deep, now fragile. Could Scott's hopes and prayers bring fulfillment for both of their dreams?

"Henderson has steadily built a name for herself…
intriguing…insightful and probing."
—*Publishers Weekly*

Available in September 2004.

Steeple
Hill®

www.SteepleHill.com

SDH519-1

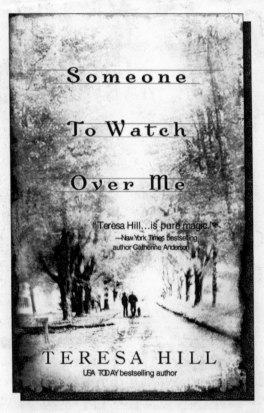

Love Inspired®

LOVE
ENOUGH
FOR TWO

BY

CYNTHIA
RUTLEDGE

Single mom Sierra Summers worked hard to
create a loving, stable home for her daughter.
Men were not part of the equation—until attorney
Matthew Dixon walked into her store with a
proposition that threatened her resolve. Neither
Sierra nor Matt were thinking marriage, but maybe
God had a different path for them....

Don't miss

LOVE ENOUGH FOR TWO
On sale August 2004

Available at your favorite retail outlet.